Hijacking of Flight 100

By

C. J. Stott

Black Thunderbird Press

Seattle, Washington

BLACK THUNDERBIRD PRESS
Hijacking of Flight 100
Clayton J. Stott

Copyright © 2014 by Clayton J. Stott
All Rights Reserved

Copyeditor: Susan Toth sue_toth@editingbysue.com
Cover Design: Cover design by Gary V. Tenuta, GVTgrafix@aol.com
Interior Design: Rich Meyer, http://quantumformatting.weebly.com

All rights reserved. This book was self-published by the author Clayton J. Stott under Black Thunderbird Press. No part of this book may be reproduced in any form, by any means without the express permission of the author. This restriction shall include reprints, excerpts, photocopying, recording and any future means or method of reproducing text and images.

To reproduce this book by any means, please seek prior permission by contacting the author.
Published in the United States of America by Black Thunderbird Press
ISBN-13: 978-0692290538 (Black Thunderbird Press)
ISBN-10: 0692290532 (Black Thunderbird Press)

This fictional work is dedicated to the hapless and innocent victims who tragically died as a result of an inflight explosion of Trans World Airlines Flight 800 on July 17, 1996. The Boeing 747 aircraft was enroute from JFK Airport in New York to Paris, France. The plane broke up into three pieces and plunged into Long Island Sound with the resultant death of all 230 souls on board.

This work was initially started in 1990, well before September 11, 2001. In the era in which this novel was written, Boeing 747 aircraft were flown by three pilots, and largely were outfitted with analog guidance and instrumentation systems. Digital or "flat glass" cockpits had not yet become an industry standard. Autoflight systems essentially were the same as had been installed on Boeing and Douglas aircraft since the end of Korean war. Overwater-navigation systems were either analog Litton LTN-51 or Delco Carousel IV-A Inertial Navigation System platforms. Global Positioning Satellite systems were not yet available in commercial aviation.

More importantly, in the 1980's, airport security was largely non-existent. Most airport terminal security was provided by private contractors who staffed airport security operations with minimum wage employees.

While the airline industry and federal agencies were aware of the threat of airline hijacking or aerial piracy, little was done to deter activity against what most considered a very unlikely event. Airline anti-aerial piracy protocols in the era of this novel were largely "passive resistance" or "reluctant acquiescence."

.

UPI WIRE SERVICE - UPI STATE WIRE (FLORIDA)
June 26, 1987
MIAMI PASSES SECURITY TEST

MIAMI (UPI) - A government test of security systems at Miami International Airport detected 97 percent of the mock weapons carried by inspectors checking the system.

Lowest detection rates were found in Las Vegas at 45 percent, and Phoenix at 34 percent. The Federal Government required airports to install passenger and baggage inspection equipment in 1973 amid a rash of hijackings, generally with the destination of Cuba.

Most airports hire private security firms to operate the detection systems, which are at the entrance to the gates at all major American airports. Federal officials cited employee boredom and monotony as the most probable cause for these lapses in security. They said steps were being taken to relieve the boredom that would result in better security.

HIJACKING OF FLIGHT 100

INTERNATIONAL HERALD TRIBUNE
SATURDAY-SUNDAY
FEBRUARY 22-23, 1993
U. S. to UNDERTAKE a FULL REVIEW of AIRPORT SECURITY
New York Times Service

WASHINGTON - The US Transportation Secretary, Richard Pena, announced a "comprehensive review" of security conditions and procedures at the nation's airports. Officials in the Transportation Department said the review was being undertaken to determine compliance with recently ordered security measures and to assess the adequacy of more established procedures, including passenger screening, baggage handling and detection of explosives. The review is to be completed by the end of the year, the officials said.

NEW YORK TIMES
WEDNESDAY, MARCH 11, 1993
AIRLINE WORKERS CHARGED in COCAINE RING at KENNEDY

Federal agents and the Port Authority police said yesterday that they had broken a sophisticated ring of airline workers that had smuggled cocaine into Kennedy International Airport aboard Pan American World Airways flights from Brazil. The ring was regularly able to bring suitcases containing 50 to 90 pounds of cocaine in the country.
Last year the Federal Government indicted 22 baggage and cargo handlers employed by Eastern Airlines in Miami on charges of smuggling cocaine from Columbia, "This is the tip of the iceberg," said Sterling Johnson, New York State special narcotics prosecutor, who said the smuggling was going on at other airlines and airports.

HIJACKING OF FLIGHT 100

02:41 Pacific Standard Time
Hillsborough, California

He awoke with a start. Someone was in his airplane. In his cockpit. They wanted to hijack his aircraft. He, the aircraft commander, the Captain, was powerless to stop them. He could see fire and hear panic. He could smell smoke.

He could also smell the smoky sharp odor of spent gunpowder. He instinctively knew a great number of people could be injured. Though now awake, he could see the face of the anxious hijacker. He couldn't recognize the man, but knew this terrorist was responsible for the attack.

The hijacker held a tall, blonde Pan American Stewardess hostage, the blunt end of his pistol pressed deeply into her neck.

Confusion flooded over him. Though awake, he was not certain if he had been dreaming about the hijacking, or if the hijacking had actually taken place.

Quickly, he awakened sufficiently to realize this had simply been a nightmare. Yet, there was something that had alerted him that his dream might be a precursor of events yet to unfold.

Maybe, he thought, his dream somehow was a latent review of the anti-terrorist training he had attended last week in Los Angeles. Captain John Testrake, a TWA pilot who had been hijacked in the

Middle East, had been one of the guest speakers. Perhaps that meeting had planted a seed in his subconscious that had now surfaced.

Don Webber felt a gnawing concern about the dream's frightening reality. The dream made no sense, especially the Pan Am Cabin Attendant, who looked remarkably like Kathryn.

The dream had been so life-like. Confused, he fitfully rolled over onto his stomach, punched his pillow into a submissive ball and tried unsuccessfully to put this dream out of his mind. Eventually, he fell back into an uneven sleep. Even in his sleep, his subconscious mind roiled and struggled with the probability the nightmare would most likely return.

01

05:45 Pacific Standard Time
Hillsborough, California

The room was still dark. Just the slightest hint of light began to peek around the edges of the dark window curtains on the east windows of their bedroom. The insistent electronic chirping of the alarm brought him reluctantly awake. His imagination was still wrapped around his troubling and unfinished dream.

He silently chose to lie still and enjoy the moment.

In this sensory solitude, he could hear Kathryn saying something humorous about his prowess, "I love it when we are like this. You are so good." She chuckled deep in her throat with her lilting Norwegian inflection on the word "so."

He wondered why he was responding to his dream about Kathryn. It seemed she recently had become the central star in many of his thoughts. Or, if regrettably, it was simply an early morning indicator he needed to arise and start his morning bathroom routine.

Ruth Webber had awakened as well. She was not sure if Don was there. From habit, she reached over to see if he was in their bed. She looked for physical reinforcement to diminish the growing feeling their marriage was in pathetic straits.

Don quickly turned away. This only reaffirmed her suspicion he no longer found her attractive or desirable. This morning was like most others. Before Ruth could say a word to Don, he was out of bed. She saw only a glimpse of the muscled backside of her husband of twenty-six years as he reached for his Rolex watch. His lean, 6'-1" frame disappeared into his portion of their shared master bath.

He stood in the foggy shower and hot water and confusion washed over him. In this private place, he tried to sort out the conflicted facets in his life. He needed to find a solution to resolve his emotional conflict between Ruth and Kathryn. Scenarios ran through his mind, and he became more confused. Part of his dilemma stemmed from the fact Kathryn knew about his marriage, while Ruth could only guess or suspect there might be someone else.

Involuntarily, Don denied his guilt. "I've been a good husband and a good father." Then he added in a whisper, "It just happened I met someone else."

The water on his back turned cold as he depleted the heater's supply. The change in temperature brought him back. He finished soaking up the last of the water and reflected on the state of his affairs.

He mused, "Perhaps, this was the origin of the term 'Affairs of State.' Probably not, maybe just a play on words." He looked in the mirror and briefly rationalized the word affair had no relation to the situation that had developed between him and Kathryn.

Recently, Kathryn had become passively resistant to him. Sexually, she was compliant. But, as long as he was married, she was not eager to enter into any sort of odd, undefined, ill-conceived, non-permanent relationship.

The harder he chased her, the more ambiguous she became. From the beginning of their relationship, she had made it clear she did not intend to ever again become seriously involved with a married man. And for emphasis, she had added, "Especially, another married pilot."

Flying with different airlines, she had never been with him on any of his trips. She was certain he was a very competent, professional and conscientious aviator. In her view, and to those of her friends who had met him, Captain Don Webber was good looking, caring and an intelligent person.

Many told her they made a handsome couple; she with her Nordic beauty and he with a perpetual tan and striking white hair. Though he was twenty two years her senior, she had found him to be attractive. From the first time they had met, there was a magnetic attraction toward him. He was trim, but always battled his weight. He was pleased his uniform size was the same as when he was discharged from the United States Navy.

Kathryn, as Ruth, had found his eyes fascinating. Always a cobalt blue. They could, however, quickly and subtlety shift color with his mood. They sometimes drifted from a bottomless pool of blue light to a dark and angry color of the sky during a violent winter storm.

Don entered their bedroom and dressed quietly and quickly. He hoped Ruth had gone back to sleep. He did not want to ruin what he perceived as the beginning of a good day, a fabulous day, one in which he would end at JFK International Airport.

New York City, where he would spend tonight and most of tomorrow with Kathryn. His reverie was broken when Ruth stirred and asked, "Where are you going?" Resentment rose in him as he attempted to back down the conversation with a cold reply, "I picked up a trip to JFK."

Silently, he thought to himself, "If she paid more attention to what I did and where I was going, maybe there wouldn't be a need for me to be involved with Kathryn."

To his wife of 26 years, he rudely finished the conversation that had hardly begun, "I'm on 100 today to JFK." Without feeling, he said, "I'll be back on 99 tomorrow night."

He dressed in his dark blue uniform slacks, tasseled black loafers and white uniform shirt. He completed his attire with the regulation black knit tie.

HIJACKING OF FLIGHT 100

Carefully, he evaluated himself in the mirror and paid particular attention to the gold wings on his uniform shirt with the four gold and black stripes on the epaulets on each shoulders. He left the bedroom, opened the hall closet door and slipped on his coat.

Subtly, he had changed from Don Webber suburban male, to Captain Webber, commander of a Boeing 747 bound for New York.

Don picked up his packed black leather suitcase and matching leather navigation kit, turned and started out the kitchen door to the car.

Just as the door closed, he thought he heard Ruth say, "Good bye, Honey. I'll see you when you get home tomorrow night." Then very tentatively, "I love you."

He didn't respond, but felt a saddened sense of resentment. Ruth had taken unfair advantage of him and had made him feel even more resentment toward her as he left for the airport. He noted with growing dismay that today, he also resented the company, the trip, the airline and the world in general.

Being with Kathryn tonight would make things much better.

02

**06:15 Pacific Standard Time
Hillsborough, California**

At this hour of the morning, traffic from Webber's house was light as Don drove briskly to San Francisco International Airport. He idly listened to the weather, traffic and news on KGO radio. He then inserted a tape Kathryn had given him. The tape hissed, whirred and then started to play. It was Kathryn's voice, pleading in a little girl tone, "Hurry, Donny. I can't wait for you..."

Her voice trailed off, "...to be with me."

There was the muffled rustle of sheets moving, and then slightly out of breath, Kathryn implored, "I haven't been with you for a long time, lover. I've missed you."

Some weeks ago, Don had been unexpectedly assigned to a 747 flight to New York. He and Kathryn had not seen each other for two months. Don was elated at the prospect of being with her again. In a rush, he had called her from the airport in San Francisco, telling her he was on the way. She met him at Kennedy Airport, where they took the first available cab into Manhattan.

During that long ride, she had turned to him, and then silently opened her long coat. She clearly revealed she was wearing little under her outer garment.

Don had caught a fleeting glimpse of her breast as she continued to tease him in the cab. At the small restaurant she provoked him by brashly rubbing his thigh under the table. He had been awash with lust and had been in a rush to take a cab back to her apartment. She teased him even more by saying she wanted to walk.

He had protested, to no avail. However, he gave in when she said, "Go ahead. Take a cab, lover. I am going to walk. You will only have a longer wait for me outside my flat."

When they finally arrived at her apartment, both slightly out of breath, she became an animal. It was during this encounter that she had made the tape of them, with a small recorder on the nightstand by her side of the bed.

The next morning she presented him with the tape saying, "When we are apart, lover, listen to this tape. Listen to how good you were, how good we are and then think of us being together." Her lilting Norwegian accent seemed much stronger as she dominated the conversation.

During the past three weeks, Don had listened to the tape many times. He listened to it in his car, on his Walkman when he walked in the morning, and on his stereo at home when Ruth was gone. The effect of hearing them making love was profound. He was consumed, seeking various ways to get the airline to schedule him on a flight to New York.

Reflectively, Don thought that he had not seen Kathryn for over a month. On his last trip to New York, she had been on a Pan Am flight to Rio. When he found she was on that flight, his mood vacillated between anger, frustration and deep disappointment. Kathryn had him under her influence. She appeared to be ambivalent about the obvious fact he was married.

Suddenly, a blinding, vivid recollection forced itself on him as he pulled into the airport parking lot. The vision was of the hijacker in this morning's dream. His involuntary response came from the subconscious. Loudly and spontaneously he said with anger, "No. No. Not today. You son of a bitch."

His own voice startled him, "You'll never get away with this on my flight." He remained surprised he had spoken aloud.

As quickly as these thoughts had erupted, they eroded and were put aside. Replaced with the sense that nothing else mattered except seeing her.

03

06:15 Pacific Standard Time
San Jose, California

Guillermo Villas Guerrero had been awake most of the night. It was nearly morning. He lay on his side in a fetal position. His attempts at sleep had been largely unsuccessful. He was angry at being forced to sleep in this too small, hand-me-down bed. Throughout the night he had accomplished nothing other than constant tossing and turning. Now, he felt cold in the early hours of the morning.

At least twice during the night he thought he was going to be sick. His stomach continued its rebellion against the overindulgence in his cousin's wife's Cuban *cena*, the evening meal of black beans, rice and sausage swimming in thick grease and spices. He had washed the meal down with three or four cans of a cheap Mexican beer.

After dinner, he had gone out in their barren back yard and smoked the last of his good Acapulco Gold.

Now, in the early morning light, he lay in the narrow twin bed while his mind raced with thoughts of the things that probably would, or could, go wrong today.

One moment, he felt the hijacking was going to be a snap, a

piece of cake. The next moment he was terrified with recurring and rampant visions of failure.

The result of his dreamed failure was always the same. He would fail. He would be caught. He would go back to prison for a very long time, *prisión durante muy largo tiempo*.

Over the past days, his chronic thoughts of apprehension always ended with him being captured. Sometimes in these vignettes, he would be shot. Other times, he died. The ultimate however, was when he was captured and then sentenced to life in prison without the possibility of parole.

Reluctantly, for reasons he did not understand, there was no turning back. His brothers were depending on him. If he quit now, he would be seen as a coward, *a sustantivo*.

"Today was the day," he thought, *"Hoy era el día."* Recently, he had caught himself saying those words and that phrase many times over.

He knew that in his past, he never had succeeded at anything. He failed every time. As much as he wanted to convince himself otherwise, deep inside, he knew that today would probably be just another example of his exceptional ability to fail.

He tried to take comfort and convince himself that their plan, "The Plan" or *"El Plan"* would work flawlessly. But nagging fears of failure continued to trickle into his consciousness and erode his already low sense of confidence.

Failure was perhaps the one thing Guillermo Guerrero y Villas did best. From long experience in hard learned lessons from life, he believed that those who were failures were also losers.

Failures equaled losers and losers were fools. In his mind, being seen as a fool was unacceptable. Most people he knew, with the exception of his brothers, were fools or weaklings.

In prison, he thought most of the inmates were losers. This was especially how he felt about the effeminate ones - the *Maricóns*, the fags.

Several times while in prison, he had been the target of rough physical sexual raids during exercise periods in the yard. He had not been able to defend himself because so many inmates ganged up on him. In those moments, he could only go along with his captor's wishes. He hated himself for being so weak. He was still fearful and very angry about those frightening, and sometimes, sickening advances.

When he left prison he carried only one remembrance, his rampant and undeniable feelings of hatred and contempt toward males who demonstrated any sexual attraction toward him.

Before going to California State Prison, he liked his name, Guillermo. But the inmates made fun of him and his Latin name. Immediately after his release, a lingering aftereffect from his prison experience was that he decided to change his name and thus his identity.

He tried William. That was the closest to Guillermo. But each time he heard the name William, it reminded him of Guillermo. That always reminded him of prison. Which reminded him of terror and abuse. The name Billy was no good. To him, it was the name for a sissy.

Finally, he chose the Americanized name of Bill. He liked the connotation the name Bill brought to mind. He thought it was very strong, masculine and, most important, powerful. He could think of no losers or weaklings named Bill.

04

06:30 Pacific Standard Time
San Jose, California

After serving ten months of his twenty-four month sentence, the Superior Court of Santa Clara County mandated the Department of Corrections to place him in one of many halfway houses in and near San Jose. Guillermo believed he was being "processed" out because of his perceived innocence. In fact, he and most others were released to halfway houses solely because of overcrowding in this prison, which the California courts had deemed as being excessive punishment.

His parole officer had been successful in finding him a job as a food handler's helper with Marriott Airline Catering at the San Jose airport. After two weeks, he was laid off but was eligible for a transfer to Marriott's catering facility at San Francisco International Airport. Parole carried many conditions, any one of which, if violated, would result in his immediate return to a California Department of Corrections medium security facility.

Consistent with his history, Bill had recently been evicted from his boarding house. Though he could not accept blame for his eviction, it was clearly his fault. In less than two months, he had fallen behind in his rent.

His cousin Frank Medina offered him a place to stay, telling his wife and family, "Bill is welcome as long as need be."

Maria, his cousin's wife, did not share her husband's *me casa, su casa* attitude of traditional Latin hospitality. She genuinely did not like Guillermo. His being there ruined their already strained household food budget. This, combined with the close quarters in their overcrowded three bedroom, one bath bungalow, only made the situation worse.

Bill paid no rent. On one or two occasions, he did give money for groceries.

Bill wished he had more privacy. He wanted to be able to bring local young Mexican women back to his "place" for the evening. This was impossible because he was forced to share the smallest bedroom with his nine-year-old cousin. The tension between Bill and Maria grew daily.

Finally, in an attempt to placate Maria, he offered to babysit for them while they went out. Unfortunately, when they returned from a Spanish language movie, they found Bill unconscious on the floor, probably from an overdose of drugs, or alcohol, or both.

During the last two months, Maria Medina made it clear to her husband that Bill Guerrero was not welcome in their house. Traditionally, the husband made those decisions. But, in this case, Maria was very good at "encouraging" her husband to do as she wished.

Bill overheard their arguments and offered his opinion. "This place is no palace either, you know. All these damn little kids running everywhere. I can't, like, even leave my things out, because they disappear."

These statements did little to relieve tension in the Medina household. Maria held her ground and then gradually stepped up her campaign to evict Bill.

05

06:45 Pacific Standard Time
San Jose, California

Frank Medina later told Federal Bureau of Investigation that during this time when Maria was openly campaigning to evict his younger cousin, Bill had called his brother Juan Guerrero in Miami.

Though Frank could only hear one side of the conversation, his recollection was clear and positive,

"Yo, Juan. This is Guill.

"In 'Frisco...Yeah. Well no. I had a job at Marriott in San Jose, but I got transferred to San Francisco.

"Then, like, I don't know what, man. I get fired again.

"Yeah, well they, like, had a sweep of the employees' lockers.

"Right on, Bro...They found my stash of Acapulco Gold in my locker.

"Wait. Then, get this. My *puta* landlady threw me out, couldn't pay my rent.

"No, No...No way man, I don't want no money."

He paused, then said, "I just want to come back to Miami, and look for a job. Or something.

"This Frisco sucks. Too cold and damp.

"Maria's giving me a hard time about moving out.

"She really wants me out of here.

"How about coming back to Miami?" His face lit up.

"Yeah. Right, that sounds OK, man."

Frank sensed Juan had been trying to talk Bill into something, "Well, Frank, he scored some hot airline tickets.

"Yeah. Well, of course. they're blank.

"He says I can fill them in for like wherever I want to go."

He looked questioningly at Frank, "Right?" Frank nodded in agreement.

Guillermo continued, "So, can I, like, come back to Miami?"

A long pause followed. "Look, Juan, I don't want no trouble. I already got a little conviction record out here. You know I did some prison time and now I'm out on parole."

There was a long pause while he listened, then said, "You know that. I don't want to get, like, busted or nothin' stupid like that."

Frank said Bill again listened for a long time but said nothing while Juan talked.

Finally Bill said, "Hey, *Senorito*, that would be great. Where the hell would I get the airplane to hijack and where would I hijack it to?" He waited, then said, "That's brilliant, you dumb *burro*."

In disgust Bill tossed the telephone onto the couch. In a resigned act of finality, he picked it up. "Well just 'cause he went to a few night classes about being an airplane mechanic, don't mean I know anythin' about hijacking no fuckin' airplane."

Another pause, then Bill covered the phone and said to Frank, "He must be crazy. He wants me to hijack a plane to Cuba. Franco, my brother has lost it."

Bill's tone had been angry as he spoke to Juan, "Wait a minute.

"Hold on, man…

Let me get this straight, you want me to just think about hijacking a plane to Havana."

He paused, and then said, "Well, I've thought about it. And you are fucking *loco* man."

Bill snorted and said, "Hey, Juan, d'you know what those crazy Cuban *Guardia Civilia* guards would do to me? A Cuban who left not exactly legally?

"Just think about it, if I, like, came back to Cuba in a hijacked jet. Think about what they would do to me.

"Well that's great for you to say, Juan. You sit there in Miami and watch me to go to Havana. You don't got no risk. All you do is sit back and collect the bread. I take all the risk and I go to jail.

"I don't think that's a good idea at all. I think the whole thing is *basura*, it's garbage. It stinks."

Bill paused while Juan said something and then went on, "Right man, when you get the details worked out, like how I can get the hijacking done and not go to jail, you call me."

Finally, Bill shook his head sadly and ended the conversation with, "Yeah, man. You do that. You let me know."

After his phone conversation, Bill confided to his cousin that he thought Juan was *loco en la cabeza*, crazy in the head.

However, the seed of a plan had been set and started to germinate. Juan Guerrero thought of ways to accomplish what he needed. He knew his brother was perfect for this job. If enough money were offered, Little Guillermo was always there to pick up his share.

Juan also knew there were two parts to the plan. First, keep Bill interested. Keep him on the hook. Then second, figure a way to make the plan so attractive that Bill would beg for a chance to join in.

More than three weeks had elapsed since the first call from Juan to his brother Bill. There had been many conversations that contained offers and counter offers between Juan and Bill, all in an attempt to build their plan. Juan saved the last bit of motivation until last Saturday.

"Guerillmo, I have some great news. Joaquin is going to help us hijack a plane." Bill was stunned, but doubtful.

"Right on. I talked to him last night."

"When? Where?"

A short pause, Juan said, "In Havana. He is with us."

The brothers had been close when they lived as a family in Cuba. Joaquin was the oldest. Then came half-brothers Juan and finally, little Guillermo. All three had grown up in Zaragoza, in the hills southeast of Havana. Early after the revolution, their father, Ernesto Villas, found a way to escape to Miami, leaving his wife and their sisters in Zaragoza.

It was their homeland that Bill missed. He missed his older sisters and his mother. He would never admit to anyone that he missed his brothers. However, when Juan said Joaquin was going to help, Bill found it hard to refuse. Slowly but reluctantly, Bill agreed to consider joining them in their plan, "The Plan."

06

06:45 Pacific Standard Time
San Jose, California

Slowly, Bill half-climbed and half-rolled out of his narrow bed. The stale stench that came from him and his bed overwhelmed him. He was naked except for his stained boxer shorts.

He staggered as he tried to steer himself into the pink tiled bathroom. He bent over the cracked porcelain tub. The cascading motion and roaring sound of the shower resulted in waves of nausea. Robotically, he stepped into the lukewarm shower. He still suffered from an overpowering hangover.

As he had done many times before, he vowed once again he would stop the abuse. "No more man. I'm like completely messed up my head."

That raw thought again crossed his mind and a chill went through him. "Today's the big day. *Hoy es el gran día.*"

"I have to be cool today. I can't be puking, feeling like shit."

The nausea returned.

He thought, "If Juan and me can make this plan work, I might only be in jail in Cuba for a few days." He had never accurately considered how the brutal *Policía Federal Cubano* notoriously treated captured criminals who had taken an airplane hostage to Cuba. He didn't know or understand that most, if not all, hijackers simply dissolved into the Cuban criminal justice system. Nor did he understand there are over one-hundred-thousand prisoners in many jails in Cuba—prisoners who are essentially without identity, name or representation; effectively serving a life sentence for a variety of misdemeanor or felony offenses.

He stopped and considered, "Two weeks at the most. After that there would be plenty of time for drugs, women and booze when I get back to Miami."

He finished soaping his chest and legs and then slowly rubbed himself with his soapy hand. He did not finish the task. He felt anyone who had to resort to playing with himself was not a man, but a little boy, *un enclenque*.

Bill rinsed with barely warm water, while the moldy shower curtain continued to cling to him.

He resented the abrupt coldness of the floor that chilled him when he stepped onto the tiles. Bill dripped water on the floor and left footprints from the tub to the toilet then toward the sink.

He took the only towel in the bathroom and rubbed his back and buttocks. He felt the dampness from the last user. He wiped his face with the towel and smelled the sour and damp odor of mildew.

He dried off and unsuccessfully attempted to wrap the towel around himself. The towel would not stay in place. In a tug of anger, he threw the towel back in the corner between the toilet and wall.

Bill stared at himself in the condensation-covered mirror and saw an undistinguished Latino in his late twenties. This morning, he thought he looked like he was in his forties. His thin, acne-scared face was framed by long wet black hair. The saddest and most predominant elements of his face were his dark and deeply sunken eyes that rested in fleshy pads of discolored and swollen skin. His stare lingered on the mirror for a moment, "*Jesus de Cristo*, I look like shit."

He plunged his hands into the hot water. Maybe it was the hangover, or more probably, from minimal damage to his synapses from his chronic drug abuse. He felt no heat, nor the sharp pain from the hot water. When he finally reacted and jerked his hands from the hot water, he scraped the skin on the back of both hands on the tap. That injury also did not immediately register.

Bill could not think clearly; he could only react to external stimulus and events. The scalded skin, the contusions and the panic he felt about today's events somehow caused him to decide shaving was not important.

He recently had seen a Middle East leader on television with a checkered scarf on his head and remembered the old man needed a shave. He thought growing a beard might be a further example of his maleness and strong character. He convinced himself that he was going to be a hero.

"Yes. Today. Today, I will become a rich and powerful hero." He knew the newspapers, radio and the television stations in San Francisco and in Cuba would picture him as a successful man.

He retraced his steps to his nephew's bedroom. A cheap plastic Crucifix stared at him from the wall above the mirror on the dresser.

He had never before noticed the cross.

Pleadingly, he said, "Maybe Mary, *Madre de Jesus*, will look after me today." Old religious instructions from his childhood surfaced as he involuntarily and mechanically made the sign of the cross.

07

**07:00 Pacific Standard Time
San Jose, California**

Seated on the edge of the bed, he felt only slightly better. The nausea and dizziness had diminished. If he didn't move too quickly, he could tolerate it.

He got up slowly and opened the dresser drawer. There were only a few clothes to choose from. He pulled out two pair of under shorts, a red T-shirt, his long sleeve shiny black polyester shirt and a thin pair of black nylon socks. Then he opened the dirty clothes bag and pulled out his faded tan cotton chino pants. From under the bed he retrieved his new black work shoes that smelled of grease from the Marriott kitchens.

He looked briefly at his reflection in the dresser mirror and another wave of fear and sadness came over him again. He sadly realized, "This is the last time I'll be in California. I hope to hell everything works out OK."

He finished dressing and checked himself in the mirror for the last time.

One of the few things he needed to take was the old black Nike gym bag on the shelf in the back of the closet. He pulled the bag down and tossed it on the bed. Clouds of dust rose up. With no real consideration given to his needs, he quickly stuffed his belongings into the bag. To this meager pile, he added the pistol, two Valium tablets wrapped in a plastic baggie, six 9mm bullets, and less than twenty dollars.

He was very apprehensive about using a gun that looked like it was made from a dull grainy plastic. Again he was surprised at how little the gun weighed. At first he thought it might be a toy. The first time he pulled the trigger, he broke out in a sweat when the brittle metallic sound the firing pin struck a spent shell casing.
That hard click loudly reinforced that this was all very real.

He remembered the judge at his trial saying his sentence was lighter than usual because Bill had not used a gun in the attempted robbery. Bill's parole officer also made it clear that should he ever be caught with a gun, that fact alone would violate his parole. Bill knew a violation of his parole would result in a return bus ride back to prison.

In an attempt to settle his concerns, Juan carefully explained how to sneak the gun and ammunition past any security checkpoint at the airport. According to Juan, the gun would not be detected by the notoriously inaccurate airport X-Ray machines. As a test, Juan had sent the ammunition through airport security in Miami where he worked for Eastern Airlines. On a different day, he sent the graphite 9 mm pistol through a security checkpoint at American Airlines. Both attempts were successful.

Braced with this success, Juan wrapped the composite plastic handgun in several rags, put the bundle in an old purse and sent the package down the security conveyor belt. The antiquated X-Ray equipment detected nothing. No alarm or other type of a warning.

The seedy Lebanese who had sold Juan the graphite pistol had been correct. The plastic pistol was not particularly accurate. It was lightweight, cheap, and most important, promised to be invisible to X-ray. Juan paid $200 for the pistol and $25 more for a handful of 9 mm ammunition.

After the test, Juan sent the pistol and ammunition to Bill. He had convinced his brother if the Post Office did not discover the gun, the airport security people wouldn't either. Bill had not been impressed. He was still terrified about being caught at the airport and going back to jail.

The postal service never suspected anything and the package containing the gun and ammunition had been delivered without a problem.

Bill carefully followed Juan's instructions after he made sure the gun was unloaded.

He remembered the advice, "Put the shells in your pocket. They won't set off the metal detector. Put the gun in your suitcase. Wrap it in a jacket or pants. No problem."

Following these suggestions, he opened his cousin's drawer, took a green wool shirt and two pair of socks in which he wrapped the graphite handgun. He next bundled the socks in a pair of underwear, and then enclosed the cloth clump in the coarse wool shirt. Not seeing the gun made him feel better as he stuffed the package of clothes in the bag and zipped it closed.

Almost casually, Bill put the 9mm shells in his pants pocket, then scooped up the plastic-wrapped yellow Valium tablets and meager cash that he quickly stuffed in the other pocket.

Briefly, Bill looked at his nine year old cousin Roberto, who was still sleeping. Though he never liked the kid, seeing him for this last time made Bill feel sad. Without a word, he strode quickly out of the bedroom, down the hall and through the living room to the front porch.

08

07:05 Pacific Standard Time
San Jose, California

Once outside he felt better as he walked across the rocky dirt surface that had once been a lawn. Bill crossed the stained sidewalk and then slumped onto the passenger's seat of his cousin's old dull green and primer-colored Chevrolet.

Frank had offered Bill a ride to the airport. For once, Maria had not complained, knowing that the ride to the airport meant Bill would be gone from their home and lives.

Bill sat quietly and waited. The interior of the car was like the rest of his cousin's belongings. Torn, dirty, run-down, dusty and used up. Bill had ample time to mull over the events which he, Juan and Joaquin were going to set into motion.

He wanted to get moving. He felt tense and impatient as he waited for the car to take him away.

A wave of strange feelings rolled over him. His first reaction was tremors. He was cold and clammy while a feeling of despair and anxiety consumed him. Bill could not pinpoint exactly what was wrong. He was shaken by an incredible fear. A fear of failure. A fear of being apprehended. And most important, a fear of being returned to prison.

On the one hand, Bill desperately wanted to be on his way. Yet, at the same time, he felt saddened about leaving this place that offered security. Most of all, he wanted today's events to be over with. He wanted the hijacking behind him.

09

09:00 Eastern Standard Time
John F. Kennedy International Airport

Frankfurt Lazlo Fielding slowly and painfully struggled to drag his two hundred seventy pound body to the second floor landing on his way to his office on the third floor of the hangar. With increased frequency, he had to stop to catch his breath. Each time he stopped, he vowed he would quit smoking. First in German and then English. *"Gott helfe mir, sie aufzugeben. Ein für allemal"* "God help me, to give them up. Once and for all."

He heard footsteps coming up the stairwell behind him and he consciously but ineffectively attempted to stifle his pained and labored breathing.

It was his assistant, Becky Mariweather. She had recently graduated and had also received her FAA Dispatcher license. She was his clerk and professional protégé. "Good morning, Sir. How are you, today?"

He did not want to appear frail or incapacitated. But when he started to answer her he felt an unbridled and uncontrollable cough starting deep in his chest. The more he tried to stifle the urge, the more pronounced it became. His autonomic nervous system produced a monumental, rattling, hacking, uncontrolled thoracic explosion. Fielding, for the second time today, felt he would not survive many more of these coughing onslaughts.

His face was contorted. An ugly, dull red color filled his cheeks and forehead. Becky was embarrassed for him. She saw he was having so much difficulty breathing he was unable to answer her. She felt she should offer assistance, but did not want to offend him.

Lightly, she touched his arm, "Are you all right, Mr. Fielding? Do you want to sit on the stairs and rest for a moment? Is there anything I can do for you?"

He was able to respond only with a rasping, "Fine."

Intentionally and quite slowly, he drew in five or six deep breaths and said, "I'll be fine. As soon as I catch my breath." Though it sounded clear to him, his statement came out as a muffled and unintelligible string of wheezing consonants.

He coughed again and made that horrible sound in his throat. Without thinking, he instinctively placed his hand on his chest. Becky saw he was still a crimson color, sweating, and appeared to be in a great deal of discomfort.

He smiled and with only slightly less effort said, "I'm much better now. I just needed to rest for a minute."

"Mr. Fielding, are you sure you're OK?"

He nodded. "Fine. Thank you for your concern." He added, "Damn cigarettes."

Only partially satisfied with his explanation and rationalization, she said with a feigned smile, "All right then. If you're sure you will be OK, I'll go on upstairs and get started on the maps."

As almost an afterthought, she added, "Then I'll see about making you some tea."

"Thank you, Becky. That will be fine."

Lazlo pressed himself against the banister to let her by. He watched until she had disappeared up the stairs, and only then very slowly started up behind her. His young and lithe assistant had bounded up two flights of stairs without a missed beat.

As well she should, being almost forty years my junior, he thought.

Once he had reached the last stair, he rested for a full minute. "Oh, what I would give to be able once again to catch my breath."

He looked down the long, dimly lit hallway at his office on the other side of the World War Two era aircraft hangar. Each week, the walk seemed longer and used more of his dwindling energy.

Every day, it seemed to him that it took longer for his breathing to return to normal. The last time he counted, his respiration rate was more than twenty-five breaths per minute. To him, it felt he could never get enough air. Recently, he felt he had trouble getting the bad air out of his lungs.

Eventually, and with continued discomfort, he reached the end of the hall, leaned against the wall and pressed the call button.

On the other side of the double doors, one of the dispatch clerks heard the buzzer and looked through a small glassed window. He recognized Lazlo, reached under his desk and pressed the switch to unlock the doors. Lazlo Fielding weakly pressed against the doors that easily yielded to his weight.

10

09:15 Eastern Standard Time
John F. Kennedy International Airport

Two steps and he was inside the airline's dispatch office. This was the nerve center for the airline's entire domestic and international operation. An easy comparison could be made to the National Air Space Administration facilities in Houston.

There were not many employees. For those who worked here, their tasks were similar. The room was almost soundless. Muted conversations quietly droned across the large room and surrounded Lazlo while he slowly and intentionally headed toward his office. Out of the corner of his eye he saw Becky walk in with several facsimile weather maps from the US Weather Bureau printers.

He turned the overhead lights on and heard the Bearcat radio-scanner come to life. To him, a symphony was being played by old and familiar voices and phrases carried on fifteen Very High Frequency radio channels assigned to John F. Kennedy International Airport.

Becky stood next to his desk and waited for him to sit at his computer terminal. He rounded the end of the desk and sank into his chair. He tried to pull the chair under his desk, but could not gain any traction on the anti-static mat. The minor exertion caused his choppy and rapid breaths to return.

She turned, reached and helped him push his chair closer to the desk. Once seated properly, he leaned forward and signed in at the keyboard. He noted the time, green numerals on a black seventeen-inch monitor: 09:16. It had taken him over fifteen minutes to travel from the front of the building, by the security guard's desk, to his third floor office; a distance of less than fifty yards.

He lit a cigarette. His fifth this morning. He kidded himself that it was the first of the day at work.

Becky brought him back to reality when she returned with a steaming mug in her hand. She lightly approached him. "Here you go, Sir. A nice cup of tea." She paused, waiting for him to acknowledge her.

No acknowledgment came, so she timidly added, "and here are the NOAA maps from early this morning."

She delicately placed the damp maps on Lazlo's desk. Her face showed concern as she continued, "Careful with the 300 millibar chart, it's still a very damp."

She stood directly behind him and studied over his shoulder. Though fully licensed by the Federal Aviation Administration, she was new to the airline. She wanted to learn from her boss, an old timer. What did he first look at when reviewing the overnight weather maps? To her dismay, the first thing he looked for was his ashtray, which she had carelessly covered with the maps. She retrieved the glass ashtray and put it on top of the maps, next to his tea.

He continued to ignore her as he looked at the weather charts. He flipped through the large sheets of paper, one at a time, until he came to the damp 300 millibar chart.

With a slight German accent, Lazlo asked, "Why is it that the chart I want to see is the one that that is always wet? I can't write on this until it dries. This is dumb."

HIJACKING OF FLIGHT 100

Becky thought perhaps she should apologize, but before she could he sighed with resignation and began to study the free formed brown lines on the damp oatmeal colored paper. Lines of equal barometric pressure, temperature and wind direction; isobars, isotherms and isotachs. This chart showed NOAA meteorologist interpretations and assessments of the constantly moving jet stream at approximately 30,000 feet altitude.

Quietly, Becky stood in the background and waited. She was still on her new-hire probation period. She did not want to do anything to put her employment in jeopardy. Nor did she want to appear pushy. She had graduated with a bachelor's degree in meteorology—now called weather science. Her goal had always been to work for an airline as a dispatcher. At one time, she had considered a career as a pilot, but her uncorrected vision kept her on the ground. She rationalized that she was better suited to provide weather and flight planning information to the flight crews than to be a pilot herself.

She twisted her fingers together behind her back and pulled a #2 pencil from the bun on the back of her head. She mindlessly wondered if pencils were made in any grades other than #2. She correctly guessed his silence was just his way of studying the daily maps needed to forecast the airline's operations.

Becky thought it was strange the way he sat absolutely motionless and said nothing as he peered at the high altitude chart before him.

When Lazlo finally spoke, it startled her. "Here. Look at this."

She sucked in her breath, "Look at what, Sir?"

"This occluded front." He intently studied the brown crescent that extended from northwest of Cleveland to a position just south of Louisville. Slowly, the line became thinner, until it dissipated over the Gulf of Mexico.

It was this tan scimitar covering half the map that held his attention. Lines of pressure, temperature and wind would tell a predictable tale of weather occurrences for the next twelve to eighteen hours. Small brown half moons, nearly the diameter of a thumb nail, alternated with brown triangles on the same side of the "line" that represented the classic pictorial definition of an occluded front. The weather data on the chart indicated this afternoon's weather would deteriorate in the eastern third of the country. The worst would be in a triangle from Pittsburgh to Boston to Washington, D. C.

Preoccupied, he did not take time to explain this potentially disturbing and extensive weather pattern, but simply said to her, "Go take a look at all the arrivals in the Eastern Sector, from Cleveland to Boston to Washington."

Lazlo was not concerned that his orders might cost the airline several hundred thousand dollars in additional fuel bills. "I think the planned arrival fuels should be increased to allow each flight at least one hour additional holding fuel, plus enough fuel to their alternate."

She was surprised by his orders. This was the first time she had been allowed to program the computer flight plans. His orders were sweeping. She did not want to make a mistake. "Every arrival?" He looked at her, but said nothing.

Becky walked to her desk and took a moment to review how she would begin the arduous task to complete Fielding's orders. For the next twenty minutes, she "busted" every preplanned fuel load and in its place constructed new flight plan release fuel loads, to which she added increased holding fuel.

Lazlo Fielding lit his sixth or seventh cigarette and then pulled up the DAP screen, the Dispatch Activity Projection on the computer. Forty-one flights would arrive in his eastern sector before his shift ended at 17:30 this evening.

Ten minutes later, Becky came back into Lazlo's office with nearly 60 sheets of computer paper in her hands. She stood next to Fielding with her arms crossed and waited for an appropriate opportunity. She marshaled her courage and brought the discrepancies to his attention. "Mr. Fielding, I've reviewed all the new releases," she paused, "most of them seem to be correct." She took a breath, "But a couple have excessive increases." She paused and then said, "The worst are Flight 100 from San Francisco to Kennedy and Flight 78 from Los Angeles to Philadelphia."

"Oh? What seems to be the matter with those releases?"

"On 100, the computer went crazy. It added 45,000 pounds to the normal release."

He put his cigarette down, looked at Becky over the top of his glasses, and turned back to his computer screen. That amount was busted and the new amount of shown to be 185,000. Finally at the bottom of the screen, Lazlo read, "CAPT - WEBBER. D." He made several additional keystrokes, and instantly, the screen blinked and came to life. Silently, the computer screen came to a stop and displayed more information about Flight 100.

His thoughts interrupted his speech. He slowly continued, "Let me look at something here." With several keystrokes he instructed the computer to rework the flight plan for 100 from San Francisco to New York. Within seconds, the task was completed. Lazlo looked at the numbers and saw that the computer still insisted on ordering 185,000 pounds of fuel for Flight 100.

"You see, these new computers have a memory. It doesn't just add one hour additional holding fuel, it looks at the history of this segment from San Francisco to New York, the departure time, the arrival time, the historical fuel consumption patterns for this particular 747, the anticipated weather, winds and various altitude information, then it decides what is an appropriate fuel load." He was out of breath.

He pressed two keys and immediately the screen went blank, and then came back to life with more detailed information. He studied this latest information on Flight 100.

Becky interrupted, "San Fran ops just sent us a message on the printer about the fuel load for 100."

She waited for his response. She heard none, looked to him for a comment, then slowly said, " So...I sent a message that we were reviewing the load and would get back to them...I hope that was okay."

When she said, "okay," she winced.

Lazlo looked up at her, but said nothing.

Impulsively, he silently and quickly pressed several keys on the computer terminal. The screen blinked immediately filled from top to bottom with more data about Flight 100. The displayed data included an aircraft maintenance history, taxi fuel burn history, even a two-week history of departure and arrival delays. He gave a Germanic nod of his head and seemed satisfied. Twice the screen blinked, but then provided him with the names of the cockpit and cabin crew on Flight 100. The Captain's name was first. The list ended with last of the flight attendants.

Lazlo ran the cursor over the Captain's name and pressed a function key. The computer responded with the FEI, Flight Experience Inventory, from which Lazlo quickly determined that Captain Don Webber was quite new on the 747.

Even though Captain Webber had been to flight school on the aircraft just a year ago, he had only flown the 747 for the past five months. He had only accumulated 151 flight hours on the 747, which Lazlo considered quite low. The computer prompted Lazlo to advance the screen. He looked up the Flight Experience Inventory of the First Officer, Fredrick Paul O'Day, which showed O'Day had been on the 747, both on International as well as Domestic operations, for more than five years, with 4,169 hours accumulated total flight time.

Based on raw data for the aircraft and normal fuel consumption, the planned fuel load suggested by the computer was excessive. Lazlo gave careful consideration to Don Webber's being new on the aircraft and then carefully considered the route and arrival weather. After a moment of thoughtful deliberation, he decided not to change Flight 100's planned fuel.

The old days intruded on his thoughts. In times past, he had personally known every captain and most of the copilots. Of course, there had only been two hundred captains and copilots. Today, there were more than three thousand pilots, each with a place on the pilot seniority list. The only way to keep track of all the crews and their assigned flights was with the computer. He muttered to himself, "Vut ever happened to da good old days?"

"Beg your pardon, Sir. Were you talking to me?"

He looked at Becky quizzically. Then he paused, lit a cigarette and said, "No. No, Becky. I wasn't taking to you. I was chust mumbling to myself."

His quizzical glance changed to one of wistful thinking as he said, "Send a message to San Fran Ops. Advise them the 185,000 pound fuel load plus

11

07:05 Pacific Standard Time
San Francisco International Airport

The sun had just begun to backlight the East Bay hills and threw long shadows, with golden highlights, across San Francisco Bay. Captain Webber took a front seat in the old, converted school bus from the employee's parking lot to the hangar and terminal. He tossed his bags on the luggage rack, made small talk with the driver and settled into his seat.

Mindlessly, his thoughts drifted until memories of Kathryn Lundgren raced through his mind as he clearly remembered his last encounter with her in New York. They had gone to a small, Italian old time restaurant in the Village. He remembered the name with great clarity - Mineta Tavern on MacDougal Street in New York.

After dinner they walked half a mile back to her apartment, taking the long way back. Once inside he started to undress her, but she resisted his advances.

Don's variety of moods climbed the scale; anger, frustration and then finally an apology. Kathryn had reluctantly invited him to spend the night, but had intentionally not invited him to sleep with her.

HIJACKING OF FLIGHT 100

Don slept on the couch. After a fitful night, the next morning he decided this was the last time he was going to see her. He was not going to be pushed and pulled by anyone, even by this amazingly beautiful woman.

The next morning she walked out of the bathroom into her living room and slowly came toward him. She wore a man's long sleeve oxford cloth dress shirt. Not one of his, he recalled.

Later that same morning they left her apartment for a leisurely brunch. During the meal, they only talked about superficial things. By the end of their lunch, Don was thoroughly confused.

Kathryn laughingly dragged him back to her apartment, where they made love during much of the early afternoon until it was time for him to catch a taxi to back to the Milford Plaza, the crew hotel in Manhattan. The rough ride across the tarmac brought him back to San Francisco and his thoughts of Kathryn were placed on hold.

Don looked through a dirty window on the bus as they approached the Employee entrance at the hangar. As usual, there were no guards on duty in the small security hut adjacent to the entrance. Don mused to himself, "That probably made sense, seeing as no one had ever hijacked an airplane hangar or the crew bus."

The American Airlines Flight Attendant who had gotten on the bus at the last stop looked at him oddly as he spoke to no one in particular.

Don felt embarrassed when he realized she was watching him. To fend off these feelings of foolishness, he looked directly at her and said, "With the increases in terrorism attacks against the airlines, airport security should be stepped up."

She smiled her best. A very non-committal grin, then in a laconic and indifferent voice said, "Whatever you say, Captain."

The ancient school bus finally groaned and shuddered to a stop in front of the domestic terminal. Don waited for the American Airlines Flight Attendant to exit, grabbed his bag and navigation kit and lightly jumped off the last step onto the concrete deck. He dropped his flight kit on the ramp and slipped into his raincoat, then pressed his uniform hat squarely on his head.

He had only recently started to wear his hat, as a concession to Kathryn. She said the contrast between the dark charcoal color of his hat and his thick white hair made him look even more the part of an airline captain. "So handsome. So dashing," she had said.

In his mind's eye, he felt he was the personification of an airline captain. He smiled as he wore his raincoat collar turned up and his hat at just the right angle. Don grabbed his bags, quickly walked through the open entrance.

Don entered operations on a lower level of the main passenger terminal and was assaulted by the vibrant colors used in this part of the building. Some time ago, upper management at the airline had hired an industrial psychologist. Their professional and clinical credo must have been, "A colorful work place is a productive work place."

The consultant had been long gone from the airline business in San Francisco. However, her colorful recommendations seemed to live forever.

He rounded the last corner and nearly collided with a ramp service person. She was dressed in the dark brown pants, tan long sleeve shirt, a brown vest and a baseball cap which was set on top of her sun-bleached blond hair. Her cap held the airline emblem, a union badge, and a giant button calling for freedom of choice in abortion.

He quickly stepped aside to let her pass and apologized, "Sorry, blind intersection."

"That's okay." She paused, looked at him and asked, "Are you the Captain on 100 today?"

"Yes. Afraid so." He looked at her. She was young with an impish air about her. She queried, "You've already been fueled. Is 185 plus 5 for taxi going to be ok?"

She waited, aimlessly rocking from one foot to the other. "If it isn't, let me know. It's no big deal. I'm still hooked up."

He thought for a moment and tried to remember the last fuel load he had to New York. "I don't know. I haven't seen the weather or the flight plan for New York. I'll let you know."

Don quickly calculated that 5 1/2 hours flying time to New York at an average of 25,000 pounds per hour would be about 140,000 pounds. He looked at her. "Actually, 185,000 probably is too much."

He considered it, smiled and said, "Tell you what. I'm sure that a 185 will be okay, maybe more than okay." She made no pretense of leaving but continued to rock back and forth, "Why don't you go ahead and disconnect. I can't see that we'll need any more fuel."

She touched the bill of her cap turned and said, "Thanks a lot, Skipper. I have three other flights to fuel this morning and I'm running late."

She turned toward the hall, looked over her shoulder. "See you on your next trip." She then disappeared down the mustard colored hall. He caught a brief whiff of her sweet perfume, but thought no perfume could mask the even stronger lingering odor of jet fuel.

12

07:10 Pacific Standard Time
San Francisco International Airport

The office in flight planning was a mess as usual. The graveyard crew used this area for their break room. The desks were covered with day-old newspapers. Half-full coffee cups and yesterday's copy of the *Racing Form* scattered about on the chairs and floor. Blank air traffic control flight planning sheets, pilot bid forms for vacation slots and expense reimbursement pads. With disgust, he shoved some of the clutter toward the round waste bucket at the end of the table.

This basket had not escaped the psychologist's brush. The barrel was marked vertically, from bottom to top, in large green letters, "REFUSE." An unknown author had written in indelible felt tip pen, "I REFUSE to empty this can."

Don went to the counter and slid open the clear glass window that separated the operations dispatch clerks and flight crew schedulers from the rest of the flight planning office.

Through the opened window Don saw a pilot who he had previously seen in the employee's parking lot this morning. He was taller than Don, probably close to 6' 3". He was talking to Shirley, an overweight Teletype operator in her mid 40s. Don thought she probably was a divorced single parent, earnestly looking for a husband. She gave her rapt and uninterrupted attention to the pilot, who was telling her what appeared to be an incredibly funny story.

Don reached through the open window and across the counter, where he rummaged through the disorganized pile of envelopes until he found the manila and red flight dispatch envelope for flight 100. The top piece of paper was the completed aircraft fueling slip, on the bottom he saw a happy face plus a scrawl, "Have A Nice Day...Suzi." Don thought the notation probably had the same sincerity as a waitress' sentiment at an airport coffee shop.

Don concentrated on the documents as he scanned information regarding Flight 100. More than twenty five pages covered pre-planned routes, fuel consumption on various routes and altitudes, departure, enroute and terminal weather forecasts. He carefully read certain messages, ignored most others and then from experience, reread several pertinent items.

Without looking, Don became aware someone was standing behind him. He turned and saw another pilot. They looked at each other and he smiled. Don noticed that both of his uniform shirt pockets were filled with pens, pencils and aircraft pocket reference cards.

He seemed chunky, not thin. Maybe in his early forties. He had thinning sandy blonde hair, and his face had a pinched look. The pilot wore steel framed glasses, the lenses of which were perfectly round, but too small for his face, so much so that the centers of the lenses did not line up with the pupils of his eyes. He gazed at Don through the outer third of each lens. He looked as though he had mistakenly put on a pair of children's glasses.

They spoke at the same time. "I'm Stan Kurtz, Flight Engineer on 100 today."

"Glad to meet you. I'm Don Webber. How long you been on the '47?" Don didn't wait or pause for an answer, but continued, "I'm fairly new on the bird. Just over a year, but I haven't flown her much, been on reserve call. Any information or insights you might have would be appreciated."

Stan thought that was a nice comment for a new guy on the airplane. "Afraid I won't be of too much help in that area, I just went to school last spring."

Don smiled. "Well, I guess we'll just have to keep an eye on each other."

Stan looked at the fuel slip, tapped the happy face with his pencil, "Suzi's quite a gal. She's a good kid. Never a problem with her work, like some of the stations." Stan picked up the fuel paperwork. "It never ceases to amaze me. Look at this. She's only off by 35 gallons. In New York, they'd be doing well if they hit the fuel load within 500 gallons."

Don looked at the fuel slip, but was not clear on what Stan was talking about. "I almost ran her down in the hallway this morning."

Briefly, Don thought about the mixed smell of Suzi's perfume and kerosene. His mind wandered to Kathryn's perfume, when he realized Stan was still talking to him.

"Why do we have so much fuel today, is the weather that bad in New York? I don't remember ever having seen a Kennedy fuel load like this before."

"Sorry, Stan. What did you say?"

Stan repeated his observations and Don responded, "I don't know, I haven't had a chance to check the weather or the flight release. But like you, I can't for the life of me figure why we have so much fuel."

Stan did some rapid mental calculations and said, "Makes no sense to me either, we can't burn more than 125 or 130 tops, even if they drag us way out over the water for a Canarsie arrival. We have enough fuel to hold for over two hours. Or, we'd have enough fuel to make Atlanta our alternate. Looks like somebody wasn't doing their homework."

Don shrugged his shoulders and said, "Maybe it had something to do with the fact that 100 was supposed to have been a DC-10 and then they put a 747 on for today."

Stan looked at him through his off-centered glasses. "Don't think so. It's been set up for a 747 for the past couple of days."

Don turned his back to Stan and started to look at the weather for the east coast arrival corridor from Boston to Washington, D. C. The weather was not particularly good. Later in the forecast period, there would be a gradual dissipation, followed by a general clearing with improved visibility. Don confirmed his unwritten declaration that JFK again would have lengthy delays at their scheduled local arrival time at 17:30.

To no one in particular, he said, "We're going to be right in the thick of the evening departure rush at Kennedy."

Stan thought, "If weather were to be a problem, the departures would start to back up. Eventually, the airport would become saturated and the inbound arrivals would have to start airborne holding in established patterns near the three main airports in New York - JFK, LaGuardia and Newark."

Don shrugged his shoulders again and thought, maybe the dispatcher knows something that we don't. Stan's remarks were muffled by the roaring laughter coming from the other side of the counter.

Stan and Don both looked across the room and saw the chunky teletype operator laughing hard, so hard she wiped tears from her eyes with the back of her pudgy hands, each finger covered with a gold-colored ring.

For some reason, Don assumed that perhaps the mirth maker was his copilot.

In a harried voice, with a bit of frustration, Don spoke loudly to the pilot across the room, "Are you on 100 today?"

Fred O'Day nodded in the affirmative.

"Do you think you can tear yourself away from the ladies," then with more than a touch of sarcasm, "and give me a hand with this flight plan?" Don looked at his Rolex and snapped, "Which, I might add, leaves in less than an hour."

The copilot was put off by this rude introduction by the Captain with whom he would spend the next six or seven hours. Fred had earlier looked at the weather and the flight plan. He knew that dispatch added Pittsburgh as an alternate for JFK. He had also noticed the large fuel increase.

Casually, Fred walked over to Don and Stan, removed his uniform hat and tossed in on the counter, where it spun and slid to a stop a couple of feet from them. Fred decided the Captain's temperamental outburst probably was nothing more than the subconscious pleading of an unsure individual. Most likely one of those who verbalized their insecurities by being brusque and irritable. His outburst about planning for their 747 trip was another not-so-subtle clue the Captain was unsure of himself in the aircraft. He quietly wondered where the airline got such men.

Fred unbuttoned his uniform jacket and reached past Don and picked up the contents of the flight information envelope. He again read the information for the second time this morning. He reflected on the odd personality of Don Webber.

Fred had never heard of this captain, neither good nor bad, which probably meant that he was either new to the domicile, or to the airplane, or both. Fred glanced at the Flight Engineer, who intently poured over the contents of a four-inch thick performance manual for the Boeing 747.

"Howdy, I'm Fred. Fred O'Day, First Officer," he smiled and extended his hand to the studious engineer.

Stan peeked at Fred over the top of his steel framed glasses and raised his eyebrows, much to say, I hope this is no indication of how the rest of this trip is going to go. Stan took Fred's hand, "Stan Kurtz. Glad to meet you."

After Fred returned all the documents to the envelope, he turned and formally introduced himself to the Captain. "Hello, I'm Fred O'Day. I'm sorry about that business over there."

Fred expected the Captain to make some attempt to smooth out the atmosphere in the room, but none came forth. Instead, the

Captain only acknowledged his introduction and apology with a sour grunt.

Fred thought maybe he should say something else to let the Captain know that he what knew what he was doing. "I don't know what those gnomes in New York were thinking about regarding the fuel for this flight. I know the weather at Kennedy's not the greatest, but almost 190,000 pounds of fuel is crazy."

Fred emphasized the word, "crazy." Don showed he barely cared that Fred was standing next to him. In exasperation, Fred concluded his review of the fueling on Flight 100 with, "It's just one of those things, I guess."

A long silence covered the room like a thick wet military tarp, until broken by Fred's final attempt at making peace. "As the saying goes, the only time you can have too much fuel on board is if you're on fire."

Don's response to his humorous comment was swift and cutting. "Do you take this job seriously? We are paid a lot of money to fly the company's aircraft safely. Carrying extra fuel is wasteful and I'm of the mind to have this excess fuel removed before our flight departure."

Fred thought, "This clown is starting to remind me of Major Frank Burns on MASH."

Don Webber's mannerisms were edged with open hostility toward Fred, "What do you think of that?"

"Think of what?"

"Defueling the aircraft down to a reasonable fuel load."

Both Fred and Stan could only look at this Captain and wonder where the company had found him. He certainly didn't seem like most of the pilots they both routinely flew with.

Fred responded quietly, "You're the boss. Whatever you want is fine with me. How much time do you think it'll take to defuel?"

Stan felt the same way, but hid it better than Fred. He paused and looked directly at Don. "How much do you want to suck out from the main tanks?" He waited a couple of seconds for an answer, but received none. "So, what will our final fuel load be for takeoff?"

Fred counted a few beats. "If you want to defuel, I'll call dispatch in New York and alert that a change is in the works." Fred continued to stare at Don. "As you know, we have to have their concurrence to reduce a fuel load."

Don knew Fred was correct. Defueling would take the better part of an hour and he would have to obtain agreement from JFK Dispatch to reduce the fuel load. But it made Don angry that his copilot had such a cavalier and capricious attitude.

His feeling was overridden by the notion that an hour delay here, would result in an hour delay for their arrival at JFK, and that would add an hour before he would be with Kathryn. Warm, random thoughts of her waiting for him in New York drummed in his mind.

He rationalized the situation, saying, "Well, that probably would result in a lengthy delay... Our passengers are entitled to an on-time departure here and arrival in New York." With as flourish, he signed his name to the flight dispatch release forms.

In an attempt to reinforce his decision, Don spoke to both Stan and Fred in a grandiose voice, "Forget the fuel reduction. We'll go with the flight plan release."

Stan excused himself, "I'm going out to the plane and start the Inertial platforms." He picked up his hat and raincoat and turned toward the door. "See you on board. I'll see if I can get one of the flight attendants to start some coffee."

Four or five minutes later, Fred picked up his hat and quickly grabbed his old worn and battered flight kit. His navigation bag was festooned with several stickers promoting the Boeing 767 and another which said, "When I get home, I'm going to Disneyland."

Then, like a good copilot, he followed Don out into the hallway.

Together they retraced Don's earlier steps, down the mustard colored hallway, past the vacant security guard's vestibule and eventually, out on to the ramp.

During the fifteen minutes they had spent in the office, the sun had risen well above the horizon. The ramp smelled of wet asphalt and concrete. In the distance across the airport, both watched a United Airlines 747 lift off in the first three thousand feet of runway.

Fred remarked, "Man, they must really be light. Either no passengers or fuel, to get off the ground that quickly." Don had no response.

On their stroll out to their 747, Don glanced at the dusty electric wall clock outside the mechanic's ready-room. It showed 8:05. Less than a half hour 'til departure. That would mean 4 hours and 50 minutes after takeoff, and he'd be in New York. And then, only 45 minutes more to get to Kathryn's apartment.

All things remaining consistent, he should be with her by 6:30 Eastern Standard Time. He quickened his pace across the ramp to the aircraft, thinking of nothing other than his evening with Kathryn.

Silently, Don recalled their last time together. Tonight was going to be on his terms. No more games to be played with him. Either she backed off with her "on again, off again" attitude, or he was going to terminate their relationship.

13

**07:20 Pacific Standard Time
San Francisco International Airport**

Early morning traffic along the James Lick Freeway—US 101 northbound toward San Francisco—was horrible, as usual. Four hundred thousand commuters from San Mateo County were determined to use the same five lanes of freeway; all at the same time. Bill's ride to the airport, his cousin's old green and gray Chevy Nova, inched along. Both driver and passenger were deep in their own private thoughts.

A strong and energetic sun attempted to stream through the windshield, but the accumulated smoke residue and grime made the windshield translucent. The glare caused Bill to close his eyes. He also tried to shut out the growing fear of approaching doom. Frank looked at Bill and wrongly assumed that his pensive and unhappy cousin was asleep.

The traffic thinned and the old car gained just enough speed to cause the front tires to start an unbalanced wobble along the entry road to the airport. The vibration rattled Bill's sun visor so that it fell down and blocked the sun. In the relative darkness he opened his eyes.

Frank glanced at Bill. "How was your siesta?"

Bill sleepily looked at his cousin, "Uh." The seriousness of the day's events wore on him. "Looks like we're here."

Bill and his brother Juan had not told Frank anything about their hijacking plan. All Frank knew was that he had given Bill a stolen American Airlines ticket which was filled out one-way from San Francisco to New York. Frank Medina knew Bill and Juan were up to no good. Somehow, the stolen ticket he had given Bill apparently played a significant part in their scheme

The old Chevrolet Nova wheezed toward the green and white sign that proclaimed, "DEPARTURES in This Lane ONLY." The car pulled into the lane and then slowly climbed the ramp to the front of the passenger drop-off area.

Frank looked for a place to drop Bill off. He found none, but tried to get as close to the curb as he could. He turned off the ignition and removed the key to unlock the trunk. Both men walked around to the back of the car where Frank unlocked the truck. Bill reached in and pulled out his black nylon bag, then slammed the deck lid closed.

Frank reached out and gave Bill the "*embrazo*", the hug, "Take care, man. Whatever you're doin', don't do nothin' stupid." Both paused and thought this might be the last time they would see each other. Frank thought Bill seemed unsettled and nervous.

"Just go to the ticket counter and give 'em your ticket. Get your boarding pass and go to the plane."

He waited for Bill to respond, but all his cousin could manage was to stare at Frank with unseeing eyes.

He finished the one-way conversation with, "You wait in there for them to call your flight."

Bill Guerrero said nothing, but only slightly nodded.

With a touch of sadness, Frank added, "And be careful."

Finally, with no emotion, Bill spoke to his cousin, "Yeah, man, thanks for the ticket and the ride. I'll see you soon."

Bill knew his last words were a lie.

Bill looked at his cousin and wished that he were staying in San Jose. Actually, he wished that he were anywhere else. Anywhere, but the airport.

A skycap materialized from out of nowhere and greeted Bill. "Good morning. Sir. I'll need to see your ticket."

Bill froze with fear. He couldn't unzip the Nike bag. He could not force himself to even reach inside. Panic poured over him. He looked at the dark-skinned skycap, who waited patiently.

"Sir. Your ticket, please." After a few seconds, the skycap said, "¿Hablas Inglés?"

Hearing those familiar words in his native Spanish, Bill realized he needed to say something to the skycap. "Just a minute. I am nervous."

"That's OK, my man. Take your time."

Bill opened the gym bag and reached inside. The ticket was gone! He looked at the skycap for help. The skycap looked back at him with a smile and waited patiently for Bill to produce his ticket.

Bill remembered where the ticket was and felt for it inside his shirt. He undid his shirt buttons with a shaking hand, pulled out the damp and wrinkled ticket. He was careful to keep a firm grip on the Nike bag.

The skycap took the ticket from him, rolled it flat and checked it. The longer Bill stood on the sidewalk, the more naked he felt and more nervous he became. He thought, "What if he knows the ticket is stolen? What if he calls the cops? What if he keeps me here until the police arrest me?"

Arrest was out of the question. Suddenly, escape was foremost in his mind. If the skycap said anything about the ticket he was going to run.

Another sickening wave of fear flushed through him. He turned just in time to see the old Nova disappear down the ramp, followed by a plume of blue smoke. His only chance for escape just went down the circular driveway toward the airport exit and out of his life forever.

The skycap did not notice anything unusual about the ticket. Even if he had noticed that it had been paid for in cash and was only issued one-way, he showed no awareness of that significance. If asked, he would have only said he was far more concerned that this poor Mexican would not give him a tip.

The skycap handed the ticket back to Bill and said, "Everything is in order. Sir. You are ready to go." He waited the requisite ten or fifteen seconds then added, "Have a nice flight."

Bill glanced downward to the outstretched hand and reached in his pocket. Without looking, he retrieved a bill. He didn't know the size of the bill as he pressed the wadded and damp green paper into open palm of the skycap.

The baggage handler looked at the $5 bill, smiled and said, "Thank you. Sir. Have a good trip." Adding, "a very very good trip." The skycap turned away, looking for the next traveler. Bill walked through the double revolving doors into the terminal.

14

07:20 Pacific Standard Time
San Francisco International Airport

The immense marble airline terminal seemed to minimize the importance of any and all who passed through. Thousands of passengers moved, collided, got lost and otherwise milled through the concourse toward individual airline ticket counters. This morning, not untypical, all the counters were jammed with passengers.

The magnitude of the terminal and the frantic activity had a negative impact on him. He entered the terminal feeling insecure. The lack of familiar sounds and sights caused his unstable feelings to run free. Once again, Bill felt panic rise up. Panic then started to control his emotions.

Neither he nor his brother Juan had established any real or significant plan. The may have had a strategy, but logistics for their plan were non-existent. The only common point of interest was their agreement that Bill would get through the terminal and onto the aircraft without getting caught or arrested.

Bill walked the length of the main terminal building. He passed Delta Air Lines, United, Mexicana, TWA and Qantas. All the ticket counters looked very similar except for the uniforms of the agents. He eventually came to the end of the main terminal building. He faced a glass wall that looked out over the ramp area.

He was confused. He looked back toward the entrance he had walked through, turned and retraced his steps. Just beyond the central newsstand and airport bar, he found what he needed. A bank of television monitors with flight information listed by departure time:

Bill was relieved. He found his flight without calling attention to himself. He did this without anyone's help. He found his airline counter and joined a line of passengers who waited patiently to purchase their tickets. Bill tried to take advantage of the motionless line to rest, but he could not relax. He concentrated on the dark blue hat worn by the older woman in front of him. All the while, he constantly looked for anyone who might recognize him.

Eventually, he came to the head of the line. The counter was chest high. High enough that he could not comfortably lean on it. He tried to do so, but that put his elbows at the same height as his shoulders.

Bill looked at the man across the counter from him for some sign of recognition. The agent stared at Bill and then at his outstretched hand. He wore very thick glasses and his uniform had white crystalline accumulations of evaporated salts near and under his armpits. Nervously, Bill subconsciously rolled the ticket envelope into a tight tube.

The agent unrolled and opened the damp packet, "You already have your ticket." He stared squarely at Bill, "This line is only for passengers who wish to purchase tickets for today's flight."

Bill thought, "This is it. He's going to find out about me. ¡Mierda! I'm done."

For reasons Bill could not understand, the agent became irritated. "Can't you read? That large sign clearly says, 'Purchase Tickets Here'." He pointed to the sign using a pen in his left hand, "If you already have your ticket you need to get your boarding pass in that line. Then you go to the boarding gate, Mr. Guerrero."

He panicked. "God. Now they know my name." "*¡Dios. Ahora ya saben mi nombre!*" No sound came out of his mouth. He wanted to speak, but was unable. He was terrified, afraid the agent would identify his ticket as stolen and turn him over to the police.

The agent continued to look at him. "I'll give you your boarding card this one time. But in the future, don't take up my very valuable time by getting in the wrong line. I have other passengers to attend to. Aisle or window?"

Bill was unable to answer even this simple question. To those around him it looked as if he had not heard the question.

Fear paralyzed him. He tried to mentally review his unclear plan for the hijacking. Everything he considered was jumbled and unclear. All he knew was there was not supposed to get on the airplane and there was not to be any trouble.

"Mr. Guerrero, do you speak English? Aisle or window seat?" With growing irritation, the agent growled, "I'm speaking to you. Where do you want to sit?"

Bill coughed, "Yes. Sure. Ok."

"Which will it be? Window?"

"Smoking."

"Smoking?"

The self-important agent busied himself at his computer and then handed Bill his boarding card with a flourish.

"Here is your boarding pass, I have assigned you seat 55-8, on today's Flight 100. Since you only have a one way ticket I could not give you a return seat assignment."

The rude little agent leaned over the top of the tall counter and again pointed to his left with a pencil, then said in an exasperated tone, "Mr. Guerrero. Go to the end of the hall. Turn left and go through security."

"Security!"

The very sound of that word terrified Bill. He thought, "I can't do this."

Quickly the agent looked over the top of his thick glasses at his miniature television monitor. "After you pass through security, use the tunnel to Gate 67."

There was that word again. Security. That was all Bill heard as the bitter acid taste of panic rose in his throat. He started to sweat as his stomach pitched and rolled. He felt lightheaded as he numbly nodded to the agent.

He turned the wrong way and was immediately face to face with a line of passengers. At the conclusion of his full right turn, his bag caught on a chrome stanchion, which wobbled on its base, making sounds like a quarter being rolled on a desktop.

The metallic rolling caused passengers and employees within several feet to stop their conversations and look at the source of the noise. Most of them saw Bill Guerrero attempt to steady the noisy base then make an unsure and lurching retreat from the ticketing area.

15

07:25 Pacific Standard Time
San Francisco International Airport

Stan Kurtz walked across the ramp toward the airplane. He stood at the base of the Jetway, where he left his bags at the bottom of the stairs. The day-shift cabin cleaners would still be on board. They'd be in his way, so he decided to inspect the exterior of the aircraft first.

Outside the two-hundred and thirty-one foot aluminum hull, he started a very deliberate and intentional inspection.. He started with the twenty-four ply nose gear tires and looked for cuts and worn spots. He paid particular attention to the sidewalls. He knew a moderate cut in the sidewall was far more likely to fail than a deep penetrating cut in the tread. He examined the nose gear steering assembly, looking for Skydrol leaks.

He walked aft along the side of the fuselage and looked at various panels, static ports and *pitot* heads. He strolled to the leading edge of the right wing and continued his inspection. of the number three and four engines, where he examined various coolers, ducts, ports and carbon-coated tailpipe sections. He paid particular attention to the nacelle-mounted fire bottles. The four engine pylons each contained two fire extinguisher bottles filled with Halon 1310. He checked the pressure gauges and also the red blowout disc. Satisfied, he walked to the right wing tip and looked along the length of the leading edge of the wing toward the fuselage for bird strike or hail damage.

He continued aft to the underside of the huge horizontal stabilizer. He looked for hydraulic fluid leaks or damage to the leading edge of the primary flight control, but he found none. Everything appeared to be airworthy and acceptable. From a location forty or fifty feet aft of the aircraft, he checked the exhaust for the Auxiliary Power Unit housed below the rudder. He looked up the trailing edge of the both upper and lower rudder, again looking for "runback," a black, gritty telltale evidence of an internal Skydrol fluid leak from the rudder power packages.

The same inspections were repeated along the left side of the fuselage, wings, pylon and nacelles for engine one and two. He completed his exterior pre-flight back at the bottom of the Jetway where his walk-around had all begun.

Kurtz climbed the external stairs and was stopped by the combination keypad on the Jetway door. The secret four-digit combination had been crudely scratched into the paint on the doorframe, "1041." Stan shook his head. Once again, the purpose of the lock had been defeated. He punched the code on the keypad, opened the door and came face to face with a group of cabin cleaners, loaded down with vacuum cleaners, mops and other cleaning gear.

There was not enough room for all of them on the landing. Stan started in through the door as the cabin cleaners started to exit.

One fleet service employee was obviously in a hurry. "Hey man, let me on by." With no further comment, he rudely brushed past Stan and banged him in the knee with his vacuum cleaner.

The aircraft had been powered down over night and the three air conditioning packs had not been operating. A stale and oppressive atmosphere flooded the interior of the plane..

He entered the aircraft through the L-2 door—left hand side, second door back from the nose of the aircraft and was immediately assaulted by strident music. Cleaners had left the audio system turned up to full volume. Pounding rock music pumped throughout the airplane. Stan often was amazed that generally undereducated cabin cleaners could control and operate a very sophisticated multiplex entertainment system, yet could not properly use a simple vacuum cleaner. He approached the multi-plex audio control panel and turned the system off with finality.

Stan moved forward toward the nose of the airplane. He wrestled with his suitcase and navigation bag as he climbed the carpeted circular staircase. He dropped his bags on the dark brown rubber flooring in the upper deck galley.

The upper deck lounge was unoccupied except for a black male cabin cleaner who was reclined in a seat. The employee took a final pull on his cigarette, as he sat with his legs and shoes on the back of the seat in front of him.

He looked up and saw Stan. "Hey Bro. What's happenin'. You the mother who turned off the music?"

Stan said, "Get your feet off the seats and put out that cigarette." The cleaner sullenly stared back at him, but made no attempt to move as Stan said, "You know the rules."

The rangy black man got up out of his seat. Stan realized the employee was several inches taller than he was.

Stan said, "Clean your mess up in here."

"Who the fuck are you? Motherfucker."

Stan felt a mild sense of uneasiness when the cleaner said in a falsetto singsong voice, "Hey, Baby. You go screw yourself. I'm on my break."

"Get back to work or get out."

They stood toe to toe; both men smelled each other's breath. "I'm tellin' my shop steward 'bout you, honkey asshole. He get you white-ass fired."

Stan's was calm. "The choice is yours. Do your job or get off my airplane." The confrontation passed. Stan watched the ramp serviceman turn and slowly leave the upper deck, swearing all the way down to the First Class galley.

Aware of his rapid breathing, Stan picked up his bags and turned toward the cockpit. He used the cockpit key on his key chain and unlocked the door and entered his private domain.

16

07:35 Pacific Standard Time
San Francisco International Airport

Bill Guerrero hung back and nervously watched the security check point. Each passenger placed their handbags, carry-on baggage, brief cases, purses and miscellaneous personal treasures on the moving conveyor belt. Smoothly, the bags disappeared into a large grey humming machine. A red illuminated sign on top of the machine randomly flashed, "X-RAY in USE."

Next to the baggage X-ray equipment was a large poster in a metal frame. It was very clear and to the point.

"AIRCRAFT HIJACKING IS A FEDERAL CRIME PUNISHABLE BY DEATH."

Further below, the sign continued,

"CARRYING CONCEALED WEAPONS ABOARD ANY AIRCRAFT IS PUNISHABLE BY PRISON SENTENCES & FINES"

The last words at the bottom of the sign stunned Bill.

"PASSENGERS AND BAGGAGE SUBJECT TO SEARCH
Federal Aviation Administration,
U. S. Department of Transportation."

The message seemed to have been written specifically for him. He read these warnings as though he were being warned personally and individually. Fitfully, he worried he would bring attention to himself if he did not proceed toward security.

He took a deep breath and walked hesitantly toward the security agent.

He gripped his Nike training bag in one hand and carried the boarding card pass in the other.

He was surprised when the young agent spoke to him in fluent Spanish. *"Senor, por favor coloque su equipaje en la cinta en movimiento."* "Senor, please place your baggage on the moving belt."

She continued, this time in English, "Do you have any metal objects in your pockets?"

He shook his head, shrugged and raised his shoulders. He said nothing.

"If you do, please place them in this plastic container. *Gracias.*"

Involuntarily, he replied with the common Spanish response, *"De nada."*

She smiled professionally. "Ah, so you do speak Spanish" *"Ah, por lo que habla español."*

He placed the black bag with its contraband on the conveyor belt. Nervously, he watched the bag disappear through the long black rubber fingers that hung down from the top of the machine, dragging against the moving belt.

Worried, he reviewed his unclear hijack plan. "No panic. Just get on board and then do my thing to hijack the plane."

The security agent's perfect Spanish jolted Bill back to where he was. She invited him to step into the chrome and plastic tunnel. *"Senor, Póngase de pie allí. Manos a los lados del cuerpo. No te muevas."* Then in English, 'Sir. Please. Stand here. Hands at your sides. Do not move."

Now, more than any other time, he was convinced Juan had it all wrong. He was terrified. This machine would know or discover he had bullets in his pocket. It knew he wanted to hijack an airplane. The machine knew everything.

Again, he held back, He was fearful. He knew he was only steps away from being caught and sent back to prison.

This time with more authority she said, *"Senor, por favor, avanzar en este sentido. Otros pasajeros están a la espera de usted."* "Senor, please move this way. Other passengers are waiting for you."

"Si. Si. Uno momento, por favor." Bill took a deep breath. He blinked very hard and started up the slight incline toward the magnetically sensitive area. The square green light immediately changed to flashing red. With the red warning light came an angry metallic warning buzzer.

Bile and panic with waves of fear overtook him. He could taste the bitter acid in his throat as his stomach churned.

He was trapped between the security agent and the machine. He was convinced that this machine knew he was planning to hijack an airplane. A rolling numbness and cold sweat came over him at the thought of being captured.

Bill considered whether he should turn and run. Caution caused him to remain stationary. He was afraid if he ran, he would be shot in the back. In his terror and anxiety, he failed to comprehend that someone was speaking to him.

"Sir, Sir. Oh, hello, Sir. Please place all your belongings in this bucket. Please. Sir. You are holding up the line." She gently brushed his arm, "Sir, I'm talking to you." *"Señor, te estoy hablando a ti."*

He heard a distant voice. A woman's warm voice. She was talking to someone. Then more clearly, he slowly realized the female voice was speaking to him.

"Yo, Chica." He blinked, "What did you say?"

She was unfazed and unflattered with his attempt at familiarity, "Put your belongings in the pail. Empty your pockets. Do you have a calculator or a quartz watch?" She was patient, but pressed him, "Walk back through the archway. Now. Come back this way." She was very thorough and focused.

Bill Guerrero lethargically complied with her request and put his meager collection of coins, St. Christopher medal, a few dollars and a very small pocket knife in the dark blue plastic bucket. The bucket moved away from him on the conveyor belt.

He was very careful to leave the 9 mm bullets in his pants pocket with his Valium tablets. His shirt dampened with each deep breath. He looked at the young agent. With fortitude he did not feel, he boldly walked up the ramp into the same magnetometer.
This time, the green ready light shined its unblinking verdant color. No red light and no blaring alarm.

She smiled at him. She considered his fear to be travel jitters as she held the blue plastic bucket toward him. Bill collected his sparse personal belongings, including his small pocket knife. He walked away on legs he was sure would not support him to the end of security area. He looked back and offered a faint smile to her and her fellow security agents. They had already dismissed him and were speaking to other passengers behind him.

A black 45-year-old female contract security guard was assigned to watch the X-ray monitor. She was incredibly bored. The monotony of her job was unbearable. Initially, she thought looking into the private and personal belongings of passengers would be interesting.

In the past year, the only break in her boredom had been when baggage from notables or people with celebrity passed through her X-ray machine. Her mind was hundreds of miles away as she thought about her scheduled break in less than 10 minutes.

Several large bags entered the machine sequentially and in rapid succession, the last of which was Bill's Nike bag. The denser bags had a tendency to absorb more of the focused X-ray energy.

The bored security guard looked at the four large bags passing before her on the monitor. She saw hair dryers, shaving kits, curling irons and other metallic items. The increase in opacity of the large bags lowered the energy received by the X-ray detector and a signal was sent to elevate the output of the X-ray transmitter.

After the last large bag passed through the X-ray tunnel, she saw a faint outline of Bill's Nike bag. The increased X-ray energy, caused by the opacity of the previous bags, passed through Bill's bag with incredible force and the fluoroscope receiver was overdriven. For only three ten-thousandths of a second, Bill's bag was electronically X-rayed as a primary means to thwart aerial piracy.

The composite graphite 9 mm handgun was not fully radio transparent. The irregular shape returned only a fuzzy image. The heightened level of X-Ray energy and radiation passed through the gun at the speed of light. The only parts shown on the monitor were two small springs and an oddly shaped metal firing pin. To the bored and mindless security agent, the opaque springs and firing pin only looked like a small assortment of metal parts. She may not have even noticed these parts. If she had, she never would have remotely perceived them as being threat to aircraft security.

Bill walked away from the security checkpoint certain he would suddenly feel a hand of his shoulder, or hear someone call his name. With each passing step his terror diminished, but only minimally. He never felt fully relieved about having passed through security. After he had walked sixty or seventy feet, his breathing slowly returned to a more normal rate. Only then did he gradually relax and quicken his step to escape the watchful eye of the security personnel.

Halfway between the security checkpoint and the end of the long corridor, Bill noticed an empty boarding area. He read the sign: FLIGHT 45 -- HONOLULU - CANCELLED. The boarding area was both dark and vacant. He felt a desperate need to hide for a few moments and settle down.

Bill knew he had taken an enormous chance. He looked back over his shoulder at the security kiosk and then quickly made an abrupt turn into the vacant, but cluttered, lounge area. After a few moments, he felt safe enough to take a chance and cautiously looked

HIJACKING OF FLIGHT 100

back to see if he had been followed.

After waiting another minute, Bill incorrectly assumed there was nothing to worry about. In fact, he was here. He was in the airport. He had passed through security. He had the gun in his bag.

He felt relieved and started to whistle a mindless tune. He looked at himself in the mirrored glass window in the boarding lounge. Though he couldn't see it, he looked tired. The dark blue-green half-circles under his eyes had worsened.

He turned from the windows and walked back into the commotion and noise of the main passenger boarding areas. He looked around the concourse, found the information board and allowed himself to smile. The monitor showed Flight 100 still scheduled at 8:30. In less than 30 minutes, he would leave San Francisco for Havana.

With a new false sense of promise and purpose, Bill Guerrero intentionally walked toward Gate 67. Though his mind was in turmoil, he considered all the risks associated with his plan. He momentarily felt relieved. Now, strangely, he felt a head-rush of enthusiasm about The Plan.

To himself, he thought, "No need to look back now. I'm on my way." In Spanish, "*No hay necesidad de mirar hacia atrás ahora. Estoy en mi camino.*"

Bill's self-confidence was unfounded. If he had looked back toward the security area again, he would have seen a distinguished-looking red-haired businessman. His newly found piece of mind would have been shattered had he seen this older individual bypass all the security measures simply by showing his gold and chrome badge and an identification card to the pretty young agent who had spoken to him in Spanish.

With a gracious smile, she ushered Robert Burns past security. His hunt was for the unknown Latino in the boarding area for Flight 100 to New York.

The game of cat and mouse had begun.

Bill Guerrero didn't know it. He was the mouse. A mouse being chased in a long tunnel. There was only one way out; back the way he had just come.

17

**10:00 Cuba Daylight Time
Jose Marti International Airport
Havana, Cuba**

It was very humid and today was going to be very hot. The temperature had climbed 2° Celsius in the last hour. The last time he saw a thermometer, it was 32° and it was not even 10:00 in the morning.

Radio Havana Cuba had forecast another hot day, just like the past ten or twelve days. He felt certain by noon it would be over 39°. Joaquin Guerrero sought a brief respite from the heat by stepping into the dark coolness of the airport bar. The stench from the lack of sanitation overrode any possible benefit to be derived from the cooler temperature. It seemed to him as though the stained tiles on the walls and floor had absorbed the smells.

He walked past the empty bar and bored bartender and sat at an unevenly tiled table in a dark corner at the rear of the room. From his seat, he could see most of the room and more importantly, all who entered.

A fat waitress in a stained and torn blouse came over to his table and asked in Spanish, "You wanna drink?" *¿Quieres un trago?*

"No. Not for me. I'm just resting, trying to stay out of the heat."

"You dumb *burro*, you can't stay here if you don't spend no money. This is a bar for passengers, for paying customers. It's not good for the bar if the passengers see you sitting here without a drink at your table."

Her argument and logic were flawed. The next Cubana Airlines estimated arrival from Madrid was more than three hours away and there were no departures until after 15:00 this afternoon.

"Bring me a *Mexicola, con limon.*" The overweight waitress lumbered away from his table. With no enthusiasm, she placed his order with the bartender.

He had not entered the airport bar because he was thirsty, or even to escape the heat and humidity. He had walked into the bar for the sole purpose to escape the watchful eye of his supervisor. This was not the day to be visible, or visibly nervous. Today was the day he was going to help his two younger half-brothers with their crazy plan.

Joaquin had worked near, or at, Havana's Jose Marti International Airport for many employers since *La Revolución* in 1956. He had worked under the Bautista machine as an airport painter. He touched up the constant grime and stains in the airport lavatories, hallways and kitchens. Before and after the revolution, Joaquin studied aeronautical engineering at the *University de Cuba de Habana*, later renamed *University de Liberdad, del Popular*.

Joaquin loved airplanes and had planned to finish his aeronautical studies in America. He hoped to find employment with Boeing or Douglas, or maybe even one of the airlines.

Unfortunately for him, when Fidel Castro "liberated" the masses, his plan to work in America was abruptly crushed. His only option would have been to continue his studies in the USSR. Then, as an ex-patriot Cuban, he would have only been able to practice his learned trade for the Russians.

He had chosen to remain in Cuba, partly because he felt he should stay near his family, including his two older sisters. With his formal education terminated by Castro's *Government Popular*, his part-time painting job had become a full-time occupation. He eventually was able to find some work on the tarmac as an unlicensed mechanic for Cubana Airlines.

The rotund cocktail waitress interrupted his thoughts as she set a dirty and spotted drinking glass on the table in front of him. She made a poor attempt to keep the Mexicola in the tumbler she poured. Cola splashed on the tabletop and Joaquin's hand. She made no attempt to clean up the mess or apologize.

"*Diez Pesos.*"

He thought, "Ten pesos for a coke, a third is on my table and running on the floor." He pulled a post-revolution ten peso note, a National Peso or CUP, from his pocket and carefully laid it on a dry spot on the table.

The waitress picked it up, held it to the light coming in the door and examined it very carefully. She turned the bill over several times to verify its authenticity. Recurrent rumors persisted that America's Central Intelligence Agency continued to flood Havana with counterfeit Cuban National paper money.

After she was satisfied the bill was genuine, she returned her attention to Joaquin and offered him a crooked smile in a failed attempt to elicit a tip from her only patron. She waited several long seconds, then gave up and lumbered back to the bar carrying the empty Mexicola bottle.

He continued to drift mentally and recalled the glory days at Jose Marti International Airport. Its rich history was filled with tales of various airlines that had flown into and out of Havana. Almost all of them either failed and or otherwise stopped flights to Cuba. One of the few airlines left was *Cubana*; the national airline of Cuba. Mexicana and Iberia still flew a few flights in to and out of Havana, but that was about it. Many other airlines had left because of the rampant corruption, graft and, of course, Cuba's dead economy. The on time performance at Jose Marti airport was the worst in the Caribbean. Only two in ten departures left anywhere near on time.

Each of these airline failures had a direct impact on his finances. He was not one to easily give up, so he hung around the edges of the aviation business. He liked airports and airplanes. To a lesser degree, maybe it was because both his half-brothers worked for airlines or aviation support companies in America. Juan was employed by Eastern Airlines in Miami as a baggage handler. Little Guillermilito used to work for Marriott Food Services in San Jose or San Francisco in California.

Joaquin remembered that less than a month, but more than three weeks ago, he thought, Juan had called from Miami to tell him that Guillermo had lost his job at Marriott.

Juan was excited as he told him about the plan he and Guillermo had devised to make them all wealthy.

18

10:20 Cuba Daylight Time
Jose Marti International Airport
Havana, Cuba

To Joaquin, the plan seemed incredibly risky. Even impossible. Certainly, this looked like another senseless idea *"idea sin sentido."* He cautioned Juan to stop and consider the risks and if he still wanted to proceed to do so with extreme caution.

Juan kidded his older brother and called him a *"Pollo Grande."* Reluctantly, Joaquin eventually went along with the idea. He thought, "What the hell, if the plan goes bad, nobody will know I'm involved. I can always stay here in Havana. Everything to gain and nothing to lose. *Todo para ganar y nada que perder."*

After the first telephone call Joaquin received two letters from Juan, each with more specific ideas and plots.

Although both letters about their plan had been in English, the envelopes had been addressed in Spanish. This was part of an effort to mask the real nature of the plan. Juan used many slang terms. In his letters and conversations with Joaquin, Juan acted the part of a medical supplier who regularly shipped medical supplies through

Miami to other destinations. He was looking for a large medical shipment that was lost. His letters were intentionally vague about the contents of the shipment and the exact shipping date, except to say that it would be in the next three weeks.

Now nearly four weeks later, the lost shipment to Cuba through Miami was destined to arrive today. Still, the exact arrival time for the shipment was unknown.

No Cuban who might have listened or read the censored mail from Miami, could possibly have known the "large shipment" was actually a hijacked Boeing 747 from California.

Joaquin Guerrero felt very unsure of his personal security. His imagination caused him to believe a number of people were watching him. With growing concern about Castro's stratocracy, he fulfilled and completed his obligations as outlined by Juan in his instructions from Miami.

Juan sent Joaquin enough American dollars to be used to enlist the support of six of the *Marielitos,* dissidents who wanted to flee from Cuba.

His arrangement with them was simple. Each would be paid one hundred American dollars for about forty-five minutes of work. They were not told the nature of the work, except they would assist in unloading of an aircraft. They were not told the contents of what they were to unload. Nor were they told they would also be reloading an airplane. The final deception was the six were not told they would be adding several extra suitcases on the hijacked 747.

Recently recruited, these unemployed drifters knew the less they knew about this job, the better.

The *Marielitos* did not ask, nor were they told, the identity of their short-term employer. All they knew was they were to be paid the equivalent of ten days' pay for work that should be completed in less than an hour.

Joaquin Guerrero arranged with these locals to meet him at the side entrance of the sand-colored main terminal building at a certain time, based on the unclear and uncertain arrival of the misguided 747.

19

10:30 Cuba Daylight Time
Jose Marti International Airport
Havana, Cuba

He left his drink untouched and walked out of the *Cantina de la Aeropuerto*. He looked at the clock as he started to walk back toward the main part of the dirty terminal. Two *Guardia Civilias* patrolled the airport baggage area.

From a distance, they looked professional. He knew they were nothing more than young teen-aged kids. Their shirts which were much too large and their oversized tan pants were held up with wide ammunition belts, drawn very tight to keep their pants from falling down. Both guards wore the inevitable professional touch, the incredibly shined black knee high boots, polished like ebony mirrors.

Under Castro, there was no problem getting military supplies from Russia. Correct sizing, however, was another matter. This situation, as was the case with everything else supplied by Russia, had given rise to a Cuban saying, "Quantity Si. Correct Size, No."

Joaquin continued his casual walk toward the two unknown soldiers. "*Hola, como esta? Muy muy caliente y humido.*" The two responded about the temperature and the humidity, "Yes, that is true. It is very humid. Too hot to work." The three *Cubanos* looked at each other and laughed an understanding laugh.

Purposefully, Joaquin walked away from the two young militia guards. Once he was away from them, he sensed he had been successful in not causing any concern or alarm. He ambled to the rear of the main terminal building. He needed to verify that all the physical bits and pieces of today's event were securely in place.

He found four of the five *compadres* he had hired. The quartet sat on their haunches and waited for instructions from him.

No one said anything to him or even acknowledged his presence. He nodded to the group only find a stoic, silent response.

Joaquin felt that Juan's plan was flawed. It was Joaquin who suggested that offloading the bags presented a perfect opportunity to reload several extra bags when the passenger's baggage was reloaded aboard the hijacked aircraft.

After Joaquin agreed to help, Juan sent him money, US Dollars and traveler's checks plus some Cuban National currency, to purchase one hundred kilos of processed, cut and cleaned cocaine. Over several weeks, the cocaine was acquired and stored in lockers at the airport. Joaquin had done his work well. He divided the white drug into wrapped parcels and put them in six unmarked dissimilar suitcases.

The half-dozen pieces of luggage were hidden in the main terminal baggage room, awaiting the arrival of the hijacked Boeing 747.

As usual, the big airport terminal clock showed the wrong time. There were at least six more hours until the "large package" arrived from the United States.

He knew from past experience when Cuban radio announced a hijacking, the small towns around the airport erupted in a frenzy of excitement. The Cubans looked at a hijacking in much the same manner as the locals viewed a town hanging in days gone by.

During his adult life in Cuba, Joaquin had seen more than twenty hijacked aircraft arrive at Jose Marti airport.

One fact was a constant: confusion ran rampant throughout the airport and surrounding communities when a hijacked aircraft arrived. The excitement in the towns unleashed a sudden increase in people around the airport. He thought this was good. It would provide a strong diversion. However, with the increase in crowds, the airport guards always looked more closely for Cuban nationals who wanted to desert to America as stowaways.

He would have to be very careful if their plan was going to be successful.

20

07:45 Pacific Standard Time
San Francisco International Airport

The hectic morning pace at the ticket counter seldom relented. As departure time drew closer, the rush intensified. People seemed to arrive at the counters in growing waves. Passengers often were chronically late and therefore generally seemed to be chronically ill-tempered.

One such passenger had just been given his boarding pass on Flight 100. As he turned away from the counter, he noticed he had been assigned a middle seat, tightly crunched between the aisle and window seats.

Quickly he turned back to the agent. "Listen, "Look here." No immediate response made the passenger angrier. "I asked for an aisle seat. Some idiot has given me a seat in between two of those 'holier than thou' types."

The frazzled and harried agent reluctantly took the passenger's boarding card.

The passenger said, "Listen to me. I demand the seat I requested and if you can't accommodate me in coach, then give me a seat in

First Class, or at least Business Class."

The small agent spoke with contrived patience, "I am sorry, Mr. Shapiro. You were rather late arriving for flight check-in. I'm afraid I can't upgrade you to Business or First simply because you wanted an aisle seat."

What the agent suspected was that Mr. Shapiro wanted a freebie; an upgrade from coach without paying an additional fare.

Shapiro continued his tirade, "I know my rights. I demand," he stopped to catch his breath, and then continued, "you provide me the seat you promised."

The agent responded quietly, "Actually the specific rule is, 'If a passenger makes a specific request, all reasonable attempts must be made to accommodate that request.'" The agent's intonation said it all. He had memorized the speech through simple repetition. "If that seat is not available, other measures may be made to placate the passenger."

Mel Shapiro was not hearing anything the agent said. They both continued to speak at the same time. "I don't give a damn what your rules say. I want a seat on the aisle, First Class, Business Class, but not your Cattle Class."

The little agent paused to catch his breath and then continued, "You should have gone directly to the gate. You had your ticket, there really was no reason to stand in line. The sign over your head clearly says, 'Passengers Purchase Tickets.' Since you already have your ticket, you took up my time and wasted your time."

Melvin Shapiro glared disgustedly at the diminutive agent.

Harold continued, "I am sorry, Sir." Actually, he secretly enjoyed holding his power and authority over people like this impossible passenger.

"Really, there are no more aisle seats left on 100 today. In any cabin, be it Coach, Business or First Class." Harold emphasized this last remark and then started to busy himself with stacking and sorting random piles of tickets and travel paperwork.

Shapiro stared with unblinking eyes at Harold and held him in deep contempt. He had dealt with this type of employee before and knew they almost always relented and would buckle under pressure. Today's airlines could not stand to have passengers make a scene or cause a commotion.

Shapiro looked at Harold's badly fitted toupee and his thick glasses, then let the tirade begin. "Listen to me, you blind, bareheaded little bastard."

"Are you speaking to me, sir?"

Harold was not in the least intimidated. He raised his red-tinged hands in an attempt to placate this most unreasonable passenger. "Sir, let's try to be reasonable. Your flight was overbooked by thirty seats. We probably are going to leave with only a handful of empty seats. I'm sure there will be no spare aisle seats, because all those seats have already been assigned. There is no way I can help you. However, you might be able to trade with another passenger."

"I don't want to trade and I don't want to sit in a middle goddamned seat."

"Well then, all I can offer you is a seat on our later flight to JFK at 1:30 this afternoon." Harold waited several seconds for an answer from Shapiro, and then said, "Which will it be, sir? Do you want to take what's available on 100, or wait until later this afternoon?"

"You bald-headed little shit. I want my aisle seat and I want it now. Do you hear me?" Shapiro was in a fit of fury, the spot of white spittle clung to his lower lip. He raised his voice, "and if you can't, can't...accommodate me, then get somebody out here who can."

The cords in Shapiro's neck were throbbing and he appeared to be on the verge of losing control. He rasped. His voice seethed, "Let me talk to your supervisor." The echo of his voice rumbled through the glass and marble terminal area.

One of those who heard Shapiro was Director of Security Robert F. Burns. When he heard the racket and commotion Shapiro was causing, he intentionally walked toward the source of the noise.

Burns approached Shapiro, who now stood alone.

He first looked at Shapiro and then at Harold, then said to both of them, "What seems to be the difficulty here?"

Shapiro looked at Burns and in an abrasive tone asked, "Who the hell are you, Pop? Why don't you mind your own business?"

"I'm Director of Security here at the airport. Your tone of voice is neither necessary, acceptable nor effective."

Shapiro quickly determined he had won. Finally. He was in control of the situation. The airline had sent someone to placate him. They were about to give in. From past experience, Shapiro knew he must not let up on the pressure He had to hold the line until the airline met his demands.

Burns' next comments were totally unexpected. "If you do not calm down sir, I will have to ask you to take your travel business elsewhere." He was firm, just as he had been in San Diego, where he had been a detective for over 21 years.

Harold chuckled to himself and was glad to see the chief of security. He quickly said, "Mr. Burns, I have advised Mr. Shapiro we have no more seats on the aisle. He doesn't seem willing, or is unable, to believe me."

Burns said in an even voice, "Mr. Shapiro, we can't decide what is best for you. Only you can do that. If you accept the seat we assigned you, you are free to board. If, on the other hand, you can't comply, then you will need to make other travel arrangements."

Robert Burns stared evenly at Shapiro before he continued. "The choice is yours." Then he looked at Harold and asked, "What flight is Mr. Shapiro on?"

"100 to Kennedy."

Harold looked at Mr. Shapiro and then at his watch.

"Sir, if you are going to make your flight, you had better start for the gate now. It takes several minutes to walk to the end of the terminal where our gates are located, and you still have to go through security."

Shapiro pulled his tickets and boarding card from Harold's outstretched hand, spun and left the counter area. His tan raincoat caught on the chrome stanchion and dragged it toward the floor.

Burns grabbed at it to keep it from spinning like a top. He smiled at the Harold and said, "This is a dangerous area. It's the second time today someone has knocked this thing over."

21

08:00 Pacific Standard Time
San Francisco International Airport

Something in Burns' police-trained mind connected, but he could not immediately fit all the pieces together. Yet, there was something in this morning's happenings that had set off an internal alarm.

Then, with certain clarity, Burns knew the source of his concern. He started to say something, but his mind raced faster than he was able to speak. "What was the story on that other passenger who made such a racket when he hit these passenger restraint ropes? You know, the first passenger, the one who hit the chain."

Harold looked at the pile of tickets on the counter.

"The Mexican? Oh, I remember now. He sure did seem like an odd duck. He was very nervous and unsure of himself."

Harold stopped talking and his mind wandered over the events in the morning crush of passengers. "I don't know, sometimes you just get a feeling about a person. Know what I mean?"

Burns looked directly at Harold. "I know exactly what you mean. Do you remember where was he going?"

"No, I don't remember. Let me look." Harold tapped his

computer keyboard with the eraser-end of a pencil. Quickly, he was able to scroll through aircraft seat maps and reservation screens.

Impatiently, Burns waited. He felt there was something going on with this passenger. But what was it?

Harold looked up and smiled. "Here he is. B. Guerrero." He was a one-way to JFK. Bought his ticket with cash. He doesn't seem to have any local contact information." Harold started to speak in a clandestine conversational tone. "You're right, Sir. He was real nervous. A strange strange fellow."

Burns did not hear the rest of Harold's comments. What he had heard were four items that precisely fit a potential hijacker profile. One way ticket. Paid cash. Anti-social behavior, nervous, unsure of himself. No verifiable contact information or identification.

Burns looked at the pile of tickets on the counter. "What was his name again?"

"Guerrero. B. Guerrero."

"Thanks, Harold. I'm going to take a walk out to the gates. Do me a favor. Page him to Gate 67 and I'll check him out."

Burns looked at his watch and added, "We're getting close to departure. And I don't want to cause a delay on the flight. But I'd sure feel better if I could have a talk with our Mr. Guerrero before he boards."

Burns strode purposefully away from the counter area and disappeared around the corner, where he headed directly toward the left side of the security kiosk.

A very attractive Guatemalan security agent smiled at him as he briskly strode up to her. "Hot on the trail of another criminal?"

He only smiled and then impulsively asked, "Do you remember anything about a Chicano who went through here a few minutes ago? Mid twenties, about 5"-10'. Anything at all?"

"Not really, but we look at hundreds of passengers every hour, especially these last few mornings. Why, what's the deal with him?"

"Nothing. Just a feeling. I want to check him out, just to be safe." He showed her his airline security badge and identification card. She nodded and he headed for the magnetometer. The mass of ferrous metal in his police service revolver always set off the alarm. Today was no exception. An elderly woman had just exited the chrome and plastic tunnel when the alarm sounded. She looked startled by the strident klaxon. A security agent smiled at her, "Don't worry, the alarm was caused by someone else."

Burns looked at her, smiled and said, "That was my fault. I'm sorry about that."

The grandmother with strongly tinted blue-hair smiled back saying, "Thank goodness, I wouldn't want you to think I was a criminal." She chuckled nervously. "If it is all right, may I proceed?"

He only heard the first part of the exchange between the agent and the elderly woman. His mind was racing. It felt good to be active and involved as he hurried down the long tiled tunnel toward the gate area. His police instincts kicked in. Once again, he was on the hunt.

The public address system intruded into his consciousness, "Will New York passenger B. Guerrero please proceed to Gate 67 and pick up a white courtesy telephone for a message." The echo in the terminal died as the announcement was repeated, "New York Passenger B. Guerrero to Gate 67. Please pick up a white courtesy phone."

22

08:05 Pacific Standard Time
San Francisco International Airport

He felt somewhat better, but was still incredibly nervous. Tremors rippled and coursed through his body. His stomach convulsed. Maybe, if he got away from the crowds, he might be able to settle down. Bill ignored the milling crowds as he hurried past Gate 67's holding area for Flight 100's waiting passengers. He didn't notice the enormous Boeing 747 with its proud nose pointed directly toward the terminal windows. All he felt was a compelling need to find privacy. Seclusion might provide a remedy to hide the fear that consumed him. He did not want to fail. He did not want to get caught and end up back to jail.

A sign marked the entrance to the men's restrooms. He pressed the doors open and entered this impromptu sanctuary. As the bathroom door closed behind him, he thought he heard his name. He froze. How could it be that he heard his name being called? He rejected the possibility, entered a stall, dropped his pants and turned around, "This is crazy, man. Who would be calling me? No one knows I'm here."

He sat in the cold stall with his pants around his ankles and talked to himself, "Just get on the airplane. Don't get caught, Fool. Be cool. Wait for the right time. They don't expect nothing. When the time's right, hijack the fucking jet. Do it. Go to Cuba. Old Juan will pay the *mordida* to the Cubans." He laughed to himself without conviction. "I'll be out of prison in a week." These thoughts terrified him and caused his colon to cramp spasmodically. Deep rippling pains over took him when he thought about Cuban prisons. He wondered if the prisoners in Havana jails would pick him as a new love-slave, like they had in California.

After several painful seconds, the distress passed and he forced himself to leave the stall. He tucked his shirt in his pants and walked over to the sinks. He wet his hands and ran his fingers through his hair. The mirror told it all. He did everything he could in an effort to take his mind off the task ahead of him. He attempted not to think about the hijacking, but his mind kept coming back to the plan.

His sense of despair and shocking fear was amplified when he heard his name called on the public address system, "Passenger Guerrero please come to a white courtesy phone at Gate 67."

He felt crazy when he spoke out loud to himself, "What if Juan or Joaquin have been caught? What if the police got tortured confessions from them? What if the police were looking for me now? What if the Police and the FBI know who I am? What the hell am I going to do?"

Bill bravely tried to assure himself. "Maybe it was for some other passenger with a name like me." As that thought crossed his mind, he knew it was no good.

Someone was looking for him. Again the fear ripped at him as he stood motionless in front of the water-spattered mirror. He tried to find an optimistic answer to the puzzle, "Maybe it was a message from Joaquin or Juan to tell me the deal was off." Panic had fully taken control of him as he breathed very rapid, shallow breaths.

He could not control his breathing and started to feel lightheaded. He spoke in tight short panting breaths to the pathetic and frightened face in the mirror, "I've got to get out of here. That's it, I'll just walk out of here, out of the airport, out of San Francisco."

Sweat formed on his upper lip, "But, if I quit now, Juan and Joaquin would be in deep shit."

He knew exactly what he needed to do. Cousin Frank had given him two Valium pills. Good old Frank, the family street-pharmacist. The Valium would help him.

Frantically, he searched his pockets but found nothing. He dropped his black bag to the floor and again patted both front shirt pockets, with the same results. Nothing.

He was not thinking, he could only respond to growing fears.

He was panicked and was reacting to primal instincts. The Valiums were in the bottom of his Nike bag. He ripped open the zipper and plunged his hands past the clothes and into the rubble at the bottom of the bag. The weight and shape of the gun felt odd wrapped in the shirt, socks and underwear. His stomach muscles contracted and a chill coursed down his spine. The sweat on his upper lip coalesced into large blistered bubble of spit while he leaned against the edge of the cold sink porcelain.

He closed his eyes and squeezed his lids so tightly that he felt pain in his temples. His jaws clenched together and he breathed through his teeth.

Finally, he was able to control his breathing rate which slowly tapered off. Bit by bit, the panic and abject fear started to subside. He waited, then shook his head and opened his eyes. He was not prepared for what he saw in the mirror. The reflection showed a person consumed by terror.

With pounding nervous energy, Bill plunged his hand in the bag and again, his hand passed under the lumpy cloth-covered gun. It terrified him. He found what he wanted. He felt the sharp plastic edge of the Valium packets. Quickly he withdrew them, opened his clenched hand, to see each individual yellow 5 mg pill wrapped in its own clear plastic case. They would soon be his chemical salvation.

He split the container into two pieces and put one of the tablet packets in his shirt pocket. His mind raced, but he was not thinking. On came the water and he ripped open the plastic cover on the single tablet. He formed a cup with his right hand and filled it with water. Bill slammed the tablet into his mouth with his left hand and pressed his water-laden hand to his mouth. Most of the water ran down his sleeve and splashed on his shirt.

The Valium lodged in his throat.

Residual dampness, as well as the small amount of water he had managed to swallow, penetrated the micro coating on the tablet. The yellow tablet began to swell. He felt a swelling stickiness and then a sour burning sensation from the disintegrating tablet. The diazepam tasted like bitter almonds as it was absorbed in the soft tissue in his throat. The tablet became a sour immovable chunk stuck above his larynx. Frenzied, he cupped both hands under the water and scooped up as much water as he could.

Carefully and slowly, he raised both hands to his mouth, but still, half the water ran down his arms and into his upturned sleeves. He swallowed what water remained in his cupped hands. The act of swallowing pushed the partially dissolved tablet farther down his throat. Eventually, by repeated swallowing, he was able to breathe.

The sour burning sensation and bitter taste would remind him of the events of today. Bill swallowed two final handfuls of water, then ran his wet hands through his black hair. A final look at himself in the mirror proved that he was a mess. The front of his shirt was soaked and water dripped from his sleeves.

Slowly, almost casually, he strolled out of the rest room and turned back toward Gate 67. He knew he had to act natural. He had to appear composed and stable.

To several passengers who saw him, he appeared to be slovenly, anxious and nervous about himself and his surroundings.

The large digital clock behind the boarding gate read 08:18.

A glut of passengers were at the boarding gate, manned by a young oriental agent and his older female supervisor who were methodically checking in passengers as each produced their individual boarding pass.

Half a dozen passengers were ahead of him when he joined the line.

A single male passenger at the head of the line surrendered his boarding card, which identified him as Melvin Shapiro.

Shapiro again started his diatribe with these agents. "I was supposed to have an aisle seat, but your people at the ticket counter screwed up and put me in the middle row. Do you have any aisle seats available?"

"So sorry, Sir. Today, we are very full." He looked at the computer screen. "Frankly, Mr. Shapiro, there probably will only be a few empty seats on the entire airplane." He paused and looked at his screen, "But, at this point, I don't know which section these seats are in. Why don't you go ahead and take your assigned seat and then see if you can trade with someone once you are on board?"

The young oriental agent consulted his computer screen again, then added, "Really that is the best answer to your problem. After you board, perhaps one of the flight attendants will be able to find a passenger who would be willing to trade seats with you."

"You dumb Chink, I want my goddamned aisle seat. If I don't get what I want, I'll make a scene you'll never forget."

Shapiro jumped as he was surprised by the voice at his side. "Robert Burns at your service, Mr. Shapiro."

"I see we meet again. I thought we told you at the counter there were no more seats in the section you wanted. We also told you that you had a choice. Accept what is available, or wait for the next flight."

Shapiro looked directly at Burns as he forcefully added, "What we didn't tell you is that we are not going to put up with your rude behavior and insulting attitudes."

Gently Burns took Shapiro by the arm and led him fifty or sixty feet away from the clot of passengers at boarding gate 67 to a circular seating area, "Sit down. I want to talk to you."

Burns sternly continued his one-sided conversation. "For the last time, what is your decision going to be?"

Shapiro knew things were not going well for him. He listened to Burns, but all he heard was his pulse pounding in his head. He gave Burns no answer.

"This airline will not tolerate your belligerent attitude toward our employees. There's no reason for you to talk to our people like that. They are only trying to do their job. We have absolutely no tolerance for abusive profanity."

The unexpected response from Shapiro was swift, short and to the point. "Go screw yourself, you dumb flatfoot. You aren't even a real cop, you're just a badge-happy has-been. All you old farts care about is collecting your pension. In fact, they probably won't even give you a gun, because this airline is afraid you'll shoot yourself or someone else."

Burns took a firm grip of Shapiro's arm. He then quickly, quietly and pointedly led the unruly passenger farther away from the boarding area.

"Keep your clammy mitts off me, you son of a bitch. I'll have you fired for this." Burns was not deterred as he led Shapiro away from the boarding area.

The young oriental agent had been momentarily distracted as he watched the dialogue between Burns and that most unpleasant passenger. The high level of noise in the rotunda at the end of the tunnel kept him from hearing the end of the conversation, but it looked like Shapiro was not going to New York on 100. The agent directed his attention to the next several passengers in his line.

When flights are overbooked, a simple system is implemented. The boarding agent looks at the passenger's boarding card and reads the seat number aloud, while his partner draws an "X" through the corresponding box on a seat map. The program took somewhat longer than the computer-automated boarding system. However, it did preclude passengers boarding who did not have a specific seat assignment. This system also kept the number of boarding passengers equal to the number of seats remaining. When all the boxes were filled with individual "X's", every seat had been assigned.

Neither agent looked at Bill Guerrero when he filed through with the rest of the passengers. "Seat 55-8, Thank you. Next please."

He was on his way! It had been so incredibly easy! Euphoria washed over him. He was invincible! He had made it through the security system. Relief overtook his fears. He was on the way.

Slowly, and strangely, he felt unbeatable. The old longings for power and the need to be in control from his childhood returned. He thought, "Yes. I am so fucking cool and I'm in charge!" He was going to make it. He was going to have it all. All the things that had been denied him were now going to be his. On the Virgin's grave, he was going to be someone.

Assigned to seat 55-8, he had no perception that because of the escalating drama about seat assignments, Shapiro had become an inadvertent accomplice to the planned hijacking of Flight 100. He also did not understand that part of his euphoria was a result of the five milligrams of Valium he had ingested minutes earlier.

23

08:00 Pacific Standard Time
San Francisco International Airport

Stan Kurtz had been in the cockpit for the past fifteen minutes by himself. During that isolated time he started and completed preflight checks and necessary inspections before engine start procedure.

Stan mumbled and talked to himself as he started the Auxiliary Power Unit, "APU DC fuel valves open. APU inlet door's open. 400+ amps cranking, a good light off, here comes the 600° centigrade degree cut-off on the temperature. Watch it, she's starting to get hot."

He opened the APU bleed air valve, checked for proper duct pressure and started the three powerful air conditioning systems. After he established a source of aircraft power and air conditioning, he moved into the left hand seat in the cockpit.

He took a few seconds to savor how that felt to be in the Captain's seat. This truly was an indelible symbol of a Captain's power and authority. Stan felt respect and responsibility for the position of Captain every time he sat in the left seat.

While seated, he ran a series of system checks. He looked at the primary flight instruments for fail flags. He checked the communication console centered between the Captain and First Officer's seats. He scanned the Captain's panel, he looked for lights that should be on, but were not. Conversely, he checked for warning lights that should not be on, but were. He checked the integrity of the safety wire on the Alternate Pneumatic Emergency Brake handle. His inspection included the emergency brake pressure gauge and warning light. No light meant there was adequate pressure. The warning light was not illuminated.

Once again, he savored the feeling he always had when he was in the Captain's seat. A sense of pride, responsibility and accomplishment. Unfortunately, his access to the Captain's seat was always temporary; only a few minutes before every flight.

Based on seniority relative to every other pilot with the airline, he started eighteen years ago at the lowest pilot position. He was initially a Flight Engineer on the smallest equipment, the old Boeing 727. He was offered a Flight Engineer promotion to the old rattle trap DC-8, but would have been based in Chicago; a choice he did not even consider. In seniority order, that vacancy was then offered to the next pilot on the seniority list.

Stan eventually transferred to the obsolete 707 as a Flight Engineer, flying from the pilot domicile in San Francisco. Several years later, he was awarded a San Francisco First Officer, or co-pilot bid on the Boeing 727. That promotion had not lasted too long. One year later he once again found himself back in the Flight Engineer's seat. He often told people that by the end of his career at age sixty, he probably would have sat in every seat (Captain, First Office and Second Officer) on every type aircraft the airline operated.

Stan remained in the Captain's seat and finished the rest of preflight checks, up through the initialization and alignment of the three Delco Electronic Inertial Navigation System platforms. It was crucial that the exact position of the aircraft on the tarmac be loaded in the 3 INS platforms. He took the well-worn Lat/Long sheet from his clipboard, found the coordinates of Gate 67 at San Francisco

International Airport and read aloud, "North 37.36.8, West 122.23.1."

The cockpit door swung open. Stan turned and saw a pleasant and very pretty woman who tentatively stood in the doorway.

She wore the mixed colored outfit of the Inflight Services uniform, a tan and blue printed loose fitting blouse with the airline emblem woven into the fabric, dark blue slacks and a scarf of the same color tied tightly around her neck. The knot on the scarf was tied so it resembled a rose bud. The two magenta and tan diagonal stripes on her left sleeve indicated that she was a purser. She appeared to be ten years younger than Stan, probably late twenties or early thirties.

She was energetic. She smiled and walked forward into the cockpit, "Hi. I'm Patti Mallory." She smiled again and said, "I remember you. We've flown together before."

"You're probably right. Somewhere in our careers we've flown off to some enchanted and exotic location." He habitually played with his glasses when he talked.

He took them off and spun then in a circle, "I'm Stan Kurtz. Glad to meet you. Again." The glasses changed hands and spun in the opposite direction. "Are you the purser on our little safari today?"

"No. Actually, I was only a Purser last summer. She frowned, "You know. Before the cut backs." She smiled at him in a resigned way. "You know, in the good old days." She shook her head slowly, "But today, I'm just a regular Flight Attendant, assigned to work Upper Deck galley. So, I'll be your Upper Deck slave." She smiled at him, then shrugged her shoulders again and they both knew it was not one of the choice assignments.

Instinctively Patti said, "I really don't mind working up here, except for all the running up and down the stairs to the galley."

She finally walked to the forward part of the cockpit, "Who is the Captain today?" She rested her left hand on the back of the Captain's seat, while her fingers lightly touched his shoulder. Her height was such that she had to lean forward to keep from rubbing her hair on the overhead circuit breaker panel.

Stan smelled her perfume, Opium or maybe Shalimar. "Man, whatever you're wearing smells terrific."

She felt herself blushing. "Why Stanley. Thank you."

Without turning around, he spoke over his shoulder, "I'm really the Captain today, I'm just dressed as a Flight Engineer." He gave her a sideways smile and said, "After 18 years with this outfit, I'm certainly ready to be a Captain. However, the airline is not ready for me."

Patti smiled at this nice person. He was not like many of the pilots, who were always on the chase, to seduce or otherwise collect Flight Attendants.

Obviously, he was wearing a ring on his left hand, so he probably was married. From his attitude, she guessed he was very married. Some lady was probably very lucky to be married to him, "Do you have any kids?"

Stan blinked at her and thought what an odd question from someone he hardly knew. "Yes. Yes, I do. Two. One of each. Why do you ask?"

"No reason, I just wondered. Did you tell me the Captain's name? If you did, I don't remember. Oh, God, I'm losing my marbles."

They both laughed, "Don Webber is the skipper today. He's sort of new on the bird. I don't really know him. In fact, I just met him in the ramp office this morning. He seemed sort of uptight. There was some concern about the weather in New York and our fuel load. He was giving the First Officer, Fred O'Day, a hard time."

"Fast Freddie's the F/O today? I remember him. He's the one with the crazy sense of humor." Patti chuckled and said, "Oh dear. I hope the Captain didn't ruin Fred's day. You know, make into one of those trips."

"I don't think so. I don't there's much that bothers Fred."
Stan smiled and looked at Patti. "The Captain was probably just preoccupied with the weather in New York. Beside, with that

perfume you're wearing, you'll have him eating out of your hand in no time."

"Well, if I don't get a chance to meet either of them, tell them that Patti from Upper Deck said hello." She turned and started for the cockpit door, "Do you want any coffee? I just made a fresh pot."

"No thanks. Not right now. I've got some things to do. How about an orange juice when the commissary people load your galley?"

"That's a deal, Stan." She turned. Her hand was in motion toward the knob, when the door rapidly and forcefully swung open into the tiny cockpit. She stepped back quickly and allowed the door to swing through its arc and bang against the stop on the aft bulkhead.

Standing in the doorway was one of the most handsome men Patti Mallory had seen in a long time. He stepped lightly into the cockpit with authority and quickly surveyed his tightly defined world. Don's thin face was creased with laugh lines around his eyes. Patti looked at him carefully and could see with great clarity the smallest and finest features of his face. They were instantly and permanently etched in her mind.

Don looked at Patti with an intentional and very direct stare. His eyes were a light azure color.

She thought, the same kind of piercing and powerful blue that created opportunities for some men to become motion picture idols.

Patti thought, "If the eyes are the mirror of the soul."

Her reverie stopped when Don winked at her and unceremoniously dropped his bags on the floor. He took off his raincoat and hat then extended his right hand to Patti. "Hi, I'm the Captain. Don Webber. I'll be taking you to New York today. What's your name?"

She felt uncoordinated and tongue-tied, "Patricia. I'm Patricia." She never introduced herself at Patricia and, in fact, didn't care for that name.

Nervously, she attempted to correct herself, "Patti. I'm Patti." Her voice sounded tight and strained to her. "I'm Patti Mallory. Glad to meet you."

She felt flushed. "Captain, I'll be working the deck." She felt like a fool, as she quickly said, "I mean Upper Deck."

Don smiled again and then very intentionally looked at her. He let his eyes linger on her face. His gaze drifted to her neck and the small throbbing artery just above her collar. With no thought or self-consciousness, he momentarily stared directly at her breasts, then slowly and provocatively, lifted his eyes back to meet her gaze.

Don retained command of the situation and referred to the entry code that the Captain established on each flight for cockpit admission. "The secret code today for entry to the cockpit is two knocks."

Patti felt as nervous as a school girl. She excused herself. "I've got to get started sorting out the galley."

Don Webber smiled again. "Well, I'm glad to meet you."

Strangely, Patti made no attempt to leave the cockpit. Don looked at her again and said, "It'll take us about four hours and fifty minutes to get to the New York area. I imagine we may have to hold when we get there." Don absent mindedly added, "God knows we have enough fuel to hold for quite a while."

Stan turned to move out of Don's seat. For an aircraft the size of the 747, the cockpit was extremely cramped. Pilots joked about the cockpit being an afterthought to Boeing's aircraft design. There was precious little room for them to pass each other, as Stan moved aft toward the rear of the cockpit and Don moved toward his seat. The only way for them to pass was belly to belly. As they were pressed close to each other, Fred O'Day entered the cockpit and stood next to Patti.

He too, stooped over to keep from rubbing his head on the circuit breakers on the overhead panel.

Fred saw these two adult men moving as though they were involved in an ancient mating ritual. He leaned very close to Patti and loudly whispered, "I'm authorized to perform wedding ceremonies, but it looks like those two have started to celebrate the honeymoon without benefit of my blessing." Patti failed in her attempt to stifle her laugh.

Fred continued, "I wonder, do you think they know each other?, Or is this just another one night stand?"

Don Webber looked at his First Officer and guessed Fred probably meant no malice with his inopportune remarks.

Patti smiled and felt her stomach ripple as she laughed and said, "You are dreadful."

Fred said, "I'm dreadful? Think how they must feel being caught in a compromising situation like this."

Patti laughed out loud, "I've really got to get out of here and back to work. Do any of you want anything?"

Fred looked at Stan and Don, then at Patti. "I'll take a juice. Any kind is okay and bring them an Early Pregnancy Test kit."

Stan squeezed past Don and slid into his seat. Fred placed his bags in the baggage stowage area outboard of his copilot seat, under the side window. Patti left, but continued to chuckle to herself as she walked aft to the Upper Deck galley. She thought, Fred really is a character, as she remembered his sense of humor and quick wit.

She began the mindless task of counting the meals in the Upper Deck galley ovens and then remembered Stan and Fred wanted something to drink. Quickly Patti opened her bar drawer and took out two cold cans of orange juice. She poured juice in two Styrofoam coffee cups, opened one of the ice bags, retrieved several ice cubes with her tongs and dropped the ice in each of the cups. Orange juice splashed on her hand and she thought, "I hope this isn't going to one of those days."

Patti took the two cups to the cockpit but found the door was locked. She remembered Don's secret code and lightly kicked the bottom of the door twice. Immediately, the electrically operated solenoid clicked and the door unlocked. She pressed against the door with her hip, opened it and entered the cockpit. "Here are two cups of cold orange juice."

Fred looked back from his seat on the right side of the cockpit.

"Did you squeeze that yourself?"

"Right, Fred. I have an orange tree growing in the upper galley."

Fred reached back toward Patti and took the juice, then looked at Don, "Don't you want something to drink, partner? It's going to be mighty dry out there on the trail. Better get something to wet your whistle. You know, to kill off the trail dust."

Don looked at Fred, who was smiling as he offered Don his cup of juice. "Maybe I'll have a coffee when she gets a chance."

Fred looked at Patti. "He says he'll have a coffee when you get a chance. If I find out how he wants it, I'll send you a note."

Fred's humor and his attempt to cheer Don failed as a long silent pause drifted over the cockpit.

Stan looked at his instrument panel clock, 08:23. "Captain, it's time to go to Nav Mode on the platforms. We only have seven minutes 'til departure." Stan thought some operational conversation might ease the tension he felt.

"Fine, Stan. Go ahead and be sure to note the time in the log book," Don turned in his seat and continued, "Patti, I would like some coffee, there's no hurry." With a flourish, Don turned back forward in his seat, looked at Fred and said, "Read me my check list."

Patti retreated. She actually backed out of the cockpit. As she passed Stan's seat, she looked at him. She smiled, raised her eyebrows, looked at Don and shook her head. She mouthed the words, "Hope things smooth out up here."

Stan smiled, nodded and then quickly readied his instrument panel for engine start.

24

**08:10 Pacific Standard Time
San Francisco International Airport**

The Jetway tunnel from the terminal to the aircraft is a coupled series of elongated boxes, eight feet wide and nine feet high. Each section is twenty feet long and telescopes one into the next. At the end of the Jetway is a ten foot diameter by ten foot high rotating cab, articulated to allow precise vertical and horizontal alignment with different aircraft. A series of powerful electric motors are used to raise and lower the cab to accommodate various aircraft door threshold height configurations.

The Boeing 747 main cabin floor is sixteen feet above the ground. In order to reach that height, the Jetway tunnel floor is sloped upward gradually from the terminal to the 747 door threshold.

This unevenness of the floor caused the hijacker to experience equilibrium and balance problems, as he was pushed and absorbed into the crowd moving toward the aircraft. He stepped into the relatively dark tunnel and carefully placed each foot in front of the other. He felt he was falling, because the incline threw off his balance.

Momentarily disoriented, he felt trapped. His sense that he was falling became more acute.

Sweat ran down his sides and his stomach continued to churn. Uncoordinated, he bumped into an elderly couple in front of him. The husband turned and looked at him with suspicion.

He did not apologize, but instead, talked loudly to himself. "Hey man, be cool. Don't get tricked. You'll be OK. Take it easy."

Later, during investigations with several federal agencies, this couple would testify about what they had seen on this day and this flight. They would recall they had seen a disheveled Latino who appeared to be in his early to mid-twenties.

Some remembered his shirt and front of his pants being wet. Others would recall that his hair was unruly and messed, plastered to his head. All who were interviewed individually agreed he was disoriented.

To some, the most peculiar affect were his slow, odd rhythmic motions. His upper body and hips rotated in a very slow circle as he stood near other passengers. He circumscribed a slow deliberate arc, even though his feet were firmly planted on the rubber flooring in the Jetway.

An elderly first-time traveler spoke to him. "Son, are you all right?"

The women in the front of them added, "Perhaps if you take my arm, I can steady you."

"No lady. I'm straight. I'll be all right. Just tired." He giggled at humor only he could understand. "Tired and nervous."

Slowly, the cluster of passengers moved up the Jetway. Again, nausea rolled through him and he thought he would vomit.

Eventually, he and the passengers around him reached the cab of the Jetway, where they entered a much wider area. The light was brighter, and that made him feel less confined. He could begin to see inside the aircraft. A slight cooling breeze leaked between a thick rubber gasket and the aircraft's aluminum exterior.

The Jetway auto-leveling system was in Standby Mode. It waited for a signal from the floor sensor that the tunnel was out of alignment with the threshold of the aircraft. Without notice, the auto-leveler sensed a misalignment and moved the Jetway upward. The movement caused a nervous reaction from several passengers as the floor tilted under their feet.

Valium is often given to relieve anxiety. However, some who take the drug experience troubling and paradoxical side effects. Frank had told him to take one of the stolen Valium, but only if he felt nervous or anxious. Neither Frank nor Bill had any knowledge of the many unwanted side effects from Valium. Some of include confusion, hallucinations, unusual thoughts or behavior, unusual risk-taking behavior, decreased inhibitions and most critical, no fear of danger.

The Valium he ingested quickly passed the blood/brain barrier and reached his cerebellum. His chemical reactions should have been predicable and consistent, but were not. He felt dizzy and again suffered a sense of motion sickness.

Even in the stuffy seventy-degree air, he was cold, but, was sweating profusely. To him, the Jetway felt like a roller coaster. He grabbed a stainless steel passenger assist handle and hung on. When he looked out a long vertical side window, he felt better. Out on the ramp, he could see the roundly formed side of the fuselage and that somehow calmed him. As long as he held tight to the railing, his stomach was more settled and the peristaltic waves of nausea diminished.

Passengers directly ahead of him were patiently prepared to board this enormous aircraft and typically concentrated on the flight attendant who checked their boarding passes. Two elderly passengers in front of him hadn't noticed that he had stopped moving with the rest of the crowd. However, passengers who were behind him went around him as he hung onto the assist railing, motionless. No one stopped to offer assistance. Instead, they detoured around him much like passing a stalled car on the highway.

He looked outside at the area immediately below the belly of the jet. He saw the left nose tire. A mechanic in coveralls and a set of headphones over his uniform cap walked across the ramp toward the airplane.

He continued to stare out across the tarmac, but had no comprehension of anything he saw. Later, passengers would comment that he appeared to be oblivious to everything around him.

"Sir. Excuse me. Sir Are you going with us today?"

Guerrero jerkily looked to his right. He reluctantly released his grip on the railing and faced the person who had spoken to him.

He was very tall. A distinguished looking Mexican dressed in the standard airline issued uniform: the dark blue trousers, with a light tan shirt, magenta tie and camel colored blazer. A nametag below the emblematic airline wings bore his name: Amelio Perez—Purser.

Perez spoke to Guerrero for the second time, first in English and then in Spanish; "Sir, it is departure time. If you are going with us today, you better board now." "*Sir, es el momento de la salida. Si usted va con nosotros hoy en día, es mejor abordar ahora.*"

In a thickened voice, "I am going to New York. What time does the flight get there?" His voice sounded as though he were speaking in slow motion and resonated with a metallic echo. His voice seemed to come through a long dark tunnel. He was puzzled by his own voice, yet the voices of those around him sounded normal.

He thought, "I must talk normal. I don't want to cause no attention to me." He said, "Fine. Fine. I'm OK. I just was trying to relax. I'm good, *Amigo*."

Amelio heard these rapid phrases, spoken in a semi-falsetto voice. He initially thought this was an attempt at making a rude and tasteless comment about Amelio's rather obvious feminine characteristics.

On reflection, Amelio later concluded the passenger was probably strung out on something and that he certainly needed to be watched.

"Come along with me, sir. Let's see your boarding pass, please."

Bill froze. He couldn't remember where his ticket or boarding pass was. He knew he was asking for his paperwork in order to get on the plane. He was inert, he could not think or move. He was unable to do anything other than stare at Amelio Perez.

"Do you have your boarding pass? We need that if you are flying to New York with us today."

Bill stood with his back to the window in the Jetway.

Amelio again asked him for his boarding pass, but he could only stare at Amelio.

Guerrero abruptly raised his arm, his elbow hyper-extended. He was holding his black bag in his right hand. The bag came to rest chest high.

Amelio was taken aback by his sudden lurching motion. Obviously, this odd duck was trying to offer his carry-on bag to him. Amelio assumed the bag contained his boarding pass for today's flight.

Guerrero knew he was in trouble. This steward would not let him board without a ticket. In his slowed, compromised and diminished mental state, Bill knew if he did not let him on the airplane, he would end up back in the terminal. If that happened and tried to retrace his steps through the terminal, he knew he would get caught.

His sense of panic increased. "Just a minute."

He thought to himself, "Think, that's what I got to do. Get control. Look and act straight."

"Hey man, I'm sorry. I'm all messed up. I took a pain pill."

Bill implored Amelio to understand. "See, I was at the dentist and he done a tooth canal. He gave me these pills for the pain. I guess they really knock you on your ass."

Quickly, in what seemed like a perfectly normal voice to him, "I'll be OK." To Amelio, he sounded strung out.

His voice became much louder. "I'm FINE. I'll just get on and go to sleep."

"I am sorry for your discomfort sir. But it is departure time. I need your boarding pass. Now." Then in Spanish, "*Necesito su tarjeta de embarque. Ahora."*

"Here. Here it is. It's in my bag here. I'll get it."

With both hands, Bill clutched the bag to his stomach as though it were a giant beach ball. Carefully, he wrapped his right hand and arm around the bag, then slowly and clumsily pulled at the zipper. Eventually, the zipper parted. Both men could hear each individual zipper tooth on the track as the lock passed each piece. For some reason, Bill found this hilarious and started to laugh.

Guerrero felt the sharp, hard edge of the gun through the fabric as he rifled through the bag looking for his ticket.

His laugh stopped, replaced by a panic that rolled over him.

He had to remain calm. He could not get caught. He had come this far. He had to keep their plan going. With forced concentration he ignored the gun in his bag. Then with much fanfare and flourish, produced his rumpled and disheveled boarding pass.

"Yo, man. Here you go. Got it right here. I wouldn't shit you." *"No hay problema para usted o para mí,"* "No problem for you or me."

Amelio quickly examined the bent pasteboard boarding pass. He took a long, experienced and objective look at Guerrero, then said, "Listen to me very carefully. Go through this door to the other side of the aircraft. Then turn right and walk back three cabins. Your seat is in the middle of the third cabin. Please hurry. If you need any assistance, one of my Main Cabin Flight Attendants will assist you."

Bill retrieved his boarding card, walked passed Amelio and said, "Hey, Compadre. No sweat. I'll be a good passenger." He thought of his plan to take control of the aircraft again and that made him giggle again.

25

08:25 Pacific Standard Time
San Francisco International Airport

Bill took several steps. To Amelio, they appeared normal. But to Bill, they seemed to be huge, high, slow-motion strides. He felt like he was wearing swim fins.

Amelio watched him. The comment about being a good passenger and then the inappropriate giggling set off another alarm. "I'll have to remember to tell whoever is working E-Zone to keep an eye on this character. It's a shame that he is so screwed up. He really is quite attractive."

Bill slowly walked through the mid-ship galley and became confused. He could not remember which way to turn. He looked for a sign, found none and turned left toward First Class.

One of three Flight Attendants who were busy handing out menus looked at him. Instinctively, she knew he did not belong in First Class. "Sir. Where are you sitting?"

His voice was thick, "I don't 'member exactly."

"Do you have your boarding pass? May I see it, please?"

He still had the rumpled, rolled and damp boarding pass in his hand. "Sure, *Chica*. Right here." For the forth or fifth time this morning, he produced his beat up boarding card.

She took a quick practiced glance at the lower right hand corner of his boarding pass. With a firm hand on Bill's right shoulder, she turned him around and forcefully aimed him toward the tail section and said, "Walk almost to the end of the airplane. Your seat is in the third cabin. If you get lost, or need help, ask one of the Attendants in the back."

He slowly turned back toward her, "Thanks, *Chica*."

A quiet fury overtook her. "Don't refer to me as '*Chica*'. I don't like it and I won't put up with your Mexican-macho bullshit. Got it?" Then instantly, her look changed, she smiled her most enchanting and radiant smile, "Have a nice day, Sir."

Confused, he turned and disappeared into the crowded aisle. The cabins were filled with passengers putting their belongings under, over, or on the floor by their assigned seats.

A rather large woman in a yellow dress blocked the aisle as she attempted to put her Pullman-sized suitcase in the overhead. Seven or eight passengers stood between him and the woman, waiting.

She looked back at the growing line of people. In frustration, she tried to shove her bag in the overhead. A third of the bag stuck out into the aisle, head-high. Pleased with herself, she brushed her hands together as though she were wiping toast crumbs from her palms. With a triumphant smile and look of satisfaction, she took her seat immediately beneath the precariously balanced bag.

While Bill waited for the people in the aisle to move, then looked down at the aisle seat next to him and saw 37-7. He tried to figure how many rows from here to his seat. One of the Valium's unanticipated consequences was it fogged his ability to do this simple calculation in his head. He mindlessly started to follow passengers toward the back end of the cabin. He reached the very end of the last section in coach, where he found nothing but a series of rest rooms and coat closets.

Near the coat closet, he saw a male Flight Attendant hanging up a garment bag. Bill reached out and touched the very tall cabin attendant's shoulder, who turned and looked directly at him with large, effeminate brown eyes.

The blond haired, brown-eyed cabin attendant pursed his lips for a brief second, then smiled. A nice smile, except for a discolored incisor. The look he gave Bill left no doubt in either of their minds that he found Bill attractive.

Abruptly and compulsively, Bill backed away to keep his distance. He glanced at the attendant's name badge. It read, "Carlton Marsh – Flight Attendant." Above his name badge was a rainbow striped ribbon with a five sided star in the middle.

He produced his boarding pass and asked, "Hey man. Where am I at?"

Carlton Marsh answered in a lilting musical voice, "Well, let's see." He looked at Bill's boarding pass, "It's supposed to be back here somewhere. But, but, maybe they moved it." Carlton laughed at his joke and held his hand over his mouth.

Then he studied Guerrero. First, he looked at Bill's eyes, then at his overall build. He inspected him as he would inspect a piece of meat in a butcher shop. He saw a thin, lanky person of Latin heritage. He wore no wedding ring. Then somewhat breathlessly, inexorably and inevitably, Carlton's gaze drifted to the front of Bill's pants.

"Forgive me, Sir. I'm just being silly. You are in that seat just over there." He waved toward an empty seat, theatrically emphasized the general direction of a vacant seat by extending a single finger from his hand held above his forehead. Quickly, he added in lush tone, "You'll be in my section. My name's Carlton, that's what all my friends call me. What's your name?"

"Guillermo. Guillermo or Bill. Bill Guerrero."

"No problem, Bill. I always take good care of my passengers and I'm going to good care of you, very good care." Then with a wink and a slight nod, "Where are you staying when you get to New York?"

Bill was shocked. His prison experiences had taught him that homosexuals, the *Maricóns*, were to be avoided. They were the object of cruel jokes. He could not understand how anyone could be like that. He found this cabin attendant's attention upsetting.

"What's the matter, Bill?" Carlton grinned at him. "Cat got your tongue?"

Bill was sickened. "No. What did you say?"

Bill had to get away from him, "Look, I'm sort of screwed up." He turned in the direction of his seat. "I took some shit and it makes me weird."

Carlton Marsh felt a rush caused by the raw attraction he felt. It probably was the swarthy roughness and bravado. He felt awash with excitement as he thought to himself, "I'm not going to let this one get away."

"Where did you say you're going to stay in New York? I didn't hear what you said." Another grin, followed by, "Our layover hotel is the Milford Plaza – but we call it the Mildew Plaza. It's in Times Square."

"I don't know. Maybe with my cousin. I don't really got no place." How could he talk to this faggot, this *Maricón*? He had never thought about New York. He wasn't going to New York. He was going to Havana!

He headed back toward the middle part of the last few rows in coach. He could barely follow Carlton's directions. He ultimately found an empty seat in Row 56.

He looked at his boarding pass and dimly saw he had been given row 55-seat 8. That seat was taken. He took the seat behind the one assigned to him. He did not want to make a scene. He dropped into his seat and felt incredibly tired.

Carlton finished hanging coats and garment bags. He heard the inter-station chimes, and saw the pink blinking light that indicated his zone in the aircraft was being paged.

He stepped several feet to the telephone handset, "E Zone, Carlton Marsh at your service."

When Carlton said service, the sibilance was overpowering. He literally hissed the "s" sound in the word service. "Carlton. This is Amelio. You have a young Mexican in your area. I don't remember his name, but he's in seat 55-8."

Carlton peeked around the coat compartment, looked for Bill, but was unable to see his prize.

"I certainly do remember him. He's just gorgeous in a rough sort of way."

"He seemed very disoriented and confused when he boarded. How does he seem to you?"

"Divine."

Amelio's voice tightened. "Carlton. This is serious. I want to know how he is. Is he behaving himself?"

Carlton's voice hardened. "I spoke with him. He seemed OK. I'll keep an eye on him."

With the telephone in his hand, Carlton strained and pulled himself up on his toes. He stretched the phone cord as he peered around the center aisle bulkhead. The crowd thinned out enough for Carlton to see the back of Bill's head, "Actually, Amelio, he looks like he's asleep."

"All right, Carlton. Listen, I think it's probably a good idea that we cut him off from the liquor and wine. He seemed pretty out of it when he came by me during the boarding. In fact, I wonder how he got past the agents in the terminal." Amelio paused. "If he gives you any trouble, let me know."

"Whatever you say, lover. I'll keep an eye on him."

Carlton smiled to himself, thinking, "I'll follow all your orders to the letter. In fact, I'll see to it that I take extra care of Bill, to make certain he is no trouble."

26

08:35 Pacific Standard Time
San Francisco International Airport

Amelio Perez placed the handset back in the cradle. No sooner had he done so, than the inter-station chimes warbled several times at his station.

"First Class, L-1 Door, Amelio."

"Amelio, this is Captain Webber."

"Yes, Captain. Is everything all right?"

"Actually, that's why I'm calling. We're about ready to go up here, but still have two cabin open door lights on. What's the delay? Why aren't the cabin doors closed?"

"Well, Sir. They are still boarding the last few passengers here at L-1. Commissary is just now closing the R-1 door."

Amelio spoke and the R-1 cabin door light on Stan's Auxiliary Panel went out. The extinguished light was confirmed by all three pilots. They heard the muffled "thwump" of the door being closed and confirmed the door-open light was no longer illuminated.

Don continued, "Okay, I see it's out now. Any idea how much longer for L-1, for the rest of the passengers?"

"Captain, the Jetway looks clear. I do not see any others coming, Wait, here comes the agent with the final paperwork and manifest."

Through the intercom handset, Don could hear the agent's conversation with Amelio, "Here you are. There are only thirty-nine empty seats in Economy Class. First and Business are full."

Amelio nodded, then said to the Captain, "Looks like we should be ready in a couple of minutes. I will call you when the cabin is secured for departure."

"Roger."

Don stowed the intercom handset at the rear of the center radio console.

Stan compulsively lifted the receiver and uncoiled the tangled cord, then replaced the handset and said to no one in particular, "It never fails. We are always the last to know what's going on. At least, on the DC-10 you could open the cockpit door and see what was happening in the cabin. With this hog, we really never know what's doin' unless one of the Flight Attendants tells us."

Fred smiled and said, "Flying this thing is like working in a branch office. Do your own thing. Nobody knows or cares."

The interphone chimed and then came to life with a loud crackling sound, "Ground to Cockpit. You there, Cockpit?"

The mechanic by the nose gear said, "You ready to rock and roll, Captain?"

Stan was the only one of the three pilots who had been listening for the mechanic's call. Stan looked directly at the Captain and said, "Don. Ground's calling on the interphone."

Don reached for the selector panel and brushed against his cup of coffee that rested nearby. The cup tilted and a small amount of coffee sluiced onto the forward console as the cup righted itself. Silently, he swore to himself.

Fred added, "That was close. Hope the rest of the trip goes better than this."

Fred watched the miniature typhoon in the coffee cup, "It's a good thing we have Doris Day back in the cabin." He referred to an old Doris Day movie *Julie*, in which she landed a crippled airplane, damaged by spilled coffee.

Don ignored Fred and spoke in the microphone, "Go ahead, Ground. This is the Captain."

"Good morning, Sir. You are cleared to check your hydraulics and flight controls."

Don turned to Stan. All three pilots knew the drill. Pressurize each of the four separate hydraulic systems and determine that both Auto Pilot systems integrity was secure. Quickly, Don lifted the "A" Autopilot bat-handled switch to the ON position. He disconnected the "A" autopilot with the thumb button on his control yoke. Immediately, the "A" Autoflight disconnect warning sounded. He pressed the red autopilot switch on the control column again and the warning stopped.

Don Webber lifted the bat-handled switch for the "B" autopilot. When he was satisfied with the system integrity, he deferred the rest of the checks to Fred. "She's all yours."

Fred applied adequate pressure with the control column to verify he could override the autopilot and then disconnected the "B" Autopilot. Once again, the auto flight disconnect wailer sounded. Fred silenced the warning by pressing the autopilot disconnect button on his control column. With his left hand, he reached to the rear corner of the center console and tested both aileron and rudder trim control switches.

Fred smiled, looked at Don and said, "I'm satisfied if you are, Doctor. I think the patient will live to fly again."

Don ignored his First Officer. "Let's finish the Engine Start Checklist."

Stan rolled the plastic-coated checklist in the holder attached to the seatback on Fred's chair and read each of the items in order, to which Fred responded. Within 30 seconds, all three pilots confirmed the 747 was ready for engine start.

Don picked up the microphone and started to call the ground mechanic, when the interphone chime sounded.

Fred quickly reached aft and pulled the handset from its cradle, "Front office. Who is this?"

"Amelio, Sir. The L-1 door is closed and the cabin is secured. We are ready for departure."

"You obviously have made a serious mistake calling me sir. You must want to talk to the Captain."

Don heard the conversation in his headset, spoke in his microphone. "Thank you, Amelio. I appreciate you calling us. We should be pushing back in just a couple of minutes."

Fred grinned and then looked to his left, "Are we ready to go?"

Don said, "Yes, I'm ready. Call the company and tell them we're ready to push back from Gate 67."

Fred said, "It's Showtime, folks." With microphone in hand, in a very professional voice, he said, "San Francisco Operations, 100 here. Ready to push from 67."

Predictably, the operation folks in the airline's mini-tower looked at, around and behind 100. "You are released and cleared to push off of Gate 67. Contact SFO Ground Control for taxi clearance."

"Company says we're cleared to push and to contact Ground."

Don nodded, "Very good."

"Good morning San Francisco Ground Control. This is 100 ready to push back from Gate 67 at our terminal. We'd like to push back for New York."

The FAA controller who managed to keep all the taxiing aircraft sorted out at SFO said, "100. You are cleared to push." She waited a second or two, then added, "Cleared to taxi to Runway 28 Right or 28 Left. Your choice."

Don started to reprimand Fred for his unnecessary chatter, when ground gave them a choice of departure runways. Don immediately said, "Tell them we'll take 1 Right."

Fred looked at him with a questioning glance, "Don, the choice was 28 Left or Right. Not 1 Right. Which do you want? 28 Left or 28 Right? Or, do you want me to request 1 Right?"

Don picked up his microphone. "Ground this is 100. We'd like 1

Right, if it's available. If it's not, then we'll take 28 Right."

"Actually, 100, your clearance was for 28 Right or 28 Left." Don sat rigid and fumed.

Ground Control continued, "1 Right was never requested when your company filed your flight plan. It was never part of your clearance. If you are requesting 1 Left or 1 Right, we'll see what we can do. In the future, you should have your company make that request so we can fit you into the North Departures."

Don said nothing. He was embarrassed. Heat caused by his humiliation spread across his face. "100. State your intentions. Will you be using the 28's or are you still requesting 1 Right?"

Fred looked at Don. He waited. This was not a good moment to say anything.

"100? Are you there? Say your intentions." Seconds passed, "Over."

Don pressed his microphone button, "100. We'll take 28 Right." Then added, "Sorry for the confusion."

"No problem 100. Monitor Ground on 121.80 until you are in the run up area for 28 Right."

Don's pulse quickened. He was still embarrassed. And he was very irritated at Fred. He thought he might be being taunted by his First Officer because he was fairly new to the 747.

"Fred, give the mechanics a call and tell them we are cleared to push back. Also, tell them that we're going to be using Runway 28 Right and we need to be headed North or East."

Fred nodded, "Hey. You still down there? We have our clearance for Runway 28 Right. The Captain wants us headed North or East. Got all that?"

"Roger." The static returned. "Release the brakes and we'll shove you out of town."

The parking brake warning light was on and the brake pressure checked. Don twisted in his seat and looked back at Stan, "Stanley, turn ADP #1 ON for body gear steering and #4 Electric pump ON for brake pressure."

HIJACKING OF FLIGHT 100

Stan had anticipated this as Don spoke, and turned two control switches. Three thousand pounds of hydraulic pressure surged through systems 1 and 4.

Don pressed down on the toe brakes and the parking brake locking mechanism clicked off and then released. The aircraft rocked slightly as loads were relieved on the main landing gear.

Don said, "Brakes released. We're cleared to push back." Then to Stan, "Mark the time."

27

08:40 Pacific Standard Time
San Francisco International Airport

Two mechanics are assigned to dispatch each flight. One walked alongside the nose gear, while the other drove the tractor. Both mechanics wore communal headsets and could hear each other as well as the instructions from the cockpit. Slowly, the two mechanics walked the aircraft away from the terminal.

Don said, "Tell the mechanics we're ready to go."

Fred called the mechanics on the interphone. "We are ready to go."

Fred faced Don. "Maintenance says they want to know who is going to get charged with a delay."

Don looked at his Rolex and saw 08:42. "Give them schedule at 08:30."

Fred looked back at Stan then said to Don. "We can't do that because of ACARS. It knows what time we left the gate. And it never lies."

Stan chuckled. "It lies today. It's still broken. San Francisco's finest mechanics were supposed to fix it. But I still get a NO COMM light and it's covered with MALF stickers."

Don said, "Then give them 08:30 for departure Stan." Then he added to both pilots in the cockpit, "I'm sorry, fellas. I guess I was a little short back there."

Fred could not contain himself. "No, I don't think you're too short. I make you to be about six foot give or take a little."

Laughing, Fred quickly added, "Apology accepted. Trust me, Don. I won't do anything to lead you down the primrose path. Don't forget. My butt's strapped in this hunk of aluminum too."

The ground mechanic called on the ships interphone, "Hey Skipper, are the brakes off?"

"Yes Sir."

The ground tractor's turbo-charged diesel engine coughed and then labored under the strain of getting the heavy 747 rolling. A cloud of unburned black diesel fuel trailed the ground tractor. Very slowly, the aircraft started to roll backward on the ramp away from the passenger gates.

Don and Fred watched the size of the aircraft's reflection diminish in the terminal windows with each increasing foot. Slowly, the tug's four wheels turned in unison to allow the aircraft to be turned 90° to the terminal. Now, the 747 faced north toward the hills across the Bayshore Freeway.

"Parking Brakes on, Captain."

"Roger that." Don looked at the pressure gauge and added, "Brake Pressure Checks." All three pilots knew that if the brake pressure dropped and the airplane started to roll, there would be no way to stop the aircraft other than to use the emergency pneumatic brakes.

The ground mechanic called, "You're cleared to start engines 4, 3, 2 and 1."

Don made one final check of the numerous system indicators in the cockpit. Satisfied that everything related to engine start was ready. He saw his Flight Engineer had done his job properly.

Don commanded, "TURN 4."

The First Officer reached up and held down the #4 Engine START switch. Numerous circuits were energized and a green start valve OPEN light came on. Fred said with no trace of humor, "#4 Valve OPEN."

Stan watched the pneumatic duct pressure decrease by thirty percent and saw the N2 tachometer on the #4 engine slowly start to move. When the N2 tachometer indicated the twenty percent, Don smoothly and quickly lifted the #4 engine start lever and called to Stan, "#4 Start Lever UP."

Stan responded, "#4 Fuel Flow 1,100 pounds and steady," an indication the initial fuel surge into the burner section of the engine was not excessive. The engine continued to accelerate to just over 45% N2, when the pneumatic starter disengaged.

Don, Fred and Stan repeated the ritual for the three remaining engines.

Both Fred and Don intently watched outside as the signalman walked to a location forty-five degrees off the nose of the aircraft on the Captain's side. The mechanic looked strange with his head and most of his face covered with a baseball cap and enormous sound suppression earmuffs, and large Ray-Ban sunglasses. He stood with flashlight wands crossed in an "X" high on his chest that indicated it was unsafe for the aircraft to move.

Slowly, the tractor backed away from the nose gear, pulling the twenty foot long tow bar. Even at a speed of less than two miles per hour the tractor bounced on the uneven pavement as it made its way back to the terminal.

After the mechanic made sure there was nothing near the aircraft, he saluted and then held one arm straight out in the general direction the aircraft was to taxi. He fanned the other wand in a circular motion to indicate movement.

Don eased the four throttles forward and each engine tachometer responded. The mass of the 747 required a moderate amount of thrust to start rolling. Once the aircraft was under way, substantially less power was required to keep her rolling.

HIJACKING OF FLIGHT 100

Don spoke to Stan. "Look and see if we have a dragging brake. She's taking a lot of power this morning to get her rolling." As he spoke, Stan had already started to check the brake temperature monitors.

"Too early to tell. All the brakes are still cool." Slowly, the 747 started to move away from the ramp area.

Fred handed Stan the paperwork required for takeoff, while Don called for the After Engine Start Checklist, to which Stan challenged and Fred responded to the litany of over twenty items.

During a brief lull in the workload, Fred said, "Captain, I think we should give our illustrious Engineer a gold star for his exemplary reading of the check list. He definitely is Captain material."

Stan reached up and turned the Auxiliary Power Unit controller to OFF. "Captain, APU's secured."

"Very good. Thanks."

Don smiled at Fred's comment about Stan and thought maybe this was going to be a good trip after all.

His First Officer probably was harmless and didn't mean anything by his remarks. Don briefly whistled a mindless tune as he taxied this seven hundred and fifty thousand pound aluminum tube full of people, fuel and cargo toward the runway.. He let his mind wander as he settled into his seat and guided the 747 with the nose gear tiller.

He casually considered the prospects of today's flight, the enroute time and the destination weather, then with no provocation Don said, "Probably going to have some rain in New York for our arrival."

Both Fred and Stan were surprised by his unsolicited comment.

Fred said carefully, "I don't know about that. I'm not sure the rain will get there before we land. But it'll definitely be raining by tomorrow morning. It never fails, I wanted to go for a walk in New York, maybe do some shopping. Looks like the weather fairy has struck again."

When Don heard the word morning, thoughts of Kathryn

suddenly bounded into his mind. Mornings and Kathryn seemed to go together. Don thought about their last morning together and mused there had to be a better way to keep their relationship on a more even keel. A half-hour ago he was going to terminate the affair and now he was thinking about tomorrow morning with her.

The thought of being with her this evening and tomorrow made his pulse race. He had once complained to Kathryn that Ruth was sexually old-fashioned. The last time they had been together he remembered how Kathryn's stomach muscles rippled every time she neared a climax. Her entire body bucked and twisted under his attention...

"Don. We were supposed to stay on the INNER. Then we're to turn left on taxiway PAPA. You missed the turn."

Don snapped back at Fred, "What?" He couldn't believe it. "I did what?" He instinctively stopped the aircraft and let it rock slowly on the landing gear.

Fred repeated what he had just said. "Our clearance was to stay on the INNER Taxiway FOXTROT, then via PAPA to the 28 Right Run Up Area. You missed PAPA. PAPA's behind us. Taxiway NOVEMBER is ahead, just over there." He pointed in the general direction of the end of Runway 28 Right. "I'll call Ground Control and tell them."

Don sat tightly, "Don't tell them a thing. We'll just go to NOVEMBER and make the turn."

Fred was not comfortable with Don's apparent disregard of Ground Control's instructions. "You sure?"

Don repeated his command. "Yes, God dammit, I'm sure. Don't say anything to Ground Control."

Don was irritated by his mistake. He had not been paying attention. His daydreaming had fogged his concentration.

It was time for him to pay attention to the job at hand and think about Kathryn later. He taxied 'til the cockpit was well past the entrance to taxiway NOVEMBER. When the nose tires were lined up with the curved apron throat, he deftly pulled the tiller full aft, which directly turned the nose gear into the opening for NOVEMBER.

San Francisco Ground Control called them on the radio. "100. It appears you have entered taxiway NOVEMBER, instead of PAPA."

Fred thought, and then said, "We're busted."

Don swore under his breath.

SFO Ground Control continued in a stern and officious manner, "In the future 100, if you are unable to comply with our instructions, please advise."

Fred moved uneasily in his seat then said, "Aw shit, Don. They caught us at our little game. Now, do you want me to say anything to them? Like maybe apologize?"

"I'll handle it." Microphone in hand, Don used his most cooperative tone of voice. "San Francisco Ground, we are sorry about the mistake. You are absolutely right. I was distracted looking at the departure chart and missed PAPA. It looks like no harm was done. Sorry for the mix up."

The ground controller continued to grind as he said, "We'll let it go this time, 100. But, be advised Taxiway NOVEMBER was closed all of last week for work in progress. There is a published NOTAM about the construction and closure. If it had been closed, you would have been stranded out there with no way to turn around. In the future, please pay attention to where you're going."

Fred thought to himself, "Oops!"

Don sighed then apologized, "Roger. It won't happen again. Sorry for the mistake."

Without thinking Stan said, "Hell of a way to start a trip." He immediately knew that was a mistake.

Don turned and gave him a disdainful stare. "Just do your job, Stan."

"Yes sir."

"Fred and I'll take care of flying the airplane. I don't appreciate your unsolicited comments."

Again, Fred settled in his seat and busied himself with

nonessential business. Quickly, he looked over his shoulder at Stan and quietly smiled, as if to say, "Hang in there. In five hours, we'll be in New York."

Embarrassment welled up in Don. It turned to mild self-criticism. He thought to himself, Making a mistake was bad enough. But having to admit it and then publically apologize was horrible. Competence is my motto. I have never thought of myself as being incompetent. I had best clean up my act, an airplane is no place for foolish distractions.

As an addendum to his self-ridicule, he thought, Forget Kathryn for the time being. Plenty of time to worry about her later.

28

08:40 Pacific Standard Time
San Francisco International Airport

Ten minutes after Flight 100 pushed back from the gate and started taxiing, Robert Burns recalled what prompted him to make the trip out to Gate 67 at the end of the terminal. It had been to locate and interrogate Guerrero.

He swore to himself, "Damn, that was sloppy police work. I never should have let Shapiro sidetrack me like that. What the hell's the matter with me, I was after someone else."

He filled out the lengthy Passenger Incident Report as it applied to Shapiro's denied boarding. He filled in most of the numerous blanks on the legal-sized document.

Burns was not convinced by his thin rationalization and excuse about the error of his ways. He was bothered by his lapse in police protocol. He attempted to quietly cover his mistake. "Maybe he was going to New York to look for a job and didn't plan on to returning to San Francisco." Intuitively, though, he knew he was rationalizing a bad decision and a glaring lapse in protocol.

Burns' deep concern caused him to speak loud enough that

Shapiro overheard some of his comments, "Or, maybe he's a hijacker, on his way to God knows where."

Shapiro responded to Burns' subconscious remark. "Not only are you a has-been, a retired ex-flat foot, you are senile, too. I have a round-trip ticket from New York to San Francisco and back to New York. What in the hell are you mumbling about? Me a hijacker?"

Burns looked at his obnoxious detainee and smiled, "Have a nice day, Mr. Shapiro. I hope American Airlines will be able to accommodate you and your travel needs. By the way, sir, we have a record of today's events. Should you chose to travel with us in the future, please be advised we will not tolerate any more of your outrageous behavior."

He folded the paperwork and put it in his coat pocket, as Mel Shapiro got up to leave.

"See you around, Pops. The next time I ride on your airline you won't be around, 'cause I'm going to have you fired. You can take your airline job and shove it."

29

08:45 Pacific Standard Time
San Francisco International Airport

Bill Guerrero was falling and could not stop. He grabbed at anything that was flying past him. He continued to fall. The place into which he was falling was a tunnel that had walls covered by stringy gripping vines and damp, dark rocks. He fell faster. He was being jostled and then felt a shuddering jolt. Cautiously, he opened his eyes, but the feeling did not go away. He sat upright in his seat and grabbed the armrest. The cabin spun.

He took deep breaths. The speed of the revolutions slowed, reversed direction and then gradually stopped.

Now, he slowly realized he was in the middle of hundreds of people. Not one of them paid the slightest attention to him. He sensed he was different from everyone else. Again, he felt uneasy. Unknown to him, he was experiencing another example of the unintended side effects of the Valium; disorientation and unfocused paranoia. Around the cabin, he continued to look to see if anyone watched him.

He thought, "Be casual. Don't attract no attention to yourself."

He turned his head far to the left and saw the faggy Flight Attendant who looked directly at him. The *"afeminado"* caught his eye, smiled and then winked at him.

He was disgusted by this blatant overture. He wondered why the *Maricón* was so interested in him. Then Carlton approached his seat, "Did you have a nice nap? You were really sleeping very soundly."

Bill was only able to stare at Carlton. He was unwilling and unable to speak, afraid that if he did say anything it would call attention to himself.

Not one to be deterred by a lack of conversation, Carlton smiled at him. "Can I get you anything?" Finally Bill began to understand that Carlton was speaking to him. "Yeah. Water. Some water. In a glass."

"I'm not allowed to give you a glass. It's just against all the regulations. I'll see if I can find a paper cup for you." Carlton turned and was gone in one fluid movement.

Strong, pulsing terror was all Bill felt. Slowly, came the realization that fear had taken over again. He tried to think about options, but the Valium slowed his rational thinking. He wanted to go back to the plan, but his mind was a roiling caldron of jumbled facts and fears.

He sat very still. He tried to decide what to do, but was unable. He weeded out seemingly unrelated ideas. He was left with only a few choices, none of them acceptable. He could do nothing. Maybe he should fly to New York and disappear. Or, he could wait and see how the flight went. If he found the right opportunity, then he could go with the plan. Once again, his thoughts would not settle down.

Brother Juan told him he borrowed money from the drug buyers in Miami to pay for the gun and other stolen items. Bill knew if their plan didn't work, Juan would be in deep trouble with his narcotic customers.

Bill's concentration was interrupted when Carlton returned and put a soft hand on his shoulder. "Here's a nice paper cup filled with water. Wet and cold. Especially for you."

He could not speak, but his mind screamed, "Get away from me you fucking fag."

Carlton leaned over him, his hand casually spread over Bill's seat back. "I just love cool water, don't you?"

Carlton ached for a physical encounter with this stunning treasure. He wanted him to pick up on the idea of cool water. Then he could bend the conversation toward taking a shower, perhaps, together. Carlton had used this approach many times, often with great success.

Bill intentionally ignored Carlton. In an impulsive act, he reached into his pants pocket and removed the remaining yellow Valium tablet and tore open the plastic covering. He avoided Carlton's gaze as he extended his hand and then took the small cup of water. He compulsively tossed the tablet into his mouth and drained the water from the cup. Bill swallowed this tablet with far less difficulty than he had with the first one.

Carlton remained in front of him and watched his ritual ingestion. "Do you like to do drugs?"

Bill's head snapped back as he looked at this angularly shaped blond haired man. "Hey, man. None of your fucking business."

Carlton was embarrassed and a little more than put off by this hostile and aggressive attitude. He tried to placate him, saying, "Well, I only wanted to help you. There's no cause to get hot with me."

After he waited a few long seconds, he dropped his gaze toward Bill. "That is, if you want my help." Carlton was starting to become aroused. He was very tempted to casually brush against Bill's arm. All he would have to do is just step a little closer, and then thrust up against Bill.

Carlton stood there and deliberated about his ingenious courting ritual, when the aircraft stopped abruptly. After a moment or two, it seemed that maybe the Captain was slowly taxiing back to the terminal. Carlton bent down in front of Bill to peer out the window. In an exaggerated move, he dropped his right hand onto Bill's left shoulder.

His hand remained there while he fussed about what was going on. "Honestly. I just don't know what is the matter. I hope we aren't going to be delayed getting to New York." Carlton squeezed Bill on the shoulder gently.

Bill's reaction was forceful and abrupt as he knocked Carlton's hand away, his voice full of intense anger, "Hey, asshole" he roared, "You listening to me? You keep your hands off me. I don't like fuckin' fairies."

The volume of his voice was conspicuous enough that passengers turned to see the source of commotion. Bill bellowed, "Keep away from me and keep your hands off me. Understand?"

Sadly, in a frightened frame of mind, Carlton looked down at him. Bill had overreacted. There was no need for him to have pushed him away so forcefully. That was mean, rejecting him so harshly. The verbal outburst and abuse simply were not called for.

The strong physical attraction Carlton experienced a few minutes ago still remained. If anything, the physical rejection made his sexual stirrings even stronger.

To Bill, the situation was out of control and this *Maricón* was going to screw everything up. He knew he would end up being caught and arrested. He felt trapped.

In all his conversations with Juan, the one thing they all agreed on was that he was to remain calm and not call attention to himself. This *afeminado* was doing exactly that. Because the *Maricón* couldn't keep his hands off of him, Bill had been forced to lash out at him. That caused many passengers to pay closer attention to Bill and the flight attendant. In Bill's mind, it was all Carlton's fault. No matter what happened, Carlton would be to blame.

Many travelers in Carlton's zone wondered what was going on with the flight attendant and the unruly passenger. Passengers in the aft section of "E" cabin had an excellent view of Carlton, as he fussed over the thin, tall Chicano. Several saw the Mexican suddenly backhand the Flight Attendant. The blow had been swift and effective. Even at a distance, the overtones of their conversation clearly indicated the passenger was angry about something the Flight Attendant had said or done.

Carlton was crushed by Bill's abusive rejection. He spun toward the rear of the aircraft, but stopped to say, "You are probably just tired. Get some sleep. I'll wake you before we get to New York."

Bill realized that he had made a serious mistake. In little under an hour, he had taken two Valium tablets. He did not know the strength of the tablets, but he knew he had to remain alert. He needed the *Maricón's* help. Maybe, somehow, he could use the fairy, much like he had been used in prison.

Carlton straightened up from having knelt down to check his door, then turned to check on his passengers. His gaze quickly zeroed in on Bill, which was met with a prolonged and direct stare. Bill looked around to see if anyone was watching him and then quietly and quickly motioned for Carlton.

Carlton could hardly contain himself as he rushed toward Bill, "Yes. Yes. I'm here. What is it you want?"

"Hey listen. I'm sorry about jumping you and all that shit, man."

Carlton smiled.

"I'm like sort of uptight. Know what I mean? Anyway, I want to take a nap for a while."

Bill looked at the delicate and feminine watch Carlton was wearing, "If I fall asleep, wake me up in an hour, man."

Here was the chance Carlton had been waiting for. He was absolutely beside himself. He would, indeed, wake his wonderful passenger at whatever time he said.

Carlton suspected he might be on a sexual roll and didn't want to do anything to antagonize Bill. He considered Bill's request about a nap and affectionately asked, "I'll be glad to wake you. Do you want a pillow, or perhaps a blanket? They really are for the First Class passengers, but I'll be happy to get one for you."

Bill felt the effects of the Valium and could hardly keep Carlton's face in focus as he said, "No. Ok. If I fall asleep, wake me in a while." He did not recognize his own voice. It sounded to him like he was speaking at half-speed.

In a dull and rapidly dimming awareness, he remembered when he flew from Miami to San Francisco it was about six hours. So he incorrectly assumed San Francisco to Havana was six hours too.

He knew he was going to fall asleep or pass out, but he was not certain which. Dreamily and euphorically, he thought everything was going to be just fine. If he fell asleep, the *Maricón* would wake him and then he would put the plan into action.

The effects of the Valium hit in waves. At first, he felt warm, relaxed and didn't have a care in the world. What he didn't know about, he didn't matter Then, some obscure thought would flash in his consciousness, over which he would obsess. He could not focus, nor could he hold onto an idea or concept. His stream of consciousness was like the sea at low tide, his thoughts rolled in, stopped and then rolled back out. Physically, his eyes felt very dry and when he closed them he quickly became incredibly tired.

Bill leaned back, now fully relaxed and settled deeply into his seat. He had no feeling or awareness of his surroundings nor any concept of time. In his semi-conscious state he was mildly aware of the aircraft's distant soft rolling motions. Far, far away, he heard the subtle whine of engines. Days, hours or minutes later, Bill's seat felt like a marble slab, covered with a rough canvas material. The marble was cold and ungiving. His last dim perception was the slab on which he was laying was being moved, turned and then lifted.

30

08:59 Pacific Standard Time
Runway 28 Right San Francisco International Airport

The two nose gear tires of the Boeing 747 straddled the eighteen inch wide white dashed centerline on Runway 28 Right at San Francisco International Airport. Don Webber aligned the aircraft on a magnetic heading of 283.7°, the precise magnetic heading of the runway.

Through two-inch thick laminated windshields Don Webber and his crew looked down the two and one half mile-long by two hundred foot wide runway. Even in the early morning light, the concrete shimmered from the absorbed heat so the last several thousand feet of runway looked wet.

Don said to both Fred and Stan, "I'm still sort of new on the aircraft. I'll fly us to Kennedy." He looked to his right at Fred. "Tomorrow you can fly us back to San Fran."

Fred said, "Fair enough." Then turned and said to Stan, "Such is life for the lowly copilot."

Don returned his attention to the job at hand and asked, "Everybody ready?" Then he quickly glanced over his shoulder at Stan.

Stan replied, "Yes Sir. I'm ready, Boss."

Continuing his instructions, Don then gave the standard before takeoff review. "Fred, call out 80 knots, V-1, V-R and V-2." Fred nodded his understanding.

"If there is a reason to abort the takeoff, I'll make the decision."

"Stan, if you see anything that doesn't look right, let me know."

"If we abort below V-1, Stan, I want you to pull all four throttles back against the idle stops. Fred I'll want you to call out airspeeds and anything else you see that is not normal." Don took a deep breath and asked, "Got it?"

Both pilots, in unison said, "Yes, Sir."

Don ending his instructions with the traditional, "If either of you see anything you don't like, speak out. Loud and clear."

"If you both are ready, let's get the takeoff check list out of the way."

Stan turned the roller shade checklist to BEFORE TAKE OFF, and read each item, to which Fred responded.

After Stan was satisfied that all the systems were properly set for take-off, he said, "BEFORE TAKE OFF checklist is complete."

Stan swiveled his seat to the full forward position and directed his attention to the four engines. Even at idle, their combined thrust exceeded fifty thousand pounds.

To the uninformed, the Standard Instrument Departure from San Francisco sounded like someone speaking in a foreign language.

TAKEOFF RUNWAYS 28L/R: Climb on SFO VOR/DME R-281 to the NORMM INT/SFO 13 DME. Expect RADAR vectors to assigned route/fix. Expect further clearance to filed altitude 10 minutes after departure.

LOST COMMUNICATIONS: If not in contact with departure control after reaching 3,000 feet, continue climb to filed altitude and proceed to assigned route/fix.

Fred repeated the clearance and placed a bug pointer on his compass directly under the cursor, his reference for maintaining runway heading after they were airborne. Then he selected HDG for heading references both Flight Directors. Finally, he set 3,000 feet in the window of the altitude arm and alert system and for the autopilot/flight directors. These actions would keep the aircraft on the assigned heading and at the proper altitude after the autopilot was engaged.

Fred looked at Don. "Whatever happened to the good old days? You know? Where you went out to the airport, jumped in the airplane and took off?"

Stan said, "These are the good old days. Just wait till you're old and gray. You'll look back at these times with fond memories." He finished the last three checklist items and then repeated, "BEFORE TAKE OFF checklist is complete."

Three air conditioning systems spooled down and the cockpit immediately started to heat up. Heat from cabin climbed the circular staircase and was sucked into the cockpit by equipment cooling fans. Radiant heat from hundreds of incandescent lights, instruments and control panels and windshield heaters added their collective heat to the cockpit environment.

Don, Fred and Stan felt an increase in cockpit temperature as they waited for their take off clearance from San Francisco Tower.

Fred continued the conversation with Stan. "I know, but it seems the company makes everything we do so difficult. We flew these things for years without all this altitude alert equipment. Sometimes I wonder how we flew from A to B without the Flig..."

San Francisco Tower interrupted, "100. Cleared for takeoff Runway 28 Right. Maintain runway heading. Climb and maintain 3,000 feet."

After a short pause, the expected meteorology advisory, "Wind is 300 degrees at 12 knots."

The windsock always told the truth regardless of the wind direction and velocity reported by the tower. Today the sock confirmed the tower report. The brisk wind blew almost directly down the runway, only 20° off the Runway 28 Right heading.

Fred looked at Webber, who nodded and rested his right hand

on the four thrust levers. Fred picked up his microphone and said, "Roger. 100's on the roll."

Don had not been listening to what Fred was saying about the good old days. He had been listening for the takeoff clearance. After the tower called, he instinctively looked at Fred and then at Stan.

"Ready, boys?"

"Yes, sir."

"Stan, trim the throttles between 60 and 80 knots. Fred hold forward pressure on the yoke and call out the targets for the V-1, V-R, V-2 and minimum safe climb speed."

Smoothly, slowly and deliberately, Don advanced the throttles. Typically, Pratt and Whitney JT-9D engines do not spool up evenly. Due to age differences, hours since overhaul, jet fuel controller adjustments and throttle rigging, each engine accelerates at its own rate. Don advanced the throttles approximately eighty percent of their forward travel and then waited for the engines to stabilize.
Essentially, this was a high-idle condition. After two seconds, he carefully advanced the levers to the target EPR's, Engine Pressure Ratios.

Don said, "EPR, Fuel Flow, Temperatures, N-1's all look good." At less than 40 knots, commanded, "Trim 'em."

Stan reached forward and made normal minor adjustments to each of the 4 thrust levers. Satisfied, he called out above the quadruple compressors' roar, "Trimmed at 60."

Fred had been holding slight forward pressure on the control column that placed a modest down load on the nose gear that improved nose wheel traction and steering. As the 747 slowly gathered speed, Fred relaxed his forward pressure and allowed the yoke to return to its neutral position. Hydraulically, the immense slab elevator returned to a position of neutral aerodynamic lift.

Don steered with the nose gear tiller, a lever that protruded through the cockpit bulkhead just below his left window. He made minute movements to the tiller and 3,000 pounds of hydraulic pressure directed the nose gear steering cylinders to slightly move right or left. All three pilots could hear the one of the nose tires as it rolled over the centerline runway lighting. A rhythmic thumping with decreasing intervals as the aircraft speed increased over each runway light.

Don heard Fred call out, "80 Knots." Don moved his hand from the nose gear tiller and put his left hand on the control yoke. He too said, "80 Knots." This confirmed both airspeed indicators were active and reasonably close indications.

At precisely 142 knots, Fred called, "V-1. Decision Speed," and then gratuitously added, "It's all downhill from here."

At V-1, the 747 had reached a speed at which a decision had to be made. If any one of the four engines failed precisely at this speed, Don would have to decide whether to continue the takeoff, or abort. Aerodynamically, the aircraft had the capability to become airborne from the amount of runway remaining on three engines. Conversely, if the pilot flying decided to abort, the 747 had the capability to stop on the remaining runway.

Every professional airline pilot knew most takeoff accidents occurred because of unsuccessful abort attempts. Don had always thought that given a choice, he would continue the takeoff rather than botch an abort.

Fred called, "156 knots. V-R. Rotate."

Don waited for this call and subconsciously tightened his grip with both hands on the yoke. He repeated Fred's call, "V-R."

At 156 knots, Don gently, consistently and intentionally pulled the control column toward his stomach.

As he pulled, the hydraulic systems started to move the leading edge of the horizontal stabilizer downward. This downward pressure on the elevator caused the aircraft to start a rotation around a predetermined aerodynamic center-of-lift through the wing and fuselage.

Slowly, the aircraft's full weight and subsequent pressure on the nose tires diminished. Inexorably, the nose gear bounced on the runway. Don pulled aft until the fuselage visually started to rotate upward. The traditional training center wisdom was that the aircraft rotation should be no more than three degrees per second. In the 747, a too-rapid rotation, if overdone, could result in a tail strike on the runway. The goal was to gently fly the airplane away from the runway surface.

Five seconds after he started the rotation, the aircraft was pitched up to precisely fifteen degrees above the horizon.

With a practiced eye, Don scanned each of flight instruments for normal indications and values he expected to see. Consistent with his anticipation, he saw the IVSI, the Instant Vertical Speed Indicator show an initial positive rate of climb.

The 747 flew away from the runway and the engine reflected roar diminished as the sound no longer bounced off the ground. As the noise level dropped, Don called to Fred, "Gear Up."

Fred looked at his airspeed indicator, which showed they had accelerated to the minimum safe flying speed of 168 knots. Fred called to Don, "V-2." He also verified a positive rate of climb. Satisfied, he reached over and pulled the landing gear handle out of the down detent and swiftly raised the lever to the full up position.

Throughout the airframe vibrations were felt. First the thump of the landing gear doors opening and then high speed vibration of the hydraulic pumps straining to raise 6,000 pounds of magnesium, titanium, aluminum and 18 wheels and tires into their respective wheel wells.

Stan Kurtz looked at the multi-lighted landing gear status panel and quickly verified through the green and amber lights, that all the individual wheels were retracting properly.

Don eased off the pressure he was holding on the control column. He trimmed out the pressure on the control column and said, "Turn off the No Smoking Sign."

Fred reached to the center of the overhead panel and pressed the illuminated 'No Smoke' switch light then said to no one in particular, "Smoke 'em if you've got'em. Suck 'em up, folks."

San Francisco tower called, "Flight 100. Contact NORCAL

Departure on 135.10. Have a good flight."

Fred picked up his microphone, "Rog, Tower. Over to Departure on 135.1." He flipped a small switch on the VHF control head, a green light indicated he had changed frequencies, "NORCAL Departure, this is 100. Were out of 900 feet on our way to 3,000."

"Roger, 100. Ident. Radar Contact. Maintain 3,000."

At less than 1,000 feet altitude above the runway the aircraft gradually changed its configuration. It transitioned from the awkward, long-legged, ungainly ground-clinging creature on the ramp; to a svelte elongated bird. She was approaching her element, the upper atmosphere.

At 1,000 feet above San Francisco Bay, Stan turned on the first of three air conditioning machines. He opened an eyeball vent above his head and hoped for cool air, but felt none.

As the 747 accelerated to a predetermined speed, Don said, "Bring the flaps up to 5°."

Fred reached over and raised the miniature flap handle from the previous detent to 5° detent. Slowly, the flap position indicator revolved and showed the trailing edge flaps retracting to 5°. The transformation of the wing was taking place smoothly and on command.

The 747 continued to accelerate and climb through 1,100 feet. Don relaxed. He habitually rolled his shoulders to relieve the tension in his upper back and neck. With his shoulders arched, he twisted his neck left and right and could hear the small cartilage in his neck click and pop as he relieved the strain. Subconsciously, even though he rolled his head left and right, he never took his eyes off of his primary flight instruments. At 1,200 feet altitude, Stan started the second air conditioning system and felt only meager cool, dry air from the vents that surrounded him.

Don made a minor adjustment to the amount of pressure he was holding on the control column and pressed his thumb on the main stabilizer trim switch. Powerful electric motors turned jack screws that slowly and effectively moved the elevator trim tabs in the tail section.

The trimming movement reduced the aerodynamic load he felt in the controls. She now climbed in excess of 2,000 feet per minute and accelerated through 190 knots over San Francisco.

At 1,500 feet altitude, Stan started the third air conditioning pack. The noise level in the cockpit increased, but all three pilots were refreshed by the modest volume of cool dry air.

At 2,000 feet, Fred called, "Out of 2 for 3," the standard required call whenever the aircraft was within a thousand feet of an assigned altitude.

In unison, several independent altimeters climbed through 2,500 feet. Micro sensors in Don's and Fred's altitude alert equipment closed and electricity energized a warning chime, the system that warned them they were within 500 feet of their assigned altitude. Don gradually eased the yoke forward and smoothly lowered the nose to the horizon. The aircraft leveled at precisely 3,000 feet. With each of her engines developing over 40,000 pounds of thrust, she accelerated rapidly. Don saw the airspeed pass through 210 knots and told Fred to bring the flaps up to 1°.

San Francisco Departure control called, "100, you're now cleared to 9,000 feet. No need to acknowledge."

At 230 knots, Don reached over and raised the flaps handle from 1° to 0°. He turned back and said, "Stan, make sure all the leading edge flaps are retracted."

Stan casually glanced at the leading edge indicator panel. Eight green lights flickered and then went out, followed by eight amber lights that came on in unison. Three seconds later, all eight amber indicator lights went out, indicating that all the leading edge flap panels were fully and properly retracted.

"Flaps are up and all the leading devices are retracted and stowed."

The after takeoff procedures continued. Within a few of minutes after liftoff, Flight 100 was climbing through 5,000 feet, accelerating toward 250 knots. Fred's elapsed time counter remained at zero hours, zero minutes and zero seconds.

31

09:20 Pacific Standard Time
Northeast of San Francisco International Airport

Fred turned to Stan and asked, "Hey Magellan, what time did you have us airborne? I made it 09:05."

"Just a minute, let me see if ACARS has a time for us." Stan stretched and reached back to press the OUT button on the Air Carrier Automated Reporting System sub panel, but all it revealed were a series of dashed lines, "Looks like ACARS is still inop."

Stan selected the #2 VHF transmitter, "ARINC. This is 100 with an off report."

"San Francisco ARINC. Go ahead, 100."

"100 was out San Francisco at 16:30 UCT. Off at 17:05 UCT. Estimating New York at 22:32 UCT. Take off fuel 183,300 pounds."

"Roger 100. Got it all ok. Have a good trip."

Stan clicked his transmit button twice and hung up the microphone. He made a note on his fuel record of the time he called Aeronautical Radio with the Off Report.

Stan leaned forward with his arm resting on the back of Fred's seat, "Well guys, it looks like we'll be in New York at 5:30. Schedule is 5:15. That's only 15 minutes late."

The airplane had climbed through 10,000 feet on the way to 19,000 when Don said, "Fred, turn off the Seat Belt Sign."

Fred automatically looked outside. No clouds. No indications of any turbulence. There had been no reported turbulence in the weather documents.

After he looked out, Fred looked at the upper center control panel. He saw Don's finger on the Fasten Seat Belt switch light. Fred's gaze proceeded down Don's arm, to his face.

Don angrily pressed the "Fasten Seat Belt" switch light, then intently stared at Fred.

After three or four seconds Don said, "Fred, when I tell you to do something, I expect you to do it. I do not expect you to second-guess me. I looked outside and I know there is no turbulence out there. Just do as you are told."

Fred was speechless.

Don pressed for an answer, "Do you understand me?"

Fred thought, I'll never understand you, but said, "Yes, Don. I understand."

Don would not let it rest, he was relentless. "From now on you will do exactly as I say. If you don't like the way I'm running this show, we can talk about it later on the ground."

Tension wafted through the cockpit. Fred could feel a pulse in his neck and his face had gotten very warm. Yet, he knew the best thing to do was say nothing. The captain would only become more angered if he attempted to explain his actions.

Don leaned over to his left and opened the top of his navigation kit. While he had his back turned, Fred and Stan simultaneously looked at each other. It was a communal look, each seeking and giving understanding and support.

NORCAL Departure Control called, "100, you are cleared to flight level 240. Proceed direct to the Linden VOR and then on course."

Company policy dictated that the pilot who was not flying

handle all the routine radio work and assist the pilot who was doing the flying. According to this policy, when the Captain was physically flying the aircraft, the First Office would make all the radio calls. Conversely, when roles were reversed and the First Officer was flying, the Captain would have the responsibility for maintaining radio contact with the Air Route Traffic Control Centers.

Don's recent outburst caused Fred to pause as he reached for the microphone and he quickly looked at Don for some signal, but none was forthcoming.

Fred read back the clearance, "Climb to 240. Proceed direct to Linden. Then on course." He paused, "Thanks for the direct clearance. That will save us a couple of minutes."

"No problem 100. We're always glad to give you a direct, if we're not too busy. Have a good one." Almost as an afterthought, "You can expect to be cleared to 370 by the next sector. Tell you what, give Oakland Center a call now on 134.95 and ask them for higher."

Fred still had his hand microphone close to his mouth. Instinctively, he repeated the clearance, "Expect 370, call Oakland on 134.95 for higher. Good day."

Fred reached down between the pilots to the center radio console and twisted the VHF radio frequency selector knobs. The left window indicated the assigned frequency of 133.80. He spun the knob and the numbers stopped at 134.85. This was a little diversion for Fred, trying to see how close he could come to the assigned frequency by spinning the tuner, instead of clicking past the frequencies one at a time.

He slowly retuned the knob two stops to 134.95, saying under his breath, "Close. But, that only counts in hand grenades and horse shoes."

"Oakland Center, this is 100. We're out of 21,000 climbing to 240. That other fellow said we could expect 370. What do you know about higher for us?"

"100, Oakland clears you to Flight Level 370. Report passing out of 240."

"Roger, cleared to 370 and we'll check with you when we're out of 240."

FAA rules and company policy dictate that all clearances be repeated by the pilot flying and Don laconically said, "Cleared to 370."

The Pratt and Whitney engines on the 747 are very sensitive to external environmental changes. A 1° change in outside air temperature will make a significant change in the thrust output. The 9-foot diameter first stage N-1 compressors ingest an incredible amount of air every second. Cooler air molecules are closer together. Denser air will produce more thrust with the same amount of fuel.

Predictably, outside air temperature, or OAT, will decrease 2 degrees for each 1,000 feet of altitude gained. Throughout the climb phase of flight, Stan Kurtz was kept busy adjusting the thrust levers to keep all four engines producing the maximum amount of thrust for a given OAT.

Stan lined up target EPRs but, with each one thousand foot gain in altitude, the throttles again required realignment. Each time Stan reached between Don and Fred to trim the throttles, he could feel the unspoken tension and hostility that passed between the two pilots like electricity.

Stan thought, "This is one hell of a piss-poor way to run an airline."

32

09:30 Pacific Standard Time
San Francisco International Airport

Robert Ford Burns reread the denied boarding Incident Report, grinned to himself and thought, "Mr. Shapiro really did belong on American Airlines." Idly, he wondered if Shapiro also knew the President of American Airlines as well as he claimed he knew the upper management here.

Situated near the door in the employee cafeteria, he sat and drank his third cup of weak Sanka for the morning. He tried to remember this morning's events with better and clearer detail. There was something in the back of his mind that bothered him, yet he could not put his finger on the source of his concern.

He felt uneasy. There was something, indeed bothering him. It had to do with the fact that he had let something slip away during the verbal altercations with Mr. Shapiro. His years of police training and experience drove this feeling there was a need to continue his investigation in more detail. He could not suppress his instinctive compulsions.

He sat there by himself. He knew he should have been stopped and interrogated Guerrero. Perhaps detaining him for further investigation would have been warranted.

He abruptly left the Employee Cafeteria. He strode past several ticket counters, until he came to his company's deserted counter.

Between the Delta Airlines ticket counter and his counter was a 3 foot gap, which allowed agents and other employees access to the work rooms behind the counters. He deftly undid the hidden latch and lifted the Formica-covered counter section. Once behind the counter, he faced a plain, unmarked door. Predictably, the door was locked. Just to the right of the door, along the jamb was a penciled message, "Call 1034 for a good time." Silently, he slowly pressed 1 0 3 4 on the keypad, heard the electric solenoid click and leaned against the door.

The hallway, like the counter, was also deserted. The door closed behind him and the locking latch clicked firmly as he walked the length of the corridor. He neared the end of the hall and found the door he wanted, "Employee Lounge."

Bob opened the door. He was ignored by three ticket agents who were killing time while on their break. Two were seated in recliner chairs and one slouched on a black vinyl couch.

He recognized the agents, but did not know their names.

Burns spoke to the closest to him, "Excuse me, do you know if Harold is still around this morning?"

The heavy, middle-aged, oriental supervisor looked up from her Chinese newspaper, "Yeah. He was here. Earlier. Maybe half hour ago."

Then quickly she asked, "Did Harold do something? Is he in trouble?"

"No. No. Not at all. He's fine. I have some concerns about one of our passengers this morning on 100 and wanted to talk to him about it."

Another agent responded, "You mean that rude asshole from New York?"

Another agent, a black female, piped up, "Where do we get these jerks? We don't have to take that kind of crap."

Bob smiled at them, reached inside his suit jacket and pulled out a small spiral bound notebook. He held the notebook in his right hand, gave his right wrist a short, practiced flip and the notebook popped open.

The opened page had the name "GUERRERO, B - Flt 100" written in his bold hand. After consulting his notebook, he said, "Actually, I'm looking for information about a passenger Guerrero. He was tall and young, probably Mexican."

"Seems as though he bought a ticket to New York, one way. Paid for it in cash and he appeared to be quite nervous and agitated."

Two agents said in unison, "Profiler." The airline insider term for a passenger who fit a basic and well-published potential hijacker profile.

"Just the same, I would like some help in checking this Guerrero out." Burns spoke with intensity and authority, "Does anybody know if Harold is here? Or, not?"

"He was lead agent on this morning shift. He's probably in the cash room, counting his receipts and balancing his drawer. He should be done in a few minutes."

The third agent who had been reading *People* magazine, commented without looking up, "Don't count on it. The way Harold keeps his cash drawer, he may be in there for several days." Everyone laughed, including Burns.

33

09:45 Pacific Standard Time
San Francisco International Airport

Behind him a door opened, and he heard the sound of a metal box being slid into a locking drawer safe. Bob turned around and Harold walked toward the center of the room. Without the ticket counter to hide behind, Harold looked like a pear. His upper torso appeared to have been made from warm wax, which had slowly settled around his waist and then congealed. His legs were thin with knees that excessively bowed out. Harold's glasses were perched on the bulb-end of his nose. In this indirect light, his toupee was not easily detected.

Harold stopped mid-step when he saw Burns. Bob sensed Harold's uneasiness and attempted to quell that as he said, "Hello, Harold. Nothing real important. I just stopped by to talk to you about one of our passengers on 100 this morning."

He heard what the Airport Security Chief said. He was not satisfied with Burns explanation and thought he was there to talk to him about the $186.00 shortage last week. This talk about a passenger on 100 was probably a sham to put him at ease and then he would start in on him about recent shortages.

Burns reassured him again and Harold slowly started to perceive that maybe this company detective was not interested in the cash shortages after all, "Who's it you want to talk about? Do you want to talk here? Or, somewhere else?"

"Well, actually, I want to see Guerrero's ticket and I want to hear whatever you," he waved his arm expansively, "and the rest of you think about him."

Through his thick and dirty glasses, Harold peered at Bob while he considered his options. Eventually, Harold cautiously said in a very measured way, "All the flight coupons come back to me from the gates and are in my report to the cashier. That's locked in the safe room. I don't have a key to the cash safe. I'll have to get my supervisor to open it." Now, he was rushing as he spoke. To Burns, he sounded nervous. To Harold, he thought he sounded calm and on top of the situation.

Harold jerked his head toward the bank of locked agent's boxes and added, "I wish you told me before I put my cash envelope in the lock box."

Burns was amused that he had been foiled by his own design and smiled at Harold, "Well, lets get your supervisor over here, so we can get this investigation underway." He was surprised he had used the word investigation. Up until now, this had only been a routine check on a passenger.

Harold slowly and intentionally turned toward an unmarked and closed door, knocked and heard the one-word invitation. "Come."

He entered the room and carefully closed the door behind him. Several seconds later, he emerged with a snap ring which contained forty or fifty keys. He carefully selected the proper key. With a flourish he unlocked the metal bar that locked all the agents' cash drawers. Harold retrieved his cash drawer from the morning shift and then carefully snapped the self-locking metal bar.

He walked away from the safe. He stepped toward his supervisor's office door, knocked and again heard the monosyllabic invitation. "Come."

Harold disappeared into the supervisor's office to quickly return the keys. After only a second or two, he returned to the agent's lounge as the supervisor's door silently shut behind him.

Burns sat at sturdy square table in the center of the room. He cleared enough clutter into the trash to make room for Harold to put down his own agent's strongbox. Harold looked at Burns and saw kindly blue eyes with a twinkle of humor. People who knew of his reputation said Burns had been a tough and thorough cop. Now, Harold suspected that even though he was retired, he was still tough.

Burns' demeanor tended to put people at ease by his grandfatherly, quiet retired attitude. He looked as though he might have retired from a Midwest manufacturing plant, or perhaps from a job as a shoe salesman at Nordstrom's.

While Harold visually evaluated Burns he continued to gaze around the room. When he was satisfied that no one was looking, he cupped his left hand and quickly turned the combination dial on the strong box.

The lock opened and Harold lifted the lid to the large grey steel box. Inside Bob saw several loose ball point pens. He also recognized large manila envelope, with a red and black dashed border, that read, REVENUE ACCOUNTING - DO NOT DELAY.

The front of the envelope was a grid of squares, on which Harold had written pertinent information regarding the tickets enclosed therein, Date, Ticket Count, Total Revenue and finally, Harold's last name, first initial and payroll number.

The envelope was sealed. Again, Harold quickly glanced around the room. The other 3 agents were not paying the least attention to either Harold or Burns.

Harold took the glued flap, pulled it from the back of the envelope, up-ended it and unceremoniously dumped the contents on the tabletop. Burns saw all the used flight coupons had been separated by individual flight numbers, wrapped with several rubber bands. He also saw a smaller sealed envelope that he presumed contained the cash and credit card vouchers for today's sales. Stapled to the cash envelope was an accounting form that recorded Harold's transactions for the morning shift. Burns also noticed several tickets which had heavy parallel diagonal lines drawn on the face of each used flight coupon.

For the first time since he and Burns had been together, Harold spoke without being spoken to, "Who are you looking for? "What was his name? "Uhm. Let's see. Oh yes, Shapiro."

A brief smile crossed Bob's face when he considered that he was not the only one who was mislead by Shapiro.

"Actually no. Shapiro was denied boarding he took his business elsewhere. I'm looking for Guerrero. He's the one I'm interested in. Remember, you paged him for me?"

In a withering and sarcastic tone Harold said, "Sure. Oh sure, I do." Harold looked at Burns through his thick glasses. "I only processed about eight hundred passengers this morning."

He shook his head at the incredible amount of work he accomplished every day. He gratuitously continued to educate Burns, "The only passenger I remember was that idiot Shapiro." After a second or two, Harold reconsidered, "Now that I think about it, I guess I sort of remember paging someone for you, but that's all."

From his experience with witnesses, Burns wanted to help Harold remember much more about Guerrero. But for time being, he just wanted to take a look at Guerrero's ticket.

"Can you get me his ticket?"

Harold picked up the stack of banded flight coupons, his hands the same red color as the backs of most of the tickets. With a practiced hand, Harold fanned through the stock of several hundred tickets. With a half-hearted flourish, Harold stopped the fan and reached in the jumble, from which he produced one flight coupon, "Here you are. B. Guerrero, to New York. One way."

Slowly and carefully, Burns examined the ticket. Hand written in black ink, one way to New York. The other three remaining flight leg boxes were blank.

He handed the ticket back to Harold and said, "If you were to write this ticket, would it look like this?"

Harold casually glanced at the ticket. A slight frown creased his brow. He looked quizzical, then concerned and finally, quite alarmed.

"There are several things wrong with this ticket. It was validated by TWA at the airport in Phoenix. But the passenger traveled from San Francisco to New York. That's not too unusual, except it is American Airlines Travel Agent Ticket stock and should have been validated by the travel agent, or American Airlines." He paused a couple of seconds, "But, never by TWA. By all rights, TWA probably has never seen this ticket."

Burns looked at Harold with newly found admiration, "How can you tell?"

"Well, if American had written this ticket at an Airport or City Ticket Office, it would have American's ticket stock numbers along the bottom."

"However, as I said before, this was written on American Agent travel agent stock. Those are the blank tickets American issues to its travel agents."

Burns was following the conversation as it went, but still did not fully understand the significance of what Harold was saying.

Harold continued, "And one more thing, no agent would ever write a one way ticket on 4 leg stock and leave the last 3 legs blank."

"Why not?"

"The passenger could write any destination in the last 3 coupons and the agency would be liable for the uncollected fare."

Thinking as he spoke, he said, "Harold, I need a photocopy of this ticket. Make that two, please. And next, I need to talk to American about this ticket. I think it might be stolen. What do you think?"

Harold was slow to answer. He was fearful that if he agreed that the ticket was stolen, that somehow he would be involved, implicated or worse, blamed, "I don't know, Sir. There are a lot of things wrong with the ticket. But I don't know if I could say it was stolen."

Burns carefully considered what Harold said, stood up and smiled at Harold, "You have been a great help and I'm going to commend you to your supervisor. Why don't we go in and talk to him?"

Harold felt a genuine gripping uneasiness about the sudden turn in how this conversation was going. He hated to have attention drawn to himself and did not want a commendation. He just wanted to get through this day, the next day, next year and then retire on the $267,450.69 he had slowly, carefully and painstakingly removed from the airline during his 23 years as an agent.

"Tell you what, Mr. Burns, he's busy right now. Why don't you forget the praise. He knows who is doing a good job and who isn't."

"Suit yourself. Your modesty is commendable, but I don't mind waiting a few minutes to see your boss."

"However, if you'd rather I not do that, I'll respect your wishes."

Actually, Burns did not want to wait for Harold's supervisor, he wanted to get moving. He had a passenger who fit the security profile of a hijacker. He now had compelling evidence that he probably had used a stolen ticket. At a minimum, the man was a stowaway.

Harold considered how neatly he diverted Burns from his supervisor and quickly stood up, "Thanks for the offer. But if you don't mind, I'll just make your copies and let you be on your way."
Both men shook hands, as Burns said, "Thank you for your assistance and cooperation. I'll have my secretary drop your supervisor a note commending you for your help."

"Not necessary. But, thank you anyway." Harold thought a note would be perfect, never hurt to have a letter of commendation.

Bob looked at his watch, which indicated 9:54 and mused, "Not too bad of a day. I've been at work just over two hours." Smiling, he added, "So far, I have denied boarding to a harmless, but obnoxious passenger. Only to turn around and let a stowaway, who fits the hijacker profile slip past."

34

10:40 Mountain Standard Time
Northeast of Denver, Colorado

In the spring of each year the predominant direction of the jet stream in the northern hemisphere generally is from west to east. This meandering stream of high-speed wind is controlled by high-pressure bubbles and low-pressure troughs in the upper atmosphere. Today, the jet stream entered the United States well north of Seattle, proceeded almost directly over Denver, then northeast to Chicago. From Lake Michigan the jet curved south over Pittsburgh to Washington, D.C. and then turned out to sea.

Being three dimensional, the wandering wind also changed altitude and was generally defined by the upper limit or height of the troposphere.

Flight 100 leveled off and cruised at an altitude of thirty-seven thousand feet. In the parlance of pilots and air traffic controllers, they were "Level at 370." Her environmental envelope was affected by today's tropopause, a thin transitional layer between the stratosphere and the troposphere at thirty-four thousand feet.

Predictably, the air in the tropopause was not temperature stable.

Warmer air being less dense than cool air directly affected the lift generated by the 747's wings. The result, as felt by crew and passengers alike, was a rough, punctuated and choppy ride.

The chop was significant and all three pilots could hear the airframe go through minor flexing caused by these strong and sudden changes in compressional loads on the wings. Stan sensed and felt one particularly strong jolt. He heard the muffled "humph" caused as the wing spar unloading the stress imposed by changing air density. Several moments passed. All on board the 747 were uncomfortable by these rapidly sequenced vertical shifts in wind and temperature.

Silently, the 747 flew through a an unstable mass of air that resulted in a short staccato of turbulence strong enough to bounce Stan's steel rimmed glasses down to the tip of his nose. He impatiently pressed them back in place, only to have them pushed down by the next encounter. Stan knew if the Captain reduced the aircraft's speed by twenty or thirty knots - to the Boeing-determined Turbulence Penetration Speed - the ride would improve. At lower airspeeds the 747's semi-flexible wings could more slowly unload the stresses placed on them.

After another series of sharp jabs, Stan could stand it no longer, "What do you think, Don. You want to skin 'em back to turbulence penetration speed?"

"I don't know, I keep thinking that we are going to run out of this chop any minute." He no sooner said that, then the 747 juddered again.

"Fred, call the center and ask them for any ride reports in the area."

Stan said to no one in particular, "You know, if this chop is from being at the edge of the 'trop,' we could be in this stuff for the next fifty or a hundred miles."

Don said, "Yeah, I know. But, I still think it might be associated with a mountain wave."

"I don't think so, Don. I've been watching the temperature and the last fifteen minutes, the Outside Air Temperature has warmed up about 6°. That sounds like we've flying in the bottom of the 'trop.'"

Fred felt as though he was caught in the middle, he wanted to comply with Don's wishes and certainly didn't want to second guess him. The nose of the 747 wallowed several degrees to the left and then the whole length of the fuselage was angrily shaken.

Fred waited no longer, "Hey, Denver. 100 here at 370." No immediate response came from the air traffic controller at Denver Air Route Traffic Control Center, located in Aurora, Colorado.

He continued, "We need some Federal Aid. Do you have any ride reports in your sector? We are getting banged around pretty good."

"Roger, 100. Understand. What are your flight conditions?"

Without thinking, Fred said, "Well, we have little white caps on the coffee. We're in the clear. No clouds. Just a lot of bumpy air."

As Fred said, "air" the aircraft entered another micro-pocket of unstable air.

Everyone on board Flight 100 had an uncomfortable sensation of feeling their heads, hands, arms and legs feel heavy. An increase in 'G' loads, or apparent gravitational force, caused by the aircraft's nose pitching up.

All heard and felt the second Whumph.

Stan said, "Come on Don, what do you say? Let's slow this turkey down to turbulence penetration speed and give the folks in the back a better ride." Without saying anything, Stan dialed in 65° on the cabin temperature selector. He knew that passengers are less susceptible to air sickness if the cabin air temperature is kept cool.

Don ignored Stan's suggestion.

Seven or eight sharp jolts were felt throughout the aircraft. Pitching movements were felt most strongly in the tail and in the cockpit. Aerodynamic physics were similar to being on a teeter-totter. The ride near the fulcrum was much less abrupt than at either end of the board.

Another thud, "Whump."

Fred felt the restraint of his seat belt against his legs and stomach. His seatbelt harnesses pulled at his chest and shoulders.

He was uncomfortable. He waited until he could stand it no longer, "Aw, horseshit. Don! Let's slow this son of a bitch down. There's no goddamned reason to be running at Mach .85 banging our brains out in this kind of unstable air."

Fred had no regrets about his speaking out to the Captain, after all hadn't Don made the ritual speech about "being new on the airplane and needing all the help he could get...."

Don looked at Fred, then back at Stan, but made no attempt to reduce the airspeed.

The three pilots sat in the choppy air for another two or three minutes, without a word being said. The ride had not improved at all. Don reached for the public address system and said, "Ladies and Gentlemen, this is your Captain. I apologize for the bumpy ride. We are in contact with the controllers on the ground and are looking for a smoother altitude."

The aircraft flew through another series of short, choppy and energetic masses of unstable air. Throughout the cabin, the passengers' reactions were all the same, an involuntary gasp and a tightened grip on whatever was close at hand.

Don continued with his announcement, "I would like to ask our Flight Attendants to take the nearest empty seat. I don't think this is going to last too much longer.

"For the time being, folks, I want everybody in the cabin to remain seated, with their seat belts firmly fastened."

The Denver Center called. "100, a United flight at 370 is about a 125 miles ahead. They have the same chop as you are experiencing since they left Denver. Based on that information, it doesn't look too good for you."

At 490 knots, just over 600 miles per hour, it would take Don's aircraft over twenty minutes to reach the same position of the United aircraft. Even with that information, there still was no promise the ride would improve.

To all three pilots, there were only two answers. Look for a smoother altitude and/or slow to turbulence penetration speed.

Neither Stan nor Fred could remember flying with a Captain who refused to reduce airspeed when they encountered moderate turbulence. It almost seemed as though Don was maintaining this speed just because Fred and Stan had suggested he pull the power back to the recommended turbulence speed.

"Fred, ask 'em if they have any ride reports at 330." Don looked back at Stan. "We're too heavy for 410, right?"

"That extra fuel did us in. We won't be light enough to climb to 410 for over two hours." Stan voice bounced as the 747 continued to slog eastward in the unstable air.

Fred immediately picked up his microphone and said, "Denver, this is 100 again. We hope you have some good news for us. We would like to find out about the ride reports at 330. If the ride's okay, we would like to descend to 330."

"100, Denver Center. Do you want to go to 330 now?"

Don felt like he was going to explode at his First Officer. He could not just do anything he was told. He just had to make a joke of everything.

Don angrily grabbed his microphone, glared at Fred, "No Denver. Right now, we just want to know what the ride reports are at 330. If others are getting a better ride, then we'd like to request 330."

"Roger roger, 100. Got it. Stand by."

Fred said, "That's one of the things I do best is to stand by." A thickening and oppressive curtain of tension again descended over the cockpit.

Stan busied himself with recording various aircraft parameters and readings on his work sheets as the turbulence continued.

"Flight 100, a TWA L-1011 is about thirty miles ahead of you at 330, reports their ride is fine. He was also at 370 and descended about fifteen minutes ago. What do you want? You want to go to 330?"

Fred and Don both reached for their microphones at the same time. Both said in unison, "Fine, yes that will be fine. We'd like 330."

Electronically, both pilots cancelled each other out. Fred looked at Don and smiled.

Don looked at what he perceived to be a real hazard to aviation, his copilot, and said, "I've got it."

The ATC facility at Denver called, "Flight 100, you were blocked. Say again."

Don said in a clipped tone, "Denver, this is Flight 100. We'd like to descend to 330." Another angry jolt hit the airframe, "Now."

"No problem 100. Descend to Flight Level 330 and report reaching."

35

11:00 Mountain Standard Time
East of Denver, Colorado

The autopilot had done a moderately good job of maintaining altitude during the turbulence - within one hundred feet of the selected altitude. When moderate turbulence is encountered, 747 autopilots often will fly an aircraft into an 'out of trim' condition. When the autopilot is disconnected, or the Altitude Hold is disengaged, the instantaneous lack of input from the autopilot computer will cause the aircraft to pitch or buck. During the eleven minutes 100 had flown through unstable air the autopilot had significantly loaded up, to the point it was seriously out of trim.

Experienced 747 pilots know better than to disconnect the Altitude Hold without first neutralizing the Auto Pilot trim. Don reached up and disengaged the Altitude Hold switch on the "A" autopilot. Out of the corner of his eye, Fred saw Don's hand reach for the Altitude Hold switch, but before Fred could say anything, the deed was done.

The nose of the 747 abruptly pitched up. At 600 miles per hour, a rapid 1° change in pitch will result in swift and dynamic change in the gravitational force placed on the aircraft. Every passenger suddenly felt as though they were in an elevator that had without warning rocketed them toward the roof of a skyscraper as they were slammed into their seats.

Don swore under his breath as he disconnected the "A" autopilot. That triggered the 747's aural warning, a wailer. He silenced the warning horn by pressing the autopilot disconnect button again. With a firm grasp on the controls, he released some of the back pressure on the control column. He overshot slightly. Now, passengers felt very light. Each felt their seatbelt restrain them as they started to lift off their seat cushions.

Fred looked at Don, laughed and said, "Whooo-Whee-e-e, Daddy. That was fun. An "E" ticket at Disneyland. Can I go on the roller coaster again?"

Don could not help but smile at the analogy between the pitch over and a ride at the amusement park.

Fred picked up his mike, "Denver. 100 here. We're out of 370, on our way to 330. We'll call you level at 33."

Eleven minutes earlier, the invisible turbulence had started. Now, just as suddenly, it stopped. Inexplicably, the aircraft's ride completely smoothed out. No more chop, pitching oscillations or abrupt changes.

Fred looked back at Stan, "What a guy. Most Captains wouldn't have been able to handle a problem like this. He's magic. I can see the headlines now, 'Jet Pilot saves Giant 747 from killer air pockets.'"

Don let the 747 settle toward its selected altitude of 33,000 feet at a rate of 3,000 feet per minute. Twenty-five seconds later, Don lightly raised the nose to the horizon. The altimeter slowly unwound and the vertical speed indicator gradually changed from 3,000 feet per minute to less than 100 feet per minute change in altitude.

After Don leveled the 747 at 33,000 feet, he re-engaged the autopilot. Satisfied with the autopilot's performance, he flipped on the Altitude Hold lever ON. A green light confirmed the autopilot knew it was to hold the aircraft at this chosen altitude. Fred remembered the center's request and said, "Denver, 100. Well, we did it. We made it all the way to 330. The ride smoothed out at about 35.5."

Don turned in his seat and said, "Stan, tell the gals they can get up and resume their cabin service." As an afterthought, "And apologize for the ride back there. Tell them that sometimes we can't accurately predict what the ride is going to be like."

Stan took the public address system handset, pressed the "PA" button twice, heard the anticipated click and said, "Ladies and Gentlemen, this is one of your pilots. We believe the unstable air is behind us and think we'll have a smooth ride for the rest of our trip to New York. Our Flight Attendants can now resume their cabin service. Again, we'd like to apologize about the bumps back there. Sometimes, we just don't know they're coming our way. Flights ahead of us have reported smooth air."

He paused, "As a matter of practice, keep your seat belts loosely fastened just in case we do encounter any more unexpected turbulence. Thank you for your cooperation."

He hung up the handset and said, "The cabin's been told it's ok to resume their service. I also apologized for the unexpected chop."

"Thanks, Stan." Don said and then sat quietly for several minutes. Both Fred and Stan gain could feel the tension start to increase. It filled the cockpit like a morning mist.

Without warning, as though he had come to some resolution, Don turned in his seat and looked at Fred. In a calm and measured voice he said, "Fred, I don't want to tell you again, clean up your act. I don't like frivolity and lack of attention in the cockpit."

Fred pulled himself up in his seat. He sat with his back erect against the lumbar support in the chair and stared straight ahead. Next, he looked out the cockpit window.

From this vantage point, he could see over one hundred miles in a 270° arc. He thought he would love to be anywhere he could see, rather than here with this strange pilot. He didn't know how to react. All he could do was solemnly say, "Right. You're the Captain.

Whatever you say."

36

**11:15 Central Standard Time
East of Denver, Colorado**

A roaring and choking sound awakened Bill. Though drugged, he eventually realized the sound was his own snoring. The two Valium he ingested had taken their toll.

Bill's reaction to the Valium continued to be clinically abnormal. The Valium depressed him, but also made him feel paranoid about those around him. He was confused, but at the same time, ambivalent.

Though he was partially awake and knew he should be doing something, he could not clearly focus on what it was he supposed to do. He knew he was on the airplane. He knew he was supposed to hijack it. Yet, mentally, he was unable to decide what to do. He had no idea of how to go about it. His mind was filled with confusing images and thoughts.

Unintentionally, he slipped back into the safe and comfortable escape of sleep. He dreamed an attractive young woman was sitting next to him. She made it very clear that she was attracted to him. In his dream, she boldly took his hand and placed in her lap. Then, strangely, the *Maricón* moved her to another seat and he was alone.

Bill drifted in and out. Suddenly, he felt very heavy. He could not hold his chin off his chest. His arms were weighed down as they pressed against the blue and red vinyl armrests. In his sleep, he had crossed his feet, now the weight of one foot on the other immobilized him. Heavy pressures forced his shoes into the carpet, so much so that he was unable to move his feet. Waves of fear took control of him. The terror quickly transformed to anger. Once again, he tried to raise his right arm. It felt like he had a fifty-pound weight on the back of his hand. The cords in the back of his neck were stretched from his head being forced onto his chest. It felt like an enormous hand was pressing him downward into the seat..

To him, the heavy weight lasted for a long time. He was a prisoner to this pressure that held him down. An unusual side effect of the Valium was a complete lack of comprehension of time. He had no sense of what time it was, how long he had been in the airplane or even if it was day or night. He could not remember ever having been without this pressing weight.

As quickly as the weight had pressed down on his head, body arms and hands, it was gone. Now he rose above most of the passengers. His feet untangled. He gradually felt himself come up and out of his seat. The elevation lasted long enough for him to see the entire length of his zone in the aft cabin. He saw most of the passengers' heads in front of him move in unison. They all tilted to the left and then immediately to the right, as the aircraft oscillated and rolled around its longitudinal axis.

A firm, loud and authoritarian voice spoke directly to him. He thought the voice had picked him out of the crowd. The pilot was talking only to him in a very powerful and deliberate voice.

He worried, "The voice knows about me and the plan. Maybe this was the end. They are going to discover me."

The commanding voice said, "Fasten your seat belts… sorry for the bumpy ride… out of this soon."

He was relieved, "The voice only wanted me to put on my seat belt." The effect of the Valium made him wonder, "How did the pilot know I didn't have my seat belt on?"

An incredibly powerful urge swept through him. If he could just close his eyes and never wake up again, that would be good. He wanted to be left alone. Just to go to sleep. Sleep and privacy. A safe place to be. No risk. No fear.

Contrary to his wish, however, he now was wide awake. The aircraft shuddered. There were metallic buzzing sounds he could hear when he put his head against the seat back. He was afraid to move. He was afraid he would hurt himself or the airplane if he touched anything.

Several rapid jolts shook the 747 that weighed over seven hundred and fifty thousand pounds. The Boeing was being shaken like a toy in the mouth of a playful puppy. His armpits were wet and he could feel his sweat running down his sides. The belt loops on his pants were now wet. He had a very unpleasant taste in his mouth. His face felt warm and he was breathing in faltering breaths. His face was soaked and his skin felt a sticky between his shoulders. He was sweating all over.

Again, he became aware of the loud voice, "Flight Attendants... any available seat near... at the same time I want everyone in their seats... won't last too...thank you."

Carlton had been busy in the aft cabin, preparing for meals that were about to be delivered from the lower galley. While he waited, he prepared extra coffee, made a pot of hot tea and filled two other coffee pots with ice and water.

The chimes sounded from the lower galley.

He answered, "E zone."

She spoke quickly, efficiently and directly. "Carlton, Honey, this is Roz. My friend, I am going to start sending food carts up your way in a couple of minutes. I'd appreciate you getting them out of the lift as soon as they come up, so I can get the rest of these up and out in the cabin."

Carlton smiled and said, "Why yes, Roz. Just give me a little ring when you send them up and I'll rush right to the lifts. I'm all alone back here, but I'll do the best I can."

"I'm sure you will, Sweetie."

He smiled. She laughed, "You always do such a good job, honey."

The ride in the tail section of the aircraft was awful. Several people got airsick and the sour smell of vomit made others feel queasy. The turbulence and the sickening parmesan cheese smell made many passengers feel nauseous.

The floor dropped beneath Carlton and he grabbed the side of the stainless steel serving counter. Abruptly, the floor came up to meet him and he felt like he weighed 350 pounds, not his normal 170. He could hear galley equipment banging. One of the food carts started to tip over. The mushroom-lock in the floor held the cart upright, but the door opened and twenty meals dumped on the floor.

The fuselage conformation was such there was a terrible air noise in the aft galleys. Carlton could only hear bit and pieces of public address announcements being broadcast throughout the cabin.

He noticed the Fasten Seat Belt sign flash and then stay on. He just started to move toward the cabin, when his chime again rang three times, "E zone, Carlton."

"Carlton, this is Roz. It's a bitch down here. I'm getting banged around pretty good."

Carlton could not resist, "Roz, I love it when you talk about getting banged. Tell me, was it good for you?"

She ignored Carlton's poor attempt at a sexual joke. "I'm going to come on up. The meals will have to wait."

The meal service started in E zone. If Roz was going to delay sending his meals up, then the entire cabin would have to wait.

"You probably ought to tell Amelio about the delay in the service, Roz."

"Listen, if Amelio wants to worry about the frickin' meals, he can just hustle his buns down here in the pit and do the work himself. I don't think it's safe down here in all the bumpy air."

Carlton hung up his handset and decided to check on passengers in his section. Secretly, he enjoyed checking seat belts. Once in a great while, he would be rewarded by finding a male passenger who welcomed the attention.

He carefully walked toward the front of his section, taking a firm hold on the two seat backs on either side of the aisle as he walked. He was two rows behind Bill when he heard the public address announcement, "… ask our Flight Attendants to take the nearest empty seat."

Carlton could hardly contain himself. This was, indeed, directed by fate. He was only too happy to follow the Captain's orders. He took two long strides and found himself adjacent to Bill's seat. He moved quickly against the shuddering and pitching aircraft and dropped into the vacant seat next to Bill. He pulled the two halves of the seat belt across his lap, and firmly engaged the lock. Through his slacks he could feel the coldness of the metal buckle.

Fate had brought Carlton here to be with Bill in this time and place. Slowly, provocatively and protectively Carlton looked over at him. Bill was diaphoretic and an ashen gray-green color. His hair was wet through and through. There was an overpowering smell of damp fear mixed with his perspiration.

Carlton reached out and put his hand on Bill's arm saying, "You'll be okay in a few minutes. Some of these air pockets are a real bitch, but they never last that long."

He gave Bill a little squeeze on the arm and continued, "I've seen it much worse than this."

Bill knew someone was talking to him. The person's voice sounded like it was coming to him on a bad telephone, like the phones when he was a child in Cuba.

The voice tried to comfort him and he became aware of a new pressure on his left arm. Bill had not consciously realized it, but his eyes were tightly shut. He forced himself to try to force them open, but they refused.

When Bill turned his head to the left, he felt the wet spot on the seat back where his head had been. With great effort, he was able to open his eyes and found that he was looking directly into Carlton's dark and forlorn eyes.

The *Maricón's* attention repulsed him. Not only did he sit next to him, he was touching him. He tried to remove his arm from under Carlton's hand, but his arm felt like it was made of lead. He commanded his body to respond, but nothing happened. He didn't know his lethargy was from the Valium, compounded from the g-loads associated with the turbulence through which they were flying.

Carlton continued, "You look much better. And as soon as the Captain says we can get up, I'll get you a cool cloth. Do you think you need something for your stomach, maybe some Coke or ginger ale?" When Carlton said "Coke," he snickered at what he hoped would be their private joke.

Confusion washed over Bill. He knew he had to get away from this fag. Then, dimly, he recalled there might have a way to use Carlton to help him with his plan. The Plan was alive.

37

11:20 Pacific Standard Time
San Francisco International Airport

Robert Burns opened the private company phone directory and found the number for Kennedy (JFK) Flight Dispatch. He dialed the thirty-two digit number that included Fielding's extension.

The phone rang three times when he heard a young woman's voice, "Flight Dispatch. Mariweather."

"Yes. I'm Robert Burns, Head of Airport Security here at the San Francisco station. Is Mr. Fielding in today?"

"Just a moment, sir. Let me check and see if he's available." He could hear her whispering, "It's the head of Security in San Fran. I think he said his name was Burr. What shall I tell him? He said he wants to talk to you."

There was a rustling as the phone changed hands, "Yes, Mr. Burr. What can I do to help you with?"

Burns instinctively corrected the mispronunciation of his last name, "It's Burns, Robert Burns, Airport Security in San Francisco. We have a passenger on Flight 100 today who was boarded with a stolen ticket. We would like to have you contact the flight and advise them he is on board. The passenger's name on the ticket is 'B. Guerrero.'"

Lazlo's mild German accent became more pronounced, "Do you know anything else about him?"

"Actually, we know little about him, other than we think he was on a ticket stolen from a travel agency in the Phoenix area. We don't know if he stole the ticket, or if he bought it from a third party."

Fielding picked up the pace of the conversation, "We certainly can get in touch with Flight 100 by radio."

Burns heard Fielding cough then said, "That sounds awful. Do you have a cold?"

Fielding crushed his cigarette in the ashtray. He deluded both of them saying, "Yes, I'm just getting over one."

Burns said, "This stowaway probably belongs in John Batchelor's shop. The flight is going to land at Kennedy and I'm going to call him when we finish here. I want this Guerrero character apprehended."

Lazlo spoke quickly, his German accent thickening, "Do you know the zeet number? Do you haff any information on him? Description, height or weight?"

Bob recalled the scene at the ticket counter, "I saw him this morning and I'd say he was 5'11", or maybe 6'0" and quite thin. Probably does not weigh more than one hundred thirty or forty pounds. He is a Mexican or Latino type, with the longer hair, poor complexion and bad skin color. He looked pale, sort of a pasty pallor. He was wearing a dark shirt, khaki pants and black shoes. He was carrying one of those small athletic training bags. As I recall, it said Adidas or Nike on the outside." Thinking hard, he said, "Black, I think."

Fielding interrupted him, saying, "Not so fast, I'm trying to copy zis down, so ve can gif it to da crew."

Burns waited thirty or forty seconds before he continued, "He was alone. He seemed quite nervous. And he..."

Lazlo interrupted, "Do you think this Gaggero is dangerous?"

Instinctively, once again, Burns corrected Fielding, "That's Guerrero, not Gaggero," He considered telling the dispatcher about the hijacker profile, but then stopped. He did not want to cause a false alarm.

Burns considered his response and selected his words carefully, "Well, now that you ask, Guerrero did fit most of the parameters of our hijack profile."

The line was quiet, except for intermittent static. He continued, "At this stage of the game, all we have is a stowaway. A stowaway who generally fits a minimum-definition hijack profile. I don't know if he has any plans for 100, but I do know that he is riding with us today, for free."

"Do you want uz to contact da crew right now or do you want we should wait until they are closer to New York?"

"I don't care. That's your call. It doesn't make a difference. I just want to see flight 100 met by our security people at Kennedy. I assume they will interrogate him and try to collect the fare for the transportation."

Lazlo Fielding considered the facts. "You did say you were going to call John Batchelor? Why don't I wait until I hear from him before I contact da crew?"

"That's fine. I'll call him right now and ask him to work out the details with you for crew notification."

"Good." Fielding's tone was official and somewhat abrupt. With finality, he said, "Good day, sir."

"Thanks for the help." Before Burns could hang up, Fielding broke the connection.

During his eight months with the airline, Burns made an ongoing attempt to meet everyone who was remotely involved with security. One of the few people he had never met face to face was John Batchelor. Both times Burns had been in New York, Batchelor was out of town on business. Batchelor was just a voice on the telephone.

For the second time today, Burns used the company land lines.

Thirty-two digits later, he heard a phone ring in New York. On the fifth ring a woman with a strong, nasally Bronx accent, "Security. John Batchelor's office."

Her name was Diane and she didn't look at all like she sounded. Her hardened telephone voice indicated middle-aged matronly woman. In reality, she was twenty seven years old, married with two children. Both times he had met her in New York, Diane had tried her hardest to make him comfortable.

"Hello, Diane, this is Bob Burns. Is your boss in today?"

"Oh. Hello, Mr. Burns. It's good to hear from you," she twanged, "John's right here. Just a second. I'll get him for you."

The wait was short, "Hi Bob. How's the weather out in San Fran? Lots of sunshine?"

"It's been pretty nice for the past two weeks. A little cold in the mornings, but by noon it's delightful."

"I'm sure you didn't call to discuss the weather. What have you got?"

"Looks like we have a stowaway on Flight 100 from San Francisco. Used a stolen ticket. Since he is going to arrive at your station, you have the pleasure, jurisdiction, authority and responsibility to collar this character."

Batchelor's voice changed as he reached for a pencil and wrote "STOWAWAY-FLIGHT 100" on his desk pad, "Give me all the information and we'll have a little reception for him when he lands here at Kennedy."

"Name on the ticket is Guerrero, B. Mid-twenties. Latino. Tall, just under six feet. Rather thin, probably one hundred forty pounds or less."

"Do you know what seat was assigned to him?"

"The agents here thought it was 55-8, but they weren't certain. Our seat-map computer isn't on-line yet. I have no way to check, other than to call central reservations."

"Standby one. I'll look at it right now." He waited and heard John quickly enter information into the computer at his side.

"Here he is, Bob. Says seat 8, row 55. No other information for his record locater. His local contact in the bay area is unknown, no telephone contact, either. Says here he bought his ticket from a travel agency. Made his reservations last week."

"John, there is something else, but I don't want to alarm you." Burns carefully chose his words, "Guerrero fits the hijack profile exactly. He meets all the parameters. I had him under loose surveillance this morning. In fact, I followed him out to the boarding area."

"Interesting."

"Unfortunately, I got involved with something else and never had the opportunity to interrogate him about his travel plans. I didn't know until after the flight departed that he was on a stolen ticket."

"Damn. That changes things considerably."

"This is your show and if the scene were reversed and he was flying from New York out here, I'd apprehend him, interrogate him and if warranted, arrest him."

"You're right, Bob. I'm inclined to do the same thing. Arrest him, that is."

"Good show. How about putting in a call to Flight Dispatch and alert them to your plans. I've already spoken with a fellow named Fielding and he's waiting for your call."

Batchelor paused, then said, "I know Fielding. I'll have him contact the flight crew and advise them having a stowaway on board. I think, just to be safe, I'll tell them he meets the profile. Then, I'll call Callahan over at the Port Authority Police at Kennedy and bring them into the loop."

"Thanks for the assist. If you turn anything on him, let me know. I'll contact the travel agency and tell them that one of their stolen tickets has surfaced." He laughed and said, "and that John Batchelor is in hot pursuit."

From his tone of voice, John was obviously anxious to get off the phone and get on with the surveillance and apprehension of Guerrero. He concluded his conversation by saying, "I hope this passenger's fitting the profile was just coincidence. If he's a real hijacker we may never get a chance to talk to him and ding him for the air fare."

"That's a chilling thought. Thanks for the help and the information. One of these days, we are going to have to meet face to face. Thanks again, John. 'Bye."

"See you around. Next time you're in New York, we'll have lunch. I promise. In fact, I'll buy."

Before Burns could hang up, Batchelor had broken the connection and had dialed a discrete number for the John F. Kennedy Port Authority Police. While the phone rang, he was looking for a telephone number for Flight Operations Supervisor Fielding.

38

15:15 Eastern Standard Time
East of Indianapolis, Indiana

Slowly and blankly, he came out of a restless sleep. He did not know how long he had been asleep. Nor did he know what time it was or how much longer before the flight was over. The safety belt pulled and held him in place. The more he resisted, the more uncomfortable he became.

He was disoriented and felt trapped. A butter-yellow diffused light beat through the closed window shade Carlton had pulled down for him after he had fallen asleep. Impulsively, in an attempt to orient himself, he raised the shade and looked outside. Far below he could only see small white clouds. He was able to see slowly passing green and brown patterns on the terrain. He recognized nothing on the ground.

Disorientation and confusion slowly left him as he became more awake. The seat belt restrained him. He angrily pulled and clawed at the cold metal buckle. When it released, he tossed the belt onto the vacant seat next to him. Once the belt was no longer tethered him to the airplane, he felt more at ease.

Everything appeared normal to the passengers. Some moved around the cabin after the inflight motion picture ended. During the entertainment, Carlton Marsh busied himself in the aft galley. He prepared trays of soft drinks and iced tea for passengers in his cabin. Carlton took two miniatures of rum and a crystal tumbler he had taken from the First Class beverage cart. He kept them on ice in cart, as he waited for Bill to wake up so he could offer him refreshments. During the movie, Carlton checked on him. Bill slept uneasily. To Carlton, it appeared Bill was tormented by dreams or nightmares. He thought Bill's uneven sleep might be a result of the pill he had taken earlier.

Carlton came forward along left aisle in the cabin, pushing his narrow serving cart. He stopped by each passenger seated on the aisle. Passengers were always the same. They were in a hurry for the flight to end and to get to their individual destinations. Always the same questions, "When do we get to New York?" Or, "How much longer?" Years of flight attendant experience taught him how to be responsive in a non-committal way. Without looking at his watch, he knew there was always 1:30 to 1:40 after the movie ended until they landed in at their destination, in this case, New York.

Carlton reached the forward cabin divider in the last zone in coach, the "Main Cabin." He carefully turned the service cart to cross the ship, and started aft, down the right-hand aisle. To the casual observer his path seemed random. However, to Carlton, his path would allow him to finish his service with Bill who was one of the last passengers in on the right-hand side of the cabin.

His pulse quickened. He exclusively focused on Bill. Time seemed to stop for him as he mustered his courage to press on. He stopped in the aisle next to Bill and attempted to be casual as he nervously reached across the empty seat and lowered the seat-back tray in front of Bill. He placed his arm on the back of Bill's headrest, leaned close to him, nervously smiled and said, "I have a special treat for you."

Bill looked up at Carlton's soft, sad eyes. There was a mild faint odor of onions on Carlton's breath as he spoke, "I've made you a friendship drink. I do hope you like rum and Coke."

Bill's voice croaked with dryness as he said, "I don't care. Anything cold."

Carlton was dismayed that Bill was not more responsive to his overtures and his carefully orchestrated plan. He reached into the liquor cart and produced a chilled crystal glass, half-filled with ice and dark amber colored rum. Bill took the glass from Carlton, who, with a great fanfare and flourish, added Coca Cola.

"Here's your *Cuba Libre.*" To any who might have been watching, it simply appeared that Carlton was refilling a passenger's glass with a soft drink. Bill felt shock. Fear roared through him when he heard, "Cuba."

He ignored Carlton as he took a deep pull and let the cold liquid run through his mouth and into his throat. The biting cold felt good. He took another long pull and held his half-empty glass for Carlton to refill.

Carlton took the glass, smiled most enchantingly and said, "Do you want another?" Not waiting for an answer, "I have a second one in the cart."

He was angered by Carlton's blatant and obvious focus on him. He resented the strong overtures Carlton continued to display. Disgustedly, Bill slammed his head firmly against the headrest, looked out the window, and thought, "If I ignore the asshole, or am mean to him, maybe he'll go away."

Bill was a mess. Old and familiar paralyzing fears engulfed him like a quick moving shadow. He continued to be effected by the paradoxical impact the two Valium had on him. He vacillated between despair and euphoria, languor and nervous energy.

Dimly at first, then like a drumming, hollow echo, came a brilliant answer to his problem. The object of his distant and still-formulating idea came closer, and more clearly into focus.

Carlton.

A trembling sense of clarity slowly swept over Bill when he

thought of how he could do this. He would use Carlton to do his plan.

Bill smiled and thought, "Maybe, I can do it. Maybe my plan, The Plan, will work after all."

39

15:20 Eastern Standard Time
East of Indianapolis, Indiana

He looked directly at Carlton and half-thought and concurrently half-said, "That's it. I'll use you."

"What did you say?" Carlton had heard exactly what Bill said, but wanted to confirm he had not mistaken about what he perceived to have been said.

"Nothing. I didn't say nothin' to you."

Carlton flirted with Bill and said, "Yes. Oh yes you did. I heard you. I, I think it's wonderful."

Bill pressed his back into the seat and again closed his eyes. "That's what I'll do. It happened to me in prison, I was used. Now it's my turn to use someone else."

Bill opened his eyes again and saw that Carlton was not making any attempts to leave.

He smiled at himself and then at Carlton. He thought, "This is going to be a good day, after all."

Thinking quickly, Bill said, "I don't want another drink." He turned and said, "*Paloma*, unless you get a drink and sit here with me?" Adding, "You know, we could like, have a drink together."

Carlton felt himself shaking. He felt little tremors everywhere. These feelings were much like an electric shock to him.

Even as he made the suggestion to Carlton, Bill felt a wave of revulsion flood over him at the thought of Carlton coming on to him.

Carlton was light-headed at the prospect that Bill had actually invited him to share a drink and sit with him. He was hardly able to speak.

He thought, "This was indeed a good sign, a very good sign. Not one to be passed lightly." Here was a rare opportunity for Carlton to turn another of his fantasies into some form of reality.

He flashed an enormous grin at Bill and said, "It will take me a few minutes to clean up my galley before landing. Wait right here. I'll be right back. Don't go away." He waited, giggled and then added, "Silly me. Where would you go?"

Not wanting Bill to change his mind, with eager anticipation, Carlton said, "I'll hurry."

Instinctively, Carlton knew he would be in serious trouble if he sat with Bill and had a drink with him. Drinking while on duty, while in uniform was grounds for immediate dismissal. Fraternization with passengers for sexual advancement was specifically forbidden in the Flight Attendant's Handbook and the company personnel manual.

Logically, he knew his raging attraction to Bill might result in him losing his job. But, he could not help himself. He had made a quick decision. He abruptly removed his arm from his headrest and took one last look at Bill. "I can't drink alcohol while I'm on duty. But I'll come back in a few minutes and sit with you."

Bill hardly heard what Carlton said. He was deep in thought about his plan. How he could take control of the flight. The plan would work, after all.

He looked at Carlton who had started to move away toward the rear galley. "How much longer is it?" Impatiently and boldly, he added, "Where the hell are we, exactly?"

Carlton stopped and turned toward him, while he carefully considered his response, "I think we are probably (which he pronounced "prolly") over Ohio or Pennsylvania, "I can call the Captain if you wish and ask him."

Carlton looked at his jewel-encrusted watch and said, "We only have about an hour and a half to go." Carlton took a deep breath, then timidly added, "As far as, 'How much longer is it' we have as much time as you want to spend."

Again, Bill ignored the sexual double-talk and started to run what few ideas through his mind. He thought to himself in Spanish, "*Si tenemos menos de dos horas, es mejor que me mi culo en movimiento*" If we have two hours, I better get my ass moving."

Carlton saw Bill's lips moving, but could not hear him and asked, "What did you say, lover?" Adding, "Were you talking to me?" He smiled and added, "I hope so."

Bill looked at him as he stood there balanced, poised and waiting for his response, "No. I wasn't talking to you. I guess I was like just sort of talking to myself."

Confusion overtook Carlton and he didn't know what to say or do. He wasn't certain whether to stay by Bill's seat, or return to the galley area. He was sexually intrigued. He was on the hunt. He did not want to do or say anything that would terminate this fragile encounter and what he hoped to be a budding relationship.

Bill panicked as he looked at Carlton and then said, "Hurry back. I have something I want to show you."

"Hurry back!" The words were like a siren's song to him. His pulse pounded in his head. He tried to speak, but could only smile and make a tight whimpering sound in his throat.

Carlton thought he was surely on the path to yet another new and successful encounter; a trophy that was soon to be collected. His potential lover had given him a direct command. He had actually said, "Hurry Back!" Explicit words called for explicit action.

In a sweeping motion, he pushed the heavy beverage cart down the aisle and into the aft galley. He was oblivious to passengers who looked at him as he quickly pushed the cart into the galley.

Bill's mind skipped and vividly raced as he began to put the plan into motion. His thoughts were constantly shattered by interfering and gnawing thoughts of failure. These thoughts were followed by a vibrant sense he would succeed. Emotionally, he felt like he was on a Merry-go-Round. Up then down, the back up again. Round and round. Up and down. Forcefully and dramatically, Bill decided the time had come.

No turning back.

He must act quickly.

He would use Carlton as his accomplice. Carlton would have no choice but to follow Bill's directions and help him hijack this airplane.

40

15:30 Eastern Standard Time
Miami International Airport

Juan Guerrero was nervous. There were a growing number of things that didn't make sense to him. He did not understand much of what was happening. He understood even less about what was not happening.

Important things. Events that might, or might not, be important. He couldn't tell. He just didn't know. He thought they had had a timetable to be followed, such as it was. He had made the planned telephone call from the lobby of the main terminal to learn if 100 had departed San Francisco on time.

The reservation agent had trouble finding the information because 100 did not go to Havana. It operated between San Francisco and New York. Another mistake. He forgot the flight was supposed to go to New York. Was that important? What difference did it make? He could not decide.

After the call, the agent in the Denver call center happened to mention it to her supervisor during a break, "We sure do get the weirdo's.

"I just had a call from some dumb-ass Puerto Rican who wanted to know if 100 left San Francisco on time. Then he wanted to know what time it was going to land in Havana."

The Supervisor shook her head as the agent continued, "When I finally found his damn flight in the computer and told him the flight went to JFK, he said 'he was just checking for a friend.'"

She paused and then continued, "We really get 'em. Don't we?" Her supervisor absently nodded an affirmation. She went on, "I don't know why, but I asked him for his name."

She snorted. "Get this. He says, 'Guerrero. No, I mean Garcia. Yeah that's it. Garcia.'" Her supervisor continued to ignore most of the conversation about the call.

Anticipation and jitters made it impossible for Juan to be at work today.

Even though he had called in sick and taken the day off from work, he was dressed in his dark-blue Eastern Airlines ramp uniform. Earlier in the day, he had called his supervisor with a claim he had hurt his back the previous day. Juan knew he would have to be very careful so as to not be seen by his supervisor.

Juan and Bill had planned on the hijacked 747's arrival in Miami by late afternoon or early evening after the unplanned side-trip to Havana. Juan's role was to supervise the off-loading of the six suitcases that contained the illicit cocaine while the airplane sat on the ramp.

Juan thought most hijacked flights usually came back to Miami from Havana. Miami had become the airport of choice of the airlines whose aircraft had been hijacked. Miami was a convenient location for the FBI, ATF, Department of Transportation and the FAA. These agencies had plenty of facilities to share during and after a hijacking or other diversion. They could easily question the passengers and crew regarding each hijacking.

Most passengers on hijacked flights were happy to get off in Miami; either to connect on other flights, or to rest from their recent ordeal. Or, in some cases, they just wanted off the aircraft that had just taken then to Havana and then back to Miami. Collective fear caused many passengers to react in ways that were not consistent with their normal behaviors.

He thought of himself as a master crime planner. Juan Guerrero included his inflated self-assessments and considerations as a foundation in his aerial piracy scheme.

All that had to be done now was wait for a public address announcement about Flight 100 being on the way to Havana. Guerrero didn't know that when a flight made an unscheduled stop in Havana, or any other airport, public address announcements were seldom, if ever, made. Returning hijacked aircraft were not scheduled to land in Miami, so there would be no expected or waiting family or friends. Likewise, there would be no scheduled departing passengers because that flight never operates out of Miami.

What was unknown to Guerrero was that when a flight diverted to Havana and then subsequently arrived in Miami, the aircraft was routinely searched for contraband. The jets were also closely inspected by US Customs and Immigration Service, who looked for additional passengers who were trying to escape from Cuba.
After a hijacking had ended and a fresh cockpit crew was located, the aircraft were usually ferried empty, as positioning flights back into the airline's route system.

Juan wandered through the main terminal and listened for any mention of a hijacking. Twice, he went to Employees' parking lot to listen to the Cuban news radio station in Miami. He heard nothing on *Radio Marti* or any Miami radio station about any hijacked flights. As a last resort, he turned the dial to *Radio Mambi* 710 AM. Usually, the Spanish language station would have news directly from their reporters in Cuba. Today, there were no news reports about a hijacked 747.

He was also deeply troubled because he had not heard from Bill before he got on board Flight 100 in San Francisco.

To Juan Guerrero, no news was good news. He had learned from his call to the airline that Flight 100 was airborne. He figured,

"Things should start to happen soon."

Juan needed to conceal his being on the airport while he was off-duty with work-related injury. He attempted this by skirting the outer edges of the space between the employees' lot and the main terminal buildings.

The main Miami International Airport terminal wall clock said almost 4 o'clock. His shift would be over in less than twenty minutes. He knew his supervisor had already left for the day.

Feeling better about having not been discovered, Juan wandered over to the baggage area. Once there, if discovered, he would explain he had traded to work someone else's afternoon "twilight" shift.

He wished there were some way he could call Bill or listen to the pilots on the radio. Then he would know exactly what was happening. For now, he continued to know nothing, and not knowing bothered him.

He decided that at 5 o'clock he would return to his car and again listen to the Cuban news on *Radio Mambí* for any news bulletins.

41

16:05 Eastern Standard Time
West of Pittsburgh, Pennsylvania

Carlton finished cleaning his galley quickly. Even to a casual observer, he would have appeared to have been possessed. He charged through his routine. He typically was quite dedicated, having a deserved reputation for being fastidious. That was not the case today. He wanted only to be with his latest potential conquest, Bill Guerrero.

He threw everything into any storage cubby he could find. He shoveled half-empty soda cans into the trash and threw passenger trash into craft paper bags marked "LINEN ONLY." Finally, he took one last look around the galley. This would have to be good enough. The cabin cleaners would sort it all out when they got to JFK.

Boeing Commercial Airplane Company and Norskog Industries had thoughtfully provided a small polished stainless steel mirror for Flight Attendant use and attached it to each galley bulkhead.

Habitually, Carlton looked at himself every time he passed the mirror. Based on what he saw, he continually worried about how he looked. With a large measure of insecurity and discontent, Carlton turned away from the galley mirror and purposefully and quickly walked 15 feet up the right side aisle toward the nose of the airplane.

Bill had taken advantage of Carlton's absence and thought about his Nike carryon bag. Frustrated, Bill knew why he had disassembled the plastic firearm; so he could make it through security. He needed to find a place to put it back together where no one could see him or the gun. The only place Bill thought of was one of the lavatories on the plane. Just as Bill started to pull the bag onto his lap, Carlton slithered into the seat next to him, a little breathless.

Bill again thought, "This fairy princess is going to screw up my plan." He glared at Carlton, in the hope his threatening look would make Carlton leave. Carlton only looked at Bill and smiled.

Bill then had a *"muy grande"* idea – almost an inspiration. He looked directly at Carlton and said, "I have to go to the bathroom and get cleaned up." He paused for a few seconds, shuddered, boosted his courage and said, "Wanna come with me?"

To Carlton, the interior of the cabin spun. He felt light-headed. For a moment he thought he was going to faint. Quickly, he took two or three very deep breaths to stabilize his emotional ups and downs and then sensuously looked at Bill. He tried to be demure, even bordering on coy as he said, "Yes. Yes, I would like that very much."

"Well, here's how we'll do it. You go back to the bathrooms and find one that's open. You, like, guard it, and I'll come back in a couple of minutes." Bill's voice sounded odd to him. Crystalline and metallic with no intonation. He did not recognize his own voice. The words tumbled out of his mouth, but he didn't believe he was saying them. It was like he was reading a script. It wasn't him saying these things, it was some other voice.

Carlton half-jumped and half-slid out of the seat next to Bill. Quickly, almost running, he headed to the five lavatories in the rear of the airplane. He hoped none of his passengers, or another flight attendant, would see them in one of the lavatories together.

He stepped around the curtains by the lavatories and looked over his shoulder. Bill was ten feet behind him, closing the gap quickly. Rushing, Carlton tried the first lavatory door. It was locked. The second was locked, too. Relief replaced the aching anticipation when Carlton found the center lavatory unoccupied and unlocked.

He fully opened the door just as Bill turned the corner behind him. He rushed toward Carlton, carrying his little black bag. Now they were suddenly face-to-face. Just as quickly as he had appeared, Bill brushed past Carlton and disappeared in the lavatory.

The door to Carlton's tryst unceremoniously closed in his face. Bill firmly slid the lock, so the sign above the lock said, "OCCUPIED." His muffled voice weakly came through the door, "Give me a couple of minutes and wait out there on guard. I'll unlock the door when I'm ready." Bill quickly opened the Nike bag and pulled the parts of the gun out and laid them on the countertop. He checked the bag for anything he had missed and shoved the bag in the trash container under the sink.

Carlton felt emotionally naked as he stood in the cross-ship aisle and waited for Bill to open the door for him. He would be mortified and positively die if one of his passengers saw them. He puzzled, "What would happen to him if they wrote a letter to the company?" Carlton's puzzle was abruptly broken when Bill unlocked the door and it opened a few inches.

Slowly, Carlton reached for the knob and pulled the door fully open. He peered into the small, darkened lavatory. Carlton could see Bill. Slowly Carlton started to lower his gaze. He felt an incredible rush of anticipation as he looked at Bill. His visual perusal was cut short by a charcoal gray, grease-colored, short-barreled pistol that Bill held firmly in his right hand.

Carlton started to say something, but Bill reached with his left hand and grabbed Carlton's shirt, tie and vest. With an intimidating yank, he pulled Carlton into the lavatory. Carlton stumbled as he was pulled tight against Bill. He whimpered loudly when he felt the gun barrel dig sharply into his rib cage. Bill released his grip, freeing his left hand, with which he tried to close the lavatory door.

Bill whispered to Carlton, "Listen to me, you God damned fag. Reach behind you and close the fuckin' door."

Carlton's right hand waved in circles as he tried to find the doorknob or latch. However, the door was partially blocked by a passenger that had been seated near Bill.

The businessman only needed to see Carlton pressed against Bill. In abject disgust, he put the palm of his hand against Carlton's back and shoved him all the way into the lavatory, "You two make me sick. You and your boyfriend are disgusting. If you worked for my company, I'd fire the whole lot of you. You're a bunch of sickos."

With a triumphant snort, he left the aft lavatory bay and slammed the center lavatory door closed.

Bill was caught off guard. Carlton's additional weight forced him to sit on the toilet seat with Carlton leaning over him at a sharp angle. He attempted to push Carlton off, but at the same time, did not want Carlton to try and escape. Bill roughly slammed the short, hard end of the gun barrel into Carlton's soft belly. He pushed and twisted the muzzle again until he heard a soft whimper from Carlton.

"If you make one sound or try to get away, I'll shoot your fuckin' dick off. No tricks *Maricón*. You understand?"

Carlton made mixed sounds of whimpers and then cried, "Yes. Yes, for God's sake." Blinking and in a very high, frightened voice, he cried, "Are you crazy?"

Carlton was alone with Bill, but not under the circumstances he had anticipated or imagined, "I like you and thought we were going to have a fun time together. Now look at you. You're hurting me and talking all crazy."

Bill did not relent. The pressure from the gun dug deeper into his belly. Carlton continued, "I've never done anything to hurt you."

The forward sight on the barrel had rubbed a sore spot on Carlton's ribs and he cried out, "My God, why are you doing this to me? Fearfully, he added, "Treating me like this."

Bill used his left hand and pushed Carlton against the closed lavatory door and Carlton's head rebounded with a dull thump. Carlton was so dizzy he was certain he was going to pass out.

He could not believe what had happened to him in the past few minutes. Grinding sexual anticipation had suddenly been transformed into unbridled 'wet your pants' fear. Carlton had been so certain this Mexican was going to be an easy mark for him. How could he have been so wrong? Why was he being treated so roughly? Why did Bill want to hurt him? Carlton some times liked rough sex, but this was not what he had expected.

"Carlton, you don't know it. But you and me are gonna be part of history. I'm gonna be rich." Carlton didn't understand. "You, little fag, are going to help me hijack this fuckin' airplane."

Carlton, his eyes wide, gasped, "Oh, No. Not that." He squirmed and said, "Are you crazy?"

"No. But you are if you don't help me."

Carlton tried to back up or turn away. Without any conviction, he said, "They'll catch you. They always do."

Guerrero ignored his advice, "You cooperate with me, and maybe you'll be like ok." He jabbed the gun harder into Carlton's midsection. "And maybe I won't hurt you." Carlton could only whimper that he understood.

Bill continued, "But you try to trick me and I'll kill you." For added emphasis Bill harshly jabbed the snubbed barrel just under Carlton's diaphragm.

Finally it began to sink in. They were going to be hijacked! This Mexican had taken him prisoner. Carlton tried a different attitude. "This is outrageous. You can't do this to me and my pass..."

His comment was cut short when Bill grabbed Carlton's shirt and tie and savagely slammed the back of his head against the closed lavatory door. Once again, he pushed Carlton's hard enough that he bounced off the door like a boxer's glove coming off the bag.

Carlton couldn't think. He could barely stand up. He said nothing. He tried to concentrate on his airline terrorist training. He hadn't been to security training for almost a year. Now it seemed like a long time ago. He knew he was supposed to do certain things, but now could not think of anything other than his own personal survival. He tried not to panic. He thought maybe he was supposed to only offer resistance but not cooperate. He sort of recalled his objective was to slow the hijacker down with various delaying tactics.

Right now, he was failing that assignment on every level. He could not think of a single thing to do or say. Here he was, a prisoner with an armed hijacker, locked in a lavatory.

Bill again pushed the gun under Carlton's rib cage with a angry twisting motion, "Hey *Paloma*. The little *Maricón*. I'm talking to you. You hear what I'm sayin'?" Carlton blanched as Bill said, "We. You 'n me. We're are going to hijack this fucker."

Mentally, Carlton went around the bend and broke down. He looked directly at Bill and sobbed, "I'll do whatever you say. Just don't hurt me any more."

Sobbing, he added, "All I wanted was to be your friend and now..." Great tears ran down his face and dripped on Bill's arm.

Carlton sobbed and cried out, "Oh, sweet Jesus. I don't know what to do. I'm so confused."

Bill interjected, "Shut the fuck up, *Maricón*."

He continued to sob. "I don't know what you want. I don't know why you are doing this. I don't even know what I want. Except, I know I don't want you to hurt me."

"You little pussy. You are, like, completely useless."

Carlton's long eyelashes were matted from his tears. Confusion and fear immobilized him. He wanted to get away, but could not motivate his body to move.

Bill spoke and Carlton's role was suddenly clarified, "We are going to walk out of here. Just you 'n me. You in front of me. And then we're going right to the Captain. I'll be behind you. If you say anything to anyone, I'll shoot you."

With that, Bill twisted and yanked the pistol from under Carlton's rib cage and viciously struck Carlton above his left eye. Carlton loudly cried out and thought he was going to wet his pants.

"Just take me to the Captain and maybe I won't hurt you; any more. Maybe, if you do what I say, you'll live through this... maybe."

With a marked change in voice and attitude, Bill added, "If you try to get away, I'll shoot you. Do you understand me?"

Carlton continued to cry silently. Great rivulets cascaded down both cheeks. Through his sniffles and sobs, Carlton looked at Bill and said, "I told you. I'll do what you say. Just tell me what it is you want." He sucked in a deep breath, "And, I'll do it. I'll do it for you."

42

16:15 Eastern Standard Time
West of Pittsburgh, Pennsylvania

"First, straighten yourself up. Stop you're fuckin' crying, you God-damned pussy." The enormity of what was about to happen shocked Bill as much as it frightened Carlton. It was as though someone had turned off the ignition in a race car just as the green flag dropped. Bill took a deep breath and forced himself to say, "Turn around and start walking to the front of the airplane. To the pilot. Remember, I'm right behind you."

Carlton pulled down at the bottom of his vest and without thinking, looked at himself in the mirror. The bleeding over his eye had slowed. Some of his blood had dried in his eyebrow. Quickly, he straightened his tie and placed his hand on the doorknob, slid the latch and turned toward the cabin.

Propelled by fear, he opened it.

He turned to his right and took three steps and heard the lavatory door close behind him. He continued up the right aisle, a frightful solitary walk toward the front of the airplane with the hijacker right behind him. Though he didn't look back, he could sense and even smell Bill's scent. His former potential lover stayed only two or three steps behind him.

As they passed seats in the aft cabin, several passengers looked up. Few paid any attention. Those who did look up only noticed a tall thin Flight Attendant walking briskly through the cabin toward the front of the plane. Few noticed he was being tightly followed by an equally tall dark Mexican.

To some, the dirty blond Cabin Attendant looked like he was trying to get away from the Mexican and the Mexican looked as though he were bound to keep the flight attendant within his sight and grasp. Without comment, they both walked quickly into the next zone of the aircraft.

One of the passengers in his section, the businessman, leaned over to an elderly gentleman and said in a thick southern accent, "I guess they just can't leave each other alone. I figured they had completed their bidness back there in the head."

Passengers watched the curtain that divided the two sections continue to sway after Carlton and Bill had rushed through it. The businessman continued, "I'll God damned guarantee you, I think this whole thing is disgusting." The white-haired elderly gentleman looked over at his wife and nodded his agreement.

Carlton passed three or four Flight Attendants on his way toward the front of the airplane. Each were busily engaged in specific tasks for their section. Flight Attendants later would say they saw Carlton when he strode purposefully through their zone. One of the Flight Attendants, Linda, thought Carlton looked odd, but dismissed her concern because Carlton was such a strange person most of the time.

Bill walked only a couple of steps behind Carlton, carrying his black Nike gym bag at his side. At one point, he momentarily lost sight of him when they were separated by the dividing curtain between Business and First Class.

Bill approached the curtain and rudely pushed it aside. Just on the other side of the divider, he was confronted by a young Flight

Attendant. She looked directly at him and asked, "Sir, where are you seated? Are you sitting in this section?"

Bill attempted to ignore her and continue after Carlton. The young woman said in a loud and conspicuous voice, "Sir, you will have to return to your cabin. You can't go up there. This area is reserved for First Class passengers." She waited a beat, "Only."

Bill turned and faced her. If she challenged him she would ruin everything. If she called attention to him, many passengers would look directly at him. He put his hand on the front of her apron and forced her out of his way. No talk. Just brute strength. She started to protest again, but was stifled when he slapped her sharply across the cheek and mouth, leaving a red handprint on her face.

Carlton looked behind him. Bill was detained by that "newbie" Flight Attendant. Quickly and frantically, Carlton looked around First Class and desperately tried to gain someone's, anyone's attention. Patti Mallory walked toward him, on her way to help with the cabin service in Business Class.

He looked back, just in time to see Bill slap the new flight attendant across her face.

43

16:25 Eastern Standard Time
Overhead Pittsburgh, Pennsylvania

Carlton grabbed Patti's arm and swung her around. He was out of breath. Not from exertion, but fear. His voice suggested he was near his limit. Hysteria was imminent. His sentences and thoughts came out in a jumble, "Patti, he's after me. Oh my God. It's awful."

Carlton shook as he looked behind and saw Bill coming directly toward him. Carlton's soft brown eyes revealed his abject fear. He looked at Patti and then back to Bill.

In a whispered, pleading voice, "He's crazy and wants to hijack the airplane."

Patti had not heard the first of his remarks and had simply dismissed it as part of his perpetual homosexual hysteria.

She also did not fully understand the importance embedded in the rest of his remarks. The high ambient noise level in the airplane drowned out most of his shallow whispered words.

Suddenly, all three of them were standing in very close proximity. Bill grabbed Carlton by the arm and roughly jerked him around so that they were face to face.

Patti looked on with distaste and then shock. At first, she thought that perhaps Bill was just another link in Carlton's never ending chain of sexual adventures. Yet, something in the way Bill roughly grabbed him, led her to sense this was indeed more than a lover's quarrel.

Bill virtually seethed when he said, "You fuckin' fag. You tried to tell her, didn't you?"

Carlton shook his head sideways. He was unable to even whisper his denial.

Bill paused to gather his breath, "I told you not to tell anyone. I told you I'd shoot your balls off if you told anyone. Now I'm going to do it."

Carlton started to sob. He defensively covered his crotch. This time, no sound came out. Just tears running down his cheeks and onto his vest and shirt.

Even though Patti did not understand Bill was intent on hijacking the aircraft, she seemed to instinctively know that this was an explosive situation.

She tried to break Bill's grip on Carlton's arm.

"What are you doing to him? You can't treat any of us like that."

Bill ignored her and tightened his grip on Carlton.

Patti's pulse raced as she said, "If you don't return to your seat immediately, I'll tell the Captain that you are trying to intimidate one of our cabin crew." As an afterthought, she added, "And, that's a federal offense." She searched for something else to diffuse the situation, adding, "You could go to jail."

Bill looked at her with disgust, "You do that. Go ahead and tell the Captain." He dug his fingers deeply into Carlton's arm.

Intuitively, she understood. Carlton was a prisoner in plain sight of her and everyone in First Class. In front of me. He was in open view. Right here. Right now. Her recognition what was going on was now very clear.

She knew the company recommended policy in the airline security program. She stood there and could almost repeat the entire litany of "Things to do when you are threatened."

"Intervene between a terrorist and a hostage."

"Delay."

"Passively create hurdles or speed bumps."

"Keep him off guard."

"Confuse the hijacker."

"Delay the hijacker."

"Delay the hijacker."

"Delay the hijacker."

"Delay. Delay. Delay."

Patti drew herself up and said, "Sir, I must warn you that assaulting a crew member is against company policy and also against the FAA rules." She paused then repeated herself, "You could go to jail for this kind of thing."

Patti looked for some sign of comprehension on Bill's part. None was forthcoming. "I want you to return to your seat immediately and stay there."

Patti, Bill and Carlton appeared to be locked in a live tableau. No one moved.

Bill used Carlton as a shield and propelled him forward into the galley in First Class. Patti was caught up by the momentum. All of them were tightly crowded in the narrow passageway.

Bill looked at her and said, "Listen to me, *puta*. He's my hostage. I'm gonna hijack this fuckin' airplane to Havana. You understand me, bitch? I want to see the Captain. Now."

The fear she felt caused her to hesitate.

"Open the fuckin' cockpit door."

Patti tried to assess the situation. Carlton was not going to be any help. The hijacker was agitated and she didn't know how serious he was. She fought to keep her own panic under control. She knew she was to delay the hijacker as long as possible. Keep him slowed down and keep him away from the cockpit.

She spoke with a voice that betrayed her outward confidence as she tried to delay the hijacker, "Sir, I'll tell the Captain you want to go to Cuba. But he is very busy right now. I don't think that he will be able to stop and talk to you."

Bill tightened his grip, then twisted Carlton's arm behind his back. Carlton squealed and winced at the pain.

The hijacker nervously demanded, "Take me to the Captain. I want this over with. No excuses, *puta*."

Bill dragged Carlton toward the front of First Class. A passenger coat closet was located at the extreme forward part of the cabin. Bill approached the closet and attempted to open the door, but could find no latches, nor did he see anything that looked like a doorknob. Several passengers became alarmed seeing a flight attendant being hauled through the First Class cabin by a disheveled looking Latino.

He forcefully slammed Carlton against the coat compartment, "How do you open this fuckin' cockpit door?" Bill had never been on a 747 and had no idea where the cockpit was located.

Carlton felt like he was going to faint. His eyes rolled up and he started to slump against Bill.

He taunted him and snarled, "Come on. Help me out here." Bill again threatened physical harm to Carlton as he raged, "Or, I'll make a mess of you. How do I get in the cockpit?"

Patti saw an advantage in suddenly being alone in the First Class Galley while the hijacker and Carlton were only eighteen feet away. Patti bolted from the galley and ran up the circular staircase to the upper deck. Away from the hijacker, Patti called the cockpit on the upper deck interphone.

She used the appropriate signal for the cockpit, but did not wait for anyone to answer, she just started to talk, "Captain, this is Patti, I'm on the upper deck. We have a passenger in First Class who says he wants to go to Havana and he has taken one of the cabin crew hostage."

All three pilots had been engaged in the tedium of a transcontinental flight. Don had been looking at the approach charts for JFK.

"We have a passenger in First Class who says he wants to go to

Havana and he has one of us hostage."

Don and Fred both grabbed for the interphone handset aft of the center console. Don lifted the handset out of the cradle and spoke, "This is the Captain. Who is this?"

She was out of breath. She couldn't remember the Captain's name, "Oh, Captain." She thought she was going to cry, "This is Patti. A passenger downstairs wants to go to Cuba." She sucked in great quantities of air, "He has taken Carlton hostage, too."

Patti heard Don's calm voice tighten, "Is he armed? Does he have a gun, or knife. Did he say anything about having explosives with him?"

"I don't know. He didn't say anything. But, yes, he has a gun. And he has small bag with him and he has Carlton Marsh with him in the forward part of First Class. As soon as they left the galley, when it was clear, I ran up here."

"Patti you did the right thing. You know the procedures. Keep him out of here if you can, for as long as you can. How serious do you think this guy is about going to Havana?"

"I don't know. I'm so scared. I didn't know what to do. All I know is he seemed nervous, very upset. Agitated. Carlton said he was crazy."

Downstairs, Bill banged Carlton against the closet door for the second time. Carlton was so frightened he could not speak. The best he could manage was to cough and whimper in the back of his throat.

A large black passenger, who, several years ago, had been a professional football player, sat in the first row of First Class and looked at Bill as he bounced Carlton off the coat closet door. The athlete started to get out of his seat and said in a deep resonant voice, "Hey man. Leave the little dude alone. He don't need to be treated that way."

Bill turned toward the voice behind him. He pointed his pistol at the voice. He came face to face with the torso of an immense passenger, who was still not quite out of his seat. Without thinking,

Bill moved the aiming point of the gun up toward the passenger's face.

The football player saw the gun as Bill turned toward him. He quickly sat down. Now the gun barrel was at eye level. Bill flicked the gun left and right at the athlete's face and enjoyed the sudden and immense power he felt. The size of the passenger made no difference. The gun was the equalizer.

The passenger had been in many situations like this in Detroit when he was growing up. He did the only smart thing he could think of. He said, "I don't know what your problem is, my man. But you have a gun and whatever you say is cool with me."

Several other passengers had seen the gun and a woman screamed. Bill looked through the cabin and waved the gun in the general direction of the passengers.

He then loudly yelled, "I am hijacking this fuckin' jet to Cuba." A community grasp of shock rumbled through First Class, "and I don't want no fuckin' trouble with any of you." He returned the aim of the gun to the passenger at his left, "Especially from you."

The passenger said, "I'm cool with that."

Carlton locked his knees so he would not fall or slide to the floor. He was sweating. Tears mixed with sweat ran down his face. He could not think. It seemed as though this was all a bad dream.

Bill threw his Nike bag on the floor, then reached behind and grabbed Carlton by the arm. He swung Carlton around in front of him and said in a loud whisper, "How do I get into the God damned cockpit? Tell me, you little fag, or I'll shoot you right here, right now."

Bill tightened his grip and then pressed the gun against Carlton's lower back then said, "If you don't tell me, I'm going to start shooting holes in your skinny little ass."

Tearfully, in great sobs, Carlton said half crying, "The cockpit is upstairs, I'll take you. But dear sweet Jesus, please don't hurt me any more."

44

16:30 Eastern Standard Time
John F. Kennedy International Airport

The Chief of Security at John F. Kennedy International Airport, John Milford Batchelor, wrote down the facts as Robert Burns pumped them to him during their telephone conversation. Next, he tried to contact Flight Dispatch and talk to Dispatcher Fielding. They had missed each other twice during the past two hours. Batchelor was getting ready to leave for the day. He remembered he still needed to get a message to Dispatch and ask them to relay it to Flight 100.

He dialed the number for Flight Operations and then the extension for Dispatch. Becky answered the telephone, "Dispatch, Mariweather."

"Hi, this is John Batchelor. I work in security here at Kennedy and I'm still trying to reach Mr. Fielding."

"Just a moment, Sir. I see him coming around the corner. May I tell him what this is about please?"

"Looks like we have a stowaway on 100 from San Francisco."

"Yes, Sir. We had a report of that earlier today. Mr. Fielding is aware of the situation."

She held her breath while Fielding came to his desk and sat down heavily, "Just a minute. Here he is."

Batchelor could hear a muffled, brief conversation and then the dispatcher's distinctive German-accented rumbling voice, "This is Dispatcher Fielding. What is it that we do to help you?" He pronounced "what" as "vut" and "we" as "vee".

"Well, it appears we have a stowaway on 100 this morning out of San Francisco. I think you may have talked with Robert Burns about this. The flight's due to land at Kennedy about 17:30 local time." He waited for Fielding to say something, but all he heard what his rattling breaths.

"So, I'd like you to notify the crew."

"Yes."

"Alert the cockpit that the New York Port Authority Police will meet the flight on arrival. It's my intention to apprehend the stowaway and press charges. I have asked the Port Authority PD to detain the stowaway for interrogation."

"What do you want the flight crew to do with this passenger?" Again, "vut."

"Nothing. We just want to alert them the New York Port Authority police will be waiting in the Jetway when 100 arrive at JFK."

"I vil haf Becky send und message to da crew. Vut iss the passenger's name?"

"The only name we have is Guerrero." He checked the spelling and said, "B. Guerrero, "Traveling on a ticket stolen from a travel agency."

He waited a second, then added, "Also, according to security in San Fran, this character meets the hijacker profile. However, that could just be coincidence."

When Batchelor mentioned 'hijacker profile,' Fielding felt a shock run up his back and neck. The chill lasted only a second or two, but it frightened Fielding. There was a fleeting sense of irritation. Fielding wondered why the head of Kennedy Security seemed to take this passenger so casually.

"Mr. Batchelor. As always, ve vil do our best. Are you sure there is nothing more about this passenger regarding a hijacking profile?" He waited for an answer, but got none.

He added, "Don't you think you should be doing something about him?"

"Listen, if we interrogated every passenger who appeared to fit the profile in some fashion, none of the flights would ever get off the ground.

"Dat is true."

"All I know at this time, is he was observed by our head of security in San Francisco. There was some concern. That led to an investigation about the validity of his ticket. Burns found that his ticket had been stolen a couple of weeks ago."

"Interesting."

"For now, I want to believe there is nothing more to this than random coincidence that he fits the profile."

"It's your call."

"I appreciate your concern. I'll let you know what we find out when 100 lands."

Fielding felt only slightly relieved by Batchelor's remarks. He mused to himself, "These security folks did know much more about hijackings than I do."

All Fielding knew was from his experience from the operational-side of a hijacking. Fuel remaining and fuel consumption, winds aloft, en route and terminal weather and destination airport conditions. The coordination with law enforcement logistics and regard to legal and international concerns were something he knew little about.

Fielding thought about these things, when he absent-mindedly said, "Well, we do what we can here to help you. Thank you for your explanation."

He hung up the telephone and Becky came to his desk, stopped and then looked at him in a quizzical manner, "Hijacking?"

"Probably just a coincidence. The passenger on 100 apparently fit the profile, or a part of the profile."

"What was that all about?" She realized perhaps she was being too outspoken and should have waited for Fielding to tell her when he thought it was the right time.

But then, she knew her fears were groundless when he said, "Kennedy Security was advised by San Fran Security and Flight Operations that a passenger on Flight 100 had boarded with a stolen ticket."

She nodded, but said nothing.

"They want us to SELCAL the flight and let the crew know they are going to be met by the Port Authority Police on arrival."

"So, where does the hijacking come into play?"

"As I said, Batchelor told me the passenger met some or most of the hijack profiles."

She said, "Right." She fidgeted with her hair, "One way ticket, purchased in cash?"

"Yes. But Batchelor didn't seem too concerned about that aspect of the situation."

Fielding lit another cigarette and tossed the paper match toward the ashtray on his desk. The match bounced off the heaping pile of crumpled cigarettes and skidded to a stop by his phone. As an afterthought he said, "Becky, pull up the latest in flight information from ACARS and the FAA Enroute Traffic Control Center on 100 and see how they are doing."

As he said this, Becky had already started to write on a pad, saying, "On it."

He smiled and said, "Ve have da out/off reports. Und zee if there is a revised ETA for Kennedy." Unrealized to Fielding, but not to Becky, as the tension in the room mounted his accent became thicker.

Becky spun the Lazy-Susan carousel so the computer faced her. She quickly entered commands. But had made several entry errors. She slowed down and re-entered the multiple requests on Fielding's keyboard.

"She muttered to herself about the typing errors. Clearly, my fault because I was in a hurry. Adrenalin coursed through her, giving her the shakes.

She didn't look up as he said to her, "I vil SELCAL dem und let dem know about der stowaway." He thrust his hand onto the pile of papers on his desk, found the still warm match and dropped it in the center of the ashtray. With a stronger German accent and inflection he said, "Mr. B. Guerrero. Vut vas you up to?"

As an afterthought Lazlo wondered to himself, "If Guerrero were going to hijack 100, why would he use a stolen ticket that could so easily be discovered and traced?" Mindlessly, Fielding looked out the window at the thickening clouds and asked himself, "Where vould our Mr. Guerrero want to hijack the flight to?" He could see the vestige formation of altocumulus clouds racing ahead of a southwest wind, "Certainly not to New York mit his stolen ticket."

45

16:53 Eastern Standard Time
Overhead Pittsburgh

Don Webber sat motionless. There were many things to consider. His first concern was to determine the strengths and weaknesses of the hijacker and then find out how serious he was about going to Havana.

He turned to his Stan, "Make damn sure the cockpit door stays locked at all times. I know we told the Flight Attendants during the pre-flight briefing about the proper code to gain access. I want you to make goddamn sure you look through the peephole before you open the door."

Stan thought, "This guy must think I'm an idiot."

Fred reviewed the company policy and procedure, "I guess passive resistance is the order of the day."

Don looked at Fred, "Damn it. This is no time for guessing. We have to be very deliberate in our actions."

With that, he picked up the interphone handset and pressed the appropriate button to call First Class. No one answered, so he pressed the code again. Again, he waited. And again, no answer.

HIJACKING OF FLIGHT 100

"We're always the last to know what is going on." As soon as the words came out of his mouth, Fred knew it was a mistake. Don verified Fred's assessment with the look of disgust.

Don busied himself with the ritual refolding of high altitude Jeppesen chart as he said, "We have a potentially dangerous passenger on board who apparently has expressed a desire to go to Cuba. This is no time for humor or levity." An ominous and tension-filled pall hung over the cockpit like a cloud of smoke from a summer campfire.

Patti looked at the passengers in the upper deck cabin and lounge. From outward appearances, they seemed concerned, but did not express the terror she felt. She started toward the circular staircase, but looked down just in time to see Carlton coming up, with the hijacker directly behind him. She changed her mind.

Carlton looked up at Patti and visually pleaded for her to do something, anything that might save him from this situation. He started to speak, but all that came out was a dry croak.

The hijacker interrupted Carlton's silent protestations and looked at Patti. "Did you tell the Captain I want to see him?"

Patti backed away from both of them as they ascended into the confined upper deck galley. The two forward-most passengers watched the unfolding scene with unbelieving eyes.

In an attempt to stall the hijacker, Patti said, "I can't talk to the Captain right now, he is too busy flying the airplane."

The hijacker was not put off by her delay, "If you can't talk to him, then I want to see the man myself."

Patti thought, "Dear God. I'm the only thing between him and the cockpit." She vividly remembered the single most important point in airline security training: KEEP THE HIJACKER OUT OF THE COCKPIT.

Mentally, she sought to find any excuse to keep him out of the cockpit and away from the pilots. "I'm afraid that is not possible. The cockpit door is locked. No one is allowed in there but the pilots."

Carlton started to feel that he might just get out of this without being seriously injured or worse. He added, "Yes. That's right. The door is locked. No one has a key."

The hijacker ignored him. Carlton took being ignored as a sign that Bill might believe what he had just said.

Carlton was momentarily bolstered by this good luck and said, "She's right. There are rules about being in the cockpit and no one is allowed in there but the pilots." Proud of his improvisation, he added with a flourish, "Besides, Bill, the door is locked from the inside."

When Bill heard his name, he was seized with a trembling wave of panic. He reacted and thought, "Because of this fag, they all knew his name and who he was." He concluded, there was no turning back now.

No doubt about it, he was into it now. The pale and skinny *Paloma* had tried to trap him. He would teach him a lesson. The hijacker turned and slapped Carlton across the face with the back of his hand, "You little cocksucker. You tried to trick me."

Fear and terror overrode logic as he said, "Just because you know my name, don't mean I'm going to get caught." For added emphasis and false bravado, he menaced Carlton and then sucker punched him again.

Carlton froze. He trembled as he said, "Honest, I wouldn't try to trick you." His words were pounded back into his throat as Bill viscously hit him with his fist.

Patti picked up on his name, "Bill, tell me what it is you want. Maybe we can help you."

"I want to see the fucking pilot. Now. I, uh, I want to see him now."

He paused, "Does he know I'm uh, that we're, out here?"

Carlton felt his lip swell, but said, "Really. You can't just go in there. He's so busy. Flying a big plane like this is really really hard." Carlton took a breath. His mouth and tongue felt like they were filled with cotton, "It takes three pilots just to fly this plane."

Bill panicked. He had no idea there was more than one pilot. Somehow, the odds had shifted. Now, he needed to do something, anything, that would give him an advantage. His panic transformed to a combination of fear, frustration and anger. He knew had to gain control of the situation.

He had no use for Carlton. He had served his purpose. Bill raised the graphite pistol and struck him on the on the side of his head, just above his ear. Bill could hear and feel something like dry spaghetti being broken when the pistol penetrated Carlton's skin.

46

17:00 Eastern Standard Time
East of Pittsburgh, Pennsylvania

Without any thoughts of resistance, Carlton's had completely exhausted his shaken resolve and dropped to the floor. He screamed, "Jesus. Don't hurt me. I'll do anything you want." Then pleadingly, "Anything."

Passengers on the upper deck were now inescapably engaged in a living terrorist drama. They had no options. All were now equally and inexorably linked to each other. All of their collective fates were now in the hands of the hijacker and the pilots. The only barrier between their lives and disaster was an attractive flight attendant next to a flimsy cockpit door.

Patti was filled with revulsion at the sight of Carlton lying on the floor. There was no reason for Carlton to have been viscously pistol-whipped. Bill kicked Carlton and she winced. This time, she felt like she was going to be sick.

Delay. Delay. Delay, "Please Bill. Don't hit him any more. He can't help you. Let me see what I, or we, can do."

She looked past Carlton into the lounge and saw a dozen

passengers leaning into the aisle bonded to each other by events that tied them together. Each passenger appeared to be lost in their thoughts as they intently stared at the unfolding scenario.

Each saw themselves as actors in a drama with no good outcomes. Men and women alike tried to fathom how their lives were going to be impacted by this hijacker and the female flight attendant. To a person, it was clear that the hijacker had regained control.

The hijacker looked at the cockpit door that was marked, "Flight Deck--No Admittance."

He saw the cockpit doorknob and saw a key slot on the face of the knob. He turned to Patti, "Where's the key, *puta?*"

He waited less than a second, then raged, "How do you unlock the fuckin' door?"

Patti hesitated for just a moment as she looked at the hijacker.

He returned her gaze, glared at her and said, "If you don't tell me how to open the door or find me a damn key, I'll shoot the fucking lock off the god damned door."

"Please don't do that. The pilots are right on the other side of the door. If you hurt them, no one will be able to fly the airplane and we could all die."

He stared at her. She stared back, "Is that what you want, Bill? To die? To kill all of us?"

Patti thought maybe the hijacker might be satisfied with her answer. She attempted to support her position as she said, "I don't know where the key is."

She had terrifying thoughts of what might happen if he got into the cockpit, "I normally work downstairs and I don't have any idea if there's even a key up here, or where its located."

Bill's gaze wandered passed Patti and he suddenly saw a handset that looked like a wall telephone. Angrily, he yanked the handset from the cradle, turned the handset over and saw a series of numbered push buttons like a touch pad on a telephone. Next to each number, was a small placard that listed various locations throughout the airplane.

Patty watched him look at the phone with dread. She realized that each passing second brought him closer to cockpit entry.

Bill stared at the list, "L1, R1, R4, R5, UPGLY, LWGLY, CONTCAB." None of the abbreviations made any sense to him. He dropped the handset and let it hang by the cord, "How the fuck do you call the pilot on this thing?"

Patti looked at Carlton who was still crumbled on the floor, partially leaning against the lavatory door. A trickle of blood ran down his cheek then dripped onto his shirt collar. His normally perfect hair was matted with perspiration and blood. He looked back at her, but likely did not comprehend what was going on around him. He alternated between looking like a whipped puppy and someone who was either going to remain cornered or would need to fight for his life. As she looked at him, clearly the whipped puppy had taken over Carlton's thoughts and reactions.

Bill felt the cold familiar fear that he was going to fail again. Angrily he thought, "This time it would be different." He knew if he failed, he would either be killed or go to jail. Going back to jail was not really a choice for him.

He surveyed the upper galley and companionway toward the cockpit. He was puzzled at the number of small doors and storage compartments that lined the walkway toward the cockpit. Bill was no longer thinking, he was only reacting to, and being driven by, his fear.

Bill yelled, "Goddamn it. Will somebody help me?" He looked directly at Patti then rasped, "Go downstairs and find the key, or find someone who knows where the fuckin' key is." He pointed the gun at Carlton, "Do it now. Or, I'll shoot this fucker." To Patti, it was clear that the hijacker had lost his connection with reality and was not processing much of what he was saying and doing.

After he yelled at Patti, he grabbed Carlton by the shirt front and forcefully pulled him back on his feet. He grabbed Carlton's shoulder and spun him around so that he was facing aft.

Bill stood behind Carlton and slammed the gun into his back just above his right kidney. He put his left forearm under his Carlton's chin and exerted just enough pressure to restrict Carlton's ability to breathe. Carlton rose up on his toes, trying to lessen Bill's ability to shut off air to his lungs.

Bill looked over Carlton's shoulder at the passengers and saw various stages of terror, fear, border-line panic and, in some, resignation. He didn't feel threatened by the passengers. Not like he did by the black football player downstairs.

Slowly, Bill backed up the incline until his back was against the cockpit door. Patti watched every move he made. Her hand was on the stainless banister of the circular staircase. She could not make herself leave the upper deck. She was transfixed by the drama that continued to unfold before her.

47

17:05 Eastern Standard Time
East of Pittsburgh, Pennsylvania

The level of tension in the cockpit was oppressive. It bordered on being offensive. All three pilots had reviewed and understood the security and anti-hijacking procedures to be followed. They also were deeply aware of the consequences that would befall them if those procedures failed.

Don considered notifying the FAA Terrorist Coordinator about this hijack situation. He delayed because other than one call from a Flight Attendant, he had no corroborating evidence. He decided that as soon as any additional supporting information became evident, he would put the FAA terrorist/hijack procedures into action.

Stan Kurtz had been busy. He knew exactly how much fuel remained. But as a double check, he calculated total fuel consumed which he subtracted from their original fuel load. Both figures agreed, if they remained at Flight Level 330 they had 2:40 minutes of fuel remaining, with an average ground speed of 500 knots, they could travel no more than 1,350 nautical miles. That calculated distance, however, was very optimistic. It would be reduced substantially because not all the fuel in the tanks was usable. He said out loud to him self, "I think a 1,000 nautical miles is a safer and more conservative estimate of distance, solely based on fuel remaining."

Don turned to Fred, but said to no one in particular, "I'm not looking for trouble. But, I'd sure would like to know if this character is serious, or if it's just a hoax." Neither Fred nor Stan could accept the captain's inability to make a decision. Both knew it was fundamental that every threat was to be considered viable until proven otherwise. The captain's lack of leadership was, at best, fool hardy.

Their individual concerns were jarred by the multi-tone trilling SELCAL chime. Don selected the number two VHF radio, keyed the mike and said, "100 answering SELCAL.

"This is Kennedy Dispatcher Fielding. We have a message from San Francisco and JFK Security that you have a stowaway on board. He's traveling on a stolen ticket. Our company security has alerted the New York Port Authority Police to meet your flight on arrival." There was a static-filled pause before Fielding continued, "What is your latest estimate for Kennedy?"

Fred pulled the aluminum clipboard from between the center console and the edge of his seat. He quickly glanced at the figures on the right side of the sheet, "We have been running three minutes behind the computer all along. If you add another ten minutes for an over water arrival, I'd guess we'll be there at 21:40 Greenwich."

Don spoke in to the microphone, "We're estimating our arrival at or before 22:00 Z." Then went on, "Is the weather holding up at Kennedy?"

"Good, Sir. 22:00 Zulu ETA. And, yes, the forecast for your arrival should be fine. However, the wind could shift to the northwest at about that time."

All three pilots could easily detect Fielding's German accent, "You vil be landing on 31 Right. Und, you vil be parked at gate Alpha 19, via Taxi vay November."

There was a short pause, "The passenger's name on da ticket iz

Guerrero, Mr. B. Guerrero."

Fielding wondered if he should say anything about the profile of this passenger.

"Thanks for the info." Don momentarily considered whether he should say anything about the report of the passenger in the cabin. Instinctively, he said, "Dispatch hold on a minute, I want to check something." Don turned to Fred, "Call First Class and ask what's going on."

"I think Patti said she was calling from the Upper Deck."

Don exploded, "God damn it. I don't give a shit where she called from. Just find out what the hell is going on."

Fred picked up the handset, but could not get a dial tone on the system. He pressed the Priority Pass button, but still got no response. He couldn't hear anyone talking, "One of Cabin Attendants must have left a hand set off the hook. I can't get a dial tone."

Stan offered, "Do you want me to go back and see what's going on?"

Don swore under his breath, "No. No. God Damn it, Stan. No. I don't want you to leave. If there is anything going on back there, I want you up here."

As an aside, Don looked back at Stan, "Is that door locked? Are you positive that it's locked? I want you to throw the dead bolt, not just turn the lock."

Stan reached back from his seat and checked the dead bolt, "Yes sir. The door's secured and the dead bolt's in position."

"Dispatch. This is 100 again. This is probably nothing. But, we had an unconfirmed report from a Flight Attendant that there is a passenger in the cabin who said something about going to Cuba." Don waited for a response on the radio, but none came. Fred and Stan were stunned at the Captain's underplaying the threat of a hijacking.

He continued, "For the time being, we will treat it as a non-threat situation."

He re-keyed the mike and said, "But, if we get any kind of

confirmation, then we'll consider it as a legitimate threat."

Lazlo Fielding felt the blood drain from his face. He shuddered, reached for a cigarette and then stopped, "Captain. Kennedy Security did say that the stowaway passenger did fit the hijack profile."

"Ah, shit."

"San Francisco security had him under surveillance while he was in the airport. This does look like more than coincidence."

Neither the pilots nor the dispatcher said anything, the radio hummed as everyone waited for the next bit of conversation.

The pilots and the dispatcher were all equally stunned. Their mutual silence had confirmed the other's suspicion.

Don looked at Fred and then at Stan, "Well. What do you think? Do we sound the alarm?"

Fred looked over his left shoulder at Stan. Stan looked at Don and back to Fred. No one responded until Stan said, "I'm for telling 'em. Be foolish not to."

Fred nodded in agreement, "Let's pull the plug. It doesn't cost us anything. I say, let's go for it."

Don sat with the microphone poised mid way between his lap and his mouth. He pulled on the cord, stretched it and then slowly raised the microphone, "Dispatch, this is Captain Webber. Please alert the authorities that we have a hijacker on board. We have not spoken to the hijacker. At this time, we do not know anything about him. For that matter, we are not certain the threat is real. We do not really know what he wants, or where he wants to go." Don started to sign off, then added, "We'll notify ATC, on this end."

"Understand 100. You are reporting that you have a hijacker on board and will notify ATC of your intentions, Dispatch clear."

Don looked at the bulkhead behind the Flight Engineer's panel, "Stan, get the crash axe out and put it where you can get to it."

"Sorry. The company took all of them off the '47's a couple of years ago. I think some of the other aircraft in the fleet may still have them. But we don't."

"Lovely. Just lovely." Fred looked at Don and added, That's

really too bad."

Stan continued, "Yep. They took the axes off the same time the pulled the asbestos gloves. Some bean counter probably figured it cost too much to keep them on the aircraft."

Fred said, "I'll bet those bean counter-types would think differently right now. Especially, if they were on this flight."

"How about a fire extinguisher, Stan?" "Do we have one of those here in the cockpit?"

"Right here, it's clamped to the aft bulkhead."

Don looked for the extinguisher, but his view was blocked by Stan's chair. "Pull that extinguisher off the bulkhead and stow it near you, in your desk. I want anything we might be able to use to be available."

"You were in the Marine Corps, right?"

"Yes Sir. Two tours in Viet Nam. Flew F-4 D Phantoms."

"Do you remember any of the hand-to-hand training you got in basic?"

"I don't know. It's been a long time and I'm not in the same shape I was in boot camp."

Fred added, "Me too. Way too long ago and way too many McDonald's."

"Nonetheless, I want both of you to think about maintaining control if he breaches the cockpit. Stan, you are our first line of defense. Fred, you're next. No matter how this goes down, I need either or both of you to help me get us back on the ground in one piece."

"Roger that."

"Just let us know what you want us to do."

"Damn it. Stan. That's my point. I hope you are both self-starters. I don't want to have to tell you what to do with regard to this clown. Do whatever it takes to maintain control."

Fred said, "Deputy Dan reporting as ordered, Sir!" Don ignored his First Officer, but smiled when he heard the metallic snap as the fire extinguisher clamp was released. At the same time, he also heard the cockpit door take a hard blow from outside, which everyone sensed was caused by the hijacker.

48

17:15 Eastern Standard Time
East of Pittsburgh, Pennsylvania

Bill lightened his grip on Carlton's throat and then grabbed Patti's shoulder. She winced with fright and sucked in her breath.

"Forget it. You're not going down stairs, *"perra*. "I think you know how to open the door, but you're not telling me." Bill looked at her. Fear was engraved across her face. He yelled, loud enough for some of the upper deck passengers to hear, "Open the fuckin' door. NOW!"

"I don't know how to do that. They have to unlock it from the inside. They have a switch in the cockpit that unlocks the door. I'll go downstairs and see if anyone else knows how to open the door."

Patti started to turn away from Bill's grasp, but he tightened his grip and then roughly let his fingers brush against her breast, "No tricks, *puta*. I want you to open the door, or this one," Bill jerked Carlton's head backward, "is going to get hurt real bad."

"Yes. Yes, Sir. I understand. No tricks." Patti was weeping. Her tears and mascara stained her face, "I'll see what I can do. I, uh, I'll do the best I can."

Bill directed his attention to Carlton, who was leaning against the bulkhead, awkwardly starting another long, slow slide to the floor. The hijacker stood motionless in front of both of them. Patti sensed this was an opportunity to leave and slowly eased toward the circular staircase to the lower cabin. Bill saw her, but let her go. Carlton quivered with rampant fear mixed with unrelenting anxiety.

Frustrated, Bill kicked at Carlton's leg, but missed. "Are you sure you don't how to help?"
He was angered that nothing in this hijacking was going like it was planned. On one hand, he felt invincible. But at the same time, nothing was working. Again, he kicked at Carlton, "What's the matter *Maricón*? You scared?" Carlton tried to move away, but was trapped by the bulkhead behind him.

Bill snarled with a vengeance, "You useless piece of shit, I'm tired of all this dickin' around." He threatened Carlton, "I want to talk to the pilot in the cockpit."

He looked over his shoulder at the passengers who were more engaged in the drama outside the cockpit door, "If she don't open the door, then it's up to you *Maricón*. If you don't do it. You'll be like dead." Bill raised his hand with the pistol and simulated pulling the trigger. All Carlton could do was cower and quietly pray for deliverance.

Carlton softly, almost politely grabbed Bill's hand, "Please don't hurt me any more." He paused, "Maybe, there's a way I could open the door."

Carlton twisted away from Bill and reached for the door. He twisted the doorknob, which was locked. He tried to push on the door with a gentle rattling motion. Though the door moved slightly, it remained locked.

Bill came up behind him and jammed the barrel of the gun against the occipital bone in Carlton's skull, just behind his ear. "You little fairy. Either you open this door, or I'll shoot you. Right here. Right now." For emphasis, he dug the barrel of the pistol into the tender skin behind Carlton's ear.

Carlton's flagging resolve crumbled into a state of paralysis. He couldn't move. He couldn't think. The only thing he could do was sob.

With no warning, Bill abruptly slammed his body against Carlton, who was pinned between the door and the hijacker's body. He used Carlton as a battering ram. Their combined weight caused the door to bend and deform.

49

17:20 Eastern Standard Time
South of Pittsburgh, Pennsylvania

Downstairs in the lower cabin, Patti ran into the First Class galley and grabbed the interphone handset. She keyed in the emergency number that overrode any other conversations in progress. Near panic, she obsessively and desperately needed to get information to the pilots. She started talking without waiting for an acknowledgement of her call, "Captain. Don. Captain. Please answer me. This is Patti."

No answer.

"The hijacker I told you about is on the upper deck and he has Carlton hostage. And he has a gun. And I'm in the lower galley. And he means business."

No response from the flight deck.

She continued, "His name is Bill. Mexican or Puerto Rican." She was rasping and short of breath.

No answer came from any of the pilots.

"And, I got away by telling him I would try to find someone to open the cockpit door, and then I ran downstairs. And he had a gun to Carlton's head. And Carlton is bleeding because the hijacker hit him with his gun. They are right outside the cockpit door." She finally stopped taking long enough to catch her breath.

She suddenly thought maybe the cockpit had not heard a single word she had said. What should she do?

There was a sharp metallic click, "Patti, this is the Captain. I heard most of what you said. Are you all right?"

"Yes. I'm okay. But. But Carlton's not."

"Listen to me. I want you to stay down there. I don't want any one coming to the upper deck and I want you to move all the First Class passengers as far back into coach as you can. If this guy discharges a gun, I don't want any passenger getting hurt." Don was running on adrenalin. Acting. Reacting. Thinking. Saying. Doing it all at once.

"Patti. This is critical. Do not hang up your handset. Keep it off the hook. I want an open line of communication between us. Do you understand me?"

"Yes sir. I'll keep the cabin team away from the upper deck area too. We'll move all the First Class people into coach. And I'll keep this handset open for you."

Don thought he sounded like a school teacher lecturing a kid in the sixth grade, "That's fine, Patti."

"You did a good job. And, we can monitor what is being said in your area of the aircraft."

"If you want to tell us anything, just start talking. Looks like we may be a little busy up here." He paused before he added, "Don't bother us unless it is absolutely necessary."

More tears welled up and again her cheeks were wet. She sniffled and said, "All right Captain. Whatever you think is best."

Then for reasons she did not understand, she added quietly, "Thank you."

50

**17:30 Eastern Standard Time
Overhead Morgantown, West Virginia**

Flight Engineer Stan Kurtz was startled when he heard a loud collision against the cockpit door from the cabin. Visually, he checked the lock in the center of the knob. He touched it and then closely examined the deadbolt. A small sense of relief; still secure.

In less than sixty minutes, they would be on the ground at JFK. He considered the safety JFK represented. He also realized how much he depended upon his habits. If the hijacker had his way, they might not being going to Kennedy. Based on his fuel remaining, they were going to be on the ground somewhere is less than one hundred and twenty minutes. An absolute. End of fuel supply equals end of flight. No "do overs."

Don looked back at the 747 fuel management panel and asked, "How much fuel do we have right now?"

Stan looked at the ships 'Totalizer' and checked that amount against his own figures, "Right now we have 69,800 pounds. That's about two hours and ten minutes aloft at this altitude. Assuming a straight in approach and also assuming no vectors, we conservatively have a little more than two hours of cruise fuel left. Depending on the wind, I'd guess about nine hundred nautical miles, give or take ten per cent."

Once again the captain became needlessly abrasive. "I can figure the fuel consumption as well as any one. If I want your opinion about our useful range, I'll ask you. Right now, all I want to know was how much fuel we have on board."

"Sorry, Captain. 69,650 pounds." Stan could not help thinking to himself, "What an asshole."

Don's pulse raced when he heard a second assault against the cockpit door. This time, the noise was Carlton's head as it ricocheted off the door. All three pilots heard Carlton scream in pain when he hit the door.

The deformation of the doorframe increased each time Bill slammed Carlton against the door. The aluminum deadbolt had a new, and very troubling bend in it.

Stan figured two or three more strong assaults and the deadbolt would fail.

Don looked over Stan's shoulder and saw the cockpit doorknob being rattled and twisted. Carlton shrieked after he bounced against door again. This time, Carlton hit the door with his chest and shoulders. That bent the door dead bolt even more.

Don stared out the windshield for several seconds. He said nothing. He didn't move. His hands, palms down, rested on the glare shield.

Finally, calmly, "Fred, call ATC and tell them we are under attack. Tell them the hijacker has taken a Flight Attendant hostage."

Fred said nothing. Stan said nothing. Neither wanted to suffer another angry outburst from the captain. Both thought if they didn't acknowledge the captain's order, perhaps this situation would go away.

Fred finally said, "What do we tell 'em about our destination? They'll need to develop a track for us and keep it clear."

"Damn it, we don't know what our destination is going to be."

Looking over his shoulder at the fuel totalizer, He paused, thinking, and said, "All we know for certain is that we're going to on the ground – somewhere – in about two hours or less."

"Hopefully, within the confines of an airport." Fred knew that was another mistake as he said it.

"God Damn it, Fred."

"Sorry, Boss."

Fred looked at Don and then over his shoulder at Stan. Neither pilot showed any emotion. Both looked very together. All three were professional airmen. Each was capable and willing to do whatever was necessary to protect their passengers, aircraft and crew.

Fred picked up his microphone, cleared his throat and said, "Cleveland Center. This is 100."

"Yes Sir. 100. Ident, please."

Don pressed the round Identification button on the transponder on the center radio console.

"Well, it looks like we have a passenger who doesn't want to go to New York. We have a situation developing here that is probably going to end up in a hijacking. At least one Flight Attendant has been taken hostage." He paused and went on, "They have not breached the cockpit. Yet.

"No comment from Don, and no immediate comment from the FAA Air Route Traffic Control Center in Cleveland.

Fred continued, "We don't know where they want to go. Earlier, they mentioned Havana to one of the cabin team."

"Roger. Roger, 100."

Almost in slow motion, Fred hung up the microphone, looked at Don, tipped his head, raised his shoulders until they were level with his ears and pressed his lips into a dry and laconic smile.

The unseen Cleveland Center controller replied, "100. Sorry for the delay. We understand. Are you requesting any special handling at this time?"

Fred picked up the microphone and looked at Don for guidance. Don turned his head left and right. "Negative. Nothing at this time."

Fred glanced over at Don for any direction or comment. None came forth, so he said, "Our plan is to continue to New York, as filed. If that changes, we'll let you know."

"Do you want to use any special radio frequencies? Do you want to declare an emergency at this time?"

This time, Fred did not wait for a cue from Don. Quietly, he broadcast, "No. Nope. So far, this is advisory only."

51

**17:30 Eastern Standard Time
Overhead Morgantown, West Virginia**

"Understand 100." Another metallic pause, then, "You just checked in my sector about 40 miles back and should be with me for the next 80 or 90 miles before hand you off to the next controller."

The distant metallic voice paused, then said, "If you need anything, we're standing by. Also, 100, we'll alert the company, FAA and FBI about the threat."

Don picked up the microphone, "This is the Captain. For the moment, the situation is marginal – probably going to become critical. We wanted to take advantage of our current ability to talk in the open. To let you know what is going on."

The almost mechanical voice of the controller said, "Rog, 100. We're with you. Good luck."

Stan Kurtz listened to the conversation with ATC. He felt some small measure of comfort in the knowledge that hundreds of people stood by to help them. Unfortunately, despite their good intentions, they were not able to disarm the hijacker or safely put the aircraft back on the ground.

52

**17:50 Eastern Standard Time
South of Morgantown, West Virginia**

The SELCAL chimes warbled again. Stan silenced the tone, picked up the microphone, selected number two VHF transceiver and said, "100 answering SELCAL. Go ahead."

A German accented voice responded, "100. This is Flight Dispatch. We need some information from you if you are able to give it to us at this time."

"Dispatch. Standby one for the Captain."

Stan looked and saw the Captain deeply reviewing his Jeppesen manual. He didn't want to disturb him, though the SELCAL from company dispatch was important. Stan interrupted Don's concentration and said, "Don, Dispatch is on number two and wants some information from us. Do you want to talk to them, or what?"

Don never looked back at Stan, but said, "Tell them the same thing we told ATC. We have an on going situation. We don't know where we are ultimately going to end up."

He waited and then said, "Tell them we'll keep them advised."

All Stan could manage was, "Roger."

And, tell them not to initiate any more calls to us unless it's an emergency. We have enough to worry about without those God damned chimes going off all the time."

Fred smiled at Don's displeasure with the interruption from the company.

Stan considered the Captain's irritation as he said, "Dispatch, we have no real news. The hijacker has taken one of the cabin crew hostage."

No response from Dispatch.

"He may be armed with a gun. We have not spoken to him directly. We know he's outside the cockpit door. He has taken at least one, or more, cabin crew hostage at this time."

VHF radios are fairly quiet, but the combined background 400 cycle hum, static, cockpit wind noise, plus Fiedling's accent made it difficult for Stan to understand his next comment, "100, from zis end, it looks like da hijacker's name is Guerrero, initial B."

Kurtz wondered why the company was telling them the hijacker's name. "Makes no sense," he thought.

"Okay. We got that, Dispatch. We'll keep you posted as things devel..."

Far to Stan's right, in the periphery of his vision, he saw something move, "Don, I don't know how much more abuse this door can take."

The Captain said nothing. He looked over his shoulder as the door was slowly being destroyed by the hijacker.

It was the mirror of the back of the cockpit door that Stan had seen move.

He helplessly watched the door's rotation. The plywood door deflected and then started to fail as Carlton was once again slammed into it by the increasingly angry hijacker.

53

**17:55 Eastern Standard Time
South of Morgantown, West Virginia**

Stan still had his microphone poised near his mouth, but did not speak. He froze as he looked, transfixed, at the flimsy cockpit door. He could see light from the upper deck galley and cabin through the gapping and deformed void at the top and bottom of the door.

The only thing that kept the door closed was the thin, badly bent aluminum dead bolt. He watched the cockpit door flex one last time as the hijacker slammed Carlton into the door. The deadbolt gave way.

"Shit," Was all he had time to think or say.

The deadbolt failed completely and showered Stan with bits of plywood and sharp metal fragments from the doorframe.

Other pieces of aircraft hardware that had been designed to keep the cockpit safe from intruders came raining down on Stan. The cockpit filled with the smell of freshly cut plywood. Fine particles of dust mixed with larger chunks of wood, pieces of Formica, plastic and rubber rained down on Stan. Some of the pieces hit Fred's back.

The sound of the door being breached caused Don to again snap his head around. He looked over Stan's shoulder just as Carlton and Bill violently tumbled and fell into the cockpit.

Carlton looked terrified. He had been badly beaten. He looked like a wet rag-doll as he tried to resist the hijacker. The door banged against the stops and harshly bounced back against Carlton, who had slumped on the floor in an ungracious heap. He wriggled and tried to crawl away, but the hijacker kicked him and then viciously stepped on his calf, securing him to one spot on the floor.

Fred looked away from the unfolding drama at the rear of the cockpit and became intensely interested in his flight instruments, clock, altimeter, Horizontal Situation Indicator. Anything that would keep him from seeing and focusing on the events that had just happened in the past thirty seconds.

Fred, like every other experienced airline pilot, knew the primary rule of aviation survival was, "Fly the Airplane First." Untold accidents and multiple deaths had happened because the pilots forgot this rule. The old and proven axiom for aviation survival was true, 'Aviate. Navigate. Communicate.' Right now.

Especially now, that was ever-present in Fred's mind.

Fly the airplane.

Keep it in the air.

Keep it safe.

The hijacker looked around the cockpit and was surprised by its small size. He wrongly thought an airplane the size of a 747 would have an enormous place for the pilots. In reality, he saw the three pilots were tightly bunched together into the narrowing and wedged-shaped horizontal pyramid. There was a sloping ceiling and little excess room anywhere except a narrow walkway behind the Flight Engineer's panel, to the cockpit emergency exit door.

The hijacker waved the pistol toward Carlton and then toward Don. "I want to go to Habana. I want to go to Cuba. Take me to Cuba."

54

**18:05 Eastern Standard Time
South of Morgantown, West Virginia**

He spoke with a strong Spanish accent. His voice was stressed. His voice was a tension-induced falsetto. It sounded like he was mentally stretched beyond his ability to control himself or the situation. He seemed to emphasize each syllable with a downward stroke of his pistol, an arc that covered Don's back and Carlton.

Don tried to sound calm and at the same time authoritative as he said, "Listen, my friend. We'll take you anywhere you want to go. You don't need to threaten us, or try to hurt us. Remember, without us you're not going anywhere but down. You're dead."

Fred muttered under his breath, "Straight down."

Sweat stood out on the hijacker's forehead, "You the pilot?"

"Yes. I am the Captain."

Don nodded toward Fred, "This is my First Officer," then looked back at Stan, who was still holding the microphone in his left hand and said, "this is my Second Officer."

Guerrero looked at each of the pilots and thought, "*Caramba!* I never knew it took three pilots to fly the plane."

Don spoke. His voice inflexible and very tight. "If you want to go to Havana, that's okay with us. But, we have to prepare. We have to make changes if our flight is going to Havana instead of New York." He waited a second. "Is that what you want to do? Is that where you want to go?"

The hijacker was confused by how easy this was, "Yes. That is want I want."

A questioning pause, then, "I want to go to Habana."

Don looked past the hijacker, through the broken cockpit doorframe, into the upper deck lounge and saw the faces of several frightened passengers.

One of the passengers was a nun, in her black habit. She leaned out in the aisle and looked directly into the cockpit. Both of her hands were busy as she frantically ran her rosary beads through her fingers. Involuntarily, her lips moved in a silent prayer.

Don looked up toward the hijacker, but said to both Bill and Stan, "Close the door." As he asked, he realized there was little left of the door to close.

"My passengers don't need to watch this. Your gun. The rough treatment of my crew. That's frightening them."

Bill thought there was nothing wrong with the pilot's request and slammed the cockpit door. The forced entry had deformed the door and it would not stay closed. The locking mechanism had been divided into many parts, some attached to the bulkhead, others strewn about the cockpit floor.

Don looked back and forth between at the hijacker and his pistol. He quickly saw the gun was made from plastic. He was not sure the pistol was real.

Don thought this would be a good time to try and see how serious the hijacker was and asked, "Since we are going to do as you wish, will you put your gun away?" He added, "There is no need for that."

Immediately Bill knew why the Captain was being so nice. He wanted the gun. Once the pilot had the gun he would not go to Havana. The hijacking would be over and he would go to jail.

Bill leveled the gun directly at Don and pointed the barrel at a spot just above the bridge of his nose. Don reflexively flinched and blinked as he looked down the barrel of the nine millimeter pistol less than 15 inches from his face.

Bill raised his voice much louder and snapped, "Hey, *Hijo*, I decide about the gun." His face a contorted mixture of fear and rage, "I'm the one who says what goes."

Don's initial reaction was to argue about who was in charge. He was the captain. Captains have the ultimate authority. They made the final decision. But he realized the hijacker didn't know or care about Captain's authority. He could only say, "Whatever you say." The hijacker said nothing.

Bill finally spoke and moved the gun slightly. Bright sunlight reflected on the dull grey barrel. Don clearly saw more detail of the gun and sadly accepted the fact that the gun was not a toy. It was real.

Fred took a chance. He looked over the hijacker, "Hey man, look. We don't want to have anything happen to us, or to you. That gun makes me nervous and when I get nervous, I don't fly very well. I promise. No tricks. Whatever you say goes. You're the boss."

Don added, "He's right. No tricks. You just tell us what you want and where you want to go. We'll do it for you. We'll get you there."

Don paused and waited to catch his breath, "The only thing we have to do is make sure we have enough fuel to get to Havana. And, that the weather in Havana is acceptable for our landing."

Stan realized that he still had the microphone in his hand and felt completely embarrassed. He released the microphone key, thereby cutting the open line of communication between Flight 100 and Flight Dispatch. Though not certain, Stan thought the entire cockpit conversation over the past several minutes had been broadcast to the company.

55

18:05 Eastern Standard Time
North of Roanoke, Virginia

The Captain made Bill feel uneasy. He didn't like the way he looked directly at him. The other pilot, the one by the other window, seemed okay.

Don thought the tension had diminished somewhat. He took a deep breath, counted several beats then and said, "If we are going to go to Havana, my crew and I have to discuss how we are going to get there."

He looked directly at the hijacker for a response. None came. No approval or disapproval. Bill stoically stood behind Don with his foot pressed down on Carlton's leg.

Don didn't know how to proceed. He didn't want to antagonize the hijacker. At the same time, he knew he had to regain and then maintain his command and control of the 747.

Not wanting to upset the hijacker more than he already was, Don blandly said, "We need to notify the traffic controllers and the company that we are not going to New York. I need to find about the weather in Cuba. We don't have an unlimited amount of fuel. We need to determine if we have enough to get to Havana. I need to start on these things right away."

Bill guessed this was probably another trick and said in a tight voice, "Never mind that shit, man."

Don realized he had made a serious error. The hijacker had no comprehension or understanding of what Don had just said.

"Listen, you say you are like the boss, *"El Jeffe"*. You got enough gasoline to go to New York. Then, *Hijo* you got enough to go to Havana. Bill was proud of himself. These *"Gringos"* weren't going to fool him There was nothing to say in response. Don, Fred and Stan could only wait for the hijacker's next comment or move. "Just fly this fucker to Cuba. You're the Captain." Bill added in a grating and sarcastic voice, "You can make it happen. You're the man. Like do it, dude."

For emphasis, the hijacker waved the pistol in a loose and irregular arc. When he waved the gun toward right side of the aircraft, Fred involuntarily flinched and ducked. Fred's thumb hit the autopilot disconnect switch on the yoke on his control column.

The autopilot Altitude Hold disengaged. A tenth of a second later, the autopilot did the same thing. These events were programmed to set off aural warnings in the cockpit. When the auto pilot disconnected, all auto flight inputs were simultaneously cancelled. Even though the autopilot was no longer flying the aircraft, her mass and inertia initially kept her level and on course. The sudden cancellation of trim inputs to the primary flight controls caused the aircraft to experience a slight jolt in the pitch axis. It felt similar to hitting a speed bump too fast. This insignificant pitch oscillation scared Bill. He was frightened by the loud and piercing wailer. He had no idea where the sound came from or what it meant.

His response was not surprising. "What the hell is that? What just happened?" He added, "Are you trying to trick me? 'Cause if you are, I'll know about it." Bill's logic was seriously flawed.

All three pilots reacted in a similar fashion. They knew the wailer was simply an alert. It was a low-level warning to tell them one, or both, of the ship's autopilots had disconnected. Don pressed the autopilot disconnect button on his yoke and the wailer immediately stopped.

Automatically, and without even thinking about the hijacker, Don reached up to the center control panel on the glare shield to re-engage the autopilot.

The aftermath of the unexpected jolt coupled with the warbling autopilot wailer destroyed Bill's ability to think clearly.

He was terrified. His voice was loud and very sharp, "Stop."

He waived the handgun, "What're you doing?" He blinked, "You are trying to trick me."

Again, he leveled the gun at the back of Don's head and said, "Listen, fucker. You don't do nothin' without you tell me first."

Don's hand stopped in midway between the "A" autopilot toggle switch and the throttles. He could feel the anger rising as he looked back at the gun in the young hijacker's dark hand.

He churned with anger. "Listen, pal. I'm responsible for the lives of those folks in the back of the airplane and I'm responsible for the lives of my crew and the safety of this flight. Hell, I'm even responsible for your safety."

The hijacker said nothing. His stare roamed between Don and Fred.

Don continued, "I'm not going to do anything that will jeopardize my responsibility." Not pausing, "I'm not going to do anything unsafe."

Fred looked at the hijacker as Don continued, "I don't have time to tell you everything that I am going to do before I do it."

He paused and then asked the hijacker, "Do you know anything about airplanes?"

The hijacker remained silent. He could not admit that knew nothing about airplanes. That would be weak and weaklings end up in prison.

A different warning sounded. The aircraft was no longer being held at a precise altitude of thirty three thousand feet. It had drifted down more than one hundred feet, which triggered a new and different warning.

Fred ingeniously said, "Captain, I need to bring the aircraft back up to our altitude." He looked at Bill, "I'm going to move the controls and silence the altitude alert. Is that ok with you?"

Bill had no understanding of what was happening all around him. He realized he knew nothing about anything in the cockpit. He could only rely on his instinct and *machismo*.

Fred asked again, "Well? I have to bring the airplane back on altitude. If I don't we could hit another aircraft below us."

Bill looked out the window and saw nothing but blue sky and a few cirrus clouds. He paused and said, "Ok. But no bullshit ideas or tricks."

Fred looked at Don and hit the autopilot disconnect button, then re-armed the altitude alert. The audible warnings stopped. Fred gently added a bit of nose-up trim and the altimeter slowly reflected the aircraft's slow and steady climb back to FL330. When the cruise altitude was reached another chime sounded. Fred started to reach for the "A" autopilot paddle switch. He paused and looked over his shoulder and then slowly engaged the "A" autopilot and Altitude Hold. The small green light again confirmed the autopilot was satisfied with its ability to hold the aircraft at the selected altitude.

Fred felt a small amount of progress had been somehow accomplished. Unfortunately, Don broke the mood.

56

18:20 Eastern Standard Time
South of Roanoke, Virginia

To Bill, Don said, "Well, you're the one who came up with this idea." He turned in his seat to face Bill, "We will help you. But you have to let us fly this plane. We need to do what needs to be done. We need to be able to fly it without any interference from you."

He waited for the hijacker to respond. He didn't. "Do you understand?"

With courage he didn't have or feel, Don intentionally and purposefully selected a navigation mode for horizontal guidance. The aircraft made a slight roll to the left and then corrected itself, before turning even less to the right.

To the hijacker, standing in the cockpit, it looked like the aircraft were going to tip over or drop down again. "Another trick," he thought.

The hijacker remained motionless and stood there in complete silence. With one foot on the floor and the other on Carlton's leg, he considered what Don had said in the past ten seconds.

Carlton moved slightly, looked up at the hijacker and said, "For

God's sake. Listen to him. He's the Captain. He knows what he is doing. He will get us wherever you want to go."

Don took advantage of the hijacker's silence as a sign of agreement and continued with his impromptu flying lesson. "There are other aircraft in this same area. We can't just start flying to Cuba."

Don knew this was not true. Any distressed aircraft is given exceptional priority over all other aircraft in the area. He hoped the hijacker didn't know anything about flying. He continued, "We have to coordinate our plans with the flights of the other airplanes around us."

Momentarily, he looked down at the radio controls center pedestal. "I'm going to call the controllers and tell them that you,..er that we, want to go to Havana." The three pilots and Carlton waited for a response from Bill. He said nothing.

Bill felt a sudden rolling fear when the word 'Havana' was said by the pilot. He didn't know what to do; so, he did nothing. Things were happening too fast for him. He was in a world of which he knew nothing.

The hijacker made no attempt to stop Don, but threatened. "No tricks. Do anything funny and I start shooting."

Don turned to Fred, "Fly the airplane for a minute, while I call Cleveland. Hold the same heading and altitude." He turned to Stan, "Keep the same airspeed."

Fred looked at Don with some confusion. Up until now, Don had been doing all of the flying on this trip and Fred had done the "Pilot Not Flying" duties. Now, everything changed. Without comment, Fred put his hands on the yoke and looked out the windshield, wishing he were anywhere but here, covering the ground at 8 miles per minute. He said, "My airplane." Meaning he was now flying.

Don acknowledged, "Your airplane."

With a very dry mouth, Don called the controllers on the ground, "Cleveland Center. 100."

Immediately, a new voice responded, "100. Yes sir. This is

Cleveland. Go ahead."

"Cleveland Center. He's in the cockpit and wants to go to Havana. We are equipped with three Inertial Nav platforms. We'd like to go Havana. We are requesting a direct heading to Havana at Flight Level 330."

All three pilots wore their earphones and heard the Center.

"Roger, 100. Understand. We'll start on a clearance for you. For the time being, turn right to a heading of 210°, maintain 370."

Fred grabbed the microphone, "Cleveland, we're at 330, not 370."

The embarrassed controller said, "Roger that. 100. My mistake. We confirm you are at Flight Level 330, not 370. Please ident."

Fred clicked the microphone twice, the standard response. Don pressed the Identification button on the transponder panel.

Thinking and reacting, Fred picked up his microphone and said, "100 Roger. We're level at 330."

Don resumed control of the aircraft, "My airplane." Fred responded, "Your aircraft."

Don thought, "Maybe. This might just work out. Or, maybe not."

57

18:35 Eastern Standard Time
Overhead Virginia / Georgia Border

The roll-rate of the autopilot is a function of the number of degrees of change selected on the heading command and the rate with which the heading selector is turned. Unfortunately, Don spun the heading selector quickly, calling for a 90° turn to he right. Immediately, all three INS platforms compared and then recalculated the aircrafts course error with regard to the original flight plan instructions. Now, the aircraft was told to fly a different specific magnetic heading.

The nose of lumbering 747 initially remained fixed on an imaginary point, while the fuselage rapidly rolled into a thirty degree bank to the right. Everyone in the airplane felt heavier and could not help being aware something was happening. Their community thought was, "Something was out of the ordinary. Something is happening that is not normal."

When the aircraft fuselage rolled to the right, the nose made a dead level arc across the sky. The two flux gate compasses, one near each wing tip, sensed the 747's heading and sent continuous signals to the autopilot/flight director computers. The aircraft gently rolled out on a heading of exactly 200°. The 80° turn had taken exactly 25 seconds.

Fred looked over at Don and said, "The assigned heading was 210 Don, not 200."

Don growled something about being under a lot of pressure, but readjusted the heading selector to 210°. The aircraft rolled into a very shallow 5° bank to a new heading and then rolled wings level.

The Captain looked at the Cross Track Error readout on the number one INS platform. In the past thirty seconds at seven miles per minute, the aircraft had flown four miles south of its intended course to New York.

He thought to himself, "Every 30 seconds we move further from New York and closer to Havana.

His mind wondered. "What will Kathryn think if I don't call her. Will she think he had been a no-show? Or, might she think he had found someone else? Or, even worse, would she not even be concerned if he didn't show up or call?"

"What do you think about pulling the power back to conserve fuel?"

Don's thoughts about Kathryn precluded him from hearing what Stan had said. "Sorry, Stan. What did you say?"

Stan started to repeat himself when Fred added, "Great idea. What is the target airspeed for Long Range Cruise?"

"Just a minute." Stan flipped open a notebook and said, "LRC would add some time to our flight, but would save us about 5,500 pounds of fuel each hour we're in the air."

Fred laughed, "Stan, you have such a way with words."

Don looked over his shoulder at Stan and Fred and said, "Stan pull 'em back to LRC. I assume we're too heavy for Max Range Cruise?"

"We could go to MRC, but the savings are minimal over LRC and at this weight, the airplane would be very sloppy."

Without further conversation, Stan reached up and pulled each engine throttle back about fifteen percent. The aircraft slowed and the nose came up as the autopilot held their assigned altitude of thirty three thousand feet. After several minutes, the aircraft's ground speed had been reduced by well over 100 knots.

The wind noise in the cockpit kept the hijacker from hearing much of what was being said on the radio. Through an overhead speaker, Bill heard something about this flight, "100. This is Cleveland, go ahead."

After that, he didn't care. The Captain said something into a microphone and then reached up and moved a knob, but nothing happened. He turned another knob and the airplane turned hard. He could see the ground directly out the other pilot's window. It looked like he could see straight down. Just as suddenly, the earth stopped rotating. While the airplane was turning, Bill felt very heavy and nearly stumbled when Carlton moved again.

The other pilot said something, the captain moved the same knob and the airplane turned but not as steeply. He was frightened when the airplane tilted. When he looked out the side window, he felt like he was falling.

Don turned in his seat and looked back at the hijacker, "We're on our way to Havana."

Bill had no understanding of the significance of what the pilot had just said.

"The people on the ground are going to clear a path for us and move other aircraft that might be in conflict with us." Bill was unable to comprehend what was happening around him.

Carlton, lay on his side and stomach. His cheek was pressed against the harsh rubber cockpit flooring. There was a patch of dried blood on the side of his head.

No one spoke for several seconds. The silence was broken by the interphone chimes. Don took the phone off the hook and answered, "This is the Captain."

"Captain, this is Patti. Almost all of the passengers have been moved into coach."

"Keep them in their seats with their seat belts on." The

interphone was silent.

He continued, "He wants to go to Havana. So, we've turned south. Patti, do not say anything to the passengers." Almost as an afterthought, "I'll make an announcement."

"Are all of you alright? I mean he seemed so crazy, the way he was acting and then how he beat on Carlton."

Don tried to ignore how Carlton looked as he lay on the floor, "Yes, we are all fine." In a conspirator's tone, "Stay in First Class. I want to know where you are, if I need you."

Don looked at the hijacker, but he didn't seem too concerned about a conversation he could not hear. He said, "Patti, hang on a minute."

He could hear her take in a sharp breath, "Yes, what is it?"

"Just a minute,"

Don looked at Carlton, and at the hijacker. Next he looked at the cockpit door that had again swung open during the heading change.

He said to Patti, "I want you to move the passengers on the upper deck to any available seats down below. Away from First Class. Put them anywhere but First Class. If things get out of hand, I don't want them sitting underneath the cockpit floor."

Both Fred and Stan thought this was an excellent idea no one from the training center or the security folks would ever have thought about. Stan nodded in appreciation.

Bill looked at Don and slowly understood what was about to happen.

"No. Leave them people up here."

Don was not discouraged and continued, "Well, I want to get some help for him," his thumb pointed toward Carlton. "He looks terrible. I want one of the flight attendants to take a look at his head."

Carlton heard some of this conversation and thought he might get out of this alive. He drew from some small reservoir of inner strength and raised his head then looked pleadingly at Don.

Don looked at the poor pathetic hostage, "Do you think you're able to walk down to the main cabin for some medical attention?"

Before Carlton could answer, the hijacker increased the pressure against Carlton's leg and made him gasp with the pain.

"He stays here."

Don was silent.

He continued, "He don't look that bad to me. I could have messed him up real bad. He got off way easy, man." Don had not expected this. He did not want a flight attendant held hostage at the hijacker's disposal, especially in the cockpit. Carlton heard the conversation and his hopes for rescue and survival were crushed.

Don's thoughts were disrupted by Patti's voice on the hand held interphone. "Captain, are you still there?"

"Sorry. Things are not okay here. I tried to get some help for Carlton. But the answer for now is no."

Don lowered his voice and said, "Tell all the flight attendants to stay on the lower deck, unless I specifically tell them to come up here."

"Do you want me to have the upper deck passengers moved down here?"

"I'd love for you to do that. But the hijacker has said no deal."

She added, "Maybe he'll change his mind. Oh, and Amelio says he has organized the passengers in Coach to make room for the First Class passengers. Some of them will have to sit on the Flight Attendant Jump Seats."

"That's good. Take good care of your passengers. We're going to be busy. Remember to leave the First Class handset off hook. Don't call us unless it's an emergency. If I want to talk to you, I'll use the emergency chimes in the cabin or make a PA announcement."

"Okay, Captain," Patti felt herself on the verge of crying as she said, "Good luck, sir."

Don heard her voice crack, "And...and, God bless you." Then in a very timid and scared voice she asked, "Are we going to be alright? I mean really really alright?"

Don tried to sound convincing and positive, but was unsuccessful, "No problem. Everything is going to be fine."

Fred and Stan did not share Don's optimism, real or imagined.

58

18:40 Eastern Standard Time
John F. Kennedy International Airport

Typically, the tedium of routine operations in Flight Dispatch was predictable, with one hundred fifty daily flights being dispatched and monitored. The only time the routine activity level increased was when the weather created diversions at several adjacent airports around the airline system.

After Lazlo Fielding's radio call with Flight 100 that a hijacking was in progress, the activity had increased noticeably.

Each airline had its own codified policy to be followed in the event of an incident, accident, hijack, sabotage, bomb or extortion threat. The reading was incredibly dry, outlining specific recommendations regarding lines of authority, areas of influence and down to prepared statements for the media.

Nowhere in the policy manual did it state how the flights crews were to be assisted. Assistance was presumed, but not expressed. Nowhere did the manual state what efforts were to be taken to make the hijack go as smoothly as possible.

In the 70s and 80s, many airlines had their fair share of hijackings.

From these experiences, some airlines learned and benefitted; while others elected to forget these events, most likely in the hope the problems and threats would go away.

Unfortunately, Flight 100's airline hijacking control and management protocols were not well defined. The company had not even designated or appointed a 'GO Team' to be used in situations like this.

The policy manual simply said, "Every attempt should be made to keep the hijacked aircraft on the ground. In the event that is not possible, every attempt should be made to land the aircraft as soon as possible." This was the extent of the official policy.

The current corporate philosophy seemed to suggest that with all the new security measures in place, the likelihood of a potential or actual hijacking is almost non-existent.

The office of general counsel for many airlines were perpetually concerned that any overt preparation for a hijacking, in terms of policy statements, could easily be interpreted in some courts as evidence the corporation knew of the likelihood of hijacking, but had not put adequate procedures in place. Should that legal theory be affirmed and upheld, hundreds of millions of dollars in liability claims could be expected.

Additionally, an absence of specific written hijacking protocols might be affirmed by the courts that the corporation believed the risk of a hijacking was so low, no policies were necessary or warranted. If that legal theory were followed, then direct liability might not be found against the airline, but completely placed on the shoulders of the hijacker, law enforcement and federal agencies.

In legal-speak, the airline was saying, "We don't believe there is any risk of a terrorist or hijacking attack. If a hijacking were to take place, the entire liability for that act, in fact, rests solely with the hijacker, not the airline."

This magical thinking, unfortunately, was common in many corporate general counsel offices throughout the airline community. Only a handful of air carriers had extensive protocols in place, each to be fully implanted the moment the threat of a hijacking was deemed credible.

Ultimately, all final operational decisions rested solely on the shoulders of the captain of the hijacked aircraft. Predictably, some of the strongest airline anti-terrorist policies were with air carriers that had extensive aerial piracy experience; TWA, El Al, Lufthansa and Pan American World Airways being prime examples.

Fielding placed another call to John Batchelor. He received no answer. The New York switchboard operator at corporate said she would try to reach him at home and then asked if Fielding wished to leave a message. He told her to tell Batchelor one of their aircraft had been hijacked, adding this hijacker might be the same passenger John Batchelor was waiting to arrest when 100 arrived at JFK.

Next, Fielding told Becky to run several computer model flight plans for 100 from its present position near Pittsburgh to Havana. He asked her to plug in block altitudes from Flight Level 330 to 390, all at Long Range Cruise and/or Max Range Cruise. Fielding knew fuel conservation and operational safety were inexorably linked.

After several minutes, Becky handed him the new flight plans. The first thing he looked at was fuel burn from present position to destination and frowned. The computer models included take off, climb, cruise, descent, approach and landing. Not Becky's fault. The computer simulations were inaccurate because 100 was at cruise altitude. Fielding estimated that ten thousand pounds of fuel could be saved or subtracted from any of these computer models, a significant benefit in planning the remainder of 100's flight.

He subtracted that fuel burn from the original fuel release and estimated 100 had about seventy thousand pounds on board overhead Pittsburgh. If everything went according to plan, 100 would arrive in Havana with less than sixteen thousand pounds of fuel.

Fielding wanted to call 100 and give them the computer model numbers he had generated. However, he remembered the Captain's specific words about not bothering them unless it was an emergency. He called the Flight Operations duty officer to tell him the critical fuel situation regarding 100's planned arrival fuel in Havana.

The duty officer's response floored Fielding, "Really not our problem. That's why we pay those Captains all the big money. Let him figure it out. He's a big boy."

Fielding was stunned and didn't have any argument to bring forth. "Stay with the flight until this is over. We have over a hundred other flights that need our attention. If you are sidetracked by Flight 100, get someone else to manage your other flights." After a pause, the duty officer said, "What the hell are we to do? We don't have air-to-air refueling capability. The flight crew is going to have to handle this one on their own."

Lazlo slammed his coffee cup down, spilling most of the contents on his desk.

He grumbled, "Dis duty manager iz a trow-back to da piston days. Been around for more than 35 years." Perplexed, he added, "Vut am I to do?"

Frustrated, Fielding thought of many possible options, but felt professionally constrained because of the direct order from the duty officer. In the same conversations, the duty officer had told Fielding he wanted him to remain at the airport until the hijack was concluded. Yet, at the same time, he was essentially told not to do anything to help. This was very confusing to him.

Becky came back and stood behind Fielding's desk. "What is going on?"

"We have a 747 with a nut job who wants to go to Havana. I think he has taken a Flight Attendant hostage and could be armed. The Captain told us unless it's an emergency, we mustn't call da flight on der radio. My boss is no help and I can't get anyone else to help me or the crew."

As he considered the weather and looked at the maps, he hoped 100 was on the east side of the weather, so that if they did go to Havana they would at least have a tail wind part of the way and extend their range as they flew south.

Although, while the winds might be more favorable, 100 would, at some point, have to penetrate a line of weather where these two air masses met.

It seemed to Fielding, if 100 had to do much deviating around weather, they could easily burn through their very limited reserves. Without being aware, he muttered a damning epithet in German about the entire situation.

Fielding picked up the telephone, but then put it down. He waited, and then picked it up again, but paused. With a sigh of resignation, he replaced the phone in the cradle. He looked around his desk for his cigarettes, but could find none. He patted his shirt pocket. Empty.

Again he picked up the telephone, paused several seconds. He knew the chain of command. He also knew what the consequences would most likely would happen if he went over the head of the duty officer.

Slowly, he came to the realization there was no real choice to be made. He was going to willfully disregard his immediate supervisor's instructions. For that, he certainly could be castigated, probably reprimanded, or perhaps, even terminated. To him, none of that mattered. There was a flight in trouble, and he had information which might be helpful to the pilots and passengers on 100. With Germanic stubbornness he said to his computer screen, "To hell wit da office politics around here. We're going to help 100 any way possible."

59

18:50 Eastern Standard Time
John F. Kennedy International Airport

He held the phone under his chin and turned the desktop Rolodex to the number he wanted. He took a deep breath and dialed. There was no answer. He called again and let the phone rang over twenty times. Still, there was no answer.

Lazlo flipped through the index with his nicotine-stained finger until he found another number and quickly dialed. The phone rang three times and an authoritative female voice said, "Federal Aviation Administration, Anti-Terrorist Unit."

Frankfurt Lazlo Fielding looked into the duty officer's cubicle across the room and could only see the back of his manager's head. The voice on the other end of the phone repeated the greeting, "This is the FAA Anti-Terrorist Unit. May I help you?"

Lazlo took a deep breath, coughed and said, "This is Lazlo Fielding, Senior Dispatcher with..." His voice was stopped by a heaving cough. Slowly, he continued, "One of our aircraft, Flight 100 has been hijacked. We think probably to Cuba. We were in contact with the flight before the hijack started. Apparently, there has been a demand to go to Havana. We believe the hijacker is armed and that he has taken at least one cabin attendant hostage. We also. . .

The southern-accented female voice said, "Whoa. Whoa there, Sir. Wait just a minute. Let me get this down and then I'll transfer you to the duty officer. Now, who are you and where is the aircraft?"

Lazlo's irritation made him speak very slowly, but with intensity. He felt as though he were surrounded by assassins. His German accent thickened as he said, "I am the senior dispatcher at Kennedy. I dispatched 100 from San Francisco to New York this morning." He paused, then added, "Boeing 747-200."

"About 30 or 35 minutes ago, we believe our flight was hijacked. Our best calculated guess is the aircraft is overhead Pittsburgh. We don't know the exact location for certain."

"What was, or is, the aircraft type?"

"As I said before, a Boeing 747-200."

"Sorry, sir."

"Country of Origin or Registration?"

Fielding ran out of patience. He responded with a thick German accent, "Da United States of America."

"Souls on Board?" In every emergency, the FAA invariably wanted to know the number of passengers and crew on board. Pilots through the years had sparked the FAA's ire by refusing to answer the question. The refusal was not because of the content of the question, but because of its untimeliness.

Lazlo exploded, "I do not know. I can find out. Is it critical that you know that information right this second?"

The unidentified southern accent said, "Yes Sir. I'll wait."

Lazlo swore under his breath. He held the phone under his chin and swiveled his chair to the computer. He pressed a series of cryptically coded stokes and the screen filled with rows of numbers.

Fielding spoke, "Vell, zis aircraft configuration iz four hundred und fifty six and they left San Francisco mit four hundred und seventeen. Plus da crew of fourteen. Dat iss eleven in da cabin and the cockpit crew iss mit three pilots."

"I believe I've got that, sir. Just a moment while I put you through."

While he waited, he could hear static and echo on the line. He watched the second hand on the wall clock across the room make four full rotations around the dial face.

"Mr. Fielding. Ed James here. How can the FAA help you today?"

"As I explained, one of our flights has been hijacked."

"You probably aren't going to like this, sir. But I'm going to have to ask you some questions. You know, before we can get to the meat of the problem."

He could not believe his ears. Here a flight with nearly four hundred and fifty people has been hijacked and he wants to ask questions. *Mein Gott im Himmel!*

"First, what is your name and your FAA Dispatcher's license number. And sir, is your FAA Medical certificate up to date."

He exploded and his accent became so thick even he had trouble understanding himself, "My name is Fielding. Lazlo Fielding. I'm the Senior Dispatcher here at Kennedy. I have been doing this job for the past thirty-four years."

He added, "Even before there was an FAA."

He took several deep raspy breaths, "One of our flights has been hijacked. I am not going to waste time mit your questions."

"Sir."

"There will be plenty of time when this is concluded to answer your stupid questions." In his fury, he pronounced the last two words with an even thicker German accent, "Schtoopid qvestions."

James was taken back by Lazlo's reaction and immediately felt that the dispatcher's anger was directed at him. James was correct. Fielding was not in the mood to wander through an unfathomable and bureaucratic mine field in the middle of a crisis.

Lazlo found an opened pack of cigarettes in his bottom desk drawer, took one, lit it. He became more settled. "I need your assistance and I need it now. There will be plenty of time to answer all the questions after this hijack has ended."

"Mr. Fielding, we must have these statistics for our records. We need to know how many souls are on board. We will also need to obtain pertinent information regarding the flight crew. I can wait until later for the information regarding your dispatcher certificate and FAA medical status."

Fielding rolled his eyes and again said, *"Mein Gott im Himmel"* to himself.

"If you insist on being uncooperative, you could be placing your dispatcher's license in jeopardy."

He tried, unsuccessfully, to stifle the anger he felt toward this federal idiot, "I don't give a damn about my license. Right now, my only concern is helping our flight that has been hijacked." He was yelling into the phone. "I am not going to waste valuable time with your Gestapo tactics. You don't seem to be able to help me. I want to speak to your supervisor."

James thought, "These airline types are all the same. If they don't get what they want they start threatening."

He had dealt with this before and would not be intimidated by this foreigner, "Very well, Mr. Fielding, I will transfer you to my supervisor. But you have not heard the last of this section and branch of the FAA. We expect you to cooperate with us and if you don't there will be severe consequences."

Lazlo became angrier with each word he heard from this *"schwachsinnige"* half-witted federal employee, "Do what you must, but let me talk to your supervisor immediately. Vat iz hiz name?"

"Very well. His name is Special Agent Clifton. Mr. Richard Clifton. I'll see if he's available." The line went dead after two or three ominous clicks.

Lazlo was on hold for what seemed like a long time. Again, he watched the second hand on the Greenwich Mean Time wall clock complete many revolutions around the dial.

No one returned, or came back on the line to ask if he was being helped. No one seemed to care about the hijacking, the passengers, the crew, or Fielding.

The reason Fielding had to wait so long was that Special Agent Clifton had been talking to John Batchelor.

60

**18:55 Eastern Standard Time
John F. Kennedy International Airport**

Fielding's mood had gone from frustration, to anger, to fury, to resignation and then finally back to irritation. He turned on his speakerphone and replaced the handset in the cradle.

When he heard a man's voice on the speaker he was startled, "Dick Clifton here. How can I help you?"

"I am a dispatcher with..."

"Yes sir. I just got off the phone with John Batchelor. He called to tell me about the hijacking. Is there any information you want to add that might assist us?"

Lazlo was taken back by the friendly and helpful attitude of Clifton, "I have all the specifics of the flight. I spoke with the Captain about 35 or 40 minutes ago. Where do you want to start?"

"First and foremost. Is the flight in any immediate peril? Do you know what the status is on board?"

Lazlo realized that he was all alone; out on the point. He had thrust himself directly in the middle of this situation and expected that his boss was not going to be pleased. He didn't care. Right now, all that mattered to him was the safe conclusion to Flight 100's hijacking.

"I don't know about the specific situation at this moment. When I last spoke with the crew, they told me the hijacker had taken a Flight Attendant hostage and gained access to the cockpit. They had a stuck microphone and I could hear some of the actual take over."

"What do you know about their fuel situation? How much time, in terms of fuel, do they have left?"

Lazlo relaxed and his anger subsided. His German accent diminished as he said, "That was one of the reasons I called. We don't know their exact location.

"You don't know?"

Feeling a little threatened, Fielding added, "They were overhead Pittsburgh. Ve haf not talked mit the crew in the past half hour."

"I see."

"I am concerned about der fuel remaining too. And, there is a weather front in the area mit strong winds along the western side of the front. Und I know they ver about fifty minutes out from Kennedy when ve last spoke mit them.

"We don't know when they started their turn south to Cuba."

"I can get their exact position from our ATC team."

Clifton repeated his earlier question, "What is your best guess about their fuel situation?"

"We ran several computer models and I came up with is less than thirty minutes of fuel when they land at Havana. Der problem, of course is, I don't know how much distance they have to go to Cuba."

He paused to think and then said, "And I don't know what kind of ground speed they have because we don't know their precise location." He thought, "Once we know their location, we can figure in winds aloft which will give us their ground speed."

Clifton thought quickly, "Hold the line, and let me see what I can find out for you." Clifton put him on hold and looked at a small map placed under glass on his desktop. He saw Pittsburgh,

Cleveland, Chicago, Indianapolis Air Route Traffic Control Centers.

He pressed the flashing hold button for Lazlo. "Did you say the flight was near Pittsburgh when you called them?"

Fielding had just lit another cigarette and coughed as he answered, "I think they were actually east of Pittsburgh. But again, I don't have any specifics."

"Hold on. I'll be right back."

Clifton looked at a typed display of unlisted telephone numbers. He scanned the left side of the typed list until he found Cleveland Center. He called the telephone number listed for the Cleveland Air Route Traffic Control Center.

The phone rang several times. A woman answered. In the background, he could hear the beep. This was a recorded line. "Cleveland Center, Watch Supervisor Simpson speaking."

"This is Richard Clifton, Supervisor of Security with the Agency in OKC."

"Yes, sir. What can I do for you?"

"We have two unconfirmed reports that a Boeing 747 in your sector has been hijacked to Cuba."

"Give me your telephone number in OKC, sir. I'll have the Center Chief get right back to you."

Dick Clifton knew this was to verify he was who he said he was. However, time was being wasted. He wanted a rapid confirmation and did not want to be involved in these silly bureaucratic games. Resignedly, he gave her his number and then added that the dispatcher from the airline was holding on another line and the airline's head of security was also waiting for information. He slowly pressed the line on which he was holding and disconnecting himself from the Cleveland Center.

"I've spoken to the Cleveland Center and their Section Chief is going to call me back with all the particulars.

"While we are waiting, is there anything else that you can think of?"

Fielding had become impatient and was astounded at the slow

pace with which the FAA worked in the midst of a crisis. "I have no further information until I can determine the exact location of our aircraft and their fuel situation."

Clifton's phone buzzed. He excused himself and answered the intercom. "Ed, what is it?"

"Cleveland Center's on the phone, they have some information about a hijacking. Also, I want to talk to you about the airline dispatcher I spoke with. He was uncooperative and argumentative."

"This is not the time, Ed. We'll discuss your problems after we deal with the hijacking."

Clifton pressed the second blinking light, "Clifton here."

"Well, Mr. Clifton, you were right. Flight 100 was hijacked about an hour ago. They were just west of Elwood City VOR. At 20:51 GMT, or 16:51 local time, our controllers gave them a direct heading to Havana and offered the standard assistance regarding altitude and course deviations. We also set up a standby discrete VHF frequency for their use."

"From your calculations, when do you think they will make Havana?"

"That depends on the wind and their true airspeed. Normally, they cruise between four-hundred ninety to five-hundred fifteen knots. However, if fuel is a consideration, they might go to Long Range Cruise, or even Maximum Range Cruise to conserve fuel. If they did that, their true airspeed would be reduced." He paused to look at something, then continued, "The boys at Flight Service think there probably is a pretty good wind from the south. That would make their ground speed somewhere between three-hundred seventy five and four-hundred twenty five knots, depending on their true airspeed."

Dick Clifton generally understood the conditions given by the Chief and was anxious to relay this information to Fielding, so that he could develop a better handle on the situation.

Clifton rushed his question. "Can you give me the specifics regarding the aircraft's location at this time and do you know how much fuel he has on board?"

The unknown supervisor's voice in Cleveland said, "Standby one. I'll have that for you in a flash."

Clifton could hear keys being pressed on a keyboard. In the background, he could hear muted buzz of air traffic controllers directing nearly two hundred aircraft that passed through their controlled airspace.

"Well, he must either have one hell of a head wind, or he's throttled back to save fuel. His ground speed is only three-hundred forty five knots. My guess is that he's got a fuel problem. Our computers have an ETA for him in Havana at 01:50 GMT."

"Thank you for the information," and then added, "If I need to get hold of you quickly, is there a secure number I can use and not have to go through this monkey-motion of you calling me back to verify who I am?"

The Center Chief laughed and gave Clifton his dedicated number. He also asked that Clifton only give the number to the airline dispatcher. They wanted and needed to keep his line open for minute-to-minute communications.

Dick Clifton thanked the supervisor again and pressed the button on his phone so he could relay the information to Fielding. When he attempted to take Fielding off hold, the line was dead. The dispatcher was not there. He had either been disconnected, or had hung up.

61

**18:55 Eastern Standard Time
Southwest of Atlanta, Georgia**

Don, Fred, Stan, the hijacker and Carlton settled into a routine of warily watching each other. Fred was flying, while Don studied the Jeppesen high altitude chart and maintained a listening watch on the radios. Stan appeared busy as he very meticulously monitored engine thrust, fuel consumption and fuel remaining in more than half-dozen tanks in the wings and fuselage. Even at Long Range Cruise, the Pratt Whitney JT-9D engines were consuming JP-4 jet fuel at a prodigious rate of one gallon every second.

In one of Don's earlier communications with dispatch, he had asked the company to construct several flight plans from their present position to Jose Marti airport at Havana. None of these fuel burn figures provided Stan any comfort.

Carlton remained shocked by his predicament, worsened by the violent instability of the hijacker.

Other than an occasional cryptic and staccato communication from the radios, the cockpit was relatively quiet. Minutes passed in which nothing was said. The outside air scrubbed the windshields at hundreds of miles per hour. A steady and constant aeronautical symphony was being played for the five cockpit occupants.

Bill slowly leaned forward and looked through Don's windshield. His back was directly in front of Stan. He could not comprehend the earth was moving beneath them at over five miles per minute. He could not tell if the 747 was flying over the earth, or if the airplane was stationary and the earth was turning beneath it.

From his experience in the military, Stan knew sometimes there were moments of opportunity in which an attack could be successfully attempted. Timing was key. For the first time since the hijacker had broken into the cockpit with Carlton, he had carelessly placed himself in a position where he could be attacked. Stan sensed this was a fleeting opportunity in which Bill's lack of situational awareness might provide Stan an opportunity to swiftly become the aggressor.

Very slowly and with excruciating deliberation, Stan raised the cover of his desk and put his hand on the cold red fire extinguisher he had previously hidden there.

The hijacker momentarily glanced out Fred's side window and Stan froze. If the hijacker looked to his right, back at Stan, he would be able to easily see Stan's hand in the opened desk compartment. Stan thought, if he turns back around, facing forward, it may be the only opportunity I'll have to turn the tables on this son of a bitch.

As quickly as Bill had turned and looked out Fred's side window, he shifted his gaze back to the front windshield and then quickly to the side window on Don's left.

With deliberate and measured intent, using his left hand, Stan lifted the extinguisher up and out. His angle was not ideal. He felt much like a baseball player throwing off the wrong foot. This was the only opportunity he might have. He raised the fire bottle over his head and swung it directly at the back of the hijacker's head.

Carlton saw the drama being played out directly above him. He whimpered and the hijacker looked down at him. In Bill's field of vision, he saw the red arc of the fire extinguisher swinging toward him. He defensively raised his right arm to deflect the bottle. Though the blow was somewhat diverted, the contact of the fire bottle against the radius in his forearm was excruciating. The extinguisher continued on a wobbly arc until it banged hard against the back of Don's seat back.

Bill grabbed the handle of the fire extinguisher and twisted the bottle free from Stan's grip.

Now, the hijacker had the advantage. He swung the fire extinguisher in tight arc and backhanded Stan in the face. The impact hit Stan's forehead. His glasses flew off, broken. Bill pulled hard and hit Stan again. The second blow hit him behind his left ear and produced a blinding explosion in Stan's field of view. Slowly, Stan listed to his right and fell against his seat, restrained by his shoulder harness; unconscious.

62

**19:10 Eastern Standard Time
Northwest of Atlanta, Georgia**

Don had been caught completely off guard. He had no idea what had happened. He only knew the fire extinguisher had glanced off his seat. Fred had been looking at a high altitude chart and didn't see any of the short battle. He only heard Carlton mutter something and the the sharp sound of the extinguisher hitting the aluminum frame on Don's seat.

Bill uttered a string of Spanish expletives – against Stan, Don and Carlton. His rage was uncontained. They all had tried to trick him. They all were playing him for the fool *"el embaucar"*. He knew this would happen. In his blind anger, he wanted to shoot the fool who attacked him with the fire extinguisher. Or, maybe, kill the useless *Maricón* crying on the floor.

He could not trust any of them. Especially the pilot who called himself the captain.

Carlton squirmed and tried to get out from under the hijacker's heavy black shoe. He pleaded with him, "Please. You are hurting me." Nothing changed. Carlton added, "Badly."

HIJACKING OF FLIGHT 100

Bill was frustrated and panicked. Everything had gone wrong. There was to have been no violence. No one was supposed to get hurt. This *Maricón* drove him crazy. He didn't trust the pilots. He especially distrusted the captain, the one who gave all the orders. He decided he needed to take over and make the pilots do what he wanted.

He thought, "Fly to Habana. Let me do just this one thing without failing." Now that he knew the pilots had been trying to trick him all along, he felt invincible. They had tried to trap him, but he was too smart for them. He would not fail again.

Carlton pushed on the back of Bill's knee. For a moment, the hijacker thought he was going to fall. He steadied himself against the back of Stan's chair and looked down at Carlton and said, "You touch me one more time and I will kill you. ¿*Comprende, Paloma*?"

Before Carlton could answer, Bill pointed the gun over Carlton's head, toward the side of the airplane. He jerkily waved the gun from side to side. Unintentionally and inadvertently, he squeezed the trigger too hard. The firing mechanism did its job and the metal hammer hit the pin.

Instantly, one round left the barrel at near the speed of sound to do it's damage in the cockpit. When the pistol fired, the muzzle was aimed at a point just above floor at the crew rest bunk on the left side of the cockpit directly behind the Captain.

The 9mm slug grazed the bunk blanket. Little energy was lost. The glancing and brief contact with the blanket caused the bullet to tumble. The lead projectile penetrated the sidewall in the cockpit. Rather than make a smooth, small round hole, it ripped a fourteen-inch gash through the inner panel, sound and temperature insulation and then tore a twenty-six inch long ragged tear in the outside aluminum skin.

63

19:20 Eastern Standard Time
Northwest of Atlanta, Georgia

Engineers at the Boeing Commercial Airplane Company may never have considered a live round being fired through the exterior skin of the airplane. However, their design philosophy of vertical stringers that wrapped around the fuselage like hoops on a whiskey barrel stopped the tear from elongating.

At thirty-three thousand feet, the differential pressure between inside pressure versus the aircraft's actual altitude was 7.5 pound per square inch. Most of the pressurized air inside the plane tried to escape through the ragged tear in the aluminum skin.

The sound was deafening.

Bill had no idea what he had done, but knew it was bad. He realized this was another example of his amazing ability to fail at nearly everything he tried to do.

When the gun fired, Fred, Carlton and Don were shocked. None, however, were as terrified as the hijacker.

The result of the bullet hole in the side of the fuselage was that the cabin altitude climbed at more than fifteen thousand feet per minute. The immediate loss of pressure momentarily caused the cockpit to fog severely enough that neither Fred nor Don could see each other at less than three feet apart.

Don roared above the screaming air leak in the cockpit sidewall, "Everyone on Oxygen. NOW."

He and Fred both donned their aviator's oxygen full-face masks, capable of providing 100% oxygen under pressure directly to each pilot. Don switched to interphone and keyed the oxygen microphone, "Captain on oxygen."

Fred checked in, "Roger. First Officer on oxygen."

Stan Kurtz did not hear the captain's command. Even if he had, he could not comprehend the significance of Don's words.

Bill had no idea what the pilot was yelling about.

Carlton, like most of the passengers, knew something had happened to the pressure in the airplane as their ears popped painfully.

Don looked at the Flight Engineer's cabin pressurization panel. He paid close attention to the round cabin altimeter. Initially, the hands spun rapidly, a clear indication of a cabin decompression. As Don watched, the cabin altitude slowly stabilized and then sluggishly started to descend as the large, automatic outflow valves in the belly of the aircraft did their job.

Don turned and faced forward, checked his flight instruments and saw the aircraft was still on altitude, airspeed and heading. Satisfied with what he saw, he returned his gaze to the cabin altimeter. Now, the cabin altimeter was holding steady at 6,800 feet above sea level – a normal indication. The very loud and shrill noise was, if anything, worse than before. Don and Fred could communicate only by yelling at each other.

After Don was satisfied that the airplane was going to hold together, he turned and looked back at Stan, Carlton and then Bill. He did not like what he saw.

64

**19:00 Eastern Standard Time
John F. Kennedy International Airport**

The phone receiver had buried itself deep into Lazlo Fielding's hand, as he held it to his ear for more than five minutes; the amount of time he spent waiting for Clifton to come back on the line. Frustrated, he impatiently hung up the phone. He waited a few minutes then redialed and once again run afoul of Ed James.

James was, as usual, rude. "Well, well. If it's not Mr. Fielding, our errant dispatcher. What do you expect the FAA to do for you today?"

Fielding tried to find a way around James. "I was talking to Mr. Clifton and got cut off. It's urgent. I need to talk to him about our flight that has been hijacked."

James spoke with his most patronizing bureaucratic voice. "You can tell me and I'll relay any messages you have to Mr. Clifton. Besides, Mr. Clifton is in a meeting." He paused, then snidely added, "Which I believe, is actually about your hijacked jet."

With a great foreboding, he suspected his message would never be forwarded. He said, "Tell him Mr. Fielding called about the progress of our Flight 100."

"What's the magic word?"

Fielding could not believe he was being subjected to a child's simple game. "Please."

James' voice took on a tightness. "You can be sure I'll just stop everything I'm doing and run into a closed meeting to tell Mr. Clifton you were on the phone. Is there any specific information you want me to relay to Mr. Clifton?"

"No, sir. Just tell him I called and ask him to call me back as soon as possible."

"Right. I'll do that. Thank you for calling the FAA." The line went dead for both James and Fielding at the same time.

With a practiced and experienced eye, he reviewed the high altitude and upper atmosphere winds aloft prognosis as well as terminal weather reports. Finally, the tension got to him. He had to do something. Anything was better than doing nothing and waiting for phone calls which seemed to never happen. Once again he tried to reach John Batchelor at home. Unfortunately, he had no success. Batchelor was either not at home or was not answering his phone.

He continued to feel frustrated. No one would return his calls. He was operating in a vacuum. His third attempt to contact Clifton was intercepted by a young-sounding secretary who assured him she would see that Mr. Clifton got the message right away. As soon as she hung up, she looked at her watch, and then at the General Electric wall clock with black hands and numerals and a red second hand. Both indicated it was after five o'clock; well past her quitting time. She was not Clifton's secretary and had only answered the telephone when no one else would.

She had no idea where Clifton was. She barely knew who he was, or what he actually did with the FAA. The last time she had seen him was when he walked out of his office to a large conference room across the hall.

The office idiot, Ed James, walked with Clifton and whined about some airline dispatcher in New York. She heard him loudly complaining that the dispatcher had been rude and uncooperative. Dick Clifton had not been at all interested in Ed James' overview, and much less interested in any FAA enforcement action.

The young secretary looked around the office, straightened up her desk, turned off the lights and left for the day. In the darkened room, one light on the telephone desktop console slowly blinked; the line on which Fielding continued to hold.

65

19:10 Eastern Standard Time
John F. Kennedy International Airport

John Batchelor received the call from the company operator. She seemed quite dedicated and concerned about her responsibility for the messages from Lazlo Fielding to Batchelor. She also was curious about the hijacking and asked Batchelor several inappropriate, or at least inopportune, questions about Flight 100; questions for which he had no answers.

John attempted to dismiss her as politely as possible, but was not successful. He hoped the operator was not one to hold a grudge. He paced in his living room, cordless phone under his chin, waiting for Fielding to answer.

With no fanfare, the silence was broken by a deep, rumbling German-infused voice. "Hello."

"Lazlo? John Batchelor here again. I just heard on WINS radio in New York that 100 not only was hijacked, but one of the pilots has been shot. Do you know anything about that?"

"No. No, I don't. I talked to the FAA over an hour ago, but they said nothing about that. I have tried to reach the FAA in Oklahoma

City several times, but they have not returned my calls.

" How about I call a contact I have with the FAA in OKC. I went to a couple of FBI training sessions with him. Let's see what Dick Clifton can do for us."

"Your friend Clifton is the one I have been waiting for. But, I don't think he knows I called him back. I'm certain he would have gotten back to me if he had known I was on the line."

Fielding lit another cigarette and blew the smoke toward the ceiling as he waited for a response from John Batchelor.

None came, so he said, "John, go ahead. See if you can get through to Clifton. If you can verify there was a shooting, or if any of the pilots were injured, let me know. We are running alternate flight plans. You know, various altitudes and routes to see which is the most efficient. Ze fuel situation iz, or could be, critical."

Batchelor walked to the hall closet, grabbed his coat and said, "I'll get right on it."

66

18:25 Eastern Standard Time
Miami International Airport

Nervously, Juan Guerrero milled around the Miami airport. He could not understand why there was no news about the hijacking. The radio stations always had bulletins about flights that were hijacked, especially in Miami, and especially to Cuba. Even if it wasn't like the old days when there were many flights to Cuba, a hijacking was still news for the radio stations. Twice Juan had walked to his old Plymouth in the employee parking lot and listened to the car radio. Neither English nor Spanish-language stations had any reports of a hijacking.

Finally, about 6:10 in the evening, he overheard a conversation between two ticket agents. "Another hijacked flight."

"This one was to Havana."

"Why would anyone want to hijack a plane to Cuba?"

"Especially in these times?"

The news contained in the stuttered conversation elated Juan. He did not know if the hijacked airplane was the one Bill was on. But he was sure their plan was working. He felt like telling the two agents why someone would hijack an airplane; especially this one.

Juan looked at his watch. It was half past six. He was confused because he thought the hijacking should have happened sooner. He still didn't know when the airplane would land at Jose Marti airport. A vague and foggy sense of despair covered him with a threatening gloom. He tried, unsuccessfully, to dismiss these feelings. He tried to calculate how much time would pass before he would be off-loading the six extra suitcases. Without knowing the planned arrival time in Havana, he could not guess at the ETA in Miami.

There was nothing for him to do. Wait and worry; that was all he could do. He walked to the International Arrivals Building, the IAB. He passed two bored United States Custom and Immigration agents. He went out the side door and looked across the vacant ramp. He carefully studied the tarmac with a practiced eye. He could almost see the enormous 747 taxiing slowly to an unknown gate. He thought about the loud and raucous cluster of reporters trying to gain access to the passengers.

Juan took his time. He slowly walked back inside from the ramp area. He decided to go to his car and listen to the radio again for more information about the hijacking. Perhaps there would be an estimated arrival time in Havana. He crossed the main terminal and stopped at the airport snack bar. He ordered a hamburger, fries and Coke to go, asking for the airline employee discount.

He paid for his bag of food and walked the length of the terminal. On his way out of the building, he narrowly avoided three ramp service people from Eastern Airlines, all whom he knew. They had finished their shifts and were going home.

He believed he had a plan for everything. He believed he had it all perfectly planned out. Everything was going to be fantastic. He would transfer the six suitcases to his automobile. His contact would be waiting for his phone call. After they talked, he would know the specific location for the drop. He smiled. Once the delivery was finished, he would have his money and never have to show up for work again.

HIJACKING OF FLIGHT 100

Nervously, he exited the main terminal building and walked down the palm-lined ramp toward the huge Eastern Airlines maintenance hangar. He turned the corner and came to the locked gate that opened on to the employee's parking lot.

He pressed the number code on the touch pad lock. The solenoid buzzed and he pushed the gate open. As he walked to his car, he laughed at the ironic nature of airline security. The employees' parking lot was under guard, with electronic gate locks. Here he was, inside the compound, planning a hijacking that was going to make him and his two brothers rich.

67

**18:35 Eastern Standard Time
Miami International Airport**

He found his '79 Plymouth and fished the car keys from his pocket. He got in and rolled down the windows. The temperature was stifling hot. He tossed the bag of food on the seat and then impatiently turned on the key and the radio.

Slowly he pressed each of the buttons on the radio dial. "Alive and well in Michigan." Another station, "The family said they were glad that the…"

The local news affiliate announcer said, "the Cleveland Indians look like they may take their Division." Another station, "The main ingredient for today is salt-cured pork…" "Unanswered questions about the stock market and why it took another nose dive today. The Dow Jones Average dropped more than 50…"

"This just in. A Boeing 747, with 450 passengers from San Francisco to New York has been hijacked. The pilot indicated the hijacker wants to go to Cuba. We have unconfirmed reports that a stewardess has been taken hostage." Brass trumpet music rose in the background, "When more information is available we will interrupt our regularly scheduled broad…"

He turned the radio knob searching for more facts or any information about the flight. He did not like the fact his brother had taken anyone hostage. There was not supposed to be any violence or injuries.

They had a simple plan, "Hijack the plane to Havana. Put on the six extra bags. The plane flies back to Miami. Offload the six suitcases. End of story."

He continued to roll the knob to hear more about the hijacking.

Suddenly his hand froze on the dial, "This unconfirmed report just in that the hijacker has shot one of the pilots. We now take you to Jim Key in Charleston."

Juan could not move. He was paralyzed. The only movement in his car came from his scared shallow breathing.

A deep sonorous voice filled the inside of Juan's car, "Jim Key here in Charleston. We have a listener who says he monitors the FAA Air Traffic Control emergency frequencies. He called us several minutes ago to report the hijacked aircraft transmitted on an emergency frequency that the hijacker had fired shots in the cockpit.

"We are not certain if the pilot had been shot, or the hijacker was shooting at the pilots. We have contacted the FAA at the Charleston International Airport. They declined to comment."

Waves of nausea hit him. He was shaking. He and his brother were the ones they were talking about. There was no way he could turn the aircraft back toward New York. Guerillmo had gone too far.

They were all going to be caught, arrested and go to jail. What if someone dies? They could get life sentences or even the electric chair.

The radio continued to spew more bad news, "In a phone interview with the FAA in Washington, D. C. all the Federal Aviation Administration would say was that the aircraft was proceeding to Havana. They would neither confirm nor deny a shooting had occurred on aircraft. Nor would they comment about unfounded reports that indicated the aircraft, passengers or crew were in any immediate danger. When the FAA was asked to comment on this emergency transmission about a shooting, they again declined comment. They did say other federal agencies had been alerted to the situation."

Juan could not believe what he was hearing. This was not the way it was supposed to happen.

The radio station news reader continued, "When asked if this included the Federal Bureau of Investigation, the FAA only would say that in situations like this many federal agencies are routinely alerted. In every case, that included the FBI."

Juan twisted in his seat. He wanted to get away. He wanted to undo what he and his brothers had done. It was much like trying to recall a bullet after the trigger has been pulled.

He thought, "It's too late. Too late. Too late."

68

**18:40 Central Standard Time
Oklahoma City, Oklahoma**

"Clifton, please."

"Who may I say is calling?"

"Ron Castle."

Ed James stuttered, "The, *the* Ron Castle? Ronald D. Castle? The Administrator? The head of the FAA?"

"Yes. Get me Clifton. Now."

Thirty seconds passed, "Special Agent Clifton here."

"Hi, Dick. Any news on our 747 hijacking?"

"John. John is that you?" He laughed. "You shook the place up telling them it was Castle. My staffer, Ed James, damn near wet his pants racing in here to tell me Ronald Castle was on the phone." He let out another rolling laugh, then said, "Whatever works."

"Well John, here is the latest information we have. About ten minutes ago, 100 called the Washington ATC Center and said they were having severe control problems and could not maintain a specific altitude. They requested a block altitude and requested that all other aircraft be cleared away from their southerly track."

"Did they say anything about a shooting? Anything about one of the pilots being shot?"

"I don't have the transcript here yet. Washington Center is going to send it to me. But, they did indicate the hijacker was in the cockpit, armed with a pistol. They also said the Flight Engineer had been hurt. Other than that, I don't have any more specifics, except the flight seems to generally be holding their assigned heading toward Havana."

"What do you have in mind as far as assistance goes for them?"

"Well, you know, all the standard protocols. Clear the airways, give them preferential treatment, coordinate with the FBI and State. Basically, whatever they need, they get."

"We have not heard from them for nearly an hour. Our Dispatcher Fielding tried to contact you, but couldn't get through. Did you ever get the message that he had called you back?"

Clifton looked directly at Ed James. "No. No one told me your dispatcher was on the line. I'll tell you what we'll do. We'll set up an open line with him in New York. I'll call him right now and then we'll keep the line open as long as the hijacking is ongoing."

"That's great. At least we'll have current information about the status of our aircraft. Thanks again for the help Dick. I'll look forward to seeing you soon."

"Take care." He chuckled again, "Ron Castle. That's great."

Clifton hung up the phone and stared coolly at Ed James shaking his head slowly from side to side.

"What?"

Clifton was so irritated with his assistant, he was unable to speak. He turned his back and strode from the conference room, muttering to himself under his breath.

When Clifton terminated the call, Batchelor quickly redialed Flight Dispatch. "This is John Batchelor, may I speak to Lazlo Fielding, please?"

"Just a moment, sir. I'll get him for you."

Becky put the incoming call on hold and said, "Mr. Fielding, Mr. Batchelor is on line six for you."

Fielding thanked her, lit a cigarette, punched the blinking light on his telephone console and said, "Yes, John. What did you find out from the FAA?"

"I found that Flight 100 is in serious trouble. The hijacker has gained access to the cockpit. They confirmed the report about a shooting."

Lazlo swore out loud in German, "*Gott Verdammt*."

"Clifton said they had a report that the Flight Engineer had been injured. But the FAA didn't know if he had been shot, or exactly what happened. They only know that he had been injured, presumably by the hijacker."

Fielding stubbed his cigarette in the overflowing ashtray. His Germanic accent thickened when he said, "Vell dot iz bat news. I must contact zem. I viss someone were here to make the decision for me."

"Lazlo if it'll help, I'm telling you to contact them. I need to know what is going on with the flight. I also want to find out where they are going to land. I also need an estimated time of arrival for them. On the strength of that, call them."

"I vill do it. Give me da telephone numbers ver you can be reached."

Batchelor gave him three numbers. His home number, the number of a local diner where he would be for the next hour, and his girlfriend's home number, "If you can't find me, leave a message with Sandy."

He ended the conversation. "Clifton is going to call you and set up an open line between dispatch and Oklahoma City. That way you both will have open communication capability regarding the status of 100."

Slowly, Lazlo's accent thinned. "This is excellent. Thank you for your help and for your authorization to call the flight. I vill let you know vat we find vin I talk to da captain."

Fielding considered what he wanted to say in the message to be sent to 100. He made a mental list. He needed a position report. The telephone link with the FAA would allow him to follow the flight's progress via telephone. He needed a planned destination if the flight was going to divert to somewhere else other than Havana. He also needed the fuel remaining when he talked to them. This would allow him to provide very accurate computer flight plans for 100. Ultimately, he wanted to know the crew, passengers and aircraft were going to be all right.

69

19:01 Eastern Standard Time
John F. Kennedy International Airport

After he wrote his list of questions, then called his assistant, "Becky, I want you to SELCAL 100, their code is DHAM, Delta Hotel Alpha Mike. Try them on the Eastern Region ARINC sector frequency. If they don't answer, have ARINC start a sweep broadcast of all their frequencies. Maybe in the pressure of the hijacking, they forgot to switch to the correct frequency."

Becky left with the information. She walked to the radio rack in the adjacent room. She closed the door and could hear electronic humming as she sat at a keyboard. She took a deep breath and entered, [FLT 100] [B-747-200] [VHF] [DHAM] [131.6] and pressed the send key. An amber XMITTER light flashed three times. She waited for about thirty seconds and pressed the send key again.

For the second time the amber XMITTER light flashed three times. Becky looked through the glass window and across the room at Fielding. He seemed to be sitting in his chair, waiting patiently. He simply smoked and then turned and looked at her. She gave him a quizzical look and shrugged her shoulders. Lazlo waved at her, as if to motion her to proceed with the next step. Becky returned to the radio rack.

70

19:02 Central Standard Time
Oklahoma City, Oklahoma

This time she entered, [FLT 100] [B-747-200] [VHF] [DHAM] [SCAN ALL]. She pressed the send key for the third time. The XMITTER light flashed an extended series of the blinks. After less than a minute, she pressed the send key again. Either 100 was not tuned to any of the assigned frequencies. Or, they were unable to answer the SELCAL.

Dick Clifton asked Ed James to set up the open-line conference call for him. After the connection was established, Clifton made it painfully clear to Ed James that he was solely responsible for maintaining this open connection link. He added if the connection were broken for any reason, Ed James would find himself working as a Flight Service Station clerk in Bemidji, Minnesota, at pay grade of GS-6, for the rest of his career with the FAA. Within less than five minutes, an open connection was operating between the FAA in Oklahoma City and JFK Dispatch at John F. Kennedy International Airport.

Ed James said, "Mr. Fielding is on the line, Mr. Clifton."

"Mr. Fielding. Clifton here, I'm sorry about the mix-up on the telephone. I have instructed my people to keep this line open as long as the hijack is in progress. Please ask your people to not break the connection."

They discussed the specifics of Flight 100 and then Clifton added, "The last position for 100 was just south Charleston, West Virginia and from what the ATC boys say, the flight's ground speed has dropped way off, either from one hell of a headwind, or for mechanical reasons."

Fielding thanked him and added that, he too, was going to try to contact the flight. When he concluded his conversation with Clifton, he was careful when he placed his telephone handset on the desk by the cradle. He did not want to break the connection.

To assure that, he pressed the hold key only after he pressed the conference button. Fielding was uncomfortable with the new phone system and quietly wished he had his old black AT&T desk phone back.

71

18:30 Central Standard Time
Oklahoma City, Oklahoma

The voice on the phone was officious and gruff. "Let me speak to Clifton."

Ed James answered with mock sincerity, in a lilting voice, "Who may I say is calling, please?"

"Ron Castle."

James tone changed to one of concerned fear, "Oh, Yes Sir. Oh, Mr. Castle, Sir. Good to talk to you again Sir. I'll get him for you right away."

For the second time today, Ed James had spoken with the Administrator of the FAA and was frenzied as he tried to find his boss. He located Clifton coming back from the supply room, loaded down with a large map and a stack of yellow legal tablets.

"Dick, Mr. Ronald Castle is on the phone again for you." Breathlessly he added, "He's on hold and should not be kept waiting. He sounded impatient. He's on line 3. Here, let me take those pads. Hurry. He's waiting and sounded like he was angry."

"Right, Ed. I'll get to him in a minute." Clifton knew the call was from Batchelor. Dick knew Batchelor had again used the name of the Administrator to cut through some of the bureaucratic nonsense that fuels the FAA.

Clifton put the maps and legal tablets down. Then slowly walked to the desktop call console in the outer office. He punched the flashing light on the console and said, "Security Branch here. What in the hell do you want, now?" Clifton could hardly conceal his amusement as he thought that he would catch Batchelor off guard. Ed James was shocked by his boss' lack of protocol.

The voice on the other end of the line was not amused, "Who the hell am I speaking to?" Dick Clifton knew instantly that he had made a huge mistake. The voice continued, "This is Ronald Castle and I don't find your attitude to be the kind of thing we like to foster here at the FAA."

"Is that you, Clifton?"

Dick felt a coolness drift over him as he blinked and looked at Ed James, who stared at him with disbelief written on his face.

Clifton did the only sensible thing he could, "I am sorry, Mr. Castle. I just received a call from someone who used your name and thought you were that person calling back. Please accept my apology, Sir."

Castle's interest was aroused. "Who was the individual impersonating me? Was he an Agency employee? What is his name?"

"He's not an agency employee." He paused, "I'd rather not say, sir. It was not an impersonation, just sort of a joke."

"Tell your friend that I take a dim personal view of anyone who uses my name, either inside or outside this Agency."

Dick Clifton allowed himself to breath a sigh of relief as he said, "Yes, Sir. I'll tell him. Now, Sir, what can I do for you?"

Castle launched into a tirade against the Washington press corps, "The God damned press have been all over my ass about this hijacking. There seems to be a persistent rumor that one of the pilots has been shot. Quite frankly, I'm in the dark on this."

Clifton said nothing as he waited for the chief administrator to either continue or wind down.

Castle paused for several seconds, then said, "I need a briefing in case I have to make a statement."

Clifton's response was automatic. "Yes sir, I'll bring you up to speed immediately."

Again Castle paused before continuing, "I just got a call from the White House Chief of Staff's office. They want to know what the FAA is doing about saving the lives of those people on the hijacked flight."

Clifton could easily understand the pressure Castle had experienced. "I hate it when they call, especially when I have not been briefed on the situation." With each syllable his voice got louder, until now he was shouting at Clifton, "What can you tell me about this hijacking and how is it different from all the rest?"

Clifton wanted to say that no two hijackings were the same. However, giving careful consideration to how he had answered the question, he said, "First of all. There was a radio communication from the flight that the hijacker had gained access to the cockpit and fired one or more shots."

Castle said nothing.

"There also was a report the Second Officer, the Flight Engineer, had been injured."

"Was that injury from a gun shot wound?"

"We don't have that information at this time."

Clifton continued, "The ATC controllers in the Washington Center are giving 100 all the support they can. Unimpeded clearances. Keeping the airspace around and ahead of their aircraft free of all known traffic. We are coordinating with the FBI and the airline has reached out to State. Other than that, Sir, that is all the information I have."

"Well, that's not good enough."

Clifton squirmed as Castle continued, "Damn it all to hell. I'm being made to look like a horse's ass by the press. I want you to contact that flight immediately. Find out what the hell is going on."

His voice rose both in volume and tone, "In fact, I want you to patch me into that flight. I want to talk with the pilots."

Clifton knew his response could either be a career enhancement or career ending moment. He said, "I, we, don't have the capability to patch you into the flight."

Castle considered that for a moment and said, "Dammit all to hell. I should be able to talk to any flight under FAA jurisdiction. Are you sure I can't do that?"

"Yes Sir. I mean, no Sir. We just don't have that capability. I can't even talk to the flight crew directly. I have to rely on the section chief at the ATC center that's working the flight."

"How soon will you have more information?"

"As soon as we finish this conversation, I will contact the ATC folks and get an update from them for you."

Somewhat mollified, "All right, then. I want you to get back to me at my private number and tell me what those pilots told you."

"Very good, sir. Except for two things."

"What's that, Clifton?"

"Remember, I don't have any way to talk to the flight directly. The best I can do is call the Center sector that is working the flight and talk to the controlling supervisor."

Castle didn't like that answer as he cleared his throat, "Harrumph."

"Also sir, I don't have your private number."

Castle laughed, perhaps a little too lightly, and then gave Clifton the number. "I hope you are better suited at following this hijacking, than you are at answering your damn phone."

"Yes, Sir."

Castle ended the conversation, "Don't let me down on this, Clifton. I want a full, up to the minute, briefings as this thing continues to develop." Castle hung up.

Dick Clifton hung up and noticed his hand was sweating. He thought the administrator was just like most other Washington bureaucrats. Don't embarrass them in front of the press. And don't embarrass them in front of their superiors. They just can't take the pressure. Another bunch of wussies. The real pressure was on the pilots and controllers.

Clifton laughed to himself, "I guess shit really does run down hill."

He walked back into his office saw Ed James standing immobile. He smiled at his lack-luster assistant, winked, smiled again and said, "Let that be a lesson to you."

72

19:10 Eastern Standard Time
Northwest of Atlanta, Georgia

In his head he saw flashing lights. Blue and white strobe lights that accompanied a pounding, crushing headache.

Stan Kurtz slowly came full circle from his trauma induced, semi-conscious state. He dimly recognized his surroundings and through a fog saw his steel rimmed glasses lying smashed and broken on his Flight Engineer's desk.

One earpiece was bent and stained cordova with dried blood.

His attention was jerkily drawn to a very loud and shrill sibilant whistle coming from an area between the crew bunk and the forward Additional Crew Member, or ACM jump seat. He attempted to orient himself. But, in his fogged mind, he could not determine much about what was going on in the airplane.

His concentration flagged. He looked at familiar aircraft system controls, but had no idea what he was looking at, nor could he remotely comprehend how they functioned. His mind drifted between comprehension and confusion.

Several amber warning lights shined brightly, as well as two red warning indicators. From his training, he should have been quite familiar with these, but he could not remember what they represented or if they were significant. He had no idea if these lights were system warnings or confirmations.

Air whistled shrilly as it vented overboard and kept him from hearing much of the operational conversation in the cockpit. The implication of the sound escaped him. He was startled by a noise behind him and tried to get out of his seat, but his seat belt restrained his movements.

If he sat still and didn't move, maybe he could slowly understand more about where he was. But, he still could not understand why he was in an airplane. He was sweating and it stung as it ran into the open wounds on his scalp.

He smelled something, but could not ascertain what it was or where it came from. Something smelled hot and there was smoke swirling around him. He took a deep breath and began to recognize the pungent odor. Now he knew what it was: the smell of recently fired gunpowder. The scent brought him back to Viet Nam. How well he knew that smell. It was spent gunpowder.

Explosions. Guns. Fear.

He looked around the cockpit and saw the long horizontal tear in the bulkhead on the left side of the airplane. Debris, paper, dust and smoke were being sucked out of the hole. A cockpit crew bunk pillow floated toward the rupture in the fuselage skin. Slowly, at first, and then very quickly, the small rubber pillow was sucked into the tear. As quickly as the sound had started, it quieted just as abruptly. The cockpit was now relatively quiet.

The sudden cessation of noise confused him.

The smell and how it applied to him was something he could not understand. Dimly, he continued to remember flying in Viet Nam. But, he wasn't in Viet Nam, nor was he in a US Navy F-4D Phantom he had flown for the Marine Corps. "Why am I strapped in the cockpit of a heavy transporter? Where's my F-4?", He asked himself. For a second he thought perhaps he had "re-upped" and was now flying Lockheed C-130's for the Marines.

73

19:20 Eastern Standard Time
South of Atlanta, Georgia

Slowly, without definition or meaning, as though everything in his field of vision was only two-dimensional, he saw the silhouette of an arm and a handgun being raised to the horizontal. It was aimed at the back of the Captain's head. Stan thought he recognized the captain, but could not remember his name.

He wondered why this enlisted man was going to shoot the pilot. He sensed fear as he remembered that he was also a pilot. Maybe this soldier would shoot me too, he thought.

A long-ago learned reflex took over. Without thinking or knowing why, Stan abruptly, swiftly and forcefully swung his left hand up and away. His fingers were bent to form a hard edge, with his thumb tucked under the palm of his hand. He felt no pain as the knife-edge of his hand violently struck the wrist of the gun holder. The force of his motion caused the assailant's hand to be deflected upward.

Up and away from the Captain.

Up and away from the other pilot.

Up and away from the thick, but fragile, windshields.

Stan's physical intervention caused the hijacker to involuntarily squeeze the trigger, or perhaps, the force of his attack on the gunman jarred the trigger. In either case, the pistol discharged twice in rapid succession. Both 9 mm bullets sequentially penetrated an overhead control panel. Two 9 or 10 mm holes formed in a vertical line, exactly where the bullets had gone through the panel. The two holes were less than two inches apart.

Spent black gunpowder spotted the gray plastic panel backgrounds. Hot bits of packing material melted into black guarded switch covers. One of the bullets was trapped between an aluminum fuselage stringer and a cross brace. It moved forward and down to the lower edge of the overhead panel. The deformed lead slug exited the panel and dropped harmlessly on the center radio control panel.

The bullet's short journey was not long enough to dissipate the heat of compression. The spent and deformed round lay on a navigation control panel, benignly smoking between Don and Fred.

74

19:25 Eastern Standard Time
Southwest of Atlanta

The second round did far more damage to the integrity of the 747. The 9 mm slug entered the Primary Flight Control Hydraulic Shut Off panel, then followed a winding path that bounced, ripped and tore though several control switches. Systems that were controlled by these switches received valid disconnect signals as though they had been activated by the pilots. Portions of the primary flight control systems, which include ailerons, rudders, elevators and trim tabs were all being powered down in random sequences and at varying rates.

Boeing Commercial Airplane Company engineers designed four separate hydraulic systems to power the enormous horizontal stabilizer. Two of the four systems received valid signals to remove all hydraulic power from the horizontal stabilizer actuators. Instantly, twenty-eight volt control power closed several hydraulic shut-off valves.

One third of the primary hydraulic power sources for the inboard ailerons were likewise powered off. One of the design criteria in the autopilot logic sequence was to constantly monitor primary flight control hydraulic pressure. Integrity in the hydraulic systems had to be assured before any control signals from the autopilot to primary flight controls could be sent.

The "A" autopilot recognized a loss of hydraulic power to the horizontal stabilizer and the inboard ailerons. The autopilot computer's logic circuits essentially became overwhelmed. True to design criteria, the "A" autopilot disconnected.

Three pilots, a terrified Flight Attendant and a lone hijacker all heard the autopilot disconnect warning. The autopilot was no longer flying the airplane.

75

19:25 Eastern Standard Time
West, Southwest of Atlanta

Consistent with Boeing design, the disconnected autopilot no longer had control of the primary flight control surfaces. As these systems failed, the aircraft's three primary axis for all controlled flight - heading, pitch and yaw – could only be controlled manually. If control to these three flight control panels could not be restored, the aircraft would eventually crash from uncontrolled flight into the ground.

Boeing designers could never have anticipated that random gunfire in the cockpit would result in hydraulic system controls being shot up and deactivated.

However, they had given thoughtful and intentional consideration to the probability of losing one or more hydraulic power sources. These type of failures could be from complete loss of hydraulic fluid in one system. Or, it could be the result of an engine failure or precautionary engine shutdown. No one at Boeing, or else where, had ever considered or anticipated losing numerous hydraulic backup sources to several independent flight control system at the same time.

Initially, there was no discernible change in the flight profile of the airplane. Her mass and inertia kept her moving along the same track, heading and altitude. Each of her four engines continued to produce over thirty-five thousand pounds of thrust.

The great horizontal stabilizer that had been holding the aircraft in a level flight condition was now disabled. As fuel was consumed, and when passengers moved about the cabin, the center of gravity of the aircraft shifted.

Normally, the sweptback stabilizer made constant imperceptible changes to keep the aircraft flying on a straight and level path. These aerodynamic changes were made by powerful hydraulic and electric motors. If more elevator authority was required, it would only come from the horizontal stabilizer, which no longer had sufficient hydraulic power to move. The horizontal tail surface was essentially frozen in a fixed position.

The disconnected and deactivated autopilot was no longer able to send trimming signals to the horizontal stabilizer. Slowly and imperceptibly, the nose of the aircraft started to move upward, a movement so slight that no one in the aircraft could initially sense or feel it. The nose continued to slowly rise, while the unpowered tail surface moved in the opposite direction: downward.

Eventually passengers in the aft-most section became aware of this gradual change. They began to feel the floor tilt. Passengers who walked in the aisles found themselves slowly, but inexorably, moving up or down an inclined ramp.

Their collective movements in the cabin exacerbated an already divergent and dynamically unstable aft center of gravity condition. Within seconds, Flight 100 had gone from dead level, to a positive pitch approaching 3 ½ ° above the horizon.

Instinctively, Don placed his hands on the control column and pressed forward on the two horns of the yoke. Thirty one years of flying experience taught him these instinctive reactions. Don simultaneously looked at the six primary flight instruments displayed before him. To an experienced pilot, they told the story of where the aircraft was in a three-dimensional world. His visual assessment confirmed what he sensed. He felt and saw a sustained nose-up pitch change in the 747's attitude. His artificial horizon showed a constant increase in pitch 3°, 4°, 6°, 9° then, finally 12°. Without direct and effective corrective action from the pilots, the vertical oscillation and excursion would continue until the aircraft would stop flying and enter into an aerodynamic stall.

Old flying habits never really go away, nor do they fail a pilot in times of stress. These habits had been built layer upon layer from years of accumulated aeronautical experience and training. Essentially, these habits were impossible to change or break.

Don smoothly exerted forward pressure as the nose passed through 15° nose-up. His manual inputs without hydraulic assistance did nothing to diminish the continued pitch-up. He added more forward pressure, which resulted in no discernable change or improvement.

Nothing.

Finally, Don pressed as far forward as the control column would move, yet the artificial horizon indicated almost 20° above horizon. Throughout this pitch-up, he also tried to use the electric stabilizer trim motors. However, Boeing, in their design wisdom, had included a stabilizer trim brake system. Essentially, if a pilot tried to trim the aircraft in the opposite direction in which he was exerting pressure, a mechanical pawl would stop the stabilizer from any further movement. With the nose of the aircraft well above the horizon, Don continued to exert maximum forward pressure. Because there was no hydraulic power, the stabilizer trim brake remained engaged.

Passengers who been standing were now piled in the aft area of each section. First Class passengers' belongings went tumbling into and through Business Class. Coach passengers tumbled and rolled aft to the rear bulkhead. Carry-on luggage and suitcases started to slide rearward, as they tumbled out of overhead bins. Assorted baggage piled over huddled and crumpled groups of passengers. Fearful voices were muffled by the increasing piles of luggage, carry-on baggage, computer cases, pillows, blankets, magazines and loose clothing.

Fred O'Day saw tremendous concentration on Don's face, amplified by the cords standing out on his neck. Don locked his elbows as he pressed on the control column. Fred joined Don in an effort to bring the nose of the aircraft back to the horizon.

As much from fear as exertion, Don's face was crimson and glistened. He took his eyes away from his instruments and glanced at Fred, "God damn it, Fred. Help me. Push harder. I can't get the nose down."

Fred pushed as they both applied maximum forward pressure against the opposing aerodynamic forces on the horizontal stabilizer. The elevator control column reached its forward limit stops. No matter how hard Don and Fred pushed, their control column would move no farther.

Even though the horizontal stabilizer was receiving the pilot input commands for more down force, residual hydraulic pressure essentially was inadequate to significantly move the stabilizer. Neither pilot was able to tell if the horizontal stabilizer was moving or having any effect on the pitch of the aircraft.

Pitched up, the cockpit floor was equally as unlevel as the rest of the aircraft. The hijacker moved, stumbled aft to the rear cockpit bulkhead. He came to rest against Carlton, who lay on the floor, cowering against the deformed cockpit doorframe.

The hijacker knew almost nothing about airplanes, but he knew something was very wrong with this one. His fears worsened when he heard the terror-filled reactions from the upper deck passengers through the badly deformed cockpit door.

The pressure of the moment caused Bill to momentarily forget he was armed. He was filled with terror and guessed there was a good chance the aircraft was going to crash and they were all going to die.

His feelings were solidified and amplified when he heard Carlton beg plaintively, "Captain. Captain. Oh, my God. Captain. He is going to kill me." He whined, He's going to kill us all. We're going to crash and die."

Carlton started to hysterically shriek, "My God. My God. Don't let me be killed." He wailed, "Please."

"Not now, Carlton." Don roared as he held full forward pressure on the yoke. "I'm in trouble here. Not now."

"Oh, dear Jesus," Carlton squealed. He got free by squirming and wiggling. But, he was unable to push the hijacker away from him. Bill regained his footing. Both were pinned against the bulkhead by the steep deck angle of the cockpit floor.

The airplane shuddered. A long-wave vibration pulsed from the wing root through the fuselage and cockpit floor. Fred, Don and Stan all knew that was the first warning that an aerodynamic stall was eminent.

Carlton could only manage to say, "Oh, for God's sake." Bill again waved the gun without aiming, and then intentionally menaced Carlton.

76

**19:45 Eastern Standard Time
South of Atlanta, Georgia**

Eventually, both pilots' sustained efforts exerted enough control input to slowly allow the flight controls to begin to work. Almost painfully, the nose of the aircraft stopped climbing. The unwanted rotation was halted near 20° nose up. Then, very slowly, the cockpit of the 747 started to drop back toward the horizon.

Fred pulled the four throttles back. "Don, I pulled 'em back to Max Continuous power on.

"Good thinking."

The nose of the giant 747 had now dropped 16° then slowly and almost gracefully 10°, 8°, 5°, then 3°. For a second, the enormous Boeing 747 was back in her element where she belonged; she was level with the horizon.

77

19:50 Eastern Standard Time
South of Atlanta, Georgia

In that moment, the aircraft was dead level - neither nose up nor nose down. Though they were level and Don felt better about their limited ability to control the aircraft, he wondered if he should risk releasing some of the forward pressure on the yoke. He looked at the airspeed indicator, 298 knots.

"Watch the airspeed, Fred."

Fred pulled the thrust levers back to flight idle. As he did so, he saw the nose of the aircraft start to drop. First, 1° nose down, then 2° below the horizon.

Alarm sounded in Fred's voice. "Hey, Don. Do you show level? I show we're pitching down about 2°. Make that 3°'" Fred answered his own question and the nose was now 4° down and increasing.

The high-speed Mach/airspeed warning clacker sounded. To Carlton, it sounded like Spanish castanets.

Fred swore, "Wonderful. Simply fucking wonderful."

The FAA had done it again. In their certification process they mandated that the Boeing Company design a warning system that could not be silenced. Through evolved, but flawed, Federal Aviation Administration logic, the only way to silence the over speed warning was to slow the aircraft.

Don pulled aft on the control column and from habit pressed on the thumb switches that activated the electric stabilizer trimming system.

Fred also pressed his thumb switch, but nothing changed. The same Boeing logic locked the trim system out because of the continued loss of hydraulic pressure. Don pulled as hard as he could with no change in their collective attempts. He roared at Fred to help, "Pull, start pulling and keep pulling until I tell you to stop."

Both Don and Fred pulled aft with as much strength available. "Pull, Fred. Pull as hard as you can."

Both had their feet on the footrests at the bottom of their instrument panels for leverage and pulled harder. There was no discernable pitch change as the heavy 747 accelerated. The artificial horizon showed 8° nose down, holding steady. Don reached over and banged the throttles closed. All four levers hit their individual limit stops with authority. Another old habit, he slammed the flat of his hand against the four closed throttles, though they already were at idle. With the four Pratt and Whitney engines spooling down to idle, the nose dropped even more as the deck angle increase to 10° below the horizon.

The 747 accelerated another twenty knots. The wind noise in the cockpit was deafening. The increased speed generated additional lift. Slowly and imperceptibly the fuselage started to round out the descent. The 747 had been descending in excess of 10,000 feet per minute, but that had now decreased to 2,000 feet per minute. However, their airspeed was still well above the maximum Vne – the Never Exceed speed.

Aerodynamicists call this a phugoid oscillation curve. In theory and in practice, if the nose of the aircraft is pushed over, the aircraft will accelerate. The increased speed creates more lift. Increased lift results the airplane leveling out. With the plane level, the aircraft will lose airspeed. The loss of airspeed will cause a reduction in lift and the cycle repeats itself. If not upset by turbulence or significant changes in outside air temperature, most aircraft will eventually return to a stabilized attitude and in a stabilized configuration – on speed and on altitude.

The basic Air Traffic Control system uses alternating altitudes for traffic separation. North through East through South traffic are assigned altitudes of 33,000, 37,000 and 41,000 feet. South through West through North are to maintain 31,000, 35,000 and 39,000 feet. Because of 100's inability to maintain any precise altitude, there was always a possibility opposing traffic could flying into the same airspace as was being used by Flight 100.

78

**19:55 Eastern Standard Time
Between Atlanta, Georgia and Jacksonville, Florida**

Don shouted against the increased wind noise, "Fred, call the center, tell them we are having control problems and have descended through 27,000 feet." He added, "I don't know how much more altitude we'll lose if we don't get control of the aircraft back."

The artificial horizon indicated they were pitched down 10° and holding steady. Don continued, "Tell them we need a block altitude from 310 to uh, hell I don't know, just tell them we need a block altitude."

Fred lost no time in following Don's orders, as he considered the potential for a mid air collision with another aircraft at their altitude. "Washington Center, this is 100. We are having serious control problems. We can't maintain or control our altitude. Back there, we were above 33,000 and then descending in excess of 10,000 feet per minute." He took a breath, "We're sort of level at 260, but we don't know for how long."

"Roger, 100. We've been tracking your altitude excursions."

"Roger, that."

"100. What do you want us to do?" The voice from the ground was tight, "What do you need from us?"

"Clear the decks. We're not able to control our altitude. We don't know yet, but our ability to control our heading may also become a little iffy. Keep all traffic above and below us well clear."

Don picked up the microphone, "We don't know what's working and what's not. We need an airspace cushion all around us."

"100, we've already done that as a matter of course, 'cause of your ah. . ah, diversion."

"Thanks, Washington. No conflict then with other traffic, right?"

"That's a Rog, 100. No problem with any other aircraft near you. What is your condition now?"

"We have a guy in the cockpit with a gun. He has pretty well shot up the aircraft. Looks like our Flight Engineer's been badly hurt. One of our flight attendants is being held hostage in the cockpit and has been beaten."

"Roger, 100." No empathy. No sympathy.

The Mach/Airspeed warning clacker suddenly stopped. The aircraft has slowed below its maximum, Never Exceed Velocity. Don managed to hold the aircraft reasonably level and learned he could anticipate the oscillations more by feel than by his instruments.

"Fred, thanks for calling the center. Check on Stan will you? I don't know if he's with us or not."

"100. If able, squawk 7500 or 7700 and ident."

Fred, without needing to look at the transponder, pressed the Identification button. That sent a marked message to ATC, showing altitude, flight number and airline identification.

"100. We have your ident. Can you squawk 7500 or 7700 and then ident?"

Both pilots knew the significance of either of those two transponder codes, "Don?"

"Do it."

Fred spun the selector knobs until the code in the transponder window read 7500. Once again, he pressed the Ident button.

Immediately, ATC responded, "100. We have your transponder code and your ident. Over."

"Roger."

79

20:20 Eastern Standard Time
80 miles North of Jacksonville, Florida

Fred turned full around in his seat and looked at Stan, who was looking toward the front of the cockpit, obviously not seeing much and comprehending even less. While he looked aft, Fred stole a casual glance at the hijacker and Carlton.

"How you doin', Stan?"

No real recognition at being addressed.

"Stan, can you hear me? Earth calling Stanley."

Nothing.

"Don't know, Don. I think ol' Stan's had his bell rung."

"God damn it! Can't you ever be serious? Here we are in a fucking airplane that is nearly out of control, with a full load of folks in the back and you're making jokes."

As suddenly as he had exploded, Don calmed down, "I'm sorry. Hold this thing level for a minute. I want to see what shape were in. Don't do anything without telling me first." Fred took a firm grip on the controls.

"You got it?"

"I've got it Don. Go ahead with what you're doing."

"Your airplane."

Fred rotated his shoulders and twisted his neck full range, "My airplane."

Don looked at the overhead and could see behind the panel through the holes caused by the bullets. He could smell the spent gunpowder as he looked at the Master Caution Warning panel lights. Out of 46 lights it looked like more than half were illuminated. To his practiced eye those lights indicated numerous system or subsystems had failed, were failing, or otherwise completely disabled.

The 747's airspeed slowly decreased below the minimum targeted flying speed of 270 knots. Fred applied Maximum Continuous Thrust. The nose gradually pitched up. Fred applied moderate forward pressure. Then full downward pressure on the controls.

Don hollered at Fred, "Push all the way forward. Don't be gentle with the son of a bitch." He unnecessarily added, "Watch it, or she'll get away from you."

Before he finished his sentence, Fred was pressing the controls against the stops. This time the pitch increase was more dynamic and rapid than the last. The aircraft again quickly pitched up beyond 20°.

The stall warning sounded, an electric motor with a concentric weight attached to the control column. When the airplane approached a near-stall condition, the 'stick shaker' concentric motor was energized. In the 747-200 the stall warning sounded like a machine gun being fired underwater.

Don and Fred heard and felt the deep rumbling vibration of the impending stall as Fred applied full forward pressure on the controls. They were in trouble.

It appeared no one had any control of the aircraft. Don, Fred, Stan, Carlton, the Flight Attendants, the hijacker and over 400 passengers were all in the same boat. Essentially, it seemed, they were all just along for the ride.

80

20:30 Eastern Standard Time
South of Atlanta, Georgia

He lay in an unceremonious tangle of suitcases, papers, maps and an old airline blanket across Carlton's leg and arm. He felt like he was going to throw up. To him, it looked like the floor was pointed straight up to the sky. He couldn't move. Both pilots groaned as they pushed and pulled on their controls.

Bill was terrified because the airplane seemed to completely be out of control. He promised himself if he got out of this alive, he would never get on an airplane again. It never occurred to him that he was the cause of this problem. His hijacking scheme and his gun had caused all the damage to the airplane the crew was trying to overcome.

Carlton moved. Bill tried to punch him with his elbow, but the angle of his arm and extra weight from being up on his shoulders made his blow ineffective. Carlton winced and whimpered quietly, as he lay under Bill's rump and side.

Both pilots pushed forward on the black control column, with as much strength as they could gather. This time, as in the past attempts, the mighty Boeing 747 did not appear to respond to their inputs. They both sensed she was not going to answer their commands.

Now the nose of the 747 pointed skyward. Loose items in the cockpit floated and tumbled aft. Soft, forgotten gray dust balls rolled out from under the rudder pedals. Don's suitcase slid aft and slammed into the rear cockpit bulkhead, narrowly missing Carlton and brushed against Bill Guerrero's leg.

Don instinctively knew he was losing control of the aircraft. The ailerons were very sloppy in controlling the plane's roll axis. He could feel the celebrated aerodynamic stall as it advanced. The airframe vibrations and buffeting were transmitted throughout the fuselage, then up through his cockpit seat. The enormous wings were losing their ability to produce sufficient lift to keep the bird in the sky.

Their sophisticated instrumentation showed she was pitched up well above 20°, "Goddamnit, Fred, help me push. Give it everything you've got."

"Yes sir. Boss, I'm a pushin, Master."

He looked at the air speed indicator. He was alarmed to see it still backing off. He watched with dismay as the speed steadily decreased to 240 knots. Old habits are powerful motivators. He reached for the throttles and felt Fred's hand already on the four levers. Both instinctively addressed the problem of decaying airspeed with the substantial application of thrust.

Stan Kurtz heard the familiar sound, a rapid "Rat-a-Tat-Tat-a-Tat-a-Tat."

"That sound, where had he heard it before?" Dimly, Stan tried to recall, Machine Guns...The sound of a door-mounted Gatling gun on a helicopter gun ship...He thought to himself, "No. That's not right." He felt the steep inclination of the cockpit and then again the sound, "Rat-a-Tat-Tat."

For a moment, he thought he was back in his F-4 in the Marines, but then realized he was on the flight deck of a Boeing 747. A 747 that was about to stall. He knew they were near a stall by the sharp pitch of the cockpit floor. He reconfirmed his suspicion by looking at Don's artificial horizon. Over 20° nose up.

The rat-a-tat sound continued, and then he knew what it was. It was the Boeing 747 mechanical stall warning, the stick shaker.

Stan could not believe what he was seeing. He thought, "No pilot would pull the nose up that high." Stan glanced at Fred's horizon and with great alarm, saw the same pitch up indications.

He quickly reacted and spoke without thinking, "Don, get the Goddamned nose down and get some power on this baby…" Don turned and looked at Stan, and said, "I'm doing the best I can, Stan."

Stan's eyes were automatically drawn to the airspeed indicators. He felt fire in his gut when he saw the airspeed continuing to decrease.

In quiet desperation, Stan said, "Aw shit, Don. Look at the frickin' airspeed. We're down to 225 knots. What the hell's the matter with the airplane?"

Stan became more aware of his surroundings. He saw that Don and Fred were both pressing with great force on the dual flight controls. Both were giving it their all.

His attention was diverted by the number two and four engine exhaust gas temperature indicators. Both started to flash amber warning lights.

The flashing stopped and was now a steady amber. Next they became bright red beacons. A clear warning for all to see. Multiple engine failures were just few seconds away.

"Don, we're about to over temp 2 and 4."

Don was doing everything he consciously could think of. He was doing it all. Push. Power. Rudder. Push. Power. Rudder.

"Don, two and four are steady red. Can you pull off any power?"

"Not now, Stan, we're down to 220. I've got to get the nose down before I lose any more airspeed. She's going to stall."

The nose was now pointed upward at 24°.

He looked at the telltale temperature indicator lights for each engine. Stan was right, two and four were on steady red. Number three flashed amber and then red as he looked at the other exhaust gas temperature indicators. With his hand on the throttles he pulled two and four levers back, bent his wrist and pulled three back. The telltale warning lights went out.

Don sensed the pitch of the aircraft had also changed. He looked at the artificial horizon and confirmed it, 21° and slowly decreasing.

He knew something was not right. For some reason, everything he knew or had been taught about stalls and stall recovery was not working in this aircraft. He also sensed their pitch was somehow controlled by the thrust of the four engines. He surrendered. If he did not do something quickly, they all were likely going to die.

He looked at Fred and said, "I'm going to gradually pull the power off." The thought of reducing power during a stall recovery still went counter to everything all three pilots had been taught in training.

Fred said in a small voice, "It's okay with me. Boss. 'Cause whatever we've been doin' ain't working for sour owl shit."

"Here goes." He slowly pulled the throttles back to flight idle. His assumption was correct. The aircraft pitch was largely being controlled by the thrust of the four engines. When the throttles were pulled back to idle, the nose of the aircraft eventually and gracefully fell to a point slightly below the horizon. Slowly and gradually, the 747 had found a position of balance. Her airspeed was stable at 230 knots and she was descending slightly.

Don advanced the throttles 20 % and she sluggishly responded. Her broad nose slowly rose slightly above the horizon, while her airspeed remained constant at 230 knots. He pulled off half the power he had just added and her nose settled on the horizon. For the moment, he touched nothing and just watched what she was going to do. The 747 maintained a level altitude. The altitude neither increased nor decreased. Airspeed was stable. For the moment, they were safe. The question was, for how long?

81

**20:45 Eastern Standard Time
Northwest of Jacksonville, Florida**

"I'll be damned, I've never seen an airplane change pitch because of power settings."

Obviously relieved, Fred said, "Looks like you pulled one out for the Gipper." Then he added, "Probably because we don't have much elevator authority with the hydraulics shot to hell."

Stan said, "Might also have something to do with the engines being mounted under the wings. Might be a moment created that caused the pitch changes. Don't know. Just a guess."

Fred turned in his seat and spoke to Stan, "Welcome back. How was your nap?"

Don ignored his both pilots' remarks. He pulled the control column aft slightly, but nothing happened. He exerted more pressure, but the nose remained fixed firmly on the horizon. He released the pressure and slowly her nose started to rise.

Neither pilot knew if the stabilizer had moved or not. Don incorrectly assumed the horizontal stabilizer was not functioning at all. He had, however, correctly discovered the pitch of the aircraft could be marginally controlled by changes in the engine power settings. Aircraft pitch and airspeed are inexorably tied together. Basic airmanship, "Pitch increases, speed decreases. Pitch decreases, speed increases." When the badly damaged 747 accelerated, the nose started up. And conversely, when she slowed, the nose dropped.

"Fred, it looks like we have some pitch control with power. The trick is going to be how to descend to a lower altitude while we maintain our airspeed."

"Sort of like a monkey screwing a football."

Stan laughed at Fred's remark.

Stan said, "Tell you what. As I said, I think we are seeing the change in pitch because the engines are hung under the wings. When we change power settings, the aircraft reacts with a pitch change. Normally, we don't feel it or see it because of the automatic compensation from the elevators. With no hydraulic power to the stabilizer, she's free to do whatever she wants in the pitch axis."

No one commented on Stan's remarks, but all agreed.

"Let's smoothly pull the power back and see what the sink rate and airspeed does, tell the center that we are going to make use of our block altitude clearance."

"Jacksonville Center, this is 100, squawking 7500."

"100, Jax Center. Go ahead."

"Awhile back you gave us a block altitude from 25,000 to 15,000. We just wanted to let you know that we're on our way down to a lower altitude. Don't be alarmed if you see us making altitude changes."

"100 Roger. What are your conditions?"

"Other than we can't control our pitch or airspeed very well, we're doing just fine."

Angrily, Don picked up his microphone, "Jax Center. We nearly stalled the aircraft about 20 miles back. We are stable at 26,500. We want to evaluate our control capabilities."

"Understand, 100. You were cleared to maintain a block between 240 and 330. Please advise us if you need to descend below

240."

Fred picked up the microphone, "Understand we're still cleared the block 330 to 240. We're requesting a block from 310 to 10,000 feet. Don't know if we're going to need it, but want the option."

Don twitched and settled himself in his seat as he took a firm grasp on the control column. Slowly, deliberately, with calm anticipation, he pulled all four thrust levers back to 65% power.

Without looking over his shoulder Don said, "Stan, keep 'em all even. I don't want any yaw problems."

Stan Kurtz reached forward and made slight adjustments to the throttles, so each engine was producing 65% thrust. Stan removed his hand from the throttles and heard the "C Chord" chime, the automated warning to remind them they had deviated their assigned altitude by more than 500 feet.

Stan looked at Don's altimeter. 26,470 feet, 26,400 feet, 26,300 feet. The aircraft's airspeed had increased ten knots and with the increased airspeed, her nose started to rise. The captain pushed forward on the controls firmly, with no help. He reduced the power to 60%. This time, the same command, "Trim 'em up, Stan."

The 747 descended while Fred watched Don intently, "Looking good, Don. How much pitch control do you have with the elevators?"

"Not much. But I think at these lower airspeeds, maybe coupled with denser air, we may have better control." He added, "When I get her level at 24,000 and stabilized, I'll think we'll be able to evaluate our pitch control."

"Fred, I want you to be ready to fly her, should anything," and nodded his head in the direction of Bill and Carlton, "happens, I want you comfortable with this bird."

Slowly and gracefully, the enormous 747 fell toward the assigned altitude of 24,000 feet. When she descended through 25,000 feet, Fred made the required call out, "25 for 24." Five hundred feet above Don's altitude limit, Don gradually increased the power settings.

Slowly, the bulbous nose started to climb just above the horizon.

The altimeter slowed its downward trend, stopped and then started to climb. 24,400, 24,500, 24,600.

"Watch the altitude, Don. She's climbing on you, but the airspeed's holding steady."

Don reduced the power slightly and the altimeter settled. The airspeed remained stable and Don leveled the 747 at 24,400 feet.

Fred turned in his seat, so that he faced Don, "Pretty good, Orville. Except that if we're going to land at somewhere near sea level, you landed four hundred feet in the air."

Don said, "This is just like teaching a student pilot how to shoot approaches and landings."

Fred laughed, "Why don't you try to slick her down another four hundred feet, Ace, and then land her?"

Stan noticed that Don had a slight smile by the corner of his mouth.

Don made a short gracious bow and said, "Ok, if you're so damn good, why don't you try it?"

Fred took a light grasp on the controls, "My airplane. I've got it." Don could feel Fred's inputs on his controls and released his grip on the yoke.

He watched as Fred left the outboard engines untouched and only reduced the power on the two inboard engines. The nose moved slightly, almost unnoticed.

Smoothly, deliberately, the aircraft descended to 24,050 feet. Fifty feet above the pre-determined altitude, Fred pushed engines two and three up to a power setting just higher than the outboards. The aircraft leveled at exactly 24,000 feet. The airspeed started to show a gradual increase and Fred pulled two and three back to a power setting that matched one and four.

"There you go, Boss. Nothing to it." Don was impressed with Fred's flying skills.

"Nice, Fred. Very nice. Tell you what, hand fly her for a few minutes and get the feel and tell me what you think."

Fred followed Don's request, making slight changes in the

power settings and using the ailerons to make a shallow turns. After several minutes, both pilots felt reasonably comfortable as long as nothing else went wrong.

"Jacksonville. 100 here. We made it to 240. Now we'll use that block altitude you gave us between 240 and 10 thousand."

"100. Yes sir. You're cleared to 10 at your discretion. Squawk Ident. Report reaching."

Both pilots practiced descending and then leveling the aircraft through a series of stepped altitudes on their way to 10,000 feet above the Gulf of Mexico.

Jacksonville ATC called, "100, in about 25 miles, we are going to ask you to contact the Miami Center on 134.80, they'll be expecting you. Are you alright for the time being?"

Fred picked up his microphone, "Yes. Oh my yes. We're doing just ducky. On our way to 10,000 feet, just buzzing along." We seem to have the pitch pretty well under control. We're okay, as long as we don't make any big power changes, or get cute and roll this aluminum tube into a 30 degree bank."

"Fred, can the chatter. Cut the crap."

Fred again felt like a small child that had been reprimanded by his teacher, "Sorry."

Fred paused, then said to the controller on the ground, "Jacksonville Center, if you are going to talk to next sector, pass the word to them that we are going to take it nice and easy. No steep turns and no aerial ballet."

"Roger, 100. We'll pass the word to them."

Fred's altimeter suddenly showed an angry red flag across the face of the instrument that read "**FAIL.**"

Immediately, Fred relinquished the manual flying of the ship back to the Captain, "Don, you've got it. My altimeter just went tits up."

Don quickly and instinctively said, "Work with Stan and see what you can do about trouble shooting this problem quickly. I don't like this at all… flying over water at night with only one altimeter."

Concern rose in Fred's throat as he said, "Stan, I think I've done it. I tapped my altimeter and now all I have is a bunch of red fail flags. Do you think you could take a look in your bag of tricks at the adult busy-board back there and tell me what's up?"

"Sure." Stan sounded positive in his desire to help, but suddenly could not remember even the most basic facts about trouble-shooting Fred's problem with the number 2 electric altimeter.

"Good. See what you can do for me. The captain is paranoid about people looking over his shoulder."

From force of habit Stan slowly rotated a selector knob to check and verify power flow to and from various instruments on the aircraft.

With a practiced hand, Stan moved two switches. Lights blinked and a meter reading changed, but Stan could not interpret their meanings. With no fanfare, the angry red warning flags on Fred's altimeter disappeared.

Fred looked at his altimeter and then said to the Flight Engineer, "You do nice work, Stanley. I'm going to put your name in for an air medal."

Stan said, "Thank you," but had no idea why Fred's altimeter suddenly had started to work again.

Fred smiled at his boss, who looked back and attempted to stifle a smile. Fred winked and then said to Stan, "Wait until he finds out I'm after his job," referring to the airline policy that all captains must start as copilots.

The radio crackled, "100. Jacksonville Center. Contact Miami Center now on 134.80. Descend to 8,000 feet, your discretion. Good luck."

Don reached for the microphone and said, "We're on our way to 8,000. Thanks for the help."

He hung up the microphone and said to his copilot, "Fred, go ahead and take her down to 8 grand." Don thought that maybe Fred was not so bad after all. One thing was certain: Fred was one hell of a pilot.

HIJACKING OF FLIGHT 100

Fred again slowly reduced the power on the inboard engines. He flew the aircraft precisely to 8,050 feet, reapplied the power and leveled at the lumbering 747 at squarely 8,000 feet.

Fred looked at Don, "I'm glad we got this thing under control. I thought back there that we were going to have to get our next clearance from the United States Bureau of Mines."

82

21:05 Eastern Standard Time
Abeam of Tampa, Florida

Earlier, but less than an hour ago, Lazlo Fielding and John Batchelor had been together in the Operations room at the hangar. They talked to 100 on the radio and about whether they could proceed to Havana.

Though their discussions were not fruitful, their motivations were above board. Fielding had been concerned that if they didn't cooperate, the hijacker would injure or kill a passenger or a crew member. Don was concerned about the structural integrity of his 747 and wanted to get the aircraft on the ground as soon as possible. Furthermore, he did not want to land at Havana with a badly damaged aircraft. Though he didn't know with any certainty, he suspected Havana's Jose Marti airport probably had marginal fire and rescue equipment, if any. Not Don Webber's idea of acceptable risk management. He and Fielding discussed options. Under the FAA rules, the pilot and dispatcher must agree on the destination.

"I don't want to leave a badly damaged 40 million dollar aircraft in a communist country. I'm convinced wherever we land, this bird is not going to fly for a long time. A lot of repairs will be required and I'm sure the company doesn't want Fidel's followers doing the work. The emergency equipment, training and protocols in the United States are much better than whatever they might or might not have in Havana." After reconsideration, Captain Webber added, "If we landed in Cuba, how do we get 439 passengers and crew out of the country? We don't have diplomatic relations with the Cuban government." He ended the conversation, "Havana is not an option. We are not going there."

"We still think you should consider the wishes of the hijacker." Fielding continued, "The company policy is to cooperate. What will he do when he finds you have landed in Miami, instead of Cuba?"

"Once we've landed it doesn't make any difference, I intend to have the aircraft disabled on landing, if necessary. Right now, he seems sort of quiet, he's not making any threats. He has a gun, but I don't think he's going to use it again, especially, if he thinks he's getting his way. My read is that I think he'll be all right."

Don made his decision not to proceed to Havana, but rather land at Miami, solely based on safety considerations. He considered Atlanta or Jacksonville. The duty runway at Miami was 2,000 feet longer than Jacksonville or Atlanta, and the weather was better in Miami. Most important, the wind at Miami International was supposed to be right down the runway – no cross wind. This was a critical consideration in Don's decision.

"Captain, this is John Batchelor, Head of Security here in New York. If you decide to go to Atlanta, Miami, Jacksonville or where ever, please let us know as soon as you have reached a decision, so we can coordinate with the local law enforcement on your arrival? This might turn into a dicey situation when you land, with the hijacker being armed and all."

He saw his opportunity. "You are right John. You are hereby notified that we are going to Miami. The weather is much better than Atlanta. I deem it safer to go to Miami than to proceed to Havana. Alert the troopers, we're on the way."

83

21:25 Eastern Standard Time
80 Miles West of St. Petersburg, Florida

After his radio conversations with Fielding and Batchelor, Don spoke frankly and openly to the hijacker. "As I said earlier, we have much to do here if we're going to take you where you want to go. I have to discuss things with my crew and people on the ground. You are welcome to listen. But I don't have time to ask you for permission to use all this equipment, or to talk on the radio."

There was been no response from Bill.

"What I'll do if you want, is set you up with a pair of head phones so you can listen to the radio." He turned and said, "There is an extra set of ear phones on the bulkhead."

The hijacker picked up a spare headset and tried to put it on with one hand, holding his gun with the other. What he didn't know was that there were over twenty combinations of audio sources that could be piped through the headset he held in his hand. The way the switches were set, he could only hear conversations on the ground interphone.

Once Don made the offer, the hijacker oddly seemed

disinterested in the specifics of the flight communications. After a few seconds of trying to put the headset on, the hijacker gave up and threw them on the floor.

Because of the hijacker's lack of interest, Don, Fred and Stan were able to communicate with each other through the cockpit interphone system.

He made a couple of adjustments to his instruments and and said to Fred, "Punch in the coordinates for Miami in the number three platform and give me an ETA. I would guess less than one hour."

Without a word, Fred did Don's bidding.

"The platform says 57 minutes, plus 8 minutes for the letdown and arrival. An hour and five or six should do it."

Don reselected his radio, "Dispatch, this is 100. You can expect us on the ground at Miami by 2210 local time." Not wanting an argument, Don added, "100 out."

"Well. Here we go."

Don didn't care much for what the FAA bureaucrats had said. Or, for that matter, what the company recommendations were. Going to Miami was the best of all possible choices in a very difficult situation.

The tenuous condition of the crippled 747 demanded that he land as soon as possible. To paraphrase the company policy, "Land at the nearest suitable airport, in point of time."

"Stan, you okay?"

"Yes." Twisting his neck, "I'm okay. I'm just a little worse for the bumps and bruises. I'll be ok. He thought a second then said, "Tell you what though, I'll feel much better when we get this hog on the ground."

The large lump behind is right ear made him look much the worse for wear. His hair was matted with blood and his nose had a cut from his glasses. His right eye was nearly swollen shut and had turned the color of eggplant. Stan still had a terrible headache and felt as bad as he looked. If he moved his head quickly, he was overcome by mounting waves of nausea.

The only thing that kept him going was his intense desire to keep the 747 aloft until they could safely and successfully put the bird on the ground. Stan realized he was not wearing his glasses. Looking around, he spotted them on the floor, twisted and broken. He opened his navigation bag and retrieved his FAA-required backup pair of glasses.

Fred chuckled nervously, "Preferably within the confines of an airport. And preferably a big airport with long runways."

"Come on Fred, we should be in the Miami area in the next fifty minutes. I need your utmost concentration and assistance. I don't need your poor attempts at humor."

Fred looked intently at his newly repowered altimeter and other navigation instruments and was everything was working properly. He leaned over toward Don. "How're your instruments? Everything okay?"

Don was caught off guard by Fred's concern, "Fine. Everything is fine."

Again the radio crackled in their headsets. "100. Miami Center. If possible, Ident on 3498."

Fred looked down at the transponder and saw dried blood on the window that revealed the selected codes. Fred licked his finger and wiped the blood away and turned the two concentric knobs, so the digits 3 4 9 8 showed in the window. He pressed the IDENT button and said at the same time, "Here you go, Miami. An Ident on 3498, coming at you."

"Roger, 100. Ident again."

"Rog."

"100. Can you switch to your other transponder?"

Fred twisted a selector switch and said, "There you go. Is that any better?"

Ten or fifteen seconds passed before the Miami called back, "100. Your Mode C reporting is not working. We're only getting a partial primary skin paint return for you."

Fred cursed. The controller asked, "Can you recycle the circuit breakers?"

"NO. We're barely able to keep this thing in the air, we are not going to start trouble shooting for the FAA." Don was angry at the controller's request.

"OK, 100. Just be aware we have no Idents or altitude info for you. Confirm you are at 8,000."

Fred looked at Don's altimeter, which read 7,980 feet, "That's a Rog. We're level at 8 grand."

"100, what are your intentions?"

Don seethed as he picked up his microphone and said, "We want a clearance direct to Miami. We don't know how much longer this piece of crap is going to stay airborne. We want a straight-in approach. We have very limited pitch control capabilities and roll control is not much better. No big turns." He paused, waiting for a response from the Miami ATC Sector. None came.

"We want vector to Runway 9 ILS approach. We'll track the localizer inbound. When we capture the glide slope, we'll follow it to the runway." As an afterthought, he added, "We are also requesting a GCA monitoring, as a back-up. We want someone monitoring our approach to let us know if we are too high, fast, low or slow." He paused, then said, "We also would like to have a long, extended final approach."

"Stand by 100, I'll have to check that with the arrival sector over at Miami Tracon."

"You check with whoever you want, we're about 70 or 80 miles north of the Runway 9 localizer. I intend to make a left turn and start tracking inbound. If you can't approve that, we'll declare an emergency."

The unseen controller said, "Stand by."

Don tossed the microphone on to the glare shield, "'Stand by,' my ass. Here we are in a crippled, marginally stable aircraft and those stupid bastards want us to stand by."

A new voice from the Miami Sector called back, "100. Maintain present heading until you receive the ILS for runway 9, 110.9. Inbound Front Course 092°. You are cleared for a Runway 9 ILS Approach. Proceed direct via the localizer to the airport. If able, Report GRITT Intersection. If unable, report INESS Outer Marker Inbound." A short pause, then, "Looks like you'll intercept the localizer about fifteen miles outside the outer marker."

Don, Fred and Stan considered what they had heard. The controller continued, "We have cleared all known traffic between you and the field." Almost as an afterthought, the controller said, "You are cleared to deviate as necessary. Advise your intentions."

Fred picked up his mic, "Roger. When we get a little closer. We'll also check in once we're established on the 9 ILS localizer."

"100 do you want the emergency equipment standing by?"

Fred looked at Don, "Might as well. We pay for the service. 'Tis time we collected."

"Just tell 'em we want the equipment standing by for us. No more."

"Miami, sure, we'd love to have the equipment waiting for us."

"Understand. 100. We'll alert them." Another new voice, a female controller said, "We have cleared the area for your arrival. We confirm you are cleared for an ILS approach to Runway 9. You are also cleared to land on Runway 9." She paused, waiting for 100 to answer, "I will be your controller during your approach."

Fred quickly looked on the back of the approach charts for Miami and said to Don, "Runway 9's over 13,000 feet long."

Don picked up his microphone, "Miami. Wind check."

"Current wind is 100° at 9 knots."

"Miami, any NOTAMs we need to know about for the TCA, terminal control area? Also, we have ATIS information TANGO."

Stan insistently interrupted them. "Don, we're losing the hydraulic fluid in system 4." His voice rose, "That's bad news." Stan was diagnosing the system problem as he spoke, "Split Trailing Edge Flaps. And, we'll be down to alternate braking." Stan referred to the main hydraulic power source for the trailing edge flaps was losing fluid. This would also reduce the primary source of power for the 16 wheel main landing gear brakes.

Don responded instantly, "Stan, run the Hydraulic Fluid Loss checklist and have Fred back you up."

Stan reached for the red bordered checklist, flipped the plastic sheet over and looked for the Hydraulic Fluid Loss procedure. A movement, some flicker of light caught his attention. Stan looked aft toward the Hydraulic Control Panel. Everything appeared to have returned to normal. No loss of fluid and no other discernible problems.

"That's the damndest thing. The quantity just disappeared and then returned. When the quantity went down, we got low quantity and low pressure lights on the EDP." Stan thought and said, "This is like the simulator. Blink and all the problems are resolved. Weird."

Don answered Stan, "Well, keep an eye on it. Let me know if anything else goes wrong."

Stan replaced the emergency checklist in the holder and hoped he would not need to use it again.

84

21:50 Eastern Standard Time
129 miles North of Naples, Florida

Don looked back at the hijacker, who still held his pistol inaccurately aimed Carlton's direction on the floor and aft bulkhead. Carlton either appeared to be asleep or to have lost consciousness. Clearly, he was dazed.

He spoke not only to the hijacker, but to everyone in the cockpit. "We're on our way and should be on the ground in less than twenty minutes. No tricks. We only have about forty minutes of fuel left. We're going to have to make this a good one. We have enough fuel to make one approach. That's it. No second chances. I don't want any trouble from you."

Bill looked at the Captain. He didn't know what to do. No plan. He thought, "There never was a plan. Things have turned to shit. Nothing was going my way. Nothing.

Don continued, "I want a Flight Attendant up here to help clean up this mess. I want Carlton moved away from the door." He stared back at the hijacker, "Drag him to the side there."

Bill didn't want anyone else in the cockpit. He was confused and panicked. Once again, he had lost control of the situation. He was a loser *"el eperdedor!"*

Unexpectedly, he attempted to stand and immediately lost his balance. He lurched precariously to the right and forward. He steadied himself against the back of Stan's seat. He stopped his fall with his right hand, the hand that held the pistol.

Bill's hand and the pistol scribed an arc in Stan's field of view. With explosive speed, Stan instinctively grabbed Bill's wrist with his right hand. He twisted Bill's arm and hand outward and down keeping the gun aimed away from himself. Bill was pulled off balance and Stan could feel the tendons in Bill's arm strain as he twisted harder.

When he had proper leverage, he smashed the hijacker's hand against the aft circuit breaker panel. He pounded Bill's hand that held the gun and felt Bill's warm and sticky blood as his hand was sliced on the ragged edges of the panel.

Bill screamed and swore in Spanish when two small bones in his right hand snapped, *"Dios Presa de puta madre. Hijo de puta, esto dueleony."*

The tables had turned. Internal injuries caused the hijacker to drop his gun, his only salvation, the equalizer was now gone. The gun clattered harmlessly on the top of Stan's worktable, and dropped to the floor where it clanked against the aluminum slide mechanism on Stan's chair. Miraculously, the gun did not discharge.

Stan strained to maintain control over the hijacker as he yelled, "Fred. Don. Goddamnit. Somebody help me."

Fred undid his seatbelt and shoulder harness straps, turned and started out of his seat. Before he could take one step, Carlton was on his feet behind the hijacker and grabbed him around the neck with a surprisingly quick action. Carlton was much stronger than he looked.

Despite the beating he had taken, he was able to pull up and started to suffocate the hijacker. He gagged, swallowed and ineffectively clawed at Carlton's hand and then gagged again. His breathing was a series of raspy, choking coughs. His eyes watered. He could not believe it. He was being choked by the *Paloma*. The fag, *El Maricón* was strangling him and more important, winning.

Carlton made a small, round, balled-up fist with his free hand. In a furious series of blows, pounded Bill's head. Rage overtook Carlton as he continued to slam his fist into soft tissue, bone, cartilage and flesh. His only focus was pay back to the hijacker for the terror, embarrassment and humiliation he had inflicted on him.

The visceral animal strength Bill had relied on had left him. His attempts to thwart Carlton's emotionally-driven attack ended. The hijacker's weakening and futile attempts drove Carlton to pull harder. Bill could no longer see Stan, nor anything else. He was losing consciousness. A dark cone closed in front of him as his optic nerve became oxygen-starved. In what was his final resignation, Bill knew he was screwed. He realized it was over. He had failed. Again.

Carlton angrily uncurled his free hand and grabbed Bill's face, just above his mouth and dug his fingers into his flesh. He wanted to tear the hijacker's face apart. He wanted the hijacker to hurt, to bleed. Carlton wanted to kill him.

Stan continued to hold his wrist against the bloodied table. He could sense Bill's resolve drift away as his resistance faded.

Stan instinctively knew the time was right. With his left hand, he reached up and smashed Bill in the face. His hand glanced off Carlton's fingers, who squealed when he pulled his hand away. Stan swung again, this time he connected squarely and firmly. He felt the cartilage break in Bill's nose. As quickly as it began, the fight was over. Bill collapsed against Carlton.

85

22:00 Eastern Standard Time
North of Naples, Florida

Don had seen and heard most of the short fight. "Carlton, quickly. Without looking back at Carlton, Stan or the hijacker, he said, "Get the first aid kit."

Carlton thought the Captain was crazy. This despicable person tried to kill him and now the Captain wanted the first aid kit. Carlton did not move, nor give any indication that he heard Don.

"Goddamnit, Carlton. Move!"

"Really, Captain. I don't care if he just dies. I really don't. I mean it would be fine with me if just died right here on the spot. Actually, I hope he does die, after all the terrible things he did to me." Carlton started to whimper, "He hurt me and humiliated me. He embarrassed me in front of my passengers."

"Carlton. Goddamnit. I don't care about any of that. I want you to get the nylon zip-ties from the First Aid kit. We need to restrain the bastard 'til we've landed." While Don gave orders to Carlton, he continued to shift his attention between his instruments and the physical drama in the back of the cockpit.

Slowly, Carlton understood. He ungraciously let go of Bill and watched his head bounce off the Flight Engineer's desk top. He retrieved the kit from the aft bulkhead. When he tried to open the kit, he broke a fingernail on the copper wire/lead seal. He stopped what he was doing, looked at his torn nail and cursed.

Stan watched Carlton with growing anticipation. "Jesus Christ. Hurry up. I don't want this asshole to come around before we have him restrained."

In an apologetic and contrite voice he said, "Sorry, Stan. I'll get him out of your way."

Carlton dragged the hijacker away from Stan. As soon as the support against Stan was removed, the hijacker slid down and collapsed on the floor. He lay on his back. Carlton noticed his captor had wet his pants. Stan got out of his seat and helped Carlton pull him away from the cockpit door, then dragged him toward the crew emergency exit escape hatch.

He and Carlton rummaged through the first aid kit until they found the bag of nylon zip-ties. Stan ripped open the package and grabbed several of the black handcuffs. They trussed Bill, left hand to right ankle and right hand to left ankle. For extra measure, Stan put one additional zip-tie across both wrists where they crossed below his knees.

Stan took three handcuffs and looped then together around the hijacker's right arm and a piece of formed aluminum framework. While the hijacker might be able to move slightly, he could not get anywhere near the pilots or the flight controls.

Stan pressed past Carlton, who was looking at himself in the cockpit mirror, checking to see how badly his face had been damaged by the hijacker. Stan smirked and was astonished at Carlton's obsession with his appearance.

Stan slid back into his seat and put on his shoulder harnesses and seatbelts. He noticed wet and drying blood on his panel, desktop, chair. The aft circuit breaker panel had torn pieces of Bill's flesh stuck to the dark grey surface.

With a sigh of relief and a smile, Don turned and said over his right shoulder, "Stan, that was outstanding. Good show."

"Thanks, Don." He was still a little out of breath, but repeated himself. "Thanks."

Fred added his input. "How did you know to do that? Where did you get the idea?"

"I don't know, Fred. It was just sort of like before I went to 'Nam. Back to basics from my Marine Corps training. You know, the old hand to hand stuff."

Fred grinned, "Semper Fi, brother. Semper Fi."

Don smiled again and said, "Well, I for one, am very glad you were on this trip. Both Fred and I owe you one."

Carlton turned away from the mirror. "Captain, you did all the work. You saved my life and the lives of my passengers. You were wonderful. Maybe magnificent would be a better word." He started to silently weep, sniffled and said, "I'm sorry. I am so embarrassed."

Fred smiled, "Carlton, my man, you did an awesome, stupendous, outrageous job. You were unbelievable. You are a tiger. You beat the shit out of him. Bravo!"

Carlton was pleased and at the same time, embarrassed. "Thanks, Fred." He paused, looked at all of them and said, "Well Captain, I'll go below now and help the passengers."

Don spoke reflexively, "No, Carlton, I want you to stay here and keep an eye on our hijacker. We are going to be busy and we don't want him causing any trouble." He quickly looked over his right shoulder. "Stan, do you have his firearm back there?"

Stan reached down to the floor and retrieved the pistol. "Yep. I've got it right here." He unceremoniously set it down on his desk.

Don turned around in his seat so he was facing Carlton and Stan, "Carlton, you sit in that extra jump seat and watch him. If he moves, you tell Stan."

"Stan, if he tries to move or makes any trouble, I want you to shoot the son of a bitch. Dead. Got that?"

"Yes Sir!" A look of comprehension and satisfaction

momentarily crossed Stan's face.

The battered Flight Attendant slowly nodded that he also understood. However, his understanding did not diminish the residual fear in his eyes. He was very glad there were three other people in the cockpit who would deal with the hijacker if he tried anything.

"Alright, then. Enough of this. We've got work to do."

86

22:15 Eastern Standard Time
West of Naples, Florida

Don looked along the west coast of Florida and the lights of Naples as they slipped beneath the nose of the aircraft.

He reached up and pressed the emergency cockpit call chimes. Almost immediately, there was a response, "Yes, this is Patti. Are you all alright?"

Don spoke with authority, "Thanks to Stan, we are terrific. We are going to Miami and should be on the ground in less than twenty minutes. I do not want any passengers to move. Period. Remember what I said, nobody moves. If you see anyone starting to get up, you have my permission to sit on them."

Fred smiled and looked at Don. "Does that go for me too? I would sort of like it if Patti sat on me."

Don ignored Fred and said, "Patti, I am going to make a PA announcement to the folks. I'll remind them about moving around. In about ten minutes, I want all the passengers to brace for a crash landing. You know the drill. Sharp objects stowed, pillow over the head, head down, arms over the neck."

Fred spoke, "Is this where you put your head between your knees and kiss your sweet ass good bye?"

Don allowed himself to chuckle then went on, "I'll give you notification as to landing time. We will let you know ten minutes out, five minutes out and one minute from touchdown."

"Right, Captain. We'll take care of the cabin. How are all of you? We heard gun shots and then the aircraft started to flip over."

Don handed the interphone handset to Fred. "Tell her what is going on here. Bring her up to date."

The aircraft is reasonably sound. Carlton is okay, a little the worse for wear, but he'll live to dance again." Carlton grinned when he heard Fred's comment to Patti.

Fred continued, "Stan took a rim shot to the side of the head, which has sort of spoiled his boyish good looks. The hijacker has been subdued and is lashed to the aircraft. We're doing our best to get this piece of junk on the ground in one piece. Keep the faith and we'll keep you posted."

87

22:20 Eastern Standard Time
85 Miles West of Miami, Florida

Patti and Amelio walked to the service center in the middle of the airplane. Amelio made a Public Address announcement, "Ladies and Gentlemen, This is your purser, Amelio Perez. The Captain has asked me to inform you about our plans. We are less than twenty minutes from Miami, Florida. As some of you know, one of our passengers wanted to go to Havana. He has been restrained and is no longer a problem." Amelio heard a muted cheer from the cabin.

"Our Captain has also advised we are experiencing some difficulty with controlling the aircraft." A hushed intake of collective breaths could be heard in the various sections of the airplane.

"Because of these problems, he has instructed us to tell you that every passenger must remain in their seat. No one can move about the cabin. The Captain said the balance of the airplane is critical. If anyone moves, it could throw our balance off. I needn't tell you that we do not want that to happen."

He waited a few seconds to let this information fully settle in before he continued, "We are here to help you with this situation. We are very well trained to do this. But, we need your cooperation. No one is to move from their seat.

"Don't worry about your belongings. There will be plenty of time to gather all of them later, after we land.

"We will be circulating though the cabin to help you prepare for landing in Miami. Please give the Flight Attendants in your cabin your full attention. Thank you for your cooperation and assistance."

Amelio and Patti gathered the rest of the cabin crew in the forward section of First Class to review the planned crash-landing procedures. Per company policy, the twelve attendants were divided into six teams. Each team of two was to circulate through their zone.

When two Attendants were in each zone, Amelio planned to make his ditching announcement, which he would read *verbatim* from an Emergency Red-Bordered laminated plastic card.

In less than two minutes, all of the cabin zones checked in. "Ladies and Gentlemen, this is Amelio Perez again. I want to instruct you in a practice exercise we are going to do, in preparation for our landing in Miami. As our Captain has said, we have had some problems with the aircraft. Because of these problems, we are going to do some things that you probably have never done before.

"First, you are going to take all the sharp objects out of your pockets. Objects like pens, pencils, combs, rulers and place them in the seat pouch in front of you. Please do that now." The Flight Attendants heard passengers' voices. While a few complained, most spoke with nervous anticipatory fear.

"Next, we are going to practice the impact position." Another fearful murmur swept through the cabin when Amelio said 'impact.'"

"Please give your attention to the Cabin Attendant at the front of your zone."

He waited for the noise to settle throughout the aircraft. "First, place your hands behind your head and then clasp your fingers tightly behind your head.

"Next, when I say the word, 'NOW!' I want you to bend forward and place your elbows on your knees."

Amelio looked through his part of the airplane interior and saw three flight attendants standing with their hands tightly clasped behind their heads.

"Alright, Ladies and Gentlemen. NOW!"

Immediately, almost all of the passengers swiftly knelt forward and attempted to place their elbows on their knees.

Amelio looked at the few passengers who were still looking around. They reminded him of the few parishioners who never closed their eyes in church during mass, but looked about to see who was praying.

He addressed these people forcefully and directly, "Ladies and Gentlemen, most of you did well, very well. Unfortunately, some of you did not. We are going to practice this until we all get it right." He paused and looked directly at two or three passengers around him who had not complied with his instructions.

Without warning, "NOW!"

From his vantage point he saw that everyone but one woman bent forward at his command.

Amelio walked to his passenger, "Do you understand me?" The elderly woman half smiled and nodded her head, indicating she did understand. He turned and retraced his steps to the mid-galley area. All the passengers in his zone had their eyes riveted on him.

"One more time, ladies and gentlemen. This is for your own safety and protection. Your life may depend upon you doing as you are told."

Patti looked at the elderly woman to whom Amelio had referred and now saw she was silently crying. Quickly, she walked to the passenger, "Are you alright? Is there any way I can help you?"

"I am so frightened. I have never flown before. I was on my way to my sister's funeral in New York. But now, I'm afraid I'm going to die, too."

Several passengers in adjacent seats overhead her frightened comments and murmured their general agreement with her.

Patti surveyed the situation and quickly added, "Don't be afraid.

We are all trained to help our passengers in times like these. If I didn't think it was safe, I wouldn't be flying."

Patti gave the woman her most reassuring smile, "Besides, the First Officer and I are going to get married later this year and I wouldn't want anything to spoil our wedding."

She had absolutely no idea why she said that about Fred. She remembered flying with him somewhere, but barely knew him. Her only general recollection was his quick sense of humor. But, marriage?

Her comments seemed to calm and reassure the frightened elderly passenger. She smiled at Patti and said, "Well, if you and your fella are going to get married, I'm sure this airplane with its little problems won't stand in your way." They both smiled as the woman said, "Invite me to your wedding. I'd love to meet him."

Patti excused herself from the woman. She turned and walked to the front of her zone, when she heard it again, "NOW!"

Much to her satisfaction, every passenger, including the elderly woman, eagerly bent over, touching their elbows to their knees.

Amelio spoke quickly, "Thank you everyone. That was excellent. Simply excellent. You are all good passengers. You may sit up now. We will keep you posted regarding our progress toward Miami. We will let you know when our landing is a few minutes away and then approximately one minute away. At that time, I will make the command for your cooperation."

Amelio read from the plastic card, "Please resist temptation to look out the windows, or around the cabin. It is absolutely necessary that all of you keep you heads down. We want the passengers sitting in a window seat to close the window shades next to them. This is done to help you not look outside." Throughout the cabin, over 140 window shades were closed.

"Now, please, make sure your seat belts are fastened tightly. Thank you again. We will keep you posted. Thank you for your cooperation."

All eleven Flight Attendants, including Patti and Amelio, busied themselves placing all the loose items that were not tied down in the lavatories. They circulated through the cabin, talked to many passengers and assured them there was no cause for alarm. Everything would be okay as soon as they landed in Miami.

88

22:30 Eastern Standard Time
Overhead Naples, Florida

Fred thought about what was ahead for them. The next ten or fifteen minutes should be no problem as long as the aircraft held together. There was no way of telling what could go wrong next. Even if the aircraft stayed airborne until they were ready to land, there was a very real potential for disaster. Fred knew it was up to the three of them to minimize the risk and provide the passengers with a safe conclusion to their flight.

They had almost no pitch control. Each and every time the thrust was adjusted, the aircraft adversely reacted. Fred was not sure that Don or he would be able to successfully land without incurring significant damage to the aircraft. Not to mention the potential for the loss of a great many lives. Fred idly considered what the chances were that they might just wrap this airplane into an aluminum ball at or near the end of the runway in Florida.

Don looked at Fred, and then back at Stan. He could not see Carlton who was sitting directly behind him. He had no interest in looking at, or seeing, the hijacker. "I think we have a fair chance to pull this off."

He looked again at Fred, "How does she feel to you?"

"Sloppy and sluggish, but flyable."

"Stan, you and Fred are my backups. I want you both to monitor everything. If either of you see anything that looks outside the normal parameters, call it out."

Fred grinned, "This whole airplane is outside the normal parameters."

Don smiled and said, "I agree. But we've got to do the best we can with what we've been given."

Don ran a mental checklist through his mind. For the first time, he fully considered braking and stopping the crippled aircraft. He wondered about the primary hydraulic power source for braking. He was not at all certain the "D" hydraulic system would work when he needed it most. That left the pneumatic emergency brakes.

He looked at the red emergency brake handle in front of him. For the first time, he noticed it was safety-tied with a copper wire and a lead seal. He gingerly touched the handle to test the integrity of the safety wire. It was secure. In fact, it was very secure.

He looked over his shoulder and said to Stan, "Do you have a knife or pliers? I want to break the seal on the emergency brake handle."

Stan lifted himself out of his seat and instantly regretted the strobe-like headache he had triggered. He tried to blink away the headache, with no luck. He found his small Leatherman pocketknife, pulled it out and opened the tool to expose the small pliers and wire cutter, "Here you go, Don." He handed the opened knife to the captain with the blade pointed toward himself. Don took the knife and sliced through the thin copper wire with one motion.

"Don, I'd be careful with that handle. I don't know how much play there is in the rigging. Once you open the emergency brake valve, you can't shut it off. It's either on or off." He thought and then added, "And there's no metering of the brake pressure. No Anti Skid either."

Somewhere in Don's airline training he had heard those warnings, but had paid little attention to them. They had always seemed out of context and without application. Now, he wished he had paid more attention to the inner workings of the emergency brake system. Almost as a last ditch effort, he asked Stan, "Walk me through this. Start with normal brake application, where I'll have Anti Skid protection. Is that right?"

"Just like any other landing."

Fred laughed and said, "Yeah. Right."

"Go ahead. What if I don't have normal braking?"

"I'm not sure, but I suspect you would want to get off the brakes and then open the pneumatic brake control." Stan was silent for several seconds as he considered what he thought would happen. "Here's where I'm not sure. Do you get back on the brakes, or does opening the handle fully apply brakes? I remember in some aircraft if you use the air charge and step on the brakes at the same time, you lock up all the wheels. The combination of pneumatic pressure and normal brake pressure overwhelms the system and the brakes lock up."

Fred said, "Seems to me you would only use the air brakes if the normal hydraulic brakes failed. That would make sense if they designed the airplane that way. Use the normal brakes 'til there is no more pressure and then use the air brakes."

Stan said, "But, that's not the question. The question is when do you open the pneumatic valve? Or, do you stand on the brakes first and then use the…"

"This is not the time to have this conversation. I'm going to use the normal braking. If, or when, they fail, I'll open the air brake handle. If that doesn't work, if the airplane doesn't slow, then I'll romp on the brake pedals. If that locks up all the wheels, so be it."

"That's one way to get 'er stopped. Just lock 'em up." Both Don and Stan chuckled at Fred's nervous comment.

89

22:46 Eastern Standard Time
41 Miles West of Miami International Airport

"Miami Approach, this is 100."

"100. We have you on radar as a primary skin paint return and we think we may have a visual on you. For verification, if able, flash your landing lights three times."

Fred reached for the landing light switches at the lower edge of the upper overhead panel. He quickly snapped all four landing light switches down and then back up. He repeated the cycle three times. "Miami, there you go. Do you see us?"

"Roger 100. We saw your lights. We believe we have you in visual contact. Say your position and Ident."

"We are sort of tracking inbound on the localizer. We were cleared to land by the last controller." He paused, " Be advised. We are Bingo fuel." A universal phrase that meant they only had minimum emergency fuel remaining.

"Roger your fuel situation. You are cleared to land. The equipment is standing by."

Don continued to concentrate on keeping the 747 on airspeed, on altitude and on heading. He looked over at his co-pilot. "Fred, tell the folks where we are, where we are going. Tell them about the hijacker and tell them everything is going to be okay."

"100. We have your Ident and have glasses on you."

Don said to Fred, "Roger."

Fred picked up his microphone and said, "Roger. 100."

Putting down his microphone and picking up the cabin PA, Fred cleared his throat, "Ladies and Gentlemen, this is your pilot. We have some good news and some bad news.

"First the good news, the hijacker has been handcuffed and is sleeping comfortably on the cockpit floor. A second bit of good news is that we are cleared to land at Miami International Airport. All things being equal, we should be on the ground in about twenty minutes or less.

He paused, as though to collect his thoughts, "Now for the bad news. We have suffered partial shutdowns of several of the flight control systems. Some of these systems are not used all the time and will have no impact on the rest of our flight tonight.

"However, others are important. Some of these systems are used during landing and stopping. Unfortunately, we won't know exactly what we have until we try to use them."

He paused - this time to calm himself. "We suspect the flaps may take longer than normal, so we'll extend them earlier than normal." He licked his lips, smiled and said, "When we extend the flaps, there may be some unwanted changes in the aircraft attitude like you may have felt earlier.

"When we extend the flaps, we'll do it a little bit at a time and then re-trim the aircraft. You'll probably feel those changes too.

"When the flaps are down, we'll extend the landing gear. When the gear is down, we will be committed to land." He held his breath and then said, "We do not think we will be able to raise the landing gear once it is down and locked."

Fred released the press to talk switch on the PA handset and asked, "What else do you want me to tell them? Do you want me to mention the potential problem with the brakes?"

Don said, "No. That's enough for now. Just tell them that it is important that nobody move from their seats. We have the aircraft trimmed and I don't want any unanticipated center-of-gravity related pitch changes. As you said, we want to keep this from being an "E" ticket ride at Disney World."

Fred pressed the microphone. In the cabin, a loud click was heard before Fred's voice continued, "Well, that's about it from the cockpit. Remember, it is critically important that nobody move from their seats. When we want you to get up, we'll turn off the Fasten Seat Belt sign. Patti or Amelio probably will have a few words for you. Take it away, Patti and Amelio."

90

22:55 Eastern Standard Time
11 Miles West of Miami International Airport

On the ground, the controllers and others in the tower speculated on the extent of damage to the aircraft. Many flights make a routine request to have the emergency equipment stand by. However, this one was urgent. This time, the request for the equipment could easily be a genuine necessity for survival.

The Miami tower supervisor called. A woman's voice said, "100, if you have a minute, can you tell us what the nature of your problems are? Specifically, what can the crash crews and first responders expect?"

"Tell 'em, Fred."

"For openers, we have very limited pitch control. So we don't think we are going to have much flare capability on landing. Second, our normal brake system is suspect. So, we may not have normal braking. Almost certain we won't have any Anti Skid protection. We still have the emergency backup brakes available to us. We won't know how reliable that system will be until we try to use it.

"Seems like less than half our aileron power is available, so roll control could be a problem, especially when we get down and dirty. Strangely enough, we still have both our rudder power packages and yaw dampers."

Stan coughed the words, "Landing gear?"

Fred nodded, "We don't know about the landing gear. But, we assume it won't be a problem."

A different tower operator, a male with a very strong southern accent said, "Sounds like y'all have had a fun-filled afternoon and evening." The voice paused, then said, "Y'all be careful now."

"Oh, and one other thing. The hijacker is subdued and handcuffed to the airframe. We have put our best and sternest flight attendant in charge of prisoners." As an afterthought Fred said, "I supposed if there were to be an incident on landing, you'd need to tell the first responders about this idiot's location."

In a light and almost whimsical voice, as though nothing had happened and this was just another normal approach, Fred said, "We'll see you on the ground in about ten minutes."

Stan questioned, "Don, is it time to alert the cabin?"

"Good idea. Stan. Fred, tell 'em when it's about ten minutes 'til touchdown."

Fred nodded and rang the emergency chimes, "Yes? Patti here."

"Patti, about ten minutes to run. How're things going back there?"

"Pretty well. Many of the passengers are anxious and some are very scared. Overall, everyone seems to be managing alright." She hesitated and then said, "No panic." She paused, "Yet."

"Ok. Here's the deal. I'll make the five and one minute warnings over the PA to the entire cabin. Got that?"

"Got it. Thanks, Fred." She sounded wistful, "Good luck guys."

Gingerly and slowly, Don reduced the inboard throttles on engines two and three, the inboard engines about 15% of their forward travel and said, "Let's see how we do with a little power reduction."

The 747 indicated 240 knots, level at 4,000 feet, heading 80°, sloppily wallowing inbound on the localizer. She reacted in a predictable fashion, the airspeed decreased and the nose dropped. Both pilots pulled back, added a small amount of power and she settled at 210 knots, re-leveled at 4,000 feet.

"So far, so good." Don said, "I want to extend the trailing edge flaps 1°. Stan, lockout the leading edge flaps until I tell you to reset the breaker."

Stan placed the Leading Edge Master Switch to ARM and pulled a circuit breaker that deactivated the pneumatic flap motor control valves. When he raised his head to look at the circuit breaker panel, a punishing strobe-like headache returned.

Fred lifted the black guarded Alternate Trailing Edge Flap Master Switch and placed the switch to ARM. He reached up and toggled the Trailing Edge Flap Switches to DOWN and watched the flap indicator on the forward panel. At the first sign of motion, he released the toggle switches.

"Well, what'd you think, Don? How's the trim?"

"Surprisingly, it's pretty good. No big changes. I'm going to sneak off a little more power."

Don reduced the power slightly and waited. The nose dropped, but not as steeply as before. The indicated airspeed backed off to 200 knots. With moderate backpressure, Don was able to hold his altitude.

"Give me 3° or 4° Trailing Edge Flap."

Fred reached to the overhead and held the left and right switches to EXTEND. Abruptly and aggressively, the nose of the aircraft started to pitch up.

Don said loudly, "Hold it. HOLD IT!"

Fred released the switches, while Don abruptly pulled off the power. Nicely, the 747's nose dropped to the horizon and stayed there.

Fred laughed, "I believe you've got it, Watson."

"Give me 5°."

Through this demanding action of balance and counterbalance,

Don was able to slow the aircraft to 180 knots and descend to 2,500 feet above the ground.

"Stan, can you give me all the Leading Edge flaps at once?"

"Sure. No problem."

"What if I want them back up? Back up in a hurry?"

"No problem. Just tell me what you want."

"Okay then, here we go." Don placed the flap handle to 25 degrees, which would be the final trailing edge flap setting for the approach and landing, "Ok Stan." He paused, "Do it. Now."

Stan moved several switches and saw all 8 amber UNLOCK lights illuminate in unison. Quickly, the amber lights went out and 7 green LOCKED lights started to flicker on. All illuminated except one.

"Stop, Stan. Stop it. I'm getting some roll here and having difficulty controlling it."

Stan grabbed the switch covers and flipped the ALTN LEADING EDGE MASTER back on. He held one toggle switch down, which locked the last errant leading edge panel into place. The aircraft stopped the roll motion to the right and the airframe vibration stopped.

"Nice work Stan. You did it. You got rid of the roll."

"Any time," he said and a small smile crossed his face.

91

23:01 Eastern Standard Time
6 Miles West of Miami International Airport

Don, Fred and Stan looked out the windshields and saw hundreds of emergency flashing lights three miles ahead.

The Outer Marker audio tone sounded and blue indicator light flashed in unison. The aircraft had proceeded to an exact location on the Instrument Landing System for Runway 9 profile. Standard protocols would demand that the landing gear be extended at the outer marker on a normal approach.

"Ok, men. Let's down the gear. Fred, give the cabin the five-minute warning."

Fred picked up the emergency hot microphone, "Ladies and Gentlemen, we have about five minutes 'til touchdown. Please do as your flight attendants have asked."

"Done deal, Don."

"Gear Down."

Fred pulled the long lever with the plastic wheel on the end. The lever came out of the center detent and slipped into the down detent. The whole aircraft shuddered and then a single red GEAR warning light was illuminated.

"Aw shit."

"We've got a gear door that's hung up." The normal procedure was to raise the gear and recycle it. However, today was not normal.

"Use the ALERNATE EXTENSION system."

Quickly, Stan pressed two switches and looked at the warning lights on the Flight Engineer's panel. The Nose Gear, the Left Wing Gear, the Left Body Gear and the Right Wing Gear all indicated solid green lights. They were all safely down and locked. The Right Body Gear still indicated a bright red warning light. The gear might, or might not, be down but it clearly was not locked.

"Looks like the Right Body Gear is hung." Frustrated, he said, "I'm sorry Don. Really really sorry. I'm fresh out of ideas. I don't know what else to suggest."

Fred took up the slack in the conversation, "Stan. No sweat. You did the best you could. This bucket of bolts has had a lot of crap happen to her today."

Stan continued to find a solution when none was available. All the conventional procedures and protocols were based on an assumption that there would only one problem at a time, not multiple system failures all happening at the same time. After a second, he said, "How about we do a flyby by the tower and have them check the gear?"

Strangely, Don was kind. "Stan, normally a great idea. But, I don't want to risk a go-around with all the problems we're having with pitch. A go-around's not going to happen. Right now, the aircraft seems pretty stable. I don't want to do anything that will upset the delicate balance we've got right now."

Stan considered what Don had said and agreed with his logic. "You're right."

Forcefully, Don said, "We're committed to land. We'll just set her down on the available gear."

Don thought a couple of seconds and then added, "The worst that will happen is she'll settle on the tail and right side if the main

Body Gear collapses."

Thinking, Stan asked, "Want me to tell the tower about the gear situation?"

"Sure. Go ahead. But make it quick."

Stan grabbed his microphone and said, "Miami, 100. We are on final, at on the localizer and we know we're a little high on the Glide Slope."

The tower Ground Control Approach controller who was monitoring 100's flight path on radar said, "We concur. Slightly right of course, slightly high on the Glide Slope."

Stan continued, "On top of everything else, we can't get the Right Body Gear down and locked." He waited then said, "We don't think it's an indication problem. We think the gear is actually hung up."

The female supervisor in the tower said, "We've got glasses on you and think we can see a landing gear door hanging down. We can't tell if the gear is locked or not. But, it does look like the gear is down."

"Roger, that. Thanks."

"Maybe when you get a little closer, we'll be able to get a better look. Maybe brighter lighting near the airport."

Fred said to no one, "They're a big help. They are all perfectly safe up there in the tower."

Don reduced the power. As expected the nose dropped. This time, however, Don didn't add or hold any backpressure. He allowed the 747's nose to pitch down 2°. The airspeed increased a few knots. After an increase of five knots the airspeed stabilized.

"Fred. Give me full flaps."

Fred pressed the alternate switches for the last time. The Trailing Edge Flap indicator passed through 20°. A loud horn sounded and a woman's electronic voice said over a loud claxon horn: "WHOOP! WHOOP! PULL UP!" Again, "WHOOP! WHOOP! PULL UP!"

Carlton cried out, "Oh my God. We're going to die."

92

23:06 Eastern Standard Time
1 Mile West of Runway 9 at Miami International Airport

Stan instantly knew the source and reason for the warnings. "The landing gear proximity switches are not lined up."

"Pull that damned Ground Proximity circuit breaker and while you're at it, pull the other aural warning breakers."

Stan did as Don ordered and silence returned to the cockpit.

Don and Fred's judicial application of power and elevator control forces allowed them to gently descend to less than nine hundred feet above the runway.

They all saw that they were still a little high on the Glide Slope. To both Don and Fred, it looked like less than one dot deviation on the high side with less than a half mile to touch down. Don thought, "I'd rather be a little high on the Glide Slope and be able to correct that, than be low and slow." He knew that with the landing gear extended they were committed to land.

He continued the approach, clearly understanding there were no alternatives.

The Public Address system barked in the cabin as Fred said,

"Less than one minute to touchdown." He thought 'impact' might be a better choice of words.

To no one he said, "It's a good thing Ralph Nader doesn't know about this airplane."

"Jesus, Fred. Will you knock it off," but as Don spoke, he half-chuckled at his copilot's comment.

They all looked in unison at both sides of the runway. In the darkness, they could see flashing red and blue emergency vehicle lights and sparking white strobe warnings at the far end of the "touch down zone," over half-mile away from their position over the end of the runway. With their ground speed of 140 knots, it would take less than ten seconds until they were abeam the emergency equipment.

At five hundred feet above the ground, Fred made the required call out, "Five Hundred. Airspeed 142. Sink rate 700."

Don acknowledged Fred's call out.

The crash equipment headlights illuminated an unlikely collection of ungainly apparatus. Bright lime-green trucks and hose tenders, red and white ambulances, several black and white police cruisers and Cyclops, the enormous yellow fire-fighting vehicle with four water cannons. To all three pilots, the emergency equipment flashed by and then was gone as 100 continued to descend toward the runway.

Don called out, "All landing lights on." Fred flipped the landing light and taxi light switches on.

Fred called, "100 to go." The 747's main landing gear were now 100 feet above the runway.

"Makes no difference. We're going to land." He told Fred to be ready to help him during the flare.

Stan watched the radar altimeter closely, as it measured absolute altitude above the runway. Now it read seventy feet. At the appropriate time, he was to call out the 747's radar altimeter read out in ten foot increments, from fifty feet to touchdown on the runway.

"Fifty feet."

Slowly, Don pulled off some power and the nose responded

with an immediate drop. Don anticipated the pitch change and pulled back with great concentration.

"Pull. Fred. Pull!"

Fred pulled hard, as Don pushed up the throttles and the nose rose slightly.

Stan said, with excitement in his voice, "Forty feet."

All three pilots could see they were still high on the approach and might float, putting them much farther down the runway, something to be avoided with marginal brakes.

There was no time to explain. Don slammed all four throttles closed and pulled aft as hard and as far as he could.

The nose dropped 1° or 2°, a dramatic pitch change, as the sink rate of the aircraft increased suddenly.

Stan called out, "Thirty feet."

"Twenty feet."

Stan could see and feel a high sink rate of over two three thousand feet per minute. He knew they were going to hit the runway very hard. Even the exceptionally well built and strong Boeing aircraft could not withstand a strike on the runway at such a high sink rate.

Don waited until he heard Stan call out 'twenty feet' then jammed all four throttles full forward to the stops. Every passenger, flight attendant and crewmember felt the resultant rumbling acceleration.

The timing was perfect. The nose rose just above the horizon and when Stan called out, "Ten feet."

Don slammed the throttles closed hard against the stops, while he and Fred pulled back on the controls as hard as they could.

Though not usually done, Stan called out, "Five feet."

The 747's nose gently dropped, just as the left hand Body Gear tires touched the runway, followed by both Wing Gear as they touched the concrete at the same time.

93

23:07 Eastern Standard Time
Runway 9 at Miami International Airport

The automatic spoilers partially deployed slowly when two of the sixteen main landing gear wheels spun up.

Don grabbed all four thrust reversers and pulled them against the interlocks and waited for what seemed an interminable span for the levers to unlock. Stan backed him up on secondary throttle handles in the center of the console.

Slowly, the interlocks released and Don pulled all four engines into maximum reverse. The nose pitched down with full deployment of the rest of the automatic spoilers, killed most of the lift generated by the wings. All three pilots could feel the aircraft's weight transfer from the wings to the main landing gear.

Don stepped on both brake pedals as if everything were normal. He felt only a slight deceleration and was not certain if the deceleration was from the reverse thrust or hydraulic brakes, or both.

The right main Body Gear knuckled under and collapsed inward and aft.

Gradually, the 747 slowed from her touchdown speed of 141

knots. At the same time, the aircraft slowly and inexorably drifted toward the right side of the runway.

Don attempted to control the ship with rudder, but knew as the aircraft slowed, the rudder would become less effective. He pressed as hard as he could on the brake pedals. Pain shot up both shins as his feet were fully extended forward. Above the noise in the cockpit, he yelled, "The brakes are not working. We're not slowing fast enough."

It felt like he was virtually standing on the brake pedals with little effect on their speed. He waited for any response from Fred or Stan.

Fred said, "Time for the air brakes!"

"Using emergency brakes now." Don gripped and then twisted the red handle but nothing happened. Unknown to the pilots, the handle needed to be turned well beyond the OPEN position and then back to OPEN to allow nitrogen to open the shuttle-cock valves. The nitrogen bottle would then provide more than 3,000 pounds of unregulated and unmetered brake pressure to multiple brake discs.

He turned the pneumatic control hard to the right, but no deceleration happened.

Don pulled the nose steering tiller aft and tried to steer her back to the center of the runway. When Bill shot up the cockpit, one of the "A" system hydraulic control valve switches was destroyed. This sent a signal to the valve the controlled hydraulic pressure to nose gear and main body gear steering. Through a design error at Boeing, this erroneous failure was not discernable by the cockpit crew.

The first indication Webber had was when he applied pressure to the nose gear tiller, only to find it was virtually useless. The flight crew also was unaware the Body Gear Steering had received an erroneous signal that closed its control valve, as well.

There was no backup system for nose gear or main body gear steering. The nose gear castered as the nose of the aircraft wandered toward the edge of the runway. Effectively, the cockpit crew had no more control over the direction of the aircraft than did the passengers in the back of the plane. Essentially, they all were just along for the ride.

In desperation, he reduced the reverse thrust on engines three and four on the right side, hoping the asymmetry would help keep the aircraft on the runway. It worked, but only marginally. With differential thrust, Don was only able to weakly redirect the 747's nose somewhat back toward the runway centerline.

"80 knots." Habits. Old habits took over as Fred called out their airspeed, which should have signaled Don to bring all four engines out of reverse thrust.

"70 knots."

The plane now rolled parallel with centerline of the runway, narrowly skirting the right edge of the concrete. Don tried to get more reverse thrust out of engines one and two. The airplane was swallowing up the remaining runway quickly.

Again, Don pressed on the brake pedals and with resigned finality turned the pneumatic emergency brake handle well past the 90° hash mark. This time, he could feel the sudden and dramatic reduction in the speed of the airplane as it rolled down the runway.

"60 knots." Fred's tone was concise but relaxed.

The aircraft continued to slow dramatically.

Fred called out, "50 knots."

There was no warning, other than a rumbling shudder. The 747 made a very abrupt turn to the right. Suddenly, they were headed 65° off the runway at 40 knots. As they say, "Through the weeds."

Don again tried to pull all of the engines into maximum reverse, but the reverser levers were already fully against the stops. Seven hundred and fifty thousand pounds of aluminum, fuel and human cargo continued on its errant path. Little seemed to alter her course or speed. The cockpit crew could do nothing but watch the runway disappear beneath the cockpit windows. No matter what they tried, nothing worked.

It was too late.

Fred looked out his side window and saw the white runway edge markings and lights disappear underneath him. Both he and Don felt the nose gear tires and then the right main landing gear tires roll off the pavement and onto the crushed sea shells, sand, dirt, grass and rocks.

All three pilots heard several concussive explosions from the main gear tires when they blew out. The combination of normal and pneumatic emergency air brakes had locked up several of the main landing gear brakes. Tires and wheels overheated quickly and fusible plugs in the magnesium wheel rims melted. The tire and wheel assemblies quickly disintegrated, throwing shredded tire casings and retreaded rubber, aluminum and magnesium debris along the runway and up into the wheel wells of the aircraft.

94

23:10 Eastern Standard Time
Runway 9 Excursion at Miami International Airport, Florida

Several years prior, the Miami-Dade Airport Authority had commissioned a new Southeast/Northwest runway to be built. The approach end of Runway 12 intersected with the rollout end of Runway 9. On both sides of Runway 9, a drainage collector tunnel was constructed under runway 12. The airport authority had also constructed a drainage culvert that ran parallel to runway 9. This culvert was located seventy feet from the edge of the runway on both sides. It was designed to accommodate excessive rainwater from Runway 12 and Runway 9 during tropical storms. The culvert was less than 18" deep by 48" wide. Both sides were sloped upward at a 45°.

When the nose tires dropped into the drainage culvert, the gear suffered an instant deceleration from 35 knots to 0 knots in a 1/10th of a second. The side load imposed on the landing gear strut far exceeded all design criteria established by the Boeing Commercial Airplane Company.

The nose gear assembly tore away from three attach points in the nose wheel well. Three thousand pounds of hydraulic pressure instantly emptied the seven gallon "A" system reservoir. Hot, steaming Skydrol sprayed from the broken hydraulic lines. Now, no pressure was available for the main landing gear brakes, nose gear or body gear steering.

When the nose strut failed, the gear collapsed inboard and aft. Both nose gear tires and rims ripped into the bottom of the fuselage just aft of forward L-1 passenger door. Great sections of aluminum skin were torn and ripped from the fuselage by the collapsing nose gear. Quickly the fuselage of the aircraft settled to the ground, grinding along on its belly. The underbelly of the fuselage was severely buckled and twisted. Elongated holes opened up from the friction with the ground had pulled the aluminum skin away from the fuselage stringers.

When the nose gear collapsed, though he had never experienced it before, Stan said, "Don, the nose gear collapsed."

"I know it."

Both Fred and Don could see the Runway 27 Instrument Landing System Glide Slope transmitter directly in front of the nose of the aircraft. Separately, Don and Fred both unconsciously calculated whether the aircraft would stop before or after it hit the Glide Slope building. The incapacitated Boeing 747 slid toward the cinderblock structure with square red and white checkerboard markings at over twenty miles an hour. The ride was bumpy and noisy. Pilots, Flight Attendants and passengers alike could hear metal being torn, compressed and then ripped from the crippled jet. One passenger likened it to the sound of an automobile collision that lasted forever.

Like the captain and first officer, Stan's assessment was that it was unlikely the aircraft's forward motion would stop before the airplane hit the radio transmitter building.

The 747 continued to rumble away from the right side of Runway 9. As diminished inertia pushed the fuselage along the ground, the aircraft slowed. With a growing cloud of dust, ground up seashells and coral, the slowing aircraft came to an abrupt and unceremonious stop when it collided with the cinderblock transmitter building. The west and north walls of the structure were completely demolished as were the radio transmitters inside the building.

The crippled 747 rested against the south and east exterior walls of the shack. Fred looked down through his side window and saw an upturned desk and a smoking equipment rack. The floor inside the building was littered with papers and electronic equipment.

The aircraft had stopped four hundred feet from the end of the runway, and two hundred feet off to the right side. The approach and landing had consumed over two miles of runway. More than eleven thousand feet of concrete had passed under the crippled 747 in less than two minutes.

Had the aircraft's forward momentum not been subdued by the Instrument Landing System shack, the airplane, passengers and crew would have crossed the Perimeter Road surrounding the Miami International Airport.

95

23:12 Eastern Standard Time
South of Runway 9 at Miami International Airport

Precariously, her crumpled nose rested on the destroyed concrete cinderblock building and three of the four main landing gear struts. The number four engine had failed, having been reduced to rubble by sustained contact with the runway and ground. Engines one, two and three were still running at some level.

As a matter of safety protocol, Stan secured and shut down all four engines. With a loss of Normal AC power, the EMERGENCY EXIT LIGHTS illuminated. Standby lighting flickered and came on throughout the cabin.

Following standard procedure, Kurtz pulled all four fire pull handles and discharged both Halon 1301 extinguisher agents into each Pratt and Whitney JT-9D engine nacelles.

As if in an anti-climactic moment, the nose of the 747 was slowly obscured by clouds of dirt and dust that overtook and engulfed the mortally-stilled airplane.

Don's voice boomed throughout the cabin over the emergency Public Address system, "This is the Captain. Flight Attendants assess for fire danger and passenger injuries. Assess the need to evacuate." He waited, then added, "Amelio, report to the cockpit."

Don started to hang up the microphone. He noticed he was shaking. After a second he said, "Any sign of fire, notify the cockpit immediately."

Fred reached for his radio microphone. "Tower, we're here. The nose and one of our main landing gear collapsed." With more than a bit of nervous laughter he said, "Also looks like we pretty well wiped out the Glide Slope shack." He paused, "We don't think there is any fire."

"From our position, we concur. No visible fire."

"Hurry with the equipment." He nervously paused and looked for the fire equipment. He saw none.

"I don't know how well balanced the aircraft is. Tell the emergency equipment crew not to go under the belly or tail. She may settle."

The tower came back instantly. "Can you confirm you have no fire on board?"

"Roger. As far as we know, there is no fire on board. Do you see any fire equipment near the aircraft?"

"The trucks are coming along side now. They are on your right side, behind the aircraft."

The first officer looked out his right window and still could not see the crash vehicles. After a second of peering into the dark, be began to see changing reflections from the flashing emergency lights, dimly penetrated the smoke and dust in the air.

Fred said, "Tower. If the company can bring portable stairs, we won't have to use the emergency slides. Call the company and tell them we need at least two sets of ramp stairs for deplaning."

"Good thinking, Fred. I told the flight attendants not to use the slides unless we initiated the EVAC alarm. "

They looked at each other and both started to laugh. Don spoke to Fred as if he were the Captain, looked directly at him and said, "Well, Captain, what do you think? Shall we start to have the passengers move for an orderly disembarking?"

"I believe the term is disembarkation, sir."

"Stan, how are you doing? Everything secured back there?"

"Right. All's okay here."

Don again took command, "Let's secure the cockpit. I don't know what other checklists we should complete, but let's make sure we haven't missed anything."

Stan and Fred completed the necessary tasks to secure the cockpit and then read the AFTER LANDING and SECURE COCKPIT checklist. When they had finished their litany, Stan said, "Checklists are complete, Sir."

"Thanks Stan." Then thinking, Don said, "Actually, thanks to both of you for all your help with this mission. I have never experienced anything like this and hope I never do again."

Fred said, "Ah, shucks. Gomer. I was just starting to enjoy all the excitement."

Stan added, "Fred, sometimes you need to know when to think before you speak. I agree with Don. I hope I never, ever, go through a drill like this again."

96

23:16 Eastern Standard Time
South of Runway 9 at Miami International Airport

They all three heard the muffled familiar sound of a first class door being opened. The Cabin chime and blue 'Call' light signaled someone was trying to call the cockpit.

Fred answered, "Cockpit."

"This is Amelio in First Class and all the passengers want to move to the front of the airplane. They are very restless and not very orderly. Can we get more steps up to the aircraft, maybe on the left side?"

They could hear the commotion. Passengers started to push and shove toward the only open exit door. This was the exit to their salvation. Passage through it would allow them to leave the hijacked aircraft and set foot on the ground.

Don picked up the hand held public address microphone, "Ladies and Gentlemen, this is Captain Webber. Please do not start moving in the aircraft, the balance of the ship may be unstable. Your moving around could upset that balance. Please remain in, or return to your seats. When it is safe and appropriate for you to leave the aircraft, we will advise you. Your leaving must be done in a very organized way. Please remain in your seats."

He took a long deep breath. "I can see from here that some of you are not cooperating," and thought to himself, "They don't I know I can't see any of them from up here." As an afterthought, he added, "When we leave the aircraft, we'll do it by rows. Most likely, the last rows will go first and the folks nearer the front will be the last to deplane. We're doing this because the balance of the aircraft is not known and we don't want the airplane to rock back on the tail."

Don continued, "Everybody hold your position. Do not move. There is no danger as long as the aircraft doesn't shift. We'll let you know when it's safe to leave the airplane. One last thing, when we do deplane, we want you to leave all your personal belongings behind. They'll be safe here." Don knew the reason for leaving the belongings on board was to smooth the evacuation flow. He continued, "No need to attempt to lug your carry-on baggage with you at this time. Leave it on board."

The tower called, "100. Company has advised they are sending four mobile stairs to you. I can see your forward door on the left side has been opened. When the passengers deplane, ask them to walk away from the aircraft and stand on the grass strip next to the run-up area for Runway 30."

Fred said, "Thanks. We'll tell 'em."

Then he looked at Don, quizzically, "You want to start them off the boat now? Or do you want to wait until the other steps are brought to the aircraft?"

Don considered the question, when Stan said, "Both left and right doors in First Class are opened."

"Go ahead and tell the cabin team to start the deplaning and have the passengers all start moving from the back rows toward the front, so we can keep the weight forward of the main body gear."

Fred rang the signal for the forward cabin door on the left side of the aircraft and Amelio answered immediately, "L1."

"Amelio, this is Fred. It's show time, folks. Let 'em start to deplane. Keep them moving forward all the time. We want to keep the weight forward in the airplane. Have the folks in the cheap seats in the back move forward first. Got that?"

"Jes, Fred." Amelio's Hispanic accent thickened when he was excited, "Some passengers have already started to leave. They are very anxious to get out."

"Amelio. Make another PA announcement. Tell the passengers to walk away from the aircraft and stand on the grass next to the runway on the left side of the aircraft."

"I'll do that and I'll let you know when all the passengers have deplaned."

97

23:20 Eastern Standard Time
South of Runway 9 at Miami International Airport

"Tower, this is the Captain. I want law enforcement personnel out here on the double to remove the hijacker. We have him restrained and I want him arrested."

Don turned to Carlton. "If you are able, go below and assist with the deplaning."

Carlton first looked at Don and then at Bill Guerrero. The hijacker looked like he was barely aware of where he was, or even who he was. Carlton got to his feet slowly and showed a disgusted look of contempt and disdain for the hijacker.

"I just wanted to be your friend, but you hurt me and you threatened me. You embarrassed me and humiliated me in front of my friends and my passengers. You tried to kill me. You, you. ." Carlton tried to think of the most despicable term he could confer on the hijacker. He shook his head side-to-side and said, "asshole."

In two steps, Carlton was all over him. He kicked him in the face, chest, in the ribs and finally he kicked him squarely in the groin.

Don started out of his seat to pull Carlton away from his tied adversary.

"Stop. That's enough. He can't hurt you any more. Let him be. The police are on the way to deal with him. You have a responsibility to your passengers. Now go on. Go below and see what you can do to help."

Carlton left the cockpit and gingerly walked down the spiral staircase to First Class.

"OK, fellas, it looks like we did it. Let's go below and see how the evacuation is coming along."

Fred and Stan both got up and quickly left, leaving Don and the hijacker alone in the silent cockpit.

98

23:25 Eastern Standard Time
South of Runway 9 at Miami International Airport

Bill attempted to pull himself up into a sitting position, but the restraints allowed him little freedom or motion. His right eye had already swollen shut. Carlton's pointed shoe had knocked out one of his front teeth. He had blood running from his nose and mouth. He was curled in a fetal position. His head pressed against the cockpit bulkhead. He looked up at Don, his eyes imploring him for mercy, forgiveness and compassion.

"Our courts are going to find you guilty. I am going to encourage my crew to testify against you at your trial. I hope they lock you up and throw away the key. I hope your ass rots off in jail, you miserable son of a bitch."

"Do you have any idea what you did? Do you realize we all came very close to dying because of you? Do you know that?" He raised his voice, "Do you?"

"Answer me, you dumb son of a bitch."

Bill remained absolutely silent, but his eyes changed and now revealed the abiding internal terror he felt.

Don lifted the cover on the Second Officer's deck where Stan had secured the handgun. He touched the damp and bloody pistol with disgust.

He carefully pointed the gun directly at the hijacker's head. "Did you think you could get away with this hijacking?"

His voice rose. "Didn't you know that you would have been arrested in Havana? Why did you do this?" Now he was yelling, "Did you think you could do this all alone?"

Reflexively, Bill said, "I'm not alone. I had help." He knew he should say no more. Yet, he believed if he told the Captain some of the truth, maybe things would go better for him. "I had help here in Miami and also in Havana."

The hijacker's remarks puzzled Don. How could he have help in Miami? Less than two hours ago, no one knew they were going to Miami.

He started to ask Bill about this false story, but was interrupted when what was left of the cockpit door opened and three uniformed police officers plus two civilians in suits entered.

The Miami Dade Airport Police Department officer and the others had their service revolvers drawn.

"Hey Cap. Why don't you hand me that gun? Ok, Cap?"

"Yes fine. Here he is." Don motioned to the hijacker and handed the bloody graphite pistol to the closest officer. "Do you think you could put your service revolver away, too? We have had enough guns in the cockpit for one day."

All three law enforcement officers surveyed Bill Guerrero. The uniformed officer with all the service stripes on his sleeve returned his service revolver to his holster. He turned to the others. "Cover me."

Quickly, he pulled Bill into a hobbled contorted position. With his pocket knife, the officer cut three of the nylon restraints. Now Bill could stand erect though his hands were still tied. Admiring the way the hijacker was trussed, "You did a pretty good job, Cap. We could use you in the department."

The officer reached back and pulled a pair of stainless steel handcuffs from his belt. He used his knife and cut the last restraint. With practiced skill he roughly pushed Bill against the bulkhead. Bill's face was pressed flat against the rough gray circuit breaker panel. Quickly and quietly, he slipped the cuffs on him and then tightened them until Bill flinched. The other two officers said not a word.

After he was handcuffed, one of the officers said, "If you don't mind Captain, we'd be more than glad to take him off your hands."
Don looked at Bill with contempt. "Get the son of a bitch out of here," and stood back as the uniformed officer turned Bill toward the bent and broken cockpit door and firmly pushed him into the upper deck area. Both the other officers whom Don guessed were Feds, followed.

The senior ranking officer said, "Oh, and Cap, we'll need you to make a statement when all this is over. Also, my friends here from the federal government are going to want to talk to you and to your crew."

He acknowledged the senior ranking officer. "As soon as all the passengers are safely secured, I'll gather my crew and we'll get with both of you."

Don knew that was not going to happen immediately. First he was going to call the Airline Pilots Association 800 number hotline. This was a representational service the ALPA union staffed 24 hours a day for the benefit of any members who found themselves in this predicament.

99

23:35 Eastern Standard Time
West of Runway 9 at Miami International Airport

Don left the cockpit and was shaking badly.

He realized that he had not thought about Kathryn for the past several hours and quietly wondered if she would still be waiting for him at her apartment. That no longer seemed important to him. He thought of how close he and his passengers had come to dying today.

He wanted to get away from the airplane, the airport and the crowds.

For the first time in a long time, Don thought of Ruth and wanted to talk to her; to tell her how scared he had been. Afraid of getting older. Afraid of dying today. He needed her and cared for her.

Epilogue

Captain Don Webber - The impact of the hijacking and its potential for disaster caused Captain Webber to appreciate the fragility of life and the importance of family; in particular, his wife. He terminated his relationship with Kathryn Lundgren, never seeing her again after he returned to San Francisco from Miami. He confided to his wife that he had had an affair, but that it was over. Don and Ruth Webber attended several marriage counseling sessions. However, within nine months Ruth Webber filed for divorce, which was uncontested. A final decree was ordered by the court in San Francisco County.

First Officer Fred O'Day - Was invited by his employer to become an instructor pilot in the company's training center. His natural ability to communicate and put his fellow pilots at ease has served him well in his new found career.

Second Officer Stan Kurtz - Took an extended vacation after the hijacking. He returned to San Francisco with his wife and children and was awarded a First Officer bid on the Boeing 767.

Senior Dispatcher Frankfurt Lazlo Fielding - The Federal Aviation Administration sought to have his Dispatcher's License revoked for "Insubordination and Failure to Cooperate with the Agency during an Act of Aerial Piracy - A Violation of Federal Air Regulation 121.638 (b)."

The primary proponent in the civil action against Fielding was Ed James, who strongly advocated the legal action against the dispatcher. The National Transportation Board Hearing and Appeals Board overruled the Federal Aviation Administration's petition against Fielding.

After all federal hearings were concluded, Fielding opted for an early retirement and moved to Fort Lauderdale, Florida. With medical intervention and counseling, he was successful in his attempt to stop smoking. Eight months after he retired in Florida, Lazlo Fielding died from a massive heart attack.

Assistant Dispatcher Clerk Becky Mariweather - Was promoted to the full status of FAA certified Dispatcher on the airline's domestic operation. She filled Lazlo Fielding's vacancy. The company anticipates Dispatcher Mariweather will eventually be promoted to a position of Senior Dispatcher at the Lazlo Fielding Dispatch Center at Kennedy International Airport.

Federal Aviation Administration Director of Security Dick Clifton - Was appointed to a new position as the Deputy Administrator of Federal Aviation Administration. His promotion created a vacancy in the FAA's Anti-Terrorist Unit.

John Batchelor - Eagerly accepted the vacant position of Director of Security with the FAA. This vacancy was created by Richard Clifton's promotion. One of Batchleor's first official acts was to transfer Ed James to the Engineering, Environmental and Planning department at the Ted Stevens International Airport in Anchorage, Alaska.

HIJACKING OF FLIGHT 100

Federal Aviation Administration Manager Ed James - Tried unsuccessfully to bid for the vacant position Director of Security with the FAA. Upon Dick Clifton's recommendation, the FAA offered John Batchelor his old job in Oklahoma City.

Director of Security Operations Robert Ford Burns - Spent over a year cooperating with various federal and local law enforcement agencies in their post-hijacking investigations.

He retired from the airline and was offered an attractive investigator position with a quasi-paramilitary anti-hijacking organization. He considered the offer, but graciously declined. From time to time, he consults with various entities on airline security matters.

He and his wife have returned to San Diego, California, where they enjoy being with their grandchildren, family and friends from his law enforcement career.

Cabin Attendant Carlton Marsh – Upon his return San Francisco, he began to suffer the effects of Post-Traumatic Stress Disorder (PTSD). He retained the services of a well-known San Francisco law firm that specializes in workplace liability claims.

Carlton never returned to active flying status. For several months after the hijacking he remained on sick call. Just over two years after the hijacking took place, Carlton Marsh died from the misdiagnosed, but untreatable effects of Human immunodeficiency virus infection / acquired immunodeficiency syndrome (HIV/AIDS).

Cabin Attendant Patti Mallory - Continued to fly from the San Francisco domicile. She moved to Sausalito with her newly minted husband, Fred O'Day. They are expecting their first child in May.

Senior Ticket Agent Harold Miller - Was offered a promotion to Shift Supervisor and Lead Agent at the Antônio Carlos Jobim International Airport in Rio de Janeiro. He accepted the position. His employer did a routine background check at the request of the bond company who provide bonding and insurance for all the airline's overseas employees. The investigation discovered Miller had over $250,000 in saving and checking accounts at various financial institutions in New York, Denver, San Francisco. Though never proven, several examples of transfers of over $600,000 to offshore investment institutions in Grand Cayman Islands and Bahamas were suspected.

Pursuant to their investigation and after being granted immunity, Harold confirmed he had been stealing from the company for more than 20 years. He eventually made partial restitution of in the amount of $267,450.69.

He was terminated. However, that action was later rescinded. He was given a choice of resignation or retirement in exchange for a written agreement he would not bring a lawsuit against the airline. He elected to retire, assuming he would find employment with another.

The bonding company quietly let Harold's larcenous behaviors be known throughout the airline industry. He essentially has unofficially been "blackballed" from the aviation community. He has plans to relocate to the Bahamas.

Guillermo Bill Guerrero - Was arrested, indicted and brought to trial in United States District Court in the Southern District of Florida. At trial, he was easily and quickly convicted of Aerial Piracy, with Force. He was sentenced to thirty years in Federal Prison, with no provision for parole. That conviction and prison sentence is on an automatic appeal.

He was also brought to trial in San Francisco (*in absentia*) on related charges resulting from his attempted murder of Carlton Marsh. He was convicted and sentenced to a twenty-year prison term at Corcoran Correctional Center in California. His California sentence will commence at the conclusion of his Federal sentence.

Juan Guerrero - Was implicated by Bill Guerrero, in the planning and execution of the hijacking of Flight 100. Juan Guerrero was arrested, convicted and sentenced to fifteen years in a Federal Penitentiary, in Leavenworth, Kansas.

Joaquin Guerrero - Waited in Havana for the unscheduled arrival of flight 100 until it was announced on Radio Havana that the hijacked flight had safely landed in Miami. United States and Cuban law enforcement officials jointly suspect his role in the hijacking, but have not been able to bring a case against him. Furthermore, because the 747 never landed on Cuban soil, Joaquin Guerrero was never arrested. He eventually returned and continues to work at odd jobs in an around the Jose Marti Airport in Havana.

ABOUT THE AUTHOR

For more than 25 years, C J Stott was a pilot with Trans World Airlines in Los Angeles and New York. He flew over 15,000 hours in Boeing 727, 707, 747 and Lockheed L-1011 aircraft to Europe, Africa, Asia and South America as First and Second Officer. During that same time, he also served on the Board of Directors with the Airline Pilots Association (ALPA) for over 20 years where he represented the needs of 4,500 TWA pilots and others who were represented by ALPA.

After a medical retirement from TWA, he enrolled at Pepperdine University School of Law in Los Angeles. Shortly after graduation from Pepperdine, he was recruited by the Federal Mediation and Conciliation Service where he served as a sworn Commissioner (federal mediator) in Los Angeles and Washington, DC. He provided labor/management mediation services to a wide range of national clients including major hotels in Los Angeles, Kaiser Permanente, Los Angeles Dodgers, Coca Cola, Disneyland Resorts, Staples Center, Southwest Airlines, Toyota Motor Sales and the Los Angeles Police Department, Los Angeles Fire Department.

In 2000, he was invited to return to Pepperdine University School of Law as an adjunct professor and an assistant director at the Straus Institute for Dispute Resolution. Though now retired, he continues to consult with international investment banking firms regarding labor management issues in airlines, transportation, health care and the entertainment industry.

He also consults directly with labor/management clients on negotiation coaching strategies and conflict management system design. He is a docent at the Harold E LeMay Family Collection, where he provides tours to the largest privately held collection of classic automobiles in the country. He has had an abiding interest in classic airplanes and automobiles and visits car shows and concours events. He also has been a collector of classic cars for many years.

Recently, he was honored to have been accepted by the Museum of Flight in Seattle, where he provides commentary and background information on Air Force One (Boeing 707-137), British Airways Concorde and other aircraft in the Museum of Flight collection. For many years, he has written articles and background pieces for automobile magazines, car clubs and aviation interest publications.

Though he has had a terrific series of varied and exciting professional careers; his first and continuing love is aviation and airlines. He and his wife live near Seattle, Washington.

Made in the USA
San Bernardino, CA
05 October 2014